D0436153

STEELSTRIKER

ALSO BY MARIE LU

Skyhunter

Legend
Prodigy
Champion
Rebel

The Kingdom of Back

Batman: Nightwalker

STEELSTRIKER

MARIE LU

SKYHUNTER BOOK TWO

ROARING BROOK PRESS
NEW YORK

Published by Roaring Brook Press
Roaring Brook Press is a division of Holtzbrinck Publishing
Holdings Limited Partnership
120 Broadway, New York, NY 10271 • fiercereads.com

Library of Congress Cataloging-in-Publication Data
Names: Lu, Marie, 1984– author.
Title: Steelstriker / Marie Lu.
Description: First edition. | New York: Roaring Brook Press, 2021. | Series: Skyhunter; vol. 2 | Sequel to: Skyhunter | Audience: Ages 12 to 17 | Audience: Grades 7–9 | Summary: "With her friends scattered by combat and her mother held captive by the Premier, Talin is forced to betray her fellow Strikers and her adopted homeland. She has no choice but to become the Federation's most deadly war machine as their newest Skyhunter."—Provided by publisher.
Identifiers: LCCN 2021012482 | ISBN 9781250221728 (hardcover)
Subjects: CYAC: Fantasy. | Science fiction. | Soldiers—Fiction. | Government, Resistance to—Fiction.
Classification: LCC PZ7.L96768 St 2021 | DDC [Fic]—dc23
LC record available at https://lccn.loc.gov/2021012482

First edition, 2021 • Book design by Michelle Gengaro-Kokmen
Printed in the United States of America

ISBN 978-1-250-22172-8 (hardcover)
1 3 5 7 9 10 8 6 4 2

ISBN 978-1-250-83877-3 (international edition)
1 3 5 7 9 10 8 6 4 2

For all who have weathered loss,
for all who have endured,
and for all who make it possible for others to survive

MARA
NEWAGE
N
W
E
BASEA
SUR
KAMA
KENTE
LARC
CARDINIA
CAPITAL OF THE KARENSA FEDERATION
PALACE
MAYOR
ELLAND'S
ESTATE
ARENA
NATIONAL
LABORATORY
PRISON
DISTRICT

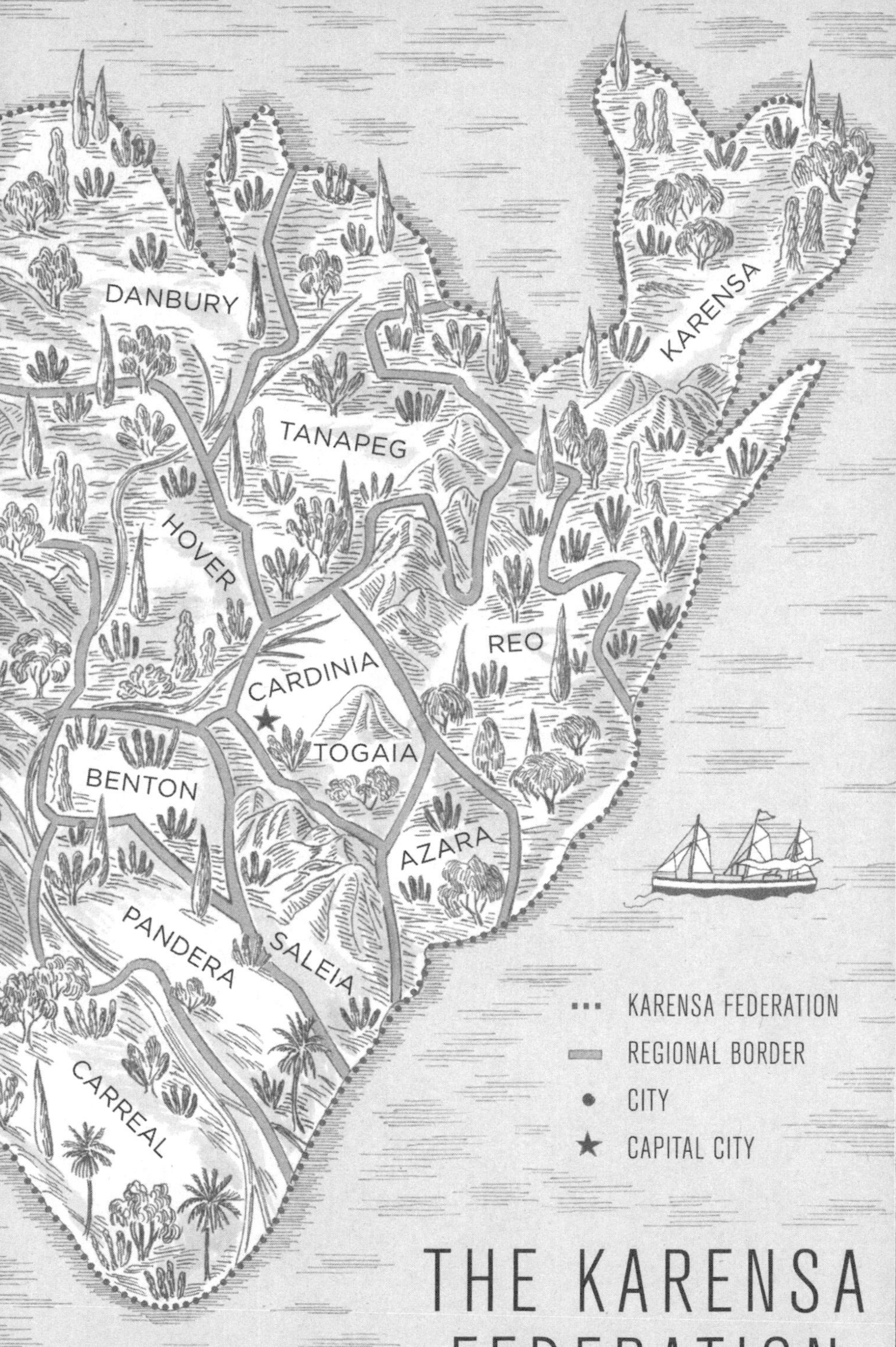

THE KARENSA FEDERATION

STEELSTRIKER

RED

YOUR FIRST LESSON AS A FEDERATION SOLDIER is efficiency.

You learn to burn down neighborhoods with ease.

You have no trouble clearing a town for train tracks in mere days.

You can execute prisoners in a steady stream, one after another, until you hardly remember who came before or after.

I see the soldiers now, down below, churning up the land around the city of Newage until the serene landscape looks no different than a salvage yard. But that's what happens when the Federation finds something they want. We come to your borders and we break you and we take it for ourselves.

If I listen closely, I can hear laughter in the soldiers' voices, jokes, stories from home.

Sure—their actions are evil, even if *they* are not inherently evil. I close my eyes and see who they really are—someone's brother, someone's daughter. Just kids, forced to choose between protecting their family or their soul.

How do I know? Because I was once one of them.

That's the thing about evil. You don't need to *be* it to do it. It doesn't have to consume all of you. It can be small. All you have to do is let it exist.

The soldiers down there laugh and joke because it keeps them from dwelling too long on what they're actually doing. But soon, the Federation will have them back on the battlefield. If you let your people think too much, give them time to remember their humanity, you risk them realizing the horror of their actions. The blood of innocents staining their hands. You risk them looking back to see the carnage they've left behind, the parts of themselves they've destroyed in the name of the Federation. You risk them falling to their knees in anguish.

Think too much, hesitate, and he locks you in a glass cage inside one of his laboratories, isolates you so there's no one to talk to but yourself. So you talk and you talk until the idea of *me* and *you* has lost all meaning, until you lose your mind.

I had too much time to think. I sat in that glass cage and thought about whether I should have spared a young girl's life, whether I was responsible for my family's deaths, how I could possibly rationalize murdering one innocent person to save another. I thought until I couldn't distinguish good from wicked anymore.

Now I'm free, but there will always be a part of me, I think, trapped in that chamber. There will always be a part of me lost to that small evil.

NEWAGE

MARA

THE KARENSA FEDERATION

Six Months After the Fall of Mara

1

TALIN

THE PLACE WHERE MY MOTHER'S HOUSE ONCE stood is now a field of scorched dirt. I have a memory of her rows of green plants, fat pea pods hanging from their vines, water dewing on the lemon-scented leaves of her sweetgrass. That's all gone.

The rest of her old street is gone too—every leaning shack, every pot steaming over a fire. The narrow alleys crowded on either side with makeshift vendors, draped with faded fabrics and rusted tin sheets, arrayed with bags of spices and salvaged tools from the scrapyards for sale, the air pungent with the smell of frying fish, grease, and raw sewage. All gone.

The slums of Newage's Outer City were never a beautiful place, but now they're nothing more than mud and earth and debris. The only footprints are those of Karensan boots, the Federation coming through for their inspections. Off in the distance, their workers are hammering down new train tracks leading straight into Newage—once Mara's capital—now another city fallen to the Federation.

The National Plaza has been taken over by a sprawl of pallets, nurses caring for injured Federation troops and Maran prisoners of war. The apartment where I used to share quarters with Red has been converted into barracks where eight Federation soldiers are bunking together. And the underground prison pit, where Red was once kept and where I'd been held upon our return to Mara, has become a massive excavation site. I can see Mayor Elland of Cardinia standing beside the churned earth, talking with the head engineer about the logistics of shipping their findings back to the capital.

The Federation believes that the Early Ones left behind a powerful, ancient source of energy in the land underneath Mara, and Premier Constantine thinks they've found it here, in the depths of what used to be our prison. Karensan engineers have exploded open the entrance and sent their drill teams down into the silo. The lowest floor is now a pit leading into darkness, the space cut by dozens of ropes and pulleys.

The changes extend to everything. The wall where I used to crouch as a small child, eyes shining and legs swinging, as Striker patrols headed out to the warfront, is completely covered with papers from Marans searching for lost loved ones. It has looked like this since the city first fell six months ago.

Lost: Damian Wen Danna, beloved father.

Has anyone seen Kira Min Calla, daughter, twelve, separated from mother in flight to the tunnels?

Errin An Perra searching for her baby, Seanine Min Perra, blue eyes, brown hair, 19 months old, separated near the south walls.

Torro Wen Marin looking for his parents, Karin An Tamen and Parro Wen Marin, both missing since the day of invasion.

On and on. The papers pile so thick on top of one another, a stack of anguished searching, that it looks like the wall itself is made of paper. I wonder if Basea's walls were like this, too, after the smoke cleared. I wonder if there was even anyone left to search for us.

Every home has a door hung with the Karensan seal. Every storefront has prices written in Karensan notes. Every corner has at least one or two Karensan soldiers, most of them looking bored as they shove their hands into the pockets of their scarlet uniforms and complain about the chill.

Six months was all it took for my memories of a free, independent Mara to fade away. I had settled into the routine of life here, hopeful that things would stay the same, until I was reminded once again of how quickly everything can vanish. One instant, there is a society, a set of steel walls, and a home. The next, there is ash.

I stand beside Constantine Tyrus, the young Premier of the Karensa Federation, in the arena where I used to train with my fellow Strikers. This place, too, has changed—its sides draped with enemy banners—but its purpose remains the same. We're here today to oversee the punishment of prisoners.

Constantine's brother, General Caitoman, stands on his other side, the two speaking in low voices. Other soldiers stay at attention near us. I cast a brief glance toward them. A few catch my eye—immediately they lower their gazes to the ground in terror, their heads hanging in bowed deference to me.

I feel a tug of satisfaction at their fear. Then revulsion washes over me. They're afraid of me because they see a monster created by their Premier.

From the corner of my eye, I can make out where the soft skin on my forearm between my wrist and elbow now has armor running underneath it. The bones of my body are now fortified with the essence of steel. My hair has taken on the same metallic sheen that Red's has. The backs of my hands bear a tattoo of a diamond shape, the symbol of something indestructible.

I am indestructible. I am stronger than any living human should be, and I can feel that strength every time I move. Where I once only saw grass, I now make out a sea of blades. The air looks like it ripples with wind. The world vibrates with a thousand new movements. My back has been torn open and rebuilt, my limbs laced with steel, my face partly hidden behind a black helmet and mask.

Only my eyes remain exposed. They are still as large and dark as ever, though they have been broken down and rebuilt into something new and superhuman. And now I see something different reflected in them whenever I pass a mirror—the presence of someone else haunting the back of my mind.

"Half of them are Marans," Caitoman says to Constantine. After the many months I spent in captivity in the labs, I have picked up enough Karenese to get by.

"And the other half?" he asks. The question sounds disinterested, but through our bond, I notice the Premier's attention pique, as if he had been waiting impatiently for Caitoman to tell him more about the prisoners.

Caitoman's lips curl into a thin smile. He is all that Constantine is not: thick muscle and height and strength, full brown hair and mischievous eyes. But even Constantine's eyes don't possess the void that his brother's have. When I look at the General, all I see is the ocean at night. Merciless and churning.

"Rebels we caught at the border states," Caitoman replies. I struggle to keep up with his rapid Karenese. "Two of them were leaders of the recent unrest at Tanapeg. One of them is from Carreal. She was heading the attempt to break Carreal from the Federation."

Rebels from the border states, Tanapeg in the west and Carreal in the south. I've been hearing about them for months, ever since I first started shadowing the Premier and protecting him. Through our bond, I sense a deep satisfaction coming from Constantine at his brother's report.

"I assume you've questioned them thoroughly," Constantine says.

Caitoman lifts an eyebrow at his brother as an unspoken understanding passes between them. "You should know that," he replies.

My hands clench and unclench, even as I tell myself to control my emotions. I have directly witnessed how General Caitoman interrogates his prisoners. Seen with my own eyes how many tools and weapons he uses, how creative he can be, how good he is at keeping people alive through it all. How that thin smile remains even after the very end.

I force my thoughts of the General away and instead look around the arena, always watchful for any threats to the Premier.

If Constantine dies, my mother dies. This is the only thought that fuels my concern for the Premier's life and health. If he is killed, a message gets relayed instantly to whatever secret location they're keeping my mother. A sniper shoots her. By the time Constantine's heart has stopped beating, so will my mother's.

So I watch for any potential assassins, spies that might harm Constantine, danger waiting in the shadows. I watch, even though it makes me sick to my stomach.

You're angry with me.

Constantine's voice in my mind jolts me out of my watch. I still haven't gotten used to this new bond between us. The Skyhunter and her master. He sounds different in these secret conversations to me from when he speaks aloud. His voice is smoother, less hoarse and more refined, perhaps how he'd sounded before his illness took hold.

I'm always angry at you, I respond to him through our link. I glance over to catch him looking sidelong at me with an expression that I hate. His eyes tell me he can sense the roiling tide of emotions, my fury with him for making me stand here and oversee this. So I fold my emotions ruthlessly back, as if I were squeezing the muscle of my heart to force it smaller.

It's one of the first things I learned after my Skyhunter transformation: My bond to the Premier's mind draws much of its strength from my emotions and his. It is why Red and I had always sensed each other's feelings so acutely, why our emotions seemed almost to feed each other. Why Red was the most powerful on the battlefield when consumed by his rage. I've found the colder I can make myself, the harder Constantine has to work to sense anything through our link. The more I hold back my emotions, the less Constantine can sense of my mind.

And Red . . .

The less I allow myself to feel, the more distant I grow from Red.

Though I can still sense the steady, faint beating of his heart from some great distance, that is all. I haven't felt a ripple of emotion from him since my transformation. Since I started to pull myself back like this. It's almost a relief. The less I feel, the less Red can feel of me. And the safer he and any surviving Strikers will be from the monster I've become.

It seems to amuse Constantine, the way I struggle to keep him at bay. But if he's aiming to get a reaction out of me, he'll have to dig harder than this.

Half of these prisoners mean nothing to you, Constantine goes on. *They are from countries you've never visited. The others are those who never treated you right. Maran nobles. Strikers who resented you for being on their patrols. Are they so sacred to you?*

My lips twist. *You're one to talk about what's sacred.*

Why? Because I'm going to make Mara a better place?

He knows what he's doing. I grit my teeth and fight to hold back my anger. *It doesn't belong to you.*

He folds his arms across his chest and nods down at the turned earth. The ornate headpiece he wears today over his shaved head sways, strings of jewels clicking and tinkling. *The energy source from the Early Ones is rumored to be so powerful that it can bring warmth and light into every house across the land*, he tells me. *Worth digging up a jail, wouldn't you say? And the people we'll execute today are war criminals, scoundrels who hoarded wealth, and zealots who pledge themselves to a nation that is no more. Worth executing, wouldn't you say?* He casts me a knowing look. *Tell me I'm wrong, Talin.*

You're wrong.

Tell me Mara would do anything differently in my position.

Wouldn't change anything if I did, would it? I bite back. I can hear the snarl of my answer echo in his mind. *You only do what you want. You ask me only to taunt me.*

He runs his fingers along the hem of his sleeve. *Truth sounds like a taunt when you don't want to hear it.*

I rest my hands against the ledge before me, waiting for my emotions to still.

Let me tell you a truth, then, I tell him in the most serene voice I can muster through our link. *You are afraid to be seen as a weak ruler.*

In an instant, I know my aim is true. He looks away from me, but through our bond, I sense his amusement flicker briefly into annoyance. We can play this game from both sides and sometimes, just sometimes, I'm the one who wins.

The hint of his irritation disappears, and he settles back into his cool demeanor. *Careful, Talin*, he tells me before looking away. *Remember who drapes you in wealth.*

I look down at my new outfit. Where before I wore the somber and refined sapphire uniform of Strikers, now I have clothes dripping in foreign luxury. Black wool and leather layered underneath with fine linen and trimmed with silver fur now covers me from neck to toe, and over my ornate sleeves are armguards fashioned in the strongest, most beautiful black steel I've ever seen, all branded with the Federation's seal.

Constantine wants his war machine to look good.

Did they dress up Red in fancy things like this too? Had he been paraded around like a puppet before he managed to escape? I find my thoughts drifting, as they often do, to the memory of him at my side. His figure, strong and seemingly invincible, crouching protectively behind me. His face, outlined by late-afternoon light in Newage's bath halls.

Is Red thinking about me out there?

I pull my thoughts harshly back. Let myself go too much, and Constantine will sense the twist of my feelings. He'll know I'm dwelling on Red again. I'd learned this the hard way early on, when I was still recovering at the National Laboratory and wept an entire night, yearning for Red. The next morning, Constantine had shown up in my chambers, interrogating me on whether I'd felt Red's location. He'd sent Caitoman scouting in the woods where I thought Red might be. I'd been wrong, luckily—my transformation had put me in such a state at the time that my mind was a haze. But it was enough of a warning.

I'm relieved the Premier can't yet compel me to obey him. The Chief Architect, the one responsible for my transformation, tells me you can't erase someone's mind without also destroying it. The kind of obedience Ghosts show so quickly to the Federation is more difficult to replicate in the mind of an alert, intelligent human. The Architect hasn't figured it out yet, but her teams are working on it.

Still, the Premier knows there's more than one way to control someone. He showed me that the day he brought my mother before me, bound and gagged, a knife at her throat. I follow his commands not because I must but because I fear what could happen if I don't.

My mother remains under guard at all hours of the day and night. Constantine has her moved to a new location every two weeks, depending on my behavior. If I am obedient and do as he says, she will spend those weeks in a luxurious place. If I displease him, he will move her somewhere much worse.

I'm allowed to visit her once every two-week period. He pretends to do this out of benevolence, but we both know it's only so I can see with my own eyes how my actions directly affect my mother's life. To make me watch her live comfortably or miserably, knowing it was my doing.

Constantine has eyes watching me everywhere, making sure I do as I'm told. So I do. I force myself to follow his orders for my mother's sake.

But my mind itself is not trapped. Not yet.

The Chief Architect warns me this won't always be the case. Every day that passes, our bond strengthens a little more. My clamp on my emotions is a little less effective.

When we return to the Federation's capital of Cardinia tomorrow, the Architect will continue to work on me in the National Laboratory. Slowly, steadily, my mind will fade, until I won't be able to tell my emotions from the Premier's.

In another year, I will no longer have control over my own mind.

Karensan troops have lined up along the rim of the arena floor, two soldiers deep. At one end of the space, a gate slides open to reveal a cluster of prisoners being shoved forward into the light.

I recognize who they are based on the rags of their former clothing.

The captured rebel leaders stand out, although their heads are nevertheless still held high. I secretly feel a sense of satisfaction at the sight. One of them has a severe limp, while another is still covered in dried blood. But even Caitoman couldn't break their spirits.

Others wear remnants of Maran silk coats and fine linen shirts. Constantine hadn't been lying when he said there were noblemen among them. Six months of wasting away in prison, laboring to clear the land around Newage and hauling supplies off Karensan trains to drag into the city, being questioned by Karensan interrogators and sentenced before Karensan judges, and then waiting, waiting, waiting for their execution dates to finally come.

A part of me is surprised that Constantine bothers coming to a mass execution like this. Surely he must have better things to do as Premier of the entire Federation than hang around Newage, delivering death sentences to Marans. And yet, here we are.

Maybe he just enjoys seeing a country fall to its knees. Maybe he wants to watch with his own eyes as rebel leaders are put to death.

Leaning against the balcony, General Caitoman smiles without smiling. I stare at him, both curious at what he must be thinking and grateful that I will never be bonded to that man's mind.

As the prisoners draw nearer, I suddenly recognize one of them. His Maran robes are in tatters, sapphires and reds now stained brown. His shoulders, once proud, are now hunched in defeat. Prison and hard labor seems to have aged him decades in mere months. The lines of his face, though, are a crueler version of Jeran.

It's his father.

My head swims at the sight of him, and I have to grasp my emotions tight to keep them from running away. Before Mara's defeat, I'd witnessed his cruelty countless times, striking Jeran with his fists or dragging his son away by his hair. I've seen Jeran's arms and face and neck bruised black and purple from this man's abuses, heard Jeran try in vain to make excuses for his father and shy away from fighting back. I've dreamed of sliding my own sword between his ribs, had to have Adena talk me down from lunging at the man.

Now he's here, about to face execution.

He looks straight up to the stands and locks on to Constantine. The hard glint in his eyes has changed to defeat, and I can see the fear sparking in him now at the sight of the Premier. Then his gaze flicks to me and catches on my face in recognition.

His lips part, as if he wants to call to me, but no sound comes out. I stare back coldly, but somewhere deep bubbles a grim glee. It's the same feeling I get when Karensan soldiers cringe at the sight of me. Talin, the Basean rat who never belonged in the Striker forces. Now I stand beside the Premier of the Federation, dressed in the black of an executioner, ready to watch this horrible man die.

Immediately, my glee melts into disgust. In that small moment, I allowed myself to ally with Constantine. And in doing so, I have become the monster he has made me. I become a Karensan standing with him.

Constantine senses the shift in my mood. *A friend of yours?* he asks me innocently.

My hands curl into fists against our ledge and I refuse to answer.

Of the other Maran prisoners, two of them are Strikers—their sapphire coats are still distinct even after so long in prison. I know both of them; they were on a patrol at the other end of the warfront, but I can still remember training alongside them in the arena, getting promoted and chosen for patrols on the same day. The girl is Sana, the boy Eres. They used to be nice enough to me. No crueler than most, at least.

I concentrate on the lump in my throat. Some of these people were horrible to me, and some were kind. But it doesn't matter. They're still going to die by the end of the day.

"Any final words?" General Caitoman calls down to them.

There is a long silence. The rebel leaders stare back in defiance. But one of the Strikers—Eres—breaks down, sinking to his knees in sobs. I take a closer look at him and I can tell that every single one of his fingers is broken, the joints twisted and black with infection. He cradles his hands gingerly.

I have a vague recollection of how elegant Eres's hands had been. I can picture the dexterity he had with his weapons back during our training days. Caitoman is good at figuring out how to take away what matters to you most.

Eres calls out for mercy. But he says it in Maran. So Caitoman just shrugs his shoulders and makes a mocking gesture at his ear, suggesting that he can't understand.

My heart breaks at the cruelty of it. I look away so I won't see Eres's pleading eyes turn to me.

How will you do it? I ask Constantine through our link. *When is your executioner going to arrive?*

Executioner? At that, the Premier shakes his head at me. *Who said they were dying today?*

His words make me turn back to him. I look at him, and there, in his eyes, I see the answer.

Of course they're not going to die. They're going to be transformed into Ghosts.

And right as I think it, the gates at the other end of the arena open.

I hear the familiar grind of their teeth even before I see them emerge, one by one, from the darkness, blinking in the glaring light of the afternoon. Ghosts, a dozen of them.

Though the beasts won't attack them, the Karensan soldiers stationed around the arena still shuffle uneasily at the sight of their approach. The largest of the Ghosts raises its head to the sky and sniffs, seemingly puzzled by its newfound freedom. Its long, tapered ears twitch, hungry for sounds to follow.

Jeran's father is a vicious abuser. But the thought of him turning into a Ghost that the Federation will then use to hunt down others makes me ill.

No. The thought shoots through me.

No? Constantine says, almost amused. *You challenge this?*

Down below, the Striker Sana has moved instinctively into a fighting stance, sliding her feet against the dirt floor. Eres remains where he is, kneeling on the ground. Beside them, the noblemen cower in terror as the monsters wander closer, searching for humans. They shrink behind the Strikers, as if this might save them.

But the rebel leaders don't move. I find myself staring at them, drawing some small strength from their stoic faces.

One of them raises her voice, her eyes on General Caitoman. It's the rebel leader from Reo.

"I have a final word for you," she calls out, her voice clear and steady. "And I'll do it in your language, General Caitoman, so you do understand." Then she smiles a little at him. "I am not the rebel leader you think you have."

Nearby, Caitoman keeps his own smile casual. But I see the slight clench of his jaw.

"I am just one of many. Remember that." Her eyes turn to Constantine. "And your Federation *will* fall. It is only a matter of time."

I feel a sharp spike of anger come from the Premier, but he doesn't respond.

Near the rebel leaders, Jeran's father lets out a strangled cry of terror as one of the Ghosts skitters closer to them on all fours. The Ghost snaps its head in their direction. Its milky eyes widen in anticipation, and it bares its jaws at the promise of nearby prey.

The other noblemen lose their nerve. They scatter, chains clacking loudly, and bolt for the edge of the arena. They skid to a halt at the raised guns of the Karensan soldiers. Trapped.

The first Ghost shrieks, and with it, the others raise their heads too. My fingers turn white as my fists curl. Every bit of my strength goes to slowing the beating of my heart, until the strain of holding back my fury feels like it might break me.

This will happen quickly.

The first Ghost lunges toward them. Its speed belies its size—in a matter of seconds, it's reached one of the two Strikers.

Sana hops to one side. Her hands still grapple instinctively for the weapons that normally hang at her hips, but they find only air. She ducks low as the Ghost snaps its jaws at her, then rolls under the creature and tries to jump on its back.

But she has no weapons except her hands, useless for tearing at a Ghost's neck, and prison has weakened her reflexes. Before she can make it onto the monster's back, the Ghost whirls around and snaps its jaws at her again. This time, its teeth find her leg.

Even now, as it bites down hard, Sana makes no sound. Our training runs deep. She opens her mouth in a silent grimace as it flings her halfway across the floor.

I flinch. The still surface of my emotions ripples. I see Corian in his final moments, lips turning blue, signing for me to end his life.

Stop this, I snap at Constantine through our bond.

Why should I? the Premier replies coldly.

Those were Strikers. Make them useful soldiers for you.

My Ghosts are *my soldiers.*

When I look at Constantine, I see an expression of steel. He watches the scene with a bitter determination churning in his heart, something that feels almost vengeful.

The rage coursing through me stretches tight against my efforts to tamp it down. On the floor, one of the noblemen tries sinking his teeth into a Ghost's neck as the creature picks him up. But then a second Ghost is upon him, and he disappears from sight as its jaws clamp down on his shoulder. Eres stays where he is until a Ghost tears through his neck. And the rebel leader who had spoken her defiance stares down the Ghost that finally hurls her off her feet.

The restraint in me snaps. I can hold back no longer. I feel the rush of rage spill from my heart into the cavity of my chest, into my limbs and mind. The wings on my back click, metal scraping against metal, as they unfurl. All I have to do is launch into the air and hurtle into them. I could cut them all to pieces right now, and no one—not even the Premier—could stop me.

"Talin," Constantine says in a low voice, this time out loud.

But I don't care. I grit my teeth and feel the strength in my veins. Down in the arena, Sana has already begun her transformation, shivering uncontrollably on the floor, her body contorting in agony, her silence finally giving way to an anguished, inhuman moan.

My wings shift down once. My feet leave the ground, and I feel myself lift into the air. Although I can't see it, I know my eyes have begun to glow with a faint light, the same way I'd once seen Red on the battlefield, ablaze with blinding fury.

"Talin," Constantine says again, his voice cutting through me like a blade. When I glance down at him, he is staring at me with a chilling look of patience.

He knows he's gotten under my skin. He has forced me to unleash my emotions. The bond between us sings with the flow of feeling, and through it, I feel his triumph over me.

Think of your mother, he tells me through our link.

Think of your mother. Think of your mother.

And it's all it takes to control me. I think of my mother then, of where she might be. I see her hands working diligently to sew up a gash on my leg I'd gotten from climbing a tree. I see her figure haloed by lantern light as she makes her own thread from sweetgrass leaves, sewing deep into the night to mend my Striker uniform. The memories cut through my rage like shears through stems.

My feet touch the ground again. My wings slide into place along my back. The tide of my fury continues to hum through my veins, leaving me in anguish. All this anger and no way to unleash it.

Constantine casts me a satisfied, sidelong glance. *Good girl*, he tells me.

I hate him. I hate him with every ounce of my strength, even as I force that hatred into a sheet of ice over my heart.

Down in the arena, the Ghosts have reached Jeran's father. He's sobbing loudly now, and his cries echo through the space. Some of the Karensan soldiers snicker at his display.

"I'm sorry," he wails, all nerve gone in the face of the Ghosts. He looks not like a former Maran Senator, but a weak old man. "Forgive me. Forgive me."

I want to look at him and feel satisfaction as the jaws of one of the Ghosts sink into his chest, as he dissolves into shrieks of pain. To savor the end of someone who had tormented one of my closest friends. But there is no joy to be found here.

Forgive me. Forgive me. Is that desperate cry meant for the son he had so mistreated? For Jeran? I will never know. Instead I watch the display and am grateful that Jeran, if he's still alive, is not here to see it. He doesn't deserve to have an image like this haunt him.

This must be why Constantine had bothered coming to this execution at all, when he could be anywhere else in his territory, dealing with his endless responsibilities. It's because he wants me to see this. He wants to be the one toying with my emotions, watching me break down. He's brought me here to see me turn my back on Mara.

Everything in me screams to tear it all apart. But instead, I stand idly by. I think of my mother and do not allow myself to feel.

The horror of facing Ghosts has forever changed for me. I will no longer have to fear being hunted down by them in the woods along the old warfront. The gnashing of their teeth and the shriek of their voices no longer threaten me. Now I have to bear a different fear, the fear of watching them turn that same viciousness against the country I'd fought so long to defend.

Once, I stood on the opposite side, facing them down. Now they are my allies, and I will watch them destroy everything.

As the scene finally comes to its awful end, General Caitoman turns and speaks quietly to Constantine. This time, his voice is not full of cold humor. He is annoyed.

"I will have that woman's words investigated," he murmurs. He means the rebel, I realize, who'd dared to speak. "They will not amass their army."

Army. I feel Constantine's emotions surge again, then settle into a careful tension.

And suddenly, with a start, I know the real reason why Constantine had come to witness these punishments. It isn't because he is bored. It isn't because he's trying to discipline me—although I know he relishes that.

It's because he needs to see these rebels' lives ended before his eyes. It's because he sees them as real threats. Because he is *afraid*. And that means he knows there must be some truth to the woman's words.

I am just one of many, she had said. *Your Federation* will *fall. It is only a matter of time.*

And I realize that maybe, just maybe, the reports of unrest inside the Federation are more serious than I thought. That the cracks might run deep enough to shatter it.

2

RED

THERE'S A WORD IN MARAN THAT I LIKE. *Restitution.*

Adena explained it to me yesterday, when we were stripping the bark off a tree to fashion makeshift weapon harnesses.

Restitution? Adena had said. *It means the return of something lost or stolen from you. A correction of wrongs.*

There's no equivalent word in Karenese. Inside the Federation, you're told that those capable of claiming something for themselves are the fateful owners. If you're too weak to hold on to what you love, the thinking goes, then maybe you don't deserve it. Maybe it belongs in the hands of someone else.

It's nice to know that this isn't what others believe. And I can't help but wonder: What else do I not know?

I crouch among the bushes lining the edge of a hill, my gaze following the double steel walls ringing Newage. This is the safest vantage point, a spot hidden in thickets and trees from which the train station set up by Karensan workers is clearly visible.

Behind us is our crowded campsite. Not that there are many who survived the siege: Two dozen are uninjured, a dozen are wounded. Jeran,

Aramin, Tomm, and Pira are among the Strikers I know here. Adena calls us—what was it?—a *ragtag* team. Not wrong, I guess—we are ragged. But everyone still keeps things tidy. Drying clothes are hung in a neat line. Shoes are lined up and polished to the best of our abilities. You have to keep morale up, right? Some sense of order.

There must be clusters of survivors in other parts of the hills sloping around the edges of Newage, although none of us can reach one another given the way the Federation has positioned its troops in the forests. Even so, we're enough of an annoyance that the Premier is still hunting for us.

Specifically, for me. His first Skyhunter. His worst mistake. Maybe I should be proud of myself.

I try to sit as still as I can. Behind me, I can feel Adena fiddling gently with my injured wings. One of them was mangled in the last siege, leaving a deep gash in the metal and severing a few of the wires and tendons servicing it. I'll be honest—I didn't think these wings would hurt if they broke. But they sure do, the wound leaving a deep ache that rings through my bones. Adena has tried to stabilize them as much as she can, but I can't open them without feeling like some goddamn knives have stabbed through my back.

"Their train's ready to move out?" she asks me as she works.

"Tomorrow, I hear." I point down at the tracks that wind away from Newage's walls and out into the hills dividing Mara from the rest of the Federation. "It looks like they have what they need on the cars."

"Cars?"

"Carriages? They are loaded," I rephrase, trying in vain to explain it in Maran. My eyes swivel briefly to the rest of our encampment, searching for Jeran. It is always harder to be clear without him translating at my side.

Adena casts me a sidelong glance. "Your accent's a little better."

I shrug. "As long as you understand."

"You still sound more formal than you need to be. You don't have to emphasize every syllable."

"How should I say it?"

She repeats the same phrase, and I try to concentrate on the differences. "See? I'm not straining each word the way you do."

I say it again, struggling. In the months since the Federation's final siege, I have learned enough Maran to communicate with the others on a basic level. But moments like these still confuse me.

Adena twists something against my back, and I feel a twinge of pain. "Tomorrow isn't much time for us," I continue. "But we don't have a choice, do we?"

She sighs. "No, we don't. That train will be carrying at least several dozen Maran prisoners of war bound for the capital. If we're going to free those soldiers and destroy that track, we'll need to do it by morning."

I'm tempted to say that it's better to leave the Maran soldiers to their fate. Even if we could free them, where would they go? You'd just delay the inevitable. General Caitoman sends more soldiers and Ghosts into the forests every day. They'd find them eventually if they continued to hide near the city. And then what?

But I don't. What's the point? If we're the only ones left to fight against the Federation, to slow them down, and we don't act, then no one else will. So I nod. "Better to do it now," I mutter in agreement.

"Damn everything, but I wish Talin were with us right now," Adena mutters. "She could sneak around better than the rest of us combined."

My thoughts turn, as always, to Talin.

For a long time after we were separated, I listened for her—hoping for her presence to come through our link. Now and then, I felt stabs of pain from her, of heartbreak and anguish. I spent many of those first nights of our separation sleepless, retching, feverish, wondering what they might be doing to her. It took every last one of the others to prevent me from going off in search of her.

Over the last few months, though, there has been little from Talin. Whenever I reach out to her, I sense only her heartbeat thrumming in rhythm with mine. Still, I'm hopeful. You have to be, right?

What would I say, if I could reach her?

Be safe. Protect yourself.

I'm sorry.

I love you.

I wait and wait. But there's nothing.

The ways they could have hurt her haunt my every nightmare. I wake each night in a sweat, whispering her name, my mind seared with the image of her left on the battlefield, when I was unable to save her. Maybe her heartbeat in our link is just a figment of my imagination. Maybe she's already dead.

And if she is, it's my fault.

I feel the edges of a deep, familiar panic at the recesses of my mind. The memories of my lost sister and father, their Ghosts snarling at me. If we go down to the walls of Newage right now, will I confront a Ghost with Talin's face?

These questions are still swirling when a sharp pain suddenly lances down my back. Instinctively I whirl, knocking Adena off-balance enough to send her tumbling.

"Ow!" I growl.

Adena props herself back up and scowls at me. "Let me know if you're going to flinch that hard!"

"Let *me* know if you're going to stab me with a knife."

"I didn't stab you with a knife!" Adena snaps as she holds both arms out.

"Well, it felt like it."

"I tried to straighten one of your feather blades, and you squawked like you just saw a lizard crawl out of my mouth."

I blink at her strange analogy. "Is that possible?"

"You've never heard that phrase before?" She stands up and dusts off her hands. "Never mind. Give your wings a try. You still won't be able to fly well, but I think you can glide."

I stand up, my wings still extended. At the sight, Adena backs away automatically, her expression wary. I may be their friend now, but it doesn't mean they think of me that way. To the rest of this camp, I'm still a Karensan war machine, one that's somehow gone rogue and ended up temporarily allied with them. No one forgives an enemy that easily. There will come a day, they must think, that I'll turn on them again.

I step back, then gingerly try to move my wings. Immediately I wince—whatever Adena thinks she did to dull my pain, I can't tell. But to my pleasant surprise, I'm at least able to fold them enough into a pair of narrow blades against my back, if not a complete and proper fit into their slots. I grit my teeth and extend them again. The pain lances through me like a ripple of heat. Still, my wings extend, casting their shadow on the forest floor beneath me until they can reach almost halfway open.

Not exactly perfect, no, but much better than before. What can I say? You take the little wins when you can.

I nod at Adena with a tentative smile. "Make sure you don't ever fall into Federation hands, all right?" I tell her. "You'd make them a valuable ham."

"A valuable what?"

I must have used the wrong Maran word. "Ham?" I try again.

Adena smiles wryly. "I think you mean *soldier*, but the words sound close enough." She holds up a small metallic cylinder, then tucks it back in her belt. "You'll just need to be able to move quickly enough to be a distraction tomorrow. Can you do it?"

At that, I give Adena a half smile. "I was literally created to be a distraction."

Adena laughs once at that. "You must have been a real pain in the ass before your transformation."

I laugh, but as I follow her back to the campsite, her words linger in my mind. A real pain in the ass. It's hard for me to remember anything about who I was before the Federation came for me and my life descended into fragments, years of torture. Before my mind bent under the weight of isolation and experimentation.

Who were you before that? I ask myself constantly. It's a question I used to grapple with back in the glass chamber, something I forced myself to answer whenever I felt my grip on my sanity fading. I would ask myself this until my voice no longer sounded like my own, but like some second being that lived in my mind, talking to me because I had no one else. That other voice echoes through my head now.

Who were you before that?

Maybe you've lost him forever. You have vague memories of a boy chasing his sister through a garden, playing a game of hide-and-seek with his father. There are pieces of your life as a boy soldier, laughing and joking with your fellow troops. Memories of friends you once had. A girl named Lei Rand. A boy named Danna Wendrove. How you all would bet on which of you could perform some stunt, just to trade guard duties or long night shifts. Danna had come over frequently for dinner. Lei once told you that you were too soft.

You live life, certain it will always stay this way, until it doesn't.

You must have been happy back then, before the Federation took that from you.

3

TALIN

AFTER THE WORST IS DONE, THE PRISONERS ARE dragged back into their cells to finish their transformations into Ghosts. As they're led out of the arena, Constantine turns to me with those steely eyes and nods up at the sky.

"Go scout the tracks, Talin," he says, "and report back to me at the National Hall. I want to make sure they are clear for the train."

Of course, I know this isn't the only reason for him to send me on this mission. Whenever I soar around the city walls, everyone looks up at my silhouette, fear naked on their faces. The people of Mara need to see the power of the Federation overhead, be reminded of why fighting back against Karensa is futile. I am Constantine's champion—and his spectacle.

Though, mercifully, I was not the one to deliver Constantine's punishment today, I remain exhausted. All I did was stand and watch. Still, the muscles of my mind tremble from the effort of holding back. Of having no choice but to obey.

Every time Constantine gives me an order, a jolt of anguish shoots through me. Will this be the time when he's displeased with me? Will this time be when he kills my mother?

So I step forward without hesitation. My fears stay held firmly in my heart, behind the barriers I've erected to keep my emotions in check. Black steel unfolds from my back, clicking as metal feathers slide against one another, until my wings have opened to their full span. I bow my head to Constantine, then lift my eyes to the sky. I launch myself up with a surge.

As I soar through the air, it's hard to resist the only part of being a Skyhunter that brings me any hint of joy. The world rushes away below me, and suddenly Constantine looks small, his slender figure disappearing from sight as I clear the height of Newage's walls, until I'm high above the city and the people below me turn into dots. In this small moment, even as my link tethers me to the Premier, I get the illusion of freedom.

Immediately, the guilt overwhelms me. During my transformation, when I lay trembling in a recovery ward on my stomach so that my back—which had been carved and opened up in preparation for steel wings—could heal, the Chief Architect told me that I would relish the feeling of my new power. That I would become addicted to the strength of being a Skyhunter, that there will be nothing more intoxicating than the realization that I can do anything I want.

I can fly. I can destroy. I can kill at will.

I told her then that I would hate it with every fiber of my being. I'd signed it through a sheen of sweat over my entire body, my vision blurring from fresh tears. She'd understood me too—she'd seen enough of my Maran sign language over the months of my captivity to parse some of what I say.

Just wait and see, Skyhunter, she'd told me, a knowing smile playing on her lips.

And here I am, not six months later, the thrill of flying rushing in my veins. My stomach twists and I push down my emotions once more.

From up here, it's easy to see the split between Newage's own architecture and the ruins it was built upon—ancient black steel blended with clean white stone, a clash between two civilizations that nevertheless looks familiar and comforting to me. Now, though, scarlet banners cut through the city's black-and-white features. Smoke trails into the air from where troops are emptying homes and throwing their contents onto bonfires. The Federation is burning remnants of Mara's rule: our flags, banners, uniforms, crests. These fires have been going sporadically for a while now, turning the evening sky a muted ash brown as fine soot rains down everywhere.

Packs of Ghosts cluster here and there, some in cages, others wandering the hills at the outskirts of the city. And the train track winds away from Newage like a snake, our carriage already prepared and waiting at the train's end. Tomorrow, that train will carry us, along with dozens of carriages full of Maran spoils—artifacts, ruins of the Early Ones, prisoners of war—back into the heart of the Federation.

This is the other reason why Constantine wants me to see the city from the sky. The view from up here offers a firm reminder of Mara's conquest, the starkest sight of a nation overtaken. It is his unspoken way of continuing to break me down. It is his way of whispering to me: *Don't forget.*

Mara no longer exists. It is only another territory in the Federation.

What little joy I'd felt from flying disappears, leaving behind the empty anguish of my new identity.

It is only here, up in the lonely wind and sky, with no one else to see me and Constantine some distance away, that I finally loosen some of the walls around my heart. I can't restrain myself any longer. I let myself relax, and the flood of emotions I've been holding back rushes through me in a tide, pouring through every inch of my body.

It's too much, this release. My eyes well with tears.

I weep in silence as I arc around the city, the wind wiping away the evidence of my grief. Up here, I can cry without a drop landing on my cheeks. My thoughts wander to my mother, then to the ever-looming question of where Constantine will decide to send her next.

Last month, I'd openly refused his order to root out a pocket of Marans who had been caught hiding in a valley outside of Newage. The next day, the Premier had my mother shipped off to one of the factories along the river winding through Cardinia. I spent our last visitation day sobbing helplessly at the bleeding scars on my mother's chained hands and the sharp hollows of her cheeks, the sight of her struggling to load cubes of stone onto the back of a wagon. Telling her I was sorry, so deeply sorry. This month must be different.

Will he reward her this time because I stood beside him in the arena today? Or will he punish her for my angry outburst? A wrenching sob bursts from me at the thought—a hoarse rattle from my lips—lost immediately in the roar of wind around me. What will happen to her? How much more will I make her bear for me?

I weep until my lungs are heavy, until the icy air pricks my eyes, until I can no longer tell whether my tears are in anguish or from the sting of flying.

Finally, my breaths slow. My fists unclench and the muscles in my back relax, smoothing my flight as I yield to the air currents. When I first started flying, I tired myself easily by fighting against the wind. Gradually, I learned to turn my body in tune with it instead, to observe the way birds used the air to their favor. My flights have gotten longer as a result. By the time I've circled over half the city, I've calmed enough to rebuild the walls around my heart, firmer after having been allowed to rest. Bit by bit, I compose myself again until my emotions feel securely restrained under the surface.

Down below, the arena comes into view behind apartment towers. I can see it changing from an execution stage to a makeshift supply station, where laborers working on the nearby prison excavation site are moving crates in order to make more room for piles of debris outside the worksite.

A closer look makes me slow momentarily in my sweep. I change my path to a tight circle over the arena as I peer at the massive pit that used to be Newage's dungeon.

The pulleys and ropes, which have long hung deep into the pit, are now hauling up something big from the depths. Cardinia's mayor stands beside the teams and peers down at it.

I frown, my heartache giving way for a moment of curiosity. Have they finally found something?

The mysterious object looks like a cylinder the size of one of the buttresses enforcing the sides of the National Hall, but judging from the way it makes the pulleys creak and the sheer number of workers struggling to haul it up, it must weigh at least ten times that. Even caked in eons of dirt, I can still see the glint of dull metal through it, catching the weak afternoon light.

Slowly, they manage to lift the object until, with one final, mighty pull, it hangs above the ground. A team scrambles to move it to one side while the pulleys lower it onto a rolling platform.

My brows furrow in concentration. Nothing else I've seen in Mara looks anything like this, not even within the Early Ones' ruins.

I stare in wonder, and as I do, I notice the faintest glow coming from it. Maybe it's my imagination or some remnant of the days I spent feverish in the Laboratory, never sure if what I was seeing in the mirror was me or a hallucination . . . but something about the object *seems* warm, as if it has an inner life of its own. A chill seeps into my bones as I watch the workers below circle the object, pointing at various parts of it and scrubbing down its sides. The energy source that Constantine claims lies buried underneath Mara. Is this what he's been searching for?

Its internal light reminds me of the first time I ever saw Red on the battlefield, on that distant night when we faced the Federation at Mara's old warfront. Red had crouched on the ground beside me and uttered a low growl from the depths of his chest, and when I looked at him, I'd seen his eyes glow with an ethereal blue light. Had known he was something more than human.

Red, I call out to him again through our bond, my permanent reflex, before turning my attention back down.

I have called to him every day since Mara first fell. I go to bed with my mind still yearning for his, my emotions alight with fire and grief and desperation, hoping for an answer that would never come. In all that time, never has he replied.

Until now.

Something familiar tugs at my mind.

It startles me so much that at first I think it's another trick of my memory, my imagination conjuring things I wish were real. No. It must just be Constantine, ready to call me back to his side.

Then the tug comes again. I turn instinctively in its direction, but it's too subtle a feeling for me to tell exactly where it's coming from. Still, its origin is unmistakable.

This pull isn't coming from the Premier. It comes from my first link, one that can never be severed.

It is the pull of emotion from a person I am all too familiar with.

It is the call of someone I've ached for every day.

It is Red.

4

RED

I FIRST SENSE HER WHEN SUNSET GLINTS THROUGH the trees over our campsite, right as I head out into the lengthening darkness with Adena and Jeran.

I blink, freezing in place at the feeling. *Talin.* My heart begins to race, and the other voice in me stirs awake.

Can't be. You must be dreaming.

For a moment, I think it's a trick of my mind. I've dreamed about her almost every night since we were separated during the invasion. Maybe this is a waking dream, a hallucination of what I wish were true. It is the faintest trickle of an emotion—an absolute, soul-deep sadness, and with it, a searing flame. The fire of anger.

Everything in me yearns for the warmth I'd always felt coming from her.

Is Talin near enough for me to sense more than her heartbeat? Does it mean she's here, in Newage?

I don't know what to do with this feeling. I don't say a word about it. How can I share this with the others when I'm not even sure of it myself? So all I can do is stand here, frozen, my breath caught in my throat as I try desperately to catch a hint of her presence again.

It's me, I call to her through our bond. *It's Red. Are you there?*

There's nothing but the ever-present pulse of her heartbeat, faint in the background of my mind.

Talin, I call again.

But she doesn't answer. Of course not. There I go again, wanting the impossible. After a minute, her emotion fades away again, leaving me once more with nothing but the fragile thread of our bond.

Jeran glances back at me as we move quietly through the woods. "All good?" he signs to me.

How can it hurt more, after so many months, to feel a phantom sense of Talin and then have it taken away? How can it be worse than not hearing from her for so long?

I think about telling him this. But then the other voice in my mind turns on me, harsh and biting. It was just a trick of your mind, it says. Just the ache of Talin's absence.

I nod and sign back, "All good."

Jeran looks at me a beat longer, eyes searching mine, but then continues along our path.

Over the past few months, we have learned all the ways through this forest. With Adena, I practiced how to step softly enough not to disturb the leaves on the floor. From Jeran, I mastered gliding from tree to tree like—how do the Marans say it?—a breath of air. They still move more stealthily than I do, but one learns survival techniques quickly when trained by the Federation's army.

By the time we reach a clearing overlooking the valley where Newage sits, the sunset has given way to twilight. Stars overhead are winking rapidly into existence. The train station's construction site near Newage's front gate is flooded with artificial light from their lamps, but otherwise, several bonfires burn across what was once the Outer City. From here, the three guard towers they've erected around Newage loom like pillars to the sky, casting long black lines of shadow in their wake.

A short distance away, Adena stirs in the shadows of an engine in the grass beside the tracks. She signs at Jeran and mercifully keeps her movements to what I've learned over the months, so I'm able to understand.

"Who's watching the walls tonight?" she asks him.

Jeran's gaze roams the area before he finds the uniforms he is looking for.

"Caitoman Tyrus and his patrols," he responds to Adena in the darkness, using the new name sign we have developed to represent the Premier's younger brother. Even though I can't see Adena's expression from here, I can tell from her silhouette that she winces.

My own memory of the General is of him smiling at me on the other side of the jail cell that I—a boy of fourteen—had been thrown into before I was sent to the National Laboratory and given to the Chief Architect. He'd listened to me as I begged him for the lives of my father and sister.

"And what would you be willing to do to save them?" he asked me.

"Anything, sir," I replied in desperation.

At that, the General's eyes widened, glinting with mischievous delight.

He ordered me taken out of my cell, then led to the prison's courtyard, where he handed me the leash of a young goat they were about to send to the kitchens. He gave me a knife and told me what he wanted me to do to it.

So I did.

That's what it takes to become a Federation soldier. You do what you're told.

Afterward, when I asked him if he would now spare my father and sister, he started laughing. He laughed until he wiped a tear from his eye.

"I just wanted to see if you would do it, boy," he called over his shoulder before walking away down the prison hall.

I swallow hard at the memory, shame filling me all over again. That is General Caitoman. I wonder what he'll do to us if he catches us here tonight.

Adena glances to where I am hiding and signs, "You have everything I gave you?"

I nod once, my hand moving to the pouch strapped to my belt. Inside, wrapped snugly, are at least a dozen small spheres filled with chemical concoctions that Adena has stolen over the months, meant to explode when ignited. My job tonight is to place them strategically along the train tracks. The next morning, the striking of the train's wheels rolling against the cylinders will set them aflame. One by one, they will light up in a spectacular show, damaging the track beyond repair. If done correctly, it should set the Federation back by months.

In the chaos, I'll attack the Karensan patrols while the others work to free the prisoners in the cars. If we move quickly enough, we can get out of there before the Federation hunts us down.

Everything that happens next is about buying time.

I creep closer now, moving from the trees to the stacks of rails that tower around the construction site. Their workers have stopped for the night, leaving the area patrolled only by a couple of guards, and I can crouch in the shadows to get a good view of the train station. My eyes linger on each of the soldiers.

Seeing those scarlet uniforms always leaves me with a strange, nauseating familiarity. I can't help but remember how that coat felt against my skin. The weight of the blades and rifles at the belt, the weary impatience at night duty. Now I find myself searching their faces, as if I might stumble across someone I once knew. Some old acquaintance.

But they are all strangers.

We wait there until the guards rotate, leaving a small window of time where no one is looking out from the guard towers. In the dark, I see a ripple of movement through the train yard as Jeran makes his way toward the closest tower to him. Even knowing that he is there, I still lose him in the shadows until I finally notice him settle into position in the shadows underneath the tower, a spot that gives him a wide view of the rest of the train yard.

Once more, something stirs in my mind, the heartbeat of someone familiar on the other end of the bridge.

I pause, frowning again. My hand comes up to rub the side of my temple.

Talin?

She can't be in Newage. They took her to the capital months ago. But my breath still turns shallow in my chest. The wild hope stirs awake in me, and I search the grounds for a sign of her. But I see no one.

I can't afford to waste time. With all my strength, I force away the nagging thought and turn in the direction of the station itself, then pick my way through the train yard until I'm crouched in the shadow of the nearest tower. Guards on top of Newage's walls have their attention trained mostly on the clusters of former Maran refugees wandering around outside the gates, picking through the destruction of their former homes in the Outer City. I see two of the refugees scuffle over something they have found on the ground. Is it some precious scrap of memories? Is it shoes? I don't know, but the incident is enough to distract nearby Karensan soldiers into heading toward them to break it up.

I don't waste the opportunity. The moment the guards leave, I move into the shadow cast by the body of the train. There, I plant the first cylinder, tucking it underneath the wood of a track. Then I plant another, and another. The work is easy, if tedious, until the guards rotate back. When they do, I pause and hide again, my eyes turned toward Jeran's tower for his signal.

His silhouette in the long grass is almost impossible to pick out.

I stare at him for so long that I almost believe he has vanished. At last, I see his head shift subtly, followed by the faint sight of his fingers moving against the moonlight.

Anyone else would be unable to make out his signs from so far away, but I have extraordinary sight, and there against the night, I can decipher his words.

"Wait thirty seconds," he signs. "The guards will rotate to the third tower, and in the gap, you can move to the other side of the tracks."

I turn my attention back to the tracks. I wait the full thirty seconds, then take a deep breath and slip between the cars to the other side of the tracks. Sure enough, the space is empty, the guards gone for a breath. I move as quickly and quietly as I can, placing the spheres at careful intervals.

Most of the cars of this train seem to be carrying back hauls of crumbled stone and twisted steel, remnants of Newage's destruction that the Federation must want to recycle and turn into better things. I glimpse cars filled with nothing but glass shards or black stone or mangled sections of metal.

Under the tower, Jeran signs again, "One minute."

I speed up my work. One sphere, then another, then another. On the opposite end of the train yard, Adena should be nearly done cycling around the station building itself. By the time we are finished and leave this site, no one will be the wiser that this entire site is rigged for destruction. The thought brings me a sense of grim satisfaction. Months of us hiding in the forest, rescuing the occasional prisoner, nothing more, while helplessly watching Karensa lay down these tracks and rebuild Newage the way they want, has eroded our confidence.

But even if we're captured, there are others out in the forest. This war is not over yet.

Talin's heartbeat comes through our link again. Stronger.

Something has changed; there is a new darkness in her, something unspeakable. I feel the weight of it, and fear fills my every cavity. Because I know that feeling. That darkness. My eyes again go back up to the city's walls, searching. She must be here. This is no longer a hallucination.

And something has gone terribly wrong.

Then, all of a sudden, I hear a commotion near the front gate leading into Newage, and I freeze, melting back into the shadows of the train.

A patrol of soldiers heads out through the gate, pausing to split into two lines. I watch closely, then glance at the tower, wondering whether Jeran has another sign to send to me. No movement from him. My eyes dart to where Adena should be by the station. She doesn't move either.

Between the two lines walks the Premier, who looks like he's here to carry out a night inspection of the grounds. But it is not his presence that opens a pit in my stomach, hollow and nauseating. It is not him who sends the world around me spinning. Instead, it is the sudden, overwhelming surge of *her* presence in my mind. The heart and emotion of a girl I have thought about every waking moment for the past six months. It is the figure I see walking alongside the young Premier as he speaks in a low voice to one of his soldiers. This figure moves in sync with the Premier, and her eyes stay forward, searching the darkness.

No. I am scarcely aware of my breath hovering in the night air. The thought squeezes my chest tight. *No.*

And that's when I see her unfurl a set of steel wings on her back, just slightly.

Talin.

I know every line of her figure and the tilt of her chin, even behind the mask and helmet she wears. The evening light outlines the profile of a young woman whose face I've taken care to memorize.

It's her.

But even as I wrestle with my disbelief, I see with horror the slight unfurling of her own wings as she faces the Premier. The way she bows her head to the Premier as he turns to her.

You know what those wings mean. You know that black armor.

In desperation, I reach out to Talin through our link. But all I feel from her is that tide of darkness, the awfulness of what has been done to her. Her anguish coats the bridge between us.

The horror seeping in is a familiar feeling. It is watching your sister transformed into a Ghost, right before your eyes. It is knowing that your own defiance as a Karensan soldier meant the deaths of your family.

When I rip my gaze away and toward the train station, I see Jeran signing at me. "What's happening?"

I can hardly bear to sign back. "Talin is alive," I tell him.

Even in the distant shadow, I can see Jeran's face brighten at my words. "She's here? Can we get to her? Is she one of the prisoners being loaded—"

But I shake my head before he can even finish. "No," I respond.

"Why?"

I turn my eyes back to the girl I used to know. "Because," I sign, "she is a Skyhunter."

5

TALIN

RED. I'D SENSED HIM.

I'd felt his presence while I soared over Newage. I'd felt the lilt of his emotions seeping through our link as I toured the grounds outside the city walls with the Premier.

I'd tried over and over again to call to him, but he must be too far away for me to speak to him. Still, I'd watched the grounds with my emotions pulled tight, my gaze sweeping for any sign of him even as I monitored the train tracks. Even as we returned to the National Hall that night, Red's familiar pull lingered in the back of my mind, haunting me.

He is here. He is *here*.

If Constantine can tell that something has shaken my feelings to-night, he doesn't say it. Instead, he walks beside me at a slower pace than earlier in the day. Even though he'd looked every inch the Premier at the arena, he finally falters as we head back into the city late in the night. I feel his weight lean slightly against me, then his voice coming through our link.

Talin.

Sir.

Hold out your arm to me.

I sense the slight fog of his emotions, the numbness of his mind as his aches plague him tonight. Even though everything in me wants to kill him, plunge one of my weapons into his chest and end his life, I instead hold out my arm and let him take it, feel his hand tremble against my armguard as he uses my strength to keep himself steady.

I hate the way he turns his weakness into a weapon against me, forcing me to help him in his moments of need, as if he isn't the tyrant of the Federation. A person who has the power to destroy every life around him. But I swallow my anger and assist him. As I do, I repeat to myself the silent promise I always make.

Someday, his illness will kill him. If it doesn't, I vow that I will.

• • •

For now, the Premier has turned our former Speaker's chambers in the National Hall into his personal rooms. It's a vast space surrounded by windows layered several panels thick, engineered to stop bullets from shattering them all the way through. There used to be Maran banners hanging on either side of the door, so I heard, but they've been replaced with maps of the entire Karensa territory.

Tonight, as I wait for Constantine to settle into bed, I stare at the maps. The Federation's land runs red on the paper, the color bleeding across an entire continent from ocean to ocean. Once, a long time ago, it covered only the northeastern part of this land. Then it leaked into Tanapeg and Hover, Kente and Larc. Basea. My eyes travel from the coast of the eastern sea across the continent to the west, across former nation after bloodied former nation, sweeping north until I finally reach Mara, newly scarlet.

A lump sits heavy in my throat. For months, I'd witnessed teams dismantling parts of this city. A small but beautiful ruin in the center of Newage, the Waterfall, was removed piece by piece, its bones groaning as workers toppled it sideways. I'd watched, numb. When I was first accepted into the Striker recruits and paired with Corian, I'd gone to the Waterfall to give my own thanks. Mara doesn't believe in gods, but we have always held up the Early Ones with a degree of supernatural awe. So I used to kneel there and wish for good fortune to guide me in the Strikers, to make it as a recruit, and to support my mother in the Outer City. I can still remember the cool breeze filtering between the structure's gaps, the cold ground seeping through the fabric against my knees.

All that's left is a field of churned dirt and mud and grass. The Waterfall is now sitting on the train to be taken back to Cardinia. Another trophy for their collection.

They'd taken the lintel from the Striker arena's front entrance too, the most obvious symbol of Newage, along with two columns from the gate of Newage's outer wall. Mara is like all these other bleeding territories, another spoil of Constantine's war. These relics of our nation will be installed in the Federation's capital for all to admire.

My mind is pulled from my grief by the twinge in my link that I'd felt earlier in the day. Red had been out there, the tug between us unmistakable. Where is he? Is he with other Strikers? I swallow, trying to still my mind so the Premier doesn't sense the emotions that the thought awakens in me. My eyes stay on the scarlet staining the entire map.

How long before our paths will be forced to cross? If he's close enough for me to sense through our weakened bond, then our reunion will be sooner than I'd like. And then what will happen?

"Talin."

At Constantine's command, I turn and walk toward his bedside. A servant is massaging his knees, while Mayor Elland of Cardinia is seated beside the head of the bed, still writing down some notes into her notebook. She peers up at me as I arrive.

"Ah!" she says, looking at Constantine. "Your Skyhunter."

Her silks drape easily against her, and her hair is silver-gray, but it's thick and luscious, piled high on her head in a series of curls. When I bow my head to her, I hear her snort. "Barely a Karensan citizen for a year, and already lowering your head to any Cardinian you meet. Eh?" When I look up again, she smirks and looks back at the Premier. Unlike the others, there's no hint of fear in her face. Nothing about my Skyhunter status seems to intimidate her.

"She knows her place," Constantine replies as he accepts a bowl of medicinal soup from his food tester. It's a recipe from the Chief Architect herself, designed to clear his head and soothe his muscles.

"I should hope so." Mayor Elland considers me before closing her notebook and standing up. She bows her head to Constantine. "I'll make sure our facilities are ready for you, sir," she says. "Everyone will want a look at those artifacts." She winks at the Premier. "Maybe they'll steal the thunder of your arrival."

I watch her go before turning back to the Premier. Through our link, I can sense the lingering ache in him. Only I really know what kind of pain lances through him on a daily basis. It is his illness that has consumed him in recent years, an ailment that eats away at his strength and leaves him unable to sleep well at night.

As I watch him lying in bed, a deep weariness comes through our link. The day's activities have exhausted him, and he will need a good night's rest before we board the train tomorrow to head back to Cardinia.

As his servants close the door and leave us alone, Constantine nods toward the maps. "You're imagining the world before us," he says in Maran. "The Federation."

His use of my languages is his way of signaling whether or not he's happy with me. Whenever he uses Basean, it is because he's upset and cruel, eager to taunt me with the sound of my old home. When he uses

Maran, though, he is in a good-enough mood to dole out small kindnesses. Or he's lonely and in need of a friend—even if it's the illusion of one.

I stare back at him without moving a muscle, hating the way he can interpret my emotions. At least he can't read my mind—yet.

He gives me a subtle, sidelong smile as he settles back against his pillows. "You must be wondering how much lovelier it was in the past." He sighs. "Before we expanded, you know, this continent was covered with warring nations. Tanapeg quarreled with Hover every decade. Larc tried to invade Kente. Everywhere, people hid behind their walls and died throwing themselves against their enemies. It's like that across the oceans too." He raises an eyebrow at me. "Did you know that?"

There's little we know about the rest of the world's nations, other than that they war too. I remember hearing about the breaking up of a country across the ocean that now exists as a dozen separate territories.

"I know you survived horrors in Basea during our invasion," Constantine tells me. "I know what you witnessed. But since the Federation united all the nations on our continent, there has never been another war. No blood shed, no battle fought. No lives lost. Do you understand?"

A lie, I want to say. There have been uprisings and riots in every country conquered by the Federation. And if today's punishments in the arena are any indication, they have only gotten worse.

I understand, I reply through our link.

"You understand, but you don't agree." He sweeps his hand idly in my direction. "The Federation has brought peace, regardless of whether you choose to believe that."

Annihilation is not peace.

"My father didn't annihilate anyone," he replies. "He saved failing nation-states by uniting them under one flag."

I think about the soldier who shot my father the night Basea was invaded, and a helpless rage floods me.

Constantine sighs, and just for a moment, I see him as a young man, slowly dying from the inside out. "Peace is a good thing, however it's bought," he whispers.

Is it peace if there are still so many rebels out there?

The topic is a thorn in his side, and I feel a brief satisfaction at the prickle of irritation that darts through our link. He narrows his eyes at me.

It is. And it will stay.

You're wasting your time trying to convince me of anything.

"Maybe it's a waste of time," he agrees. He closes his eyes. I can sense pain still pulsing through his body. "Or maybe you'll find yourself dwelling on my words at night, until they make sense."

Why do you care?

He opens his eyes briefly, and for a moment, I sense something tragic in his mix of emotions. "Everyone wants someone to believe them," he replies.

Then he turns his head away, and I head toward my adjoining room. Even as I close the door, I can still sense Constantine as if it is open, can envision his room as he might see it. The ache in his body is still there, loosening his tongue. As his exhausted mind finally lulls itself into sleep, I get the curious feeling that he meant every word.

It must be lonely, living in a world of your own lies.

• • •

It takes me hours, as always, to drift off into a light, troubled sleep. Corian, my first Shield, had always teased me about my deep sleeping habits—I used to wake in our shared Striker apartment every morning at his cheerful calls from the kitchen, followed by a pillow flung at my head.

Those happy days are only a memory now.

As my mind finally, mercifully, gives way to unconsciousness, the rope of a bridge tightens against my thoughts, tugging at me from some faraway, invisible anchor. Anxiety flitters down my chest to settle in my stomach, hollow and bitter, as I wonder if the Premier can sense this too.

I travel down the bridge. When I look down, I see a chasm extending down into nothing, cut only by a silver ribbon of a river. It reminds me of the bridge I'd crossed with my mother on the night we escaped from Basea, of the river winding below us. I feel an inkling of the same terror as I look over my shoulder, certain that the Premier is chasing after me.

But he isn't. Instead, I travel alone across the bridge until I reach a land of gray, and there, the pulse of Red's heart wraps around me, pulling me to him. Everything in me lifts in hope at the feeling. He's here, all around me. I'm standing inside his consciousness. And slowly, the world he sees in that moment comes to me, as surely as if I'm beside him.

And then I *am* Red, seeing from his point of view, standing at the edge of the foothills ringing behind Newage. He's staring without a word at the smoke still billowing from the city. Beside him are glimpses of a few other Strikers—maybe a dozen of them, their uniforms dirty and charred—settling in the darkness without fires to keep them warm or heat their food. They gnaw instead on handfuls of roots from the forest and what little provisions some of them had managed to take from the city.

Are these the only soldiers that escaped?

Beside Red comes a familiar voice. My heart surges as Red turns to look at Adena beside him, who nods down at the ramparts of Newage's steel walls. She's hunched over a Karensan gun, taking it apart bit by bit.

Even the sight of Adena's slouched figure sitting on the ground makes my throat constrict. Tears well behind my closed eyes. I've thought about her so often since my captivity, had ached for her quick smile and her homemade remedies and thoughtful inventions. I miss her even more than I thought I did.

"—not nearly enough of us to mount even the semblance of a rebellion," Adena says. "But we have to free those prisoners. We need more than just this small crew."

"How much time can they really buy for us against the Federation?" Tomm says.

Tomm had hated us not long ago, back when the Maran warfront still held. Now here he is, sitting side by side with Adena. All I can feel is gratitude at the sight of his blue coat. I suppose desperate circumstances can unite anyone.

"A month? That'd give us enough to think of a way to push back, maybe even force them out of Newage," Adena argues. "We can't defeat the entire Federation. We only want them to think Mara isn't worth the trouble."

"You don't understand," Red responds. "What we saw at the train yard changes things. None of us knew that the Premier would be on that train tomorrow. That means he will be out at the yard in the morning, when we are supposed to make our move, and Talin will be the one protecting him. She is a true Skyhunter, Adena, one loyal to the Premier." His voice quiets. "I am no match for her. None of us are."

She straightens and shakes her head at him. "Waiting isn't a luxury we can afford. You said that yourself."

If they had been near the train yards, then they are definitely close.

No wonder I felt Red's pull today. And he had seen me there. He knows what I've become.

Then I notice Red is wearing my armguard from the last battle we'd fought and lost. Except this is impossible, because I'd never taken them off. I blink and look at Adena, whose hair also seems too long given the time that has passed.

This is, after all, still a dream. I don't even know how much of what I'm seeing is real and how much is just a fantasy. Maybe only fragments are real. Maybe I can't tell what is and isn't. There were times, back during my transformation, when the agony of steel instruments working against my back and on my limbs and in my eyes had sent me into shock, had filled my head with hallucinations. Maybe I am still confused.

Maybe they're not alive at all. Maybe this is my imagination.

Red sits back, frustrated, but unwilling to argue Adena's point. At his silence, one of other figures sitting nearby stirs, and Red turns to look at him. I suck in my breath. Aramin.

"You're both right," the Firstblade says, his eyes reflecting the night. When he speaks, everyone else hushes. "Talin as a Skyhunter isn't something we bargained for. We can't fight against her. But if we're lucky, we won't have to. If everything goes as we plan, we can destroy the tracks and escape with those prisoners before she can hunt us all down."

"It isn't worth it," Red snaps. "A ruined train track and a few prisoners, for your lives?"

At that, the figure beside Aramin speaks up. It's Jeran. He looks like he has a fresh wound on his face, a scar running along his cheek that changes his beauty. His uniform is worn, fraying at the elbows, but he still looks so much like himself that I can hardly bear seeing him.

"I think there's another reason why you're holding back, Red," Jeran says in his soft voice. "I know what Talin means to you."

"Talin is not a human anymore," Red replies. His words are stated in a cold, vicious way that I recognize. It's his defense against the grief that might otherwise overwhelm him, the same habit he had when I first met him and he seemed ready to give up his life. "She is a war machine. She is designed to do one thing—carry out Constantine's orders, whether they are to protect him or kill everyone in sight. She will do as he asks without hesitation. Why do you not understand this?"

His words pierce me as painfully as a blade. My own grief wells up in me now, surging through my chest and up my throat until I can feel the pressure of a cry wanting to burst from me. *Red*, I try reaching through our link again, but he doesn't react at all.

"We understand just fine," Aramin says, his voice just as cutting.

"For what? A brief delay of the Federation's plans?"

"Do you really think we will stay here, camped safely, for another month?" Aramin narrows his eyes. "Two months? Three? How long? Meanwhile, they hunt for us in the hills. Do we let them capture us like frightened children? Or do we do something?"

"Something would have to shift the odds in our favor," Red mutters. He looks down at his feet, and now I can feel the fear flowing through him. With a start, I realize it's directed at me.

Not because he's afraid to go against me in battle. He's afraid to come face-to-face with what I really am. To be unable to help me.

"*You* are our odds," Adena tells him. "You are a Skyhunter too." She shrugs, her gaze going momentarily toward Newage in the distance. "We have to believe in something."

Red's silent. A wave of his emotions roils over me, and I gasp, drowning for a moment in his grief. He's thinking of the last time we saw each other, and the flash of that memory appears sharp in my own mind.

"We are going to do this," Aramin says in the pause that follows. "And we are going to do it quickly. In and out. Let's keep this efficient."

Red doesn't answer at first. Then, finally, he nods, his jaw tight.

"And then what?" Adena asks quietly.

"Step by step," Jeran says.

Before them, the first rays of dawn scatter purple and orange streaks behind the fallen city of Newage, and overhead, the stars are beginning to fade away. They're still so bright through Red's enhanced vision that I think their light must be heightened by the fog of my dream.

Be real, I wish. And then I think, *Don't be real.* If this is just a dream, then Red isn't really sitting at a campsite with the Strikers. If this is real, then he believes I'm now a monster. Real, not real. Either way, I lose.

Then I see Red turn to his side. His profile is framed in the shadows, but in that darkness, I make out the expression on his face. He's looking over his shoulder, his eyes lost in thought, his body blurred in mist. As if he heard a whisper from some faraway place. From me.

I wake up gasping, my face damp with tears. The dim light streaking blue across my sheets tells me it is the hour just before dawn. I tremble, my head turning instinctively toward the window, aching and hopeful and bewildered at the dream I'd just had of Red. Not a dream, no. Every detail in it was so vivid that I can still feel the tingle of Red's presence in my fingers, still feel the cold breeze at the top of the ledge where he sat with the others. It was a glimpse into something real. They are out there, and they are planning to make a move on the train tracks this morning.

I'm in such turmoil that, when Constantine's voice appears in my mind, it's too late. Through our link, I can almost feel him shifting into a sitting position in his own bed. The fog in his head has cleared. His medicine must have worked.

You are thinking about Red, he says.

He has sensed the storm of my feelings. He knows something has happened.

I can hear you whispering his name in your mind, over and over again.

I want to shake my head and lie to him. But I'm still too unsettled by my dream, still shaking off the bewilderment of sleep to hide it properly. The image of my mother appears in my mind, her back turned to me as she cooks over her old stove. I remember the guard holding a gun to her head when I first pledged my loyalty to Constantine. I think of where she might be now, in a place Constantine has yet to reveal to me.

You saw him, didn't you? he says. *You linked with him.*

I didn't, I reply. But he doesn't believe me.

You are going to tell me everything, he orders, his voice at once gentle and menacing. *And when we return to Cardinia, you will be pleased with where your mother is staying. Do you understand me?*

And I find myself doing exactly as he says.

6

RED

FROM OUR VANTAGE POINT ON THE CLIFF OVER-looking the city walls, the train yard is already active in the early hours before dawn. Adena looks on with me, while beside her, Jeran finishes sheathing his blades. Tomm and Pira are checking their weapons too.

"They're already in position," Pira mutters. "Earlier than we thought."

"If the Premier himself is going to be on that train, then we haven't even seen how crowded it's going to get," I reply. "Talin may already be out there, overseeing the train's inspection."

"Any Ghosts out?" Jeran asks.

Adena shakes her head. "Not yet. I'll be surprised if they don't make an appearance though."

"We'll wait for your move," Tomm says.

Adena looks at me. "You sure you can act alone?"

"Yes," I reply. "As long as the rest of you can handle the station and the train cars." If Talin really is going to be near the train, then it's better she run into me than anyone else.

Adena does not look convinced, but we have little choice, so she just nods and hands me a small object covered in makeshift plates of joined steel, an armored explosive she had made out of the scrap metal we had salvaged. "This isn't exactly a perfect product," she tells me, turning it gingerly in her hands. "But it should work. See here?" She touches a small length of rope at one end. "It's linked to an interior of gunpowder. If you pull the string, it lights a flint inside that will give you a brief flame. It's quick. Release it right away and toss it. It'll explode on contact."

I nod. "Pull and release immediately. I can handle it."

"Make sure it doesn't get wet." Adena takes a deep breath. "It won't work if it does, and I've only been able to make a handful of these. And don't blow it up in your face. You may be a Skyhunter, but as far as I can tell, you're not immortal."

It is my turn to give her a wry smile. "Close enough." I rise and stretch my wings slightly. The pain lances through me again, but noticeably duller.

Adena just rolls her eyes as she hops to her feet and rests her hands on her blade hilts. "No reason to keep waiting around, then. Let's go."

Below my bold façade, my fears are a living, slithering thing in my bones. The sky is clear, everything in place, and we have a plan. But it doesn't matter. The other voice shifts in my mind, stirring awake.

Somehow, you can still feel at your core that it's all about to go horribly wrong.

Talin will be down at the train yard today with the Premier. I shake my head, trying not to let thoughts of her take over my mind. There had even been an instant last night when I thought I had sensed her watching my back, looking at me from some faraway place. But I can't be sure. When you've been an experiment most of your life, it always feels like someone's watching you.

If I cross her path this morning, it's best if I face her alone. At least it should be enough of a distraction for the others to escape.

We head down to the city outskirts in the silent shadows. By the time the first hints of light start graying the sky, we have taken up our positions behind the piles of steel and wood near the train yard. A smattering of soldiers patrols the area, and the front gates are open, through which a steady stream of workers and guards head back and forth from the train station. Along with them walks a steady line of prisoners. As I look on, they shuffle out from the gates, stumbling as Karensan troops guide them one by one onto one of the train cars. A few of them are still dressed in sapphire coats. Some Strikers are mingled in with the common soldiers. With a sick feeling, I know that these are the ones the Federation has deemed *promising*, fighters they will turn over to the Chief Architect once they arrive in Cardinia. Future Skyhunters, perhaps.

Suddenly I'm reminded of my early training days, when I was a young Karensan recruit sent out for the first time on a mission patrolling the streets of a conquered city in Larc. I'd been assigned to follow a tall, gruff warrior, one who had no patience with this scrawny boy tailing her every move.

"Stay here," she'd told me that afternoon, pointing to the rubble of brick and mortar that had once been a house. "If anyone gets past me and tries to flee, you raise the alarm. Understand?"

I had nodded and stayed back as she then entered a house with several other soldiers behind her. I remember how small I had been then, how easy it was to hide in the shadow of that rubble. Waiting for her felt like an eternity. Then a shout came from the house, followed by several sobs and then the sound of a gunshot. I jumped, tense as a rabbit ready to take flight. But no one emerged, so I stayed where I was. I waited for a long time before she finally reappeared leading several men out, their hands bound tightly, their eyes blindfolded.

Please, I remember thinking. *Do not move.*

No one did. I do not know what happened to those men, nor why they had been led out. Maybe they were rebels, the same as we are now.

Whatever the reason, I lost my nerve and stole away through the rubble, silent and unseen, back to the Karensan base set up at the outskirts of the city. The female soldier I had shadowed didn't even care about my absence. She must have been relieved for my disappearance.

Now I crouch behind the tracks and will myself to become as small and invisible as I had once been. Some distance away, I can see the outline of Adena, Tomm, and Pira near the train station, while Jeran and Aramin have settled into hiding places around the farther cars of the train. They'll wait for my diversion before making their move.

In the strengthening light, I can better see exactly what this train is bringing back to Cardinia. What had looked like bits of steel and stone hauled back in cars now take on the recognizable shape of specific types of pillars or stone blocks with letters carved in them. With a start, I realize that these are artifacts of Mara that the Federation must think are worth keeping. They are trophies.

I look on grimly, recognizing one enormous stone strapped into its own car as the stone usually suspended over the Striker arena's gate. On it is engraved one of their mantras: MAY THERE BE FUTURE DAWNS. Still another car carries two pillars with carvings indicative of the Early Ones' writing. Finally, there is the car that the others will be targeting, the one loaded with prisoners.

I wait until the light has fully brightened. Somehow, the arrangement of soldiers and workers milling around out here makes me uncomfortable. I see a few teams walking alongside engineers, all inspecting the objects tied to the cars. There's a woman with them too, and I recognize her as Mayor Elland of Cardinia. She must have come here to Mara to inspect what they'll be bringing back to her city.

None of it feels right. Usually, if the Premier is headed somewhere, the patrols are more structured, ordered into neat rows to await his arrival so they can easily and safely usher him to where he needs to go. I've seen it plenty in my lifetime.

But they aren't out here. Neither is the Premier.

Had they changed their minds? Is the Premier not on this train after all? If that's the case, it will make this mission an easier one for us. Talin won't be at his side, a weapon we cannot defeat.

The light changes more. I exchange a brief look with Adena and the others near the station. They appear as confused as I am. We stay where we are until steam and smoke finally begin to pour from the train. It is going to move.

I watch as the massive machine yawns and roars, as the soldiers shout to one another and back away from the train. Then I tense for the first detonation of the cylinders hidden under its tracks, ready to move.

It doesn't come.

Neither does the second.

The explosives don't work. This is my first thought as I turn my eyes to meet Adena's stricken ones. But when I look closer at the tracks, I notice that it's not that the spheres she created do not work.

It's that they have been removed. Someone has cleared away all of them since we planted them last night.

My blood runs cold at the same time I look up to see General Caitoman emerging from the front gate. Behind him march several patrols of soldiers.

They look unsurprised, ready to attack, and to my horror, I realize that there is an entire ring of soldiers who have been waiting for us already. They appear all along the edges of the train station now, along with the hulking shapes of Ghosts.

This is the moment when it finally dawns on me that they knew we were coming. We've walked right into a trap.

Part of what makes you a Skyhunter is the rush of rage that fills you in the seconds before you attack. Now, as I gear up to move, I can feel that same rush coursing through my veins with blinding heat. Talin had told me of how my eyes glow, transforming me from a young man into something monstrous. Along with this fury comes fear.

I hate the rush. I hate the feeling. And yet, every time it appears, I can't help but want more of it, hoping that if it swallows me completely, I'd never have to know the destruction I've created. Better to hide, right? Better to lose yourself.

I close my eyes; the world around me narrows into a funnel of light.

Then I stand and extend my wings. If the others at the station see me now, they should know I am directing every bit of the soldiers' attention to me. The guard closest to me freezes, her eyes wide in terror at the sight of me. She waves frantically to the team behind her, but it's all she has a chance to do. I brace myself, then surge toward the train. If there is nothing we have to stop the train with, then I will have to attempt to inflict the damage myself.

Soldiers dart out of my path as I hurtle toward the train's massive wheels. My bladed feathers clip against their giant metal spokes, and sparks fly. The hit sends ripples of agony through me, but I grit my teeth and saw desperately into the wheels again.

My attack is no explosion—but the force of me throwing all my weight against the train makes the entire structure rock sideways with a loud groan. The wheels' spokes bend sharply at the impact, scraping hard against the wheels themselves and bringing the train to a halt.

The others seem to sense immediately what I'm doing, because when my attention shifts to them for a moment, they are already out from their hiding places and rushing into battle in an attempt to get to the train car. I see the blur of Jeran's figure. He reaches one of the patrols first and twists, blades flashing through the air. Nearby, Adena leaps against the train station's shed, scales it in an instant, and launches herself off, gun firing.

I turn to face the Karensan soldiers. All the while, my mind whirls with the same question. They knew. They knew. How did they know?

The soldiers have no time to react. All they can do is lift their blades. Some of them point their guns at me, but I slide into a crouch, one of my wings shielding me from their barrage of bullets. I seize the first soldier by the collar and fling him aside; I grab his fallen blade and swing it viciously at the second soldier.

From behind them comes the gnashing of rotting fangs. Ghosts.

They don't target me, but turn their attention on the Strikers who have come with us on the mission. I narrow my eyes, bare my teeth, and hurtle into them.

Near the end of the train tracks, an explosion rocks the earth.

The blast is so powerful that I feel the heat scalding my back. *One of Adena's bombs.* I guess they didn't catch all of them.

Screams erupt from the gate, where the patrol has been thrown back. Flames roar against the entrance's frame. Silhouetted against the chaos is Adena herself, running alongside Tomm and Pira as they draw near to the train car of prisoners. I glimpse a flash of Aramin's uniform darting through the grass.

Knives are in my hands, cutting through skin and flesh before I am even aware of my own attack. I spin through soldiers and Ghosts alike in a whirlwind of blood. The blades of my wings slice through the air until they strike bodies. I wince at each impact, but the pain fuels me now, and the threat of death pushes me to keep moving.

Some of the Ghosts are newly formed. They look more human than the others, their forms smaller but their rage fresh, their bodies flush with strength from the intense agony of breaking down. I grit my teeth, hating the look of them. It's like looking at a person who is no longer a person. Like watching the soul of your sister rot before your eyes.

Soldiers are pouring toward us from every direction now. There are far too many of them for us to face. They seem not only to know that we would stage this attack, but that I would be among them.

We have lost this battle. The others have to get out of here.

I push off from the ground and charge into a patrol of soldiers heading for the others. A bullet hits my shoulder and rockets me backward. I grimace and look in the direction of my attacker. It's Caitoman himself. His hit can't penetrate the steel under my skin, but it leaves a small wound anyway. I whirl to focus on him.

Far at the other end of the train, I see Jeran sliding the train car door open and slicing through the ropes of the first prisoner he sees.

I raise my voice at him. "Jeran!" I scream. "Retreat! Retreat!"

Jeran's eyes flicker toward me, but his jaw is set as he ignores me and goes back to freeing the prisoners. I curse. Damn bleeding hearts.

Caitoman shoots at me again. I dodge a second time, but now I can tell that they are less interested in the prisoners and more determined to keep me from escaping. I am the real prize. I narrow my eyes and dart into the crowd of soldiers, cutting anyone down in my path. But there are so many of them now.

"Strikers!" I shout again and again, blindly. *"Retreat!"*

From the corner of my eye, I see Jeran ushering some of the prisoners toward the woods. A few of them have broken past the train station and are heading straight into the forest. Jeran whirls as some of the Ghosts lunge toward them. He switches one of his blades for a gun in the same fluid movement.

Then he freezes in his path. His eyes are fixed on the first Ghost hurtling toward him. All the color has drained from his face.

My eyes flicker to the beast that has caught his attention. It was clearly transformed recently—still bearing some resemblance to the old man it once was, though its lips are already ripped and bleeding from the larger, jagged teeth growing in its mouth. Its skin has begun cracking in places, all the way down to the red muscle.

It looks familiar. And an instant later, I realize who it is.

This was once Jeran's father.

My head whips back to Jeran. "No!" I shout. "Move!" I crouch as if to rush to him, but I know I'm too far away to reach him in time. In my panic, I switch to Karenese. *"It's not your father!"*

But Jeran doesn't move. His face is locked on his father's, and his body is frozen in terror.

In that expression, you see the boy he must have once been, cowering under the cruelty of the Senator, bearing the abuse quietly. You see the same fear on his face that you'd seen in the Grid.

Jeran takes a hesitant step backward. All his Striker training seems to have left him. He drops his gun and remaining blade and raises his hands toward his face as if in self-defense. His father—the Ghost—lunges at him with jaws open.

Adena comes out of nowhere. She barrels hard into Jeran, knocking him out of the Ghost's path and clear to the ground.

At the same time, Aramin jumps down from the top of the train to land in a crouch before Jeran and Adena. His teeth are bared in a snarl; a blade shines in each of his hands.

He gives the charging Ghost a grim smile before rushing at it.

I'm forced to tear my gaze away as more soldiers try to fence me in. But even from the corner of my eye, I see blood spray. I don't know whether it's from the Ghost or from Aramin. From the top of the train shoots a net. I dart out of the way barely in time and turn toward the others again in another attempt to join them.

That is when the shadow falls over me. I know in the pit of my stomach who it is before I raise my eyes.

Talin has arrived.

7

RED

TALIN'S FIGURE SOARS ABOVE US AND LANDS a dozen yards in front of me, blocking my path to the others. I freeze, transfixed by the crouched figure before me.

She is breathtaking—I can't help but think it. Her black wings extend fully from her back, seeming to block out the sky and everything else behind her. Every line of her exudes power. She lifts her eyes to meet mine.

And there, I don't see the girl who saved me in the arena, nor the girl who once soaked in a bath a hundred feet from me, both of us lost in the quiet moment.

I see someone new and terrifying.

In this Skyhunter's eyes, I see flickers of the Premier. This is not Talin, but Constantine come to retrieve his servant of war.

It's the thought of him here, even more than the sight of Talin in her full armor, that sends a ripple of terror through me. They're here to take me back, and they know I'm no match for her.

She bolts at me before I can retreat. I whirl to one side, but she anticipates my move and hurtles into me, sending me reeling onto my back.

The force of her hit knocks the wind out of me. I cannot believe how strong she is.

"Talin—" I manage to utter, but my voice is lost in the next second as she rushes at me again. I roll aside and force myself to my feet, darting out of her path in time before her hands can lock around my throat. The Karensan soldiers have backed away, afraid to get between two Skyhunters battling it out. I am fast; I am the only one here who stands any chance against her. But there's no question that she will overwhelm me. Pain lances through my back as I attempt to stretch my broken wings as far as I can manage. I scan the area for a way out.

She locks her glowing eyes on me. Then she crouches and hurtles for me again.

I do the only thing I can think of. I lunge toward Caitoman, where he stands with his guards. Two of his soldiers try to stop me, but I shove the first aside. The second brings his gun up to my face. I grab it from his hand and strike him hard in the head. He crumples. Caitoman swings at me—I dodge around him and lock my arm hard around his neck. Then I whirl to face Talin.

"Constantine," I call out, my eyes fixed on Talin, not daring to look up to where the Premier might be watching this all play out. "Your brother's life, or mine."

For a moment, I think the Premier will not stop Talin from attacking me, that he is perfectly willing to sacrifice his brother. Caitoman bares his teeth in my grip, but even as he struggles, I hang grimly on. I wait a beat longer. Talin does not move.

Constantine must have told her to hold off.

The thought makes my heart sink. A small part of me had hoped, however foolishly, that maybe she wasn't so tightly linked to the Premier's commands. What a stupid thought. I face her, my heart pounding desperately, and for the first time since we were separated, I allow myself a good look at her.

She hesitates before me. Where before I had only seen her narrowed eyes, ready to kill, now I catch a glimpse of something else in her gaze. Recognition, at least, of who I am. And as I notice this, I sense the first inkling of something in our link that goes beyond the simple beat of our hearts.

I sense an emotion from her. Fear.

Fear of hurting me, of seeing me captured, of seeing me killed in this place. The emotion washes over me in a wave, and it is such a familiar feeling, that it takes everything in me to remember she is no longer the same person I once knew. She is a weapon of the Federation now, a danger to us all. I tighten my grip around Caitoman's neck. His hands clutch my arm in vain. Some of his soldiers step forward, uncertain what they can do to help their commanding officer, but he just moves his head stiffly at them.

Then, from behind the lines of soldiers, I hear Constantine's voice drift to us. "Let him go."

I turn my head to see his familiar silhouette framed against the backdrop of Newage, his form frighteningly thin, shadows darkening the skin under his eyes. If he is concerned for his brother, I do not see it in his steady gaze.

"I do not take orders from you," I call to him in Karenese.

"I am not ordering you," Constantine replies. "I am telling you it is the only way to save you and your friends' lives."

I glance over my shoulder. One look is all it takes to tell me that we have lost this battle bitterly. Jeran is nowhere to be seen. Had his father taken him down? Aramin struggles in the grip of Karensan soldiers. Adena has been forced to the ground, her cheek pressed hard into the dirt. Two other young Strikers lie dead near the tracks. The circle of soldiers around us presses tight, and the shrieks of Ghosts pierce the air as they shake their heads restlessly after the heat of battle.

You think you have a shot at slowing the Federation down; you think you're ready. And then you fall.

"Come back, Redlen," Constantine says, "and let me fix your wings. They must hurt you."

As if on cue, I feel the pain of the twisted steel against my back. I turn my stare to Talin. She looks at me with a pained expression now, and as we face each other, she gives me a subtle shake of her head.

Please, she says to me through our link.

I hear the word echo in my mind, a presence that I've missed for so long.

A lump rises in my throat at her presence in my thoughts. I strain to hear more, but nothing else comes.

And in a rush of grief, I understand how the Federation knew we were coming today. Talin. Somehow, she must have seen through my eyes what we were planning. The link between us must be more intact than I thought. And if she knew about it, she must have been helpless against passing the information along to Constantine.

She is—I am—the reason behind this trap.

I don't want to hurt you, she tells me now.

I know, I answer her gently.

Release the General, she says, gesturing at the other Strikers, *or you will see them bleed to death right here.*

How much control does Constantine hold over her? The Talin I knew would rather die than threaten the lives of her former companions like this. I shudder to imagine the kind of pain she must be feeling, but I sense a wall of resistance through our link. I know there is nothing I can do.

I look back at the others. Adena meets my gaze with her own, and her eyes are hollow with defeat. We have lost. It is over.

Suddenly I hear a single, final word from Talin through our link.

Go.

I don't know if it's our bond that lets me guess exactly what she wants to do, our unconscious sense of her emotions and thoughts. But I understand immediately. She's trying to help me. She knows I cannot, under any circumstances, fall back into the hands of the Federation.

Then Talin rushes at me—but she leaves me the slightest fraction of a second to act.

I sense the tiny advantage and take it. My wings unfurl in a single, snapping motion, and pain shoots through my back. I push off the ground in a burst of strength and take Caitoman with me. The General struggles in my grasp, but I grit my teeth and concentrate, using everything in me to fly as high as I can.

Behind me comes a rush of wind. Talin has taken off in pursuit of me. I push one more time with my injured wings and feel the strain in my back. It's as far as I can go.

That's when I release Caitoman.

He plummets with a strangled shout. I only dare a single glimpse down to see Talin forced to pause in her flight. She swivels in her attack, metal wings carving a mighty arc through the air, then twists to reach out for Caitoman. She catches him as I swerve into a sharp glide and hurtle away from the scene.

I don't get the chance to see what happens to the others. I don't know whether Constantine orders them all gunned down. I only see the expression on Talin's face as she looks up, the reflection of unshed tears glossy in her eyes. The other part of me, the part that speaks into the hollows of my mind, echoes loudly through me now.

You can't save them. It's the curse of your life. All you can do is run.

8

TALIN

MY FIRST THOUGHT AFTER RED HAS ESCAPED is one I hate. Did Constantine sense what I told Red? Does he know I let him escape? Will this be what kills my mother?

Did Red make it out alive? Will they hunt him down? Will the others be allowed to live?

This is what my fear of the Premier has done to me.

As Caitoman tumbles past midair, I grasp his arm and swing with him for a second, carried by his momentum. Then my other hand steadies my grip, and I hold him there for an instant before lowering him carefully to the ground. The General rolls in a shower of dust before leaping to his feet, his eyes already searching the sky for where Red might have gone.

I turn my gaze up to hunt for him too, but through our bond, I can already tell that it's no use to look. In the time it took me to save Caitoman's life, Red has long vanished.

Do I pursue him? I ask Constantine through our link.

When Constantine answers, his tone is bitter. *No*, he answers. *I want you here.* And I realize it's because he's not sure whether other invisible rebels are waiting to attack. In case there is a surprise we're not prepared for, I need to stay here to protect the Premier and his brother.

My gaze returns to Caitoman, who's still on one knee as he catches his breath. There are soldiers running all around me, dragging my friends up as they tie their hands, their figures shrouded in the train's steam and smoke that coil along the ground. But to me, the world feels slow and silent.

I am a traitor. I am a destroyer. I am the reason my friends—and my mother—will die. The guilt floods me until I can barely stand.

How had I linked with Red in my dreams? I'd worked so hard to build a shell around myself for all these months! I'd forced my emotions down, closing them off to protect us all. How had I broken my promise to myself, to keep my feelings in check to guard my loved ones from Constantine's wrath?

Sleep. Sleep is what betrayed me.

In my dreams, I have less control. I can sense it when I wake, fighting to open my eyes and build my walls up once more. My broken heart must leak through the stone of my restraint when I'm unconscious. Does my link to Red strengthen in response during those hours, connecting me to him against my will?

Is that what had happened?

Constantine had forced everything out of me once he was aware of the extent of our linking, on pain of my mother's life.

It'd gotten my friends captured. It'd almost gotten Red.

Even though I can sense the low pulse of Red's heartbeat, everything in me trembles as if I had ended his life. I could have, in that moment. If Constantine had ordered me to ignore Caitoman and kill Red, I would've had no choice but to do it.

What if he had sensed the fraction of a second I'd given Red to escape?

The thought leaves me weak with fear. Nevertheless, I force myself to clench my fists instead, opening and closing them in my steady exercise.

My mother, I think, reminding myself. My mother. My mother.

So when Constantine calls me back to his side, I force myself to go to him. I force myself to bow my head in obedience when he praises me for what I've done. I force myself to watch as Constantine turns his attention to the captured Strikers. My friends.

He doesn't order their deaths. I don't know whether to feel relieved or terrified by that. They're instead bound with rope and chain, added to the prisoners that will head to Cardinia. I search each of their faces. Tomm and Pira. Adena. Aramin.

Jeran. I don't see him here, but I don't dare utter a sound about it. Still, my eyes scan the prisoners and the grounds before I come to the realization that Jeran isn't among them. He'd been here during the attack—I'd seen him in the fray.

At first, I worry that maybe one of the soldiers had killed him. But he's far too talented a Striker for that. Had he escaped in the chaos? My heart hammers against my ribs, and I hope that Constantine associates it only with the fact that I'm seeing my companions chained before me.

Jeran and Red have escaped. I let myself hang on to this threadbare hope as I meet the gazes of the others.

What Constantine will do with them once they arrive in Cardinia, I already know. The Chief Architect will see them, just as she saw me. She'll take them to the National Laboratory and have them tested to see if they can withstand the Skyhunter transformation. Or, if they don't pass that exam, they may be transformed into Ghosts.

Or worse, he might hand them over to his brother. I tremble at the thought of what General Caitoman might do to them.

"Firstblade," he says when he sees Aramin. I expect Constantine to gloat, but instead he just shakes his head. "You should have surrendered at the warfront. So many of your talented soldiers could have found new purpose within the Federation."

Aramin doesn't respond to that, but he does keep his eyes fixed steadily on the Premier, a silent challenge.

The guard standing beside Aramin hits him so hard that he crumples to his knees, then shoves him face-first into the ground. I push down the pain of this sight, biting the inside of my lip until I taste the metallic tang of blood. Constantine watches coolly, unfazed.

My eyes go to Adena. She looks hollowed out, a shadow of who she'd been in Red's vision only the night before. She searches my gaze and finds what she's looking for in there—the truth. She knows I'm the reason why they were ambushed. Why their plan today didn't work. She knows that, somehow, I discovered what they were doing and I passed the knowledge on to the Premier.

The grief I see in her now reminds me of when her brother had first died.

Adena had gotten heavily drunk that night. She threw up everything in her and fell right outside of our mess hall. Jeran carried her half-conscious form back to the apartments, where Corian made her guzzle water before I helped her change and get into bed. As she went down, she turned to me, eyes glazed with despair.

How did you do it, Talin? she whispered to me. *Make it day after day, after Basea?*

I gave her a sad smile. *Honestly? I don't know. I don't remember many of the days after my mother and I settled in the Outer City. They blended together.* I shrugged, hesitating. *And then, one day, you realize years have passed and you're still here.*

She smiled back, her bravado surging forward for a second, and then started to cry. Her hands came up, trembling, to hide her face. *I was staring right at him, Talin*, she sobbed. *He was running right at me, and I didn't even think to run forward to get him. He watched me do nothing to save him. I feel like I killed him.*

I put a hand on her shoulder and waited for her. Finally, when she fell silent and started to wipe her tears away, I leaned forward against her bed and met her stare. *You didn't do this*, I signed to her firmly. *They did. Listen to me, Adena. You're still here. You made it. And as long as you're alive, you carry on your brother's legacy. As long as we're still alive, we can keep pushing back.*

The memory fades, and I find myself staring back into the face of the same girl. But her grief is not what it once was. She doesn't see me as the Striker who fought alongside her or who held her as she cried. She looks at me like I'm the one on the other side of the warfront, shooting her brother in the back as he runs.

And she's right. Because what else am I?

Constantine glances at Caitoman and gives him a curt nod. Caitoman snaps his fingers at his troops, that malicious smile back on his face, and the Strikers are jerked away by their ropes. I tear my eyes away from their bound figures, my heart pounding at the thought of what he might do to them.

When I look back at Constantine, he's regarding me with a curious expression. "Thank you for saving my brother's life," he says to me. But I can feel him studying me, wondering if I did anything in that moment to defy him.

Finally, he gives me a small nod. *I know you resent saving my brother. You know he is a monster.*

At that, something strange and different ripples through our link. Pity, maybe, or regret. I can't tell.

Caitoman is only what our father made him, Constantine replies.

He doesn't say more about it. Instead, he straightens and walks ahead of me to join his brother's side, listening patiently as his brother leans over to tell him something.

I watch the brothers go, not knowing how to feel. Then I realize that I don't care. I don't care what happened in Constantine's past, or why Caitoman is the way he is. I don't care to know why they have chosen to destroy everything in their paths. No matter what it is, it cannot change what they've done to me. To Red. To my friends. To my mother.

My mother. My mother. My fear for her life clouds every corner of my mind. So I let myself feel angry instead, allowing the emotion of fury to build in my chest until it overtakes my fear, until rage is the only thing Constantine could possibly feel from me. I hope the anger emanating from me haunts him. Let him wake at night, sweating, from his dark dreams.

Let him feel fear too.

9

RED

I HEAD INTO THE FORESTS AND LAND AS SOON as I can, trying to keep a distance away from our makeshift Striker campsite. No need to lead General Caitoman straight to us. There, I crouch in a high, dark nook of a tree and wait.

I don't know what for. We've lost already.

The accusing voice, the other me talking to myself, fills my head like a maelstrom.

You're back to running, it hisses. Always running. And for a while, you don't know where to go. You were supposed to have destroyed the new train tracks they are building into Newage. The prisoners they were supposed to be transporting would instead be freed, ready to join us in our growing fight.

Instead, the others have died or vanished or been captured.

You'd left them there to fend for themselves. Had anyone else escaped? Would they head back to the campsite, or is it too dangerous? Would you even be able to return to the remaining stragglers like this, alone, a useless former Skyhunter with a broken wing that they'd somehow thought would give them a fighting chance? What will they think if they see you coming back empty-handed? Would you just be leading the enemy right to them?

And Talin.

I shut my eyes in an attempt to keep the image of her out—the new metal of her wings, the black armor that encases her, the hollow tragedy in her eyes. I try to kill the other voice. I had faced her and she had faced me. She'd looked straight at me, recognized me, knew what she was being forced to do, and told me to run.

Her body has been transformed, ripped apart and put together in the way that mine is. The difference is that I'd escaped, while she remains trapped.

The Premier of the Federation has her at his beck and call and I can't free her. I couldn't take her with me. My teeth clench until I think I might break my jaw. My fists tighten until the edges of my nails slice through the skin of my palms.

You couldn't help her.

I stay frozen where I am, the shame in my heart pulling me in every direction, the voice repeating over and over in my mind. It always sounds the loudest when I'm alone, trapped and helpless, as if I'm back in that glass cage. Meeting Talin had quieted it for a time. Losing her has brought it back in force.

Then I shake my head. The voice's advice changes.

No use dwelling on your failings now. Soldiers will still be on your trail. They saw the path you took in the sky to escape. They will be out, searching. You can't afford to sit here, waiting for your mind to fall apart.

Talin took a risk, warning you to escape while you could. You don't know the depth to which Constantine can control her, but she clearly still has a mind of her own. It means there's still time.

You can still find a way to get her out. You have to.

The rest of the day gradually passes. I shift locations hour by hour, careful to stay on the move. My body aches. Sunset slides into evening and then into dawn. When I fall into an unsettled half sleep, I imagine I'm a boy soldier again, curled next to other guards and shivering on my shift. I dream someone is shaking me awake, Danna shouting that I'm late for my rotation. His voice turns into the Chief Architect's, telling me to get up, it's time for the next phase of my Skyhunter transformation. I bolt awake again and again, trembling.

Then, as the first weak rays of morning sift through the forest's canopy, I see a lone figure picking its way silently through the carpet of dotted light.

At first I think it's a Karensan scout. My muscles tense as I prepare to kill the intruder before they can find me.

Only when the figure passes under an illuminated patch of forest floor and I catch the glint of red in his hair do I recognize Jeran.

I let out my breath in a rush. My eyes quickly scan the rest of the forest around us, checking if anyone is following him. But he's alone. No one else had made it out with him.

I should be elated that Jeran escaped the trap set for us. But he looks like a shell of his former self. Bloodstains on his worn Striker coat have turned black. Judging from his walk, at least, he seems uninjured. All I can muster is a bone-weary relief.

I'm trying to figure out the best way to alert him to my presence without frightening him when his steps stiffen a dozen yards from me and he looks around. His stance shifts seamlessly into an attack position. He searches his surroundings before his eyes turn up toward the trees, locking on me.

In spite of everything, I can't help smiling. His instincts have not abandoned him.

I twist around on the branch and step against the trunk, then slide to the forest floor with a soft hush, my wings softening my descent. Even this slight use of them for a glide makes me wince. I'd pushed them hard during my escape, so even Adena's temporary fix can't stop the fire of agony that shoots up and down my spine.

I crouch on the forest floor for a moment, catching my breath, before painstakingly folding my wings and approaching Jeran.

He looks exhausted, the early light casting long shadows across his face. The knot of his hair hangs messy and loose, damp strands clinging to his forehead. For a moment, neither of us says anything. Then we exchange a silent, grim nod in unison, as if we already know what the other wants to say.

"You didn't head back to camp," he whispers, when he finally finds his voice.

I shake my head.

He studies my expression and sees my guilt. It breaks something within him. Whatever restraint had held him together as he made his way here snaps, and his face crumples. He sinks to the forest floor on his knees. His sapphire coat pools around him in a circle.

"I couldn't move," he whispers, his voice breaking. "I saw his face and I couldn't move." His words halt, and I hear him take in a sharp breath wet with tears. "I couldn't do it. And they took Adena and Aramin because of it. Because they protected me."

I wait beside him as he cries, the sounds of his weeping quiet and muffled in the silent stillness of the forest. I think of the look of fear that came across his face at the sight of his father's Ghost. I know, in that moment, he must have seen not a monster but the man who he feared, who Jeran had always protected himself from by simply bowing to his wishes.

There's nothing you can say to comfort him. You know how it is. You saw the same with your own family.

Finally, when his sobs have calmed, I say to him in a low voice, "The first time I saw my father and sister as Ghosts, I froze too. It felt like someone had plunged a hand into my mind and seized it, letting it bleed. That's what the Federation intends, you know. To recognize those you love within something you hate. They know it kills something deep inside you." My voice softens. "There was no other way you could have reacted."

He shakes his head, wiping his sleeve across his face. We sit in silence for a while, the only sound being the occasional trill of some faraway bird.

At last, Jeran reaches up to retie his hair. The neater knot seems to give him a sense of calm, and he looks at me with clearer eyes.

"They knew what we were planning because of Talin, didn't they?" He nods in the direction of the camp. "That's why you aren't going back."

I tear my eyes away from him to the thick of trees surrounding us. All I can do is nod once. The joy I'd felt connecting with Talin is nothing compared with the rage and grief that swallow me now, knowing that my joy is the reason for my sorrow.

Our link pits us against each other, and the closer we get, the more we may hurt each other.

"I can't risk it," I reply. "Talin could sense, somehow, our planning—she may even have seen a glimpse of us there. The closer I linger to the others, the more danger I put them in."

At the look on my face, Jeran reaches out to touch my elbow. "Your bond with her still works," he says. "That's a good thing. And that's something we can turn to our advantage."

"How?" I pause, letting the wind through the trees haunt us. "Her link with me is a constant danger to us."

"Aramin always told the Strikers that we can always be the hunter if we think like the hunter," he says. "If Talin can see you, then maybe you can see her, too. Maybe she can give us a look inside the Federation, into the heart of what Constantine is planning day to day." Jeran's fingers tap restlessly against the hilt of his blades, and some emotion flickers across his face. I wonder if his heart is with Aramin and Adena. "Maybe we can find a way to strengthen it."

"Our bond tightens when we are physically closer," I say.

Jeran looks at me. "Then maybe that means we should head back into Cardinia."

I'm quiet for a while. He's right, of course. Let the rest of the camp here survive on their own, free of whatever dangers I might bring back to them. We'll carry on to the Federation itself.

I nod at him. "It's where they're taking the others, anyway, on that train."

Jeran's lips tighten. "Yes," he replies. "So we don't have a choice."

And now I hear the hint of resolve in his voice, some fire burning deep and angry in his chest. The Federation is reckless in who it hurts. Perhaps someday, in some way, that recklessness will be what brings it down—recklessness that breeds strong enemies against it.

The other voice in me seems to agree, lending its strength to me.

You are still here. And that means you have a chance.

Jeran is careful not to voice aloud what we both fear. I picture Aramin, then Adena, strapped down in glass chambers, turned into Skyhunters or worse. I see them joining Talin's side, forced to strike down their own friends and companions.

"It will be easier, just the two of us traveling," I tell Jeran.

He nods, and I'm grateful that he—one of the first Marans to help me—will be at my side. The realization of leaving Mara behind to fall burdens his eyes. If we leave now, it is our acknowledgment that there is little our small group can do to take this nation back. It is him turning away from his homeland, like so many others have before him. Let things go so that we can live to fight another day.

Finally, he nods and points his boots away from the direction of the campsite. "Then let's find a way to hitch a ride."

CARDINIA

THE KARENSA FEDERATION

10

TALIN

I'M TOO SCARED TO SLEEP.

As night falls, I find myself propped against the wall of my chamber adjoining the Premier's, forcing myself to stay alert, to keep a tight handle on the walls around my heart. I pace at first. Then I pour cold water on my face, trying desperately to stay conscious. The night lengthens, the moonlight shifts across my floor. I count aloud, reciting old Basean poems or Maran folk songs, rhymes we used to say to pass the time on the warfront.

Sleep threatens to pull me under again and again. Each time, I jolt awake in a panic. No. I can't sleep. I can't dream. I can't connect to Red by accident and expose him to the Premier. Not again.

I am alone now. No one can help me in this.

At some point before dawn, I pass out against the wall. I jerk upright with the first rays of dawn, bleary-eyed and gasping for air. Had I seen Red again? Had I betrayed him again?

But when I meet Constantine, he says nothing. I must not have slept for long enough.

By the time morning comes in earnest and we head down to the station, I'm exhausted. Dark circles smudge the bottom of my eyes as we pass the soldiers checking the tracks that the Strikers had tried in vain to destroy.

We board the train in what feels like a blur. I sit across from Constantine and stare out the window as we pull slowly away from Newage, trying to remember the city that existed before the conquest. Already, it's hard for me to imagine this place without scarlet-and-black banners hanging on its walls.

Before long, we've left Mara behind and are cutting smoothly through the countryside of Basea. It is an image of what Mara will someday look like—a homeland that is no longer a homeland, but one that Karensa has stripped of its soul. I tear my gaze away from the windows.

I half expect Constantine to needle me with a taunt, to say something to me in Basean. But he is mercifully quiet, spending his time writing notes into his leather journal. Maybe he sees the dark circles under my eyes, had sensed my exhaustion and grief and decided I'd gotten enough for now. No point in completely destroying his Skyhunter's mind.

In these moments, he looks deceptively docile and sophisticated, like he's someone I'm having a pleasant journey with instead of a young warlord with blood staining his hands. A man who had shoved my friends into a train car.

Other times, he speaks in low voices with advisors who come by to talk to him. I listen in helpless silence as he discusses which Maran holidays he'll let them keep and which will be done away with, what new customs and cultures he will have installed. Among them is a change in the dress law, ordering the cutting of hair and style of clothing to more closely align with habits already in place in inner Karensa. Then there are conversations about technology to bring in. The building of new streets and tracks.

He talks as if it's nothing to rip away a country's customs and traditions. As if he's chatting about the weather, while in the train cars behind us are captive soldiers, prisoners that include my former Striker companions.

His words sit like a fire in my stomach. But there's nothing I can do except reinforce the walls around my emotions, hardening myself until it feels like anything still alive in me has died.

I reach into my pocket and pull out a small pouch of coins hanging at my waist. From them, I remove a small, silver Karensan coin. I take it out and press it facedown in my palm, so that the side showing Constantine's profile is hidden and the side displaying Karensa's Federation boundaries is up.

Mara is such a new territory that Constantine has yet to mint coins showing it within the borders of the Federation. As the Premier continues to talk with his advisors, I stare at the old lands. This has become how I remind myself that Karensa wasn't always all-encompassing, that it didn't always own Mara. I study the coin and hang on to the words of the young rebel leader before she had succumbed to a Ghost.

Your Federation will *fall. It is only a matter of time.*

There may still come a day when the Federation turns to dust and disappears into the fog of history.

• • •

We arrive in Cardinia to a celebration unlike anything I've seen in my life. It pales in comparison even with the national fair we witnessed when Jeran, Adena, and I first attempted to infiltrate the capital.

The train tracks that lead into the capital of the Federation all run along black steel bridges, something I remember from my first excursion into this place—but this time, those bridges have been painted in gold. Enormous scarlet-and-black banners hang at each entry tunnel, and as our train passes through one of these tunnels, I look up to see crowds cheering our arrival, each of them flinging basketfuls of paper confetti over our carriages. Beyond sprawls the capital, a cityscape of glass domes and towers that reach for the sky.

"The celebrations will go on for the next week," Constantine tells me as I stare at the scene. "It will escalate each day until it ends on the evening of the summer solstice. There will be a series of games throughout that time."

I look at him. *Games?*

He nods. "It's a tradition from the Early Ones, who used to host games every four years that drew participants from every part of the world."

I open one of the windows and stick out my hand to catch bits of the red paper. When I bring my arm in to look at the papers, I realize they each have the Karensan crest printed on one side, along with the flag of Mara on the other.

I glance quickly at Constantine, who gives me a smile that doesn't reach his eyes.

Welcome into our fold, he tells me through our link.

And I realize that this year, they are also celebrating their new conquest.

When Adena, Jeran, and I first came to Cardinia, I'd been so awestruck by the sight of its towers that I'd never even bothered to notice the district that circles around the inside of the city wall. This district has its own, smaller wall, with a series of gates attended by guards.

This time, as we head into the city, I turn to look back at that district. I've learned what it is now, because my mother had labored within this place just months earlier. It's the prison district, a camp so large that it runs in a ring all around the outskirts of the city. Over the top of the prison district's gates, I can see clouds of steam pouring from buildings.

It houses prisoners of war. Traitors and spies. Thieves, murderers, and anyone that has crossed the Federation.

General Caitoman oversees their interrogation.

I turn my eyes away from the sight, sickness roiling in my stomach. I'd seen the hard labor my mother did in one of their factories, had to bear the horror of her bruises and wounds. I'd witnessed prisoners shackled to that inner wall, hanging until they were dead.

What if the Strikers are sent there? What if Adena and Aramin end up hanging inside that wall?

We come off the train to a commotion. A crowd of several thousand has gathered to see their Premier step onto the train platform. General Caitoman steps off first, head high and smile confident, as if he had never been held temporarily hostage by a rogue Skyhunter. He glances back at me, meets my gaze briefly, then steps aside to make room for me and his brother.

At the sight of me, the throngs back instinctively away, and I hear the whisper of a Karensan word ripple through their ranks. *Skyhunter. Skyhunter.*

I open my steel wings slightly, to impress them, then step aside to give Constantine room to walk. A roar greets him as he emerges from the train carriage. His makeup artists have done extra work on him today, covering the dark circles under his eyes and adding some color to his tired skin. He looks young and even refreshed. Perhaps part of his glow comes from the celebration of Karensa's new region, because even through our link, I can sense his pleasure.

Beside him, Caitoman nods at the crowd. "A good day to return home, isn't it?" he murmurs to his older brother before he leaves us to manage his patrols.

A cluster of Constantine's advisors is here to greet him. They flutter around him now, all fawning smiles, jostling with one another to give him their updates. A few catch my eye and skitter away until they are on the far side of the group.

I turn my attention from them and look instead down the train, craning my neck for any sign of the prisoners being unloaded. But billows of steam block my line of sight. Here and there, I think I catch glimpses of dirty sapphire coats moving through the cloud. Beyond them, teams of workers are already hustling the Striker arena's lintel and the Waterfall onto moving platforms.

Then, at a nudge through our bond, my attention shifts back to Constantine. We're on the move again. Heartsick, I reluctantly follow the Premier as he begins to make his way along the train station's path leading into the capital.

"Tonight. It's urgent."

One of the advisor's voices floats to me. My ears, keener with my Skyhunter enhancements, catch the desperation on the man's tongue as he hurries beside Constantine with the others.

Constantine gives him a cold look, but the man continues. He's pale, his lips pulled into a worried line as he speaks: "It's about Tanapeg," he says in a low voice. His eyes dart around the platform. "And Carreal. We need to send troops immediately. Tonight, sir. They've declared independence—"

At that, Constantine turns and fixes such a cold glare at the advisor that he immediately shrinks back, dropping his eyes to the floor.

"Of course, sir," he whispers hurriedly, "we can address this later. We just need an immediate vote."

"Of course," Constantine says smoothly as he walks, but in his voice, I hear a warning for the man. He pales even more, then bows his head low and drops the subject altogether. His shuffling gait speeds up as he follows beside the rest of the advisors.

I am careful not to react too much, lest Constantine realize how much I've overheard. My emotions stay even, but my mind whirls at the news. Tanapeg and Carreal, states bordering the Federation's territorial limits. The same states whose rebel leaders had been punished in Newage.

Independence.

No doubt Constantine will order troops there, may send General Caitoman out to crush the unrest. But an outright declaration of independence?

That means the Premier didn't have enough troops to quell the beginnings of their rebellion. It means the Federation might be spread too thin, and this negligence has cost Constantine the advantage of absolute control.

How deep do these cracks in the Federation run? Where do they go?

The questions sit heavy on my chest as we go, taking root there.

The rest of the city has been covered entirely in scarlet banners and strings of golden lights. Food carts line the streets, the aroma of their sizzling meats and breads sending my stomach grumbling. I look on as children chase one another through the streets, laughing, pointing, and waving at the Premier's caravan parading toward the central palace. As sundown approaches, pink light casts a warm glow across the entire city. The distinctive glass domes that top so many Karensan buildings catch the warm hues of the light. The angle of the glass is designed in such a way that the tops of these buildings look bathed in bloody light.

It is such a contrast to Mara's black-and-white architecture or Basea's lush greenery. My heart trembles at the sight.

By the time the sun sets, we have reached the end of Cardinia's main thoroughfare, where the central palace looms. General Caitoman rides on horseback in front of his patrols, leading our procession forward. Here, I see the beginnings of a vast sculpture garden with installations taken from every conquered region inside the Federation. The hollow steel husks of the Early Ones' ancient flying machines. Bones of old buildings, mangled steel and stone, jutting up into the sky. Pieces of domes and straight white columns taken from some old ruling house.

But then there are the newer pieces: a stone statue of a beautiful woman taken from Danbury; the carved arch of what was once an enormous door, taken from the halls of Saleia's governor; a collection of matching busts that used to line the front steps leading up to Tanapeg's Senate Hill, depicting each of that former nation's leaders before Karensa came.

There must be hundreds of these sculptures, all artfully placed in this garden and surrounded by blooming flowers. The pieces then continue on down the middle of the main thoroughfare leading both ways from the palace, for as far as the eye can see.

Constantine turns to me as I stare at the structures we pass. *I preserve beauty when I see it*, he tells me casually through our bond, as if this is a valid reason for all the stolen pieces here.

I grit my teeth and look away from him. *These are haunted tombs.*

But the Premier just shrugs. *There are twenty regions in this city*, he continues, *and every single one of them will soon be adorned with sculptures. Let them remind us of Karensa's destiny, fulfilled.* He gives me a pointed look. *Best get used to it, Talin. You will have to oversee Mara's installations with me.*

I look at him, and through our bond, I see a glimmer of his thoughts—his vision of the engraved lintel from the Striker arena and the pieces of the Waterfall that were being unloaded from the train.

He means to waste no time, then. He intends them to take their places here with the rest of the skeletons, as soon as possible.

Relics of Mara's greatness. Objects that hold a place deep in a nation's psyche. Soon they will be on display here too, proof of that nation's collapse. Plate sets and family heirlooms seized from the Maran nobility will fill Cardinia's National Museum. I can see the pillared building from here, its beautiful façade hiding its stolen interiors.

Even though the memory of Mara's sneering noblemen still lives fresh in my mind, I can't muster any satisfaction at it. Their wealth and greed will outlive them, put on display behind glass while they lie buried, rotting, in the ground. So what was the use in accumulating it all?

Maybe my sadness is foolish. Mara had been the nation full of people who spat on the ground I walked over, a country that refused to let my mother past its walls and shot refugees who dared to enter its gates.

But it had also been home. It had also birthed Adena and Aramin and Jeran and Corian. It had tried, at least, to hold a greater evil at bay. So I turn my eyes away from the National Museum in the distance and let my breath out, dizzy from the war of emotions in my chest.

I stay behind the Premier as he stands up on the carriage that pulls him down the main thoroughfare toward the palace, waving to the crowds that have gathered to watch him. Dancers in scarlet costumes parade before and behind the carriage, while the one behind us brings his advisors. Even from here, I can hear their laughs and chatter. Some are already drunk, eager for the night's festivities.

We finally reach the front of the palace. The square wall running along the palace's perimeter has a gate in the middle of each side, and only the Premier and his immediate procession are allowed to enter through the front. The advisors split off from us here, heading to the side gates, while we continue forward. The gate's doors, like those I remember from the National Laboratory, are made of black steel, and as we approach it, they slide open on their own without a sound.

Here, Caitoman guides his brother off the carriage and up a set of stone steps leading to the top of the palace gate, where a rampart draped with red-and-black banners and equipped with an ornate chair is waiting for him.

The Chief Architect is already here and waiting for us. Her sleek white coat nearly touches the ground, and her hair is swept up into a simple bun. Her shoulders are hunched up in a familiar, tense gesture that makes her look eternally anxious, and her deep-set eyes are hidden behind the glare of light on her glasses. A gold ring engraved with the sun's rays flashes blindingly bright on her finger, distracting me. When she notices me looking at it, she smiles briefly at me, then offers me a cool kiss on my cheek. Beside the Premier, General Caitoman nods in smug approval.

"We are guided by light," she explains of her ring, as if quoting some Karensan scripture, "and fated by the sun. Welcome back to the capital, Skyhunter."

I shift away from her in disgust.

She startles at the sight of Constantine, as she always seems to do, but then brightens her smile into one so smooth that I almost believe it's genuine.

"The entire capital has been celebrating for the past week," she tells Constantine, her eyes darting rapidly between him and General Caitoman as we all follow her. "Word of your return from Mara spread rapidly."

Constantine smiles at her. "I've missed the city. My Skyhunter and I will come to the Laboratory tomorrow, when you can study her progress and make sure she's doing well."

"Progress" is code, of course, for asking the Chief Architect to analyze my mind to ensure that my transformation is still on track. It is a sign that I'll need to return soon to the Laboratory for her to give me more injections, to have my blood drawn for analysis. It is a reminder that eventually, my autonomy will be overtaken by the Premier's commands.

I don't react, and the Chief Architect nods her head hurriedly in agreement. There's a flicker of some emotion on her face, something that confuses me, but then it's gone.

She approaches me and holds out a small vial of pale, murky liquid. "Drink this, please," she tells me. "It will help me determine how you're doing."

So, my transformation will continue as planned. How can someone be so cordial to me while deforming my body? I have no choice but to do as she says, here, before Constantine. I take the vial from her hands and drain it in one gulp. It tastes sickeningly sweet, like something unnatural.

In spite of everything, my anger toward her has settled into a simmer. She's done all this to me, but at the end of the day, we're no different. Hadn't I turned my back on my friends in order to protect my family? Instead of glaring at her, I hand the vial back and look away.

Eyes follow me as we go. I can only guess at which of them are Constantine's spies, watching me to make sure I show the proper amount of obedience.

As we look on, Constantine steps forward with Caitoman at one side and me at the other, until we appear over the edge of the rampart so that the crowds can see us.

A roar goes up from below. People wave small scarlet flags furiously, so that it looks like an undulating sea. On cue, engineers stationed along the main thoroughfare light the series of round sconces lining the street. Sparks come from each one. I step closer to the Premier as if the sconces are weapons, but Constantine's voice comes almost immediately through our link.

Don't worry, Talin. They're fireworks.

Fireworks, like what I'd seen during our mission here all those months ago. I stay back and watch, awed, as lights shoot up in trails from the sconces and explode high in the sky, illuminating the evening and the crowds with a rainbow of colors. The sound of the bursts shakes the ground.

I look on in stunned silence at the scene. People down below dance in front of the palace while lines of soldiers watch. The Chief Architect glances at me again with a look that I cannot read. She must have all sorts of ideas about how to fine-tune my transformation. Then she's facing front again, her hands folded primly before her.

The Premier holds his hands out wide to either side. As the crowd quiets for a moment, General Caitoman clears his throat and speaks, his voice ringing out loud and reverent as he acts as Constantine's mouthpiece.

"Your Premier has returned to a new Karensa Federation, united from sea to sea!"

The crowd bursts into cheers again.

Constantine smiles slightly and bows his head to his people. I know Caitoman speaks for him because the Premier lacks the strength to shout to such a crowd, but to the audience, it must appear as if Constantine has full authority over his brother.

"With the annexation of Mara into our territory," Caitoman continues, "this new regional state can at last help us build up our energy source into something that will power us into a new age. Your Premier looks forward to continuing his work on expanding and improving our nation."

At the same time, I hear Constantine's command through our link. *Show them.*

I expand my steel wings so that they stretch behind the Premier, our combined silhouette so wide that the massive shadow it casts nearly reaches from one end of the palace to the other. The people below gasp at the sight of me.

General Caitoman goes on, a confident smile on his face. I keep my wings expanded like the circus show I am. I let his words wash over me in a numb wave, more about the glory of their enormous nation and their plans for the future, their pride in their people, and their commitment to always, always, always improving themselves. How did I become indifferent to this talk?

It takes me a moment to realize what the crowd below is chanting.

"Skyhunter! Skyhunter! Skyhunter!"

They're delighted by the sight of me. To my surprise, I feel a current of unease coming from Constantine through our link. I glance at him to see his slight frown down at the people and the furrow of his brows. It's the expression he gets when he's uncertain or concerned.

With a start, I realize that he dislikes the way the crowd is enthusiastically shouting for me. Karensans love a show of strength, and I'm making the Premier look weaker by comparison.

Enough, he tells me through our link.

I instinctively pull my wings back. The people let out a chorus of disappointed shouts.

The words of Constantine's advisor come back to me as I stand here, looking out at the people. *They've declared independence.* I keep scanning the crowds for the smallest sign of dissent, watching for whispers, people with their heads turned away from the scene before them and toward one another. Watching for more signs of the Federation's weak spots.

At first, it looks like nothing but a sea of cheering people. But then, my keen vision catches a detail here and there. Murmurs. The occasional pair of eyes that dart away the instant the Premier looks in their direction. The odd citizen who does not raise their hands in applause at something the General just said.

I watch each of them as they move away, their frowns of discontent pointing at the Premier when he's not looking and then away at the rest of the city when he is. I make a mental note of who they are.

Soon the speeches are over, and we are ushered down from the wall and back into a carriage that takes us down another thoroughfare. In the carriage behind us come the Chief Architect and General Caitoman, along with a third one of Constantine's advisors.

It doesn't take long to see where we're headed next. Some distance ahead of us, past the thoroughfare's row of installations, there is a gap between the displayed artifacts.

Sickness returns to my stomach. Already, the workers that had moved Mara's pieces off the train are here, followed by giant rolling platforms pulled by teams of horses. The Maran sculptures have arrived, the pieces of the Waterfall each laid neatly out along the ground. Engineers had sent the measurements of the objects well ahead of our train, and I can see that workers have set up proper slots in the earth for the bones of the Waterfall to stand. For the lintel, they've set up two beautiful steel pillars at least ten feet high.

The crowds hush, jostling quietly in a wide circle around the garden, as the Premier steps off his carriage and takes his place in front of the installation area. As I look on, his engineers hoist each steel bone of the Waterfall with a series of ropes and pulleys, moving them carefully into place until they slide neatly into their respective slots. Other workers rush to weld each newly installed piece securely in place while the engineers move on to the next. One after another, the Waterfall comes back into existence, until it looks exactly as it did in Mara—only instead of being a sacred place, it is now the art of a conquered land made for the enjoyment of Karensans.

Beside the sculpture, they've already placed into the ground an engraved plaque written in both Karensan and Maran.

THE WATERFALL
ORIGINALLY FROM THE INNER CITY OF NEWAGE, MARA

A STRUCTURE FROM THE EARLY ONES,
THIS ANCIENT PIECE WAS COMMONLY USED
BY MARANS AS A PLACE OF MEDITATION AND SERENITY

A feeling of rage spikes at the sight, and I feel a lump well in my throat. I look away to see workers bring a large pulley system to hoist the Strikers' lintel into place atop its pillars.

How strange it is to see the stone here, its eyes staring across the Federation's capital instead of over the hills of Newage's Inner City, watching me every morning as I entered the arena to train to protect my country. How surreal it is to read the words engraved on it, words that I used to linger on every time I stepped into the Striker arena.

The lintel's placard says this:

THE STONE OF THE STRIKER ARENA
ORIGINALLY FROM THE INNER CITY OF NEWAGE, MARA

THIS EARLY ONES PIECE ONCE ADORNED THE ENTRANCE TO
THE STRIKER ARENA,
WHERE MARA'S FAMED STRIKERS TRAINED

ITS ENGRAVED WORDS TRANSLATE TO:
MAY THERE BE FUTURE DAWNS,
THE STRIKER MANTRA

Before the lintel is lifted into place, one of the Premier's advisors steps forward holding a shallow plate filled with crimson paint. She brings it before Constantine. The crowd's silence hangs in the air as the Premier dips two fingers into the paint, then steps forward to the Waterfall. There, he touches his fingers to one of the sculpture's steel bones and marks a vertical line against it. He does the same to the lintel, painting a scarlet line straight down the stone face I know so well.

Finally, he steps back so that the stone can be hoisted onto its pillars. We watch as it slides into place with a neat click.

At this point, Constantine finally smiles and spreads his arms wide. "We welcome Mara into the Karensa Federation!" he calls out.

The people burst into wild cheers. In the midst of their thunderous applause, I find myself recalling the creed of the Early Ones, the phrase that Karensa had adopted as their own.

We sow the seeds of Infinite Destiny for our children, so that they may rule from this earth to the stars.

The words play repeatedly in my mind as the ceremony continues. I keep my head bowed so I don't have to see the lintel displayed above me. It isn't until the Premier has stepped away from the new sculptures and headed back into the carriage that I realize I'm shivering. From the exertion of standing calmly by. From the strain of watching them display shreds of Mara.

From the realization that I am complicit in this nightmare.

11

RED

THE PATH WE ONCE TOOK OUT OF MARA AND into the Federation's borders is now impossible. As I glide laboriously up to the top of the tree canopy to look out over the valley between Mara's old warfront and the territory beyond, I see that part of the wild forest where we'd previously passed through is now cut down and sprinkled with soldier camps and equipment. Here and there are cavernous dig sites, the earth churned and ruined, metal pulleys and cables extending into the pits.

They're searching for something here. Karensa always is.

I shake my head at Jeran, then descend to him. My wings hurt so fiercely now that I have to clench my jaw shut to keep my teeth from chattering.

"We have to go farther north," I sign.

Jeran points at the trees from where he'd been scouting. "They're laying down new track near the river," he signs back. "We can find a way to ride on top of the train and make it past this military campground."

I follow him. It's a cloudy night, and the darkness is all-consuming, swathing us protectively in her shadows. We make it to the train station without much trouble.

Here, they are loading something onto a train car—a cylinder maybe ten feet long, containing smaller cylinders inside. I frown at the sight of it. The artifact looks oddly familiar, although I'm not quite sure why. Hadn't they been loading a similar object onto the train in Newage, the one we'd failed to stop? Is it the sleek design—or that there is more than one of them—that makes me uneasy?

"Careful!" I hear the shout go up repeatedly in Karenese from the workers struggling to move it. It must be heavy, much heavier than its size would belie. "Careful! *Careful!*"

Another of the workers is waving at the soldiers stationed nearby.

"They'll be at it for a while," Jeran whispers beside me. When I look at him, he makes a subtle gesture at the other soldiers. "Look at the backup they're calling for."

Sure enough, a trickle of guards is hurrying over to the artifact as it starts to roll off the train ramp again. Shouts of alarm come from the workers as they struggle with the chains thrown around the object, fighting to keep it from falling back to the ground.

I study the rest of the station. The number of guards left on patrol is sparse now as the rest have rushed to help with the loading effort. I glance at Jeran and nod.

As the remaining guards keep their attention on the scramble at the tracks, we make our way in the dark of night to the shadows of the train. There, we slip between two of the cars and wait in silence.

It's not exactly a small object, but how in the world can something that size be *that* heavy?

Finally, the weight shifts in their favor and the cylinder groans onto the train car. Workers scurry to secure it, throwing new chains over its top and bolting them securely against the car's platform. It's difficult to tell in the darkness, but the object seems to have a strange, faint glow about it.

The other voice in me shifts uncomfortably. Something about it reminds you of the first time you saw yourself in the mirror after your transformation. The way your new eyes seemed lit from within. Something that shouldn't exist.

After the artifact seems securely fastened, the soldiers go back to their positions and the workers return to the train. Half a dozen of them stay on the same car as the artifact, settling beside the object in exhaustion.

We board one of the nearby train cars, flattening ourselves against its side as the wheels below us jerk once with a groan. A deafening blast comes from the train's whistle. I brace myself against the car.

A minute later, the train finally begins to pull away from the station.

Before long, we are snaking through the nighttime countryside, leaving a trail of smoke and steam behind us. As the cars roll and clank, I peer out from the side to see nothing but blackness beyond us in all directions.

Behind me, Jeran shifts closer. He can't see my hands in the night and the train is too loud for us to speak, so instead, I reach back and find his arm, then tug his wrist upward twice, hoping to signal to him that we should move to the roof. It's impossible to stay down here without being thrown from side to side. If we grow too exhausted, we might fall off and be crushed when the train cars jolt against one another.

I lead Jeran to one of the ladders against the side of the car, then pull myself up step by step. Behind me, I listen for his boots on the ladder steps, but he moves so quietly that I can't detect him at all. So I just look up and keep going.

Finally, we reach the top and are hit with a blast of wind. It's cold up here, but at least it's flat, and two metal railings running along either side of the car's roof make it possible for us to grab on to something for balance.

I look behind me to see Jeran already crouched in a small, tight ball, his figure swaying gently with the car, his grip firm against the railing. His eyes glitter faintly in the night. It's all I can really make out of him.

There's still not much light to sign to each other, so instead we stay quiet and low, holding tight. The night drags on. I fight against the sleep calling to me. But the fatigue creeps into every corner of my mind, pulling me down. My chin dips as my eyes droop—I jerk awake repeatedly as the train jolts us. Then I fade again in a cycle. *Hold tight*, I scream at myself, making sure each time that my hand is still clamped against the railing.

The other voice in me chuckles. All these enhancements they gave you as a Skyhunter—and they didn't bother to take away your need for sleep? What a waste.

• • •

Despite my best efforts, I eventually drift into a half sleep filled with hallucinations.

In most of my dreams, Talin's pulse is the ever-present rhythm in the background, and I am so used to it I think of it as infrequently as my own heartbeat. But tonight, she feels near in a way that I only remember from the days when we used to walk side by side. I still, hoping to stay in this dream. Her figure starts to flicker like a shadow in the night, so subtle a movement that I cannot tell whether or not she is there.

Then I see a glimmer of her shoulder, the angle of her chin. The faint outline of a shirt with a wide, loose collar pulled back so that it exposes the skin of her upper back and lower neck. It is only a glimpse of her, but even this is enough to make me catch my breath, and in my dream, I tense, hating that my mind has conjured her in this imaginary state just to torment me. Everything in me wants to reach out and brush strands of hair from her neck, run my fingers along the line of her arm.

The scene sharpens further. Talin is sitting alone beside a window, weak light from streetlamps outside bathing her in silver, as she arches her neck high and closes her eyes. She is still wearing that loose-collared shirt, which pulls my gaze once more to the bit of exposed back and neck it reveals. My heart aches at the sight of her. Her steel wings are partially open, the bladed feathers draping down toward the floor in a graceful arch, and in the light, she looks like a creature from another world, all lines of beauty and death. Everything around her fades into blackness, so that she and the window and the moonlight seem to float in the middle of a dark world of nothing.

Suddenly, she straightens. Her face turns to one side, and then her voice comes through the link between us, like it used to, the sound echoing in the expanse of my dream.

Red? she says. *Are you here?*

I freeze. I am dreaming. This is not real. And yet, her voice comes through to me as clearly as beads on glass, as if she can see me too. As if she can *communicate* with me.

Never have we spoken to each other in our dreams before.

Are you here? she asks again. This time, she turns around, and her eyes lock straight onto mine, as if I am standing in the room with her.

Yes, I answer, as if pushed on by some supernatural force.

I don't expect her to hear me, much less answer—but the expression on her face is just as shocked as my own.

The tears that well in the corners of her eyes are ones of fear. As we stare at each other, her words come through our link.

Go away.

In an instant, I feel the bond between us shudder, as if she's pulling herself away, shuttering her windows and walling up her heart. The emotions linking us tremble, and my vision of her blurs.

I lean forward desperately, as if my hand can now brush hers. Even though I can't truly touch her, I feel a gate break open in her chest as the ghost of my hand sweeps across the ghost of hers, and her face crumples. It is only now that I realize I have never seen Talin cry. She is not weeping just for our connection in this moment—it is the bursting of a dam that she has carefully built over the months of her captivity. She is crying for the loss of her home, another nation gone, the deaths of those she knows, and the new life she has been forced into.

Her sorrow rushes through me in a wave, strengthening our bond again, and I can feel tears wet on my own cheeks.

Is this how these dreams are happening between us? When she's unconscious enough to let down her defenses, when, in her sleep, the tide of her emotions overwhelms her . . . does she open the gates between us? Our bond, run cold after so many months, surges forward now in a desperate hunger. I can feel it tingling between us, yearning to connect us as much as that first moment had bonded us on the old Mara warfront.

No. This is dangerous. This could be how Constantine sensed that something had happened between us, how he knew about our plan at the train station. What if he senses us this time?

I pull away from her, trying to find a way out of this place, to break out of this dream. But I can't—I don't know how.

Neither of us does; Talin is still here, too, the tears drying on her wounded face. We stand apart and feel the hum of the bond between us, unable to break it.

We can't meet like this, she says, her voice trembling. *He might know.*

How can we not? I answer. *How can we break it?*

She is silent at that. Because how can you keep yourself from falling asleep? How can you control what you do in your dreams?

Can . . . , I start to ask, hesitate, then push through. *Can Constantine sense everything you think? Can he control you?*

She shakes her head. *Not yet. Constantine only controls me because he has my mother.*

I catch the unspoken warning in her answer. Not yet. The anger in me bubbles at the realization that Constantine is using her mother against us all. *Where is he keeping her?* I ask.

I never know, Talin replies. *He just moved her last week—something he does every other week. The information is kept a close secret. He chooses the location himself the day before he orders her moved, and tells no one else.* She pauses, her expression darkening. *He can sense a shift of my emotions. He'd known that you were in my dreams the last time we met like this. And through my emotions, he can assume you were up to something.*

Relief and sadness and fear flood through me at the same time. So, Constantine has not invaded all of Talin's mind yet. She can still think for herself, make her own decisions, keep things from him if she must.

You haven't lost her. Not yet.

But he is still tied to her. His mind is linked to hers as surely as mine is, able to sense her changing emotions. No wonder she's locked her heart behind walls. No wonder she's terrified.

Worse, he has her mother. Forcing her hand so that she must protect her loved ones. I think back to the way her mother could fight alongside her, the ferocity of her love a beacon to us all. The way she had managed to lay out a feast for us when she had so little.

We have to find her. We have to save her. Without her, we cannot help Talin.

Talin looks up at me and sees the fury in my expression. She gives me a sad smile. Her emotions are a wave of grief, of pained love.

She tilts her eyes down. *I'm so sorry for what they did to you.*

Even in the depth of her loss, she's thinking of what had happened to me when I'd first endured my Skyhunter transformation. She's thinking of my family. Thinking of others.

I notice something new through our bond, beyond the sadness and hope and fear, even beyond whatever affection may still exist between us, if that can be called love. She is holding back again, pulling aggressively away. I remember the tension from when we had first bonded, whenever she did not want me to know the thoughts in her mind. Now she is keeping some other secret, and I cannot begin to guess what it is.

What if they have hurt her in ways you never endured?

I desperately want her to tell me more, but she stays quiet, as if gauging how much she can even say.

I don't know why I thought it would've been how it once was, being able to talk again with Talin. Our early days bonded to each other ended the instant the Premier invaded her mind. Now we're separated by a different kind of distance. In despair, I sense the barrier go up between us.

Talin is no longer Talin, but an extension of the Premier. She will kill you without hesitation if Constantine commanded it. And you would do the same if she threatened Jeran.

What if my blood ends up on her hands? What if hers ends up on mine?

We are, once again, enemies, each of us standing on the opposite side of when we first met.

I know Talin can feel the loss in me at these thoughts. I stare at her as she stands mere inches from me, as if we are in the same room together. I want to lean toward her, feel the warmth of her breath against my skin, the silk of her hair through my fingers. If I touched her hand right now, could I really feel it? The reality conjured by the strength of our bonded minds is so clear, it's hard to tell what's a dream and what might be real.

We dare to linger in this dream for another beat. Neither of us says anything. I concentrate on the rise and fall of her breaths, knowing she could disappear any moment. She studies my face, searching for something.

I try to reach out to her.

Then our dream shudders. We are waking. The world around us blurs again.

Talin. I reach for her one more time, knowing I shouldn't, yet unable to stop myself.

And somewhere in the suspension of reality, in this haze of a moment, she fades away, and I awaken back on top of the train car, jolting and bouncing along in the night.

I gasp as my eyes open. My hand comes up to rub across my face, and I find tears. The image of her is still imprinted in my mind. She'd been so damn real. I should be relieved that we've finally broken out of our dream—where we're so vulnerable to Constantine's suspicions—but instead I'm just desperately empty. Leaving Talin feels like ripping my heart out of my chest. I wince. I can feel the pain of it as if my body is still torn open.

My eyes wander to Jeran. He's asleep. I was supposed to have stayed awake during my shift guarding us atop this train. Guiltily, I shift so that my weight is sure to block him from rolling off the top of the car, and then I look around at the rest of the train.

My gaze settles on the platform several cars ahead of us, the one carrying the heavy artifact.

I'm grateful for the darkness that hides us from the few workers stationed to guard the artifact. They are still there, swaying with the train cars. At first I think they are all clustered together in sleep—but then I see that a couple of them are holding up one of the workers as he vomits over the side of the train car, his figure hunched over in pain.

You would think they would all be used to the motion of a train by now. I'm surprised any of them could be sick because of it.

It takes me another moment to realize that the ill worker is vomiting a trickle of blood, inky black, into the night. I know what it looks like, of course—I've seen plenty of blood in darkness. As if to confirm it, I can smell the faint scent of something metallic in the wind. My insides recoil.

The worker must have some old injury. Maybe it was made worse during the struggle to secure the artifact. I look on, feeling queasy myself, as the worker continues to retch until he finally slumps backward in exhaustion.

Over on the other side of the artifact, another worker is also vomiting over the side of the moving platform. Even from here, I can hear the occasional moan coming from him.

That man, too, is retching blood.

My grief over Talin fades momentarily as I watch them. Eventually, they seem to settle back down into a restless sleep. More old injuries? Somehow, it doesn't quite make sense to me. My eyes go from their resting figures to that strangely familiar metal cylinder, and I concentrate on the faint glow it seems to emit.

Maybe it's my imagination. Maybe it's just the way the lights from an occasional village hit the artifact whenever the train curves along its track.

But something about it feels off. It's the same feeling I remember as a child, watching Karensa's parades of early Ghosts down Cardinia's avenues.

The same feeling I had during each year's solstice festivities when red paper rained down on me even as prisoners of war were hauled through the streets.

It's the unmistakable feeling of something unnatural shifting in the air. It's the feeling that something is about to go horribly wrong.

12

TALIN

MY FIRST NIGHT BACK IN THE CARDINIAN PALACE is an unsettling one. I never get used to the sheer size of this space, a maze of corridors and gates and spiraling staircases. There are moving platforms they call elevators here, steel boxes moved by pulleys up and down through the palace to get from one story to another. To the east, in a separate building connected to the main palace by a hallway, is an enormous greenhouse, a glass structure built against the marble and stone of the palace. When I'd first set foot in Cardinia with the other Strikers, the glass exhibition hall erected for the national fair had been modeled on this greenhouse. It is a luxury, a paradise of fruit trees and rainbow-hued rows of sweet-scented flowers that Constantine frequents.

The main palace's atrium features a glass ceiling, and the walls are framed with gilded edges. They're painted with elaborate scenes of Karensan history, from their earliest days as a nomadic race to the era when they built their first permanent city atop a ruin of the Early Ones along the banks of a northeastern river.

It is an estate of grotesque extravagance. Everywhere I look, there is something new and overwhelming.

My footsteps echo down the lonely halls. There must be thousands of servants in this space, but at night, I feel like the Premier is the only other person here with me.

Once again, I can't sleep. I'd dreamed of Red in my state of exhausted collapse earlier in the evening, a vivid dream so startling that I bolted out of it with tears in my eyes, Red's name still echoing in my mind. It truly felt like we'd spoken, even though that's impossible. I had looked at him and known with horror that he was really seeing me. After all, hadn't my last dream turn out to be a real vision? For a span of minutes, I'd exposed him to Constantine in my mind, had risked the Premier's sensing us connecting once more. For hours after, I forced myself to stay behind my walled heart, wondering when Constantine would turn to me and ask me about my second dream with Red.

Or worse, that I would somehow turn a corner with the Premier and see Red chained and on his knees. That somehow just glimpsing Red in my dreams would have alerted the Premier to his location and gotten him captured.

But there's been no word from Constantine this time. We may not be this lucky again.

So tonight, as I roam these empty halls, my thoughts are filled with shadows and nightmares. Fears of my private thoughts being unveiled again. Fears of being watched by spies. Fears of Constantine's mood, that my mother will suffer depending on how it swings next. On top of it all, the eternal fear that some rebel assassin might be making their move against the Premier right now, that someday, I might fail to protect Constantine from that threat, and that my mother will be executed for it.

All of these worries swirl in my stomach until the nausea becomes unbearable. I pause in my walk, then return to my chambers, where I retch in the bathroom until I have nothing left.

No matter what happens, I will suffer. There is no light at the end of these tunnels.

• • •

When morning finally dawns, I am weary and moody. I extend one of my steel wings at the young manservant sent in to assist me in washing and dressing, sending him scurrying from my chamber in fright. Guilt flits through me at the sight of his fleeing figure, but I don't have time to worry about him. Today, I'm off to see where Constantine has decided to keep my mother currently.

Before long, I'm seated in a carriage that takes me to another district in Cardinia. As we pass through the center of the city, I notice fresh paint splashed and scrawled over some of the stone bases of the sculptures that line the thoroughfares.

They distract me for a moment. As the carriage draws near them, I realize that they are rants of fury smeared against the stone.

PUPPET PREMIER
FREEDOM IS A LIE
CUT KARENSA'S THROAT

I stare at them for as long as I can, until our carriage has passed it all and the damage fades in the distance. No doubt someone will scrub them clean as quickly as they can. I wouldn't have thought much of it, except the advisor's words at the train station keep coming back to me.

Independence.

Threats against the Premier, scrawled on his precious sculptures.

The thoughts linger with me as we pull away from the city's center and into small streets.

One look at the district we drive through tells me what I need to know. This time the path to my mother's current location is a nice one—the open carriage passes through a Cardinian district shaded with mature oaks, the path paved smooth until we reach a set of ornate wrought-iron gates. The road beyond it is cobblestone studded with shining flecks of mica, leading to an estate of white marble and stone, the sound of trickling fountains sweetening the air.

Behind the walls I've put up, the knot of terror in my heart loosens somewhat, and I feel my muscles slack a little, the air flowing a little more easily to my lungs. This is how I know Constantine is pleased with me. I've accompanied him to Mara and helped him punish prisoners of war by turning them into Ghosts. I've helped defend him and our train from espionage and turned my back on Red. I've bled my soul for him. In return, my mother will live here for a short reprieve—on the grandest estate I've ever seen in my life.

"Welcome to the home of Mayor Elland of Cardinia," the driver tells me, bowing his head, as the gates open for us. He glances at me with a half-disgusted, half-frightened look. "Her servants will attend to your every need during your stay today. At dusk, my carriage and I will be waiting for you at the manor entrance."

He says more, although his Karenese is too rapid for me to understand completely. I just nod at him and turn my attention to the front of the property. Sure enough, I see a line of servants already at attention at the front of the property, their faces turned in our direction. My eyes wander to the rest of the pathway.

Constantine has never broken his promise regarding my mother, but I still worry. My fingers tap restlessly against my leg as I search for her. She's not here yet.

The servants bow low as I step off the carriage and onto the path. Behind me, my driver doesn't hesitate to urge his horses onward the instant I leave. I hear the snap of his reins, and when I look over my shoulder, his back is already turned, hunched as if bracing himself for me to attack him.

I turn to the servants. A part of me wants to extend my wings to their full span and watch these Karensans cower at the sight of the Premier's Skyhunter, to be the monster they see. But I remind myself that they are servants. Some of them might even be prisoners like my mother, or people from some other conquered land, now forced to serve the mayor. Instead, I bow my head in return at them.

They don't see me anyway. None of them dare look up at me.

"There she is, right on time!"

The familiar voice of the mayor drifts to me from the stairs, and I glance over to see the woman making her way down the steps toward me, regal in her silver-gray outfit and her thickly piled knot of hair.

"It seems you behaved well enough for the Premier to reward your mother," she calls to me. Just as I'd seen in Newage, she smirks at the forced subservience on my face. Then she scowls at the servant beside her. "Well, don't just stand there. Make sure the Skyhunter's horse is ready and show her to it."

The servant jumps a little at the command, bowing his head in a rush, then scurries off.

The mayor looks back at me and holds her hand out at the path winding along the side of the manor. "Your mother's been out riding this morning. She's stronger than she should be after such a long captivity. Maybe there's something to be said for that Basean spirit." She smiles. "Or maybe we're treating our prisoners right, after all."

My hands curl into fists at her joke, but she laughs. "Go on, then, Skyhunter," she says, waving a dismissive hand at me. "I have a full morning of tasks ahead of me, and you've already taken up enough of my time."

I'm surprised by this noblewoman's small generosity, but I don't dwell on it. Instead, I give her a quick bow of my head.

"Ah, Constantine and his games," she says, her voice almost sad. There's a glint of sympathy in her eyes. "He hasn't changed since he was a child. All right, then. Off you go."

I turn down the path and follow in the wake of the young servant that Mayor Elland had sent running. He guides me around the side of the manor. We turn the corner, and there, waiting for me along the stone wall running beside the house, is my mother.

She's on the back of a white stallion and holding the reins of a second horse at her side. Her silver-white hair falls behind her in a thick braid. To my absolute shock, she's dressed in what looks like traditional Basean clothes—a loose, billowing white shirt with easy knots twisting down the front, a pair of high-waisted pants with a wide black belt fastened by a gleaming silver buckle in the shape of a crescent moon. It's finery I've never seen her in, not even in Basea.

Everything in me floods with gratitude that today, I'm probably far enough from Constantine for him to have trouble sensing my emotions through our bond. Even if he can, I don't care right now. The sight of my mother like this brings me to tears. At the same time, a well of anger pools thick in my stomach. Last month, she'd been kept in the prison district. Now she is on the mayor's estate, indulging in food and leisure. The wounds on her hands from the prison labor have healed, and her gaunt face has rounded, the color having returned to her skin.

Constantine and his games, the mayor had said. And it's true. This is him toying with his prey, pulling these emotions out of me to train me into obedience. Perhaps even to love him, like one of his citizens.

I look around, searching for a way I could spirit my mother out of here and to safety. But Constantine has warned me of this. *I am always watching you*, he told me. Even if I cannot see them, I know there are hidden soldiers in the trees and along the horizon, snipers on the roofs of the estate, their guns trained on my mother's head. If I try something, they will shoot her dead. Even I, with all my Skyhunter enhancements and strength, cannot stop them all.

My mother smiles sadly at the look on my face. She knows that the luxury she gets to indulge in this month is solely because my obedience has pleased the Premier. And this time I can see, behind all this new luxury around her, the weight her eyes carry no matter what conditions she's in. Her safety always comes at a cost.

Still, she brushes it away. "What?" she says, a teasing lilt in her voice. "You've never imagined your mother as a Basean noble?"

Genuine relief floods me. Being trapped in Cardinia, where no one else can understand Maran sign language, with only Constantine able to comprehend everything I want to say, with my emotions held back tight within my chest, has left me a hollow shell. But on these days, I can be with my mother. I can let my heart open a little and take her in.

I suppose I can thank the Premier for that too.

"I was about to say that you look like you belong in those clothes," I sign.

She nods to the horse waiting beside her, and I hurry to it, ready to savor every minute of this day. I grab the saddle and swing easily onto the creature's back, then guide it around to follow my mother. We turn in the direction of the rolling hills that make up the rest of the estate. The breeze is gentle, the air just the right hint of warmth, and I find myself leaning into it, trying to ignore the strangeness of enjoying this perfect morning in a hostile nation.

"How is your pain?" my mother asks after a comfortable silence, and I feel myself lean toward the soothing sound of Basean on her tongue. It's a question she brings up during each of our visits. For a while, my answers had been *always*, *constant*, *never-ending*. She would see the small changes happening on my body—one month, the metallic tint of my hair; another month, the addition of bladed tips on my wings. When they infused the marrow of my bones with steel particles; when my heart was forced to grow larger and stronger to accommodate the changes in my body; when I spent those early weeks sitting up at night, gasping for breath and clutching my chest in agony, certain that my heart would burst from the strain . . . my mother saw the consequence of each week.

For all the anguish I feel in seeing my mother suffer, I imagine the sight of me causes her even more pain.

I shake my head. "Only a little, sometimes, when I'm sleeping," I answer as I drop the reins to sign. "There's not much left to my transformation now." And before we can dwell on this, I quickly ask, "The mayor's treating you well, then?"

My mother snorts a little. "That woman," she says. "Do you know how she delivered this horse to me? She waited until I was lounging in a bath, and then had the horse stick its head right through the open window to drink my bathwater. I could hear her laughing even over my shrieks. A Cardinian with a sense of humor. I'll be damned."

I laugh in surprise, the sound coming out in a thin wheeze. "I suppose someone has to be a real human being in this country."

My mother laughs too, then quiets as our horses leave the manor behind us and enter a stretch of grassland bordered by thickets of trees. "They bring me three meals a day," she says in a low voice. "Porridges fat with chicken and eggs. White buns and scented rice. Fish and stewed beef and noodles. Basean foods, Talin. All of it, as if made by some master chef. The Premier keeps his word and wants to remind us of it at every turn. And all I can think about every single day is that, somewhere in their kitchen, a chef who likely fled Basea's collapse is now making me meals in exchange for Karensan coins. By the order of the Premier." Her lips tighten as she turns her eyes to the horizon. There we can see a few silhouettes of ruins from the Early Ones, tall pillars sticking out of the ground and reaching up to nowhere. "I'm sorry, Talin, that you have to serve them because of me."

I start to shake my head. During the first couple of months, I'd lived in terror of my mother killing herself in order to spare me the torture of continuing to obey the Premier. She had become so listless, so damaged by the sight of my suffering. I'd fallen to my knees during our second visit, sobbing like I was still a little girl, and begged her to stay alive. Told her that if she died, I would too. I forced her to promise me to live. So she had lived on, month after month.

Sometimes I wonder whether I've done a terrible thing to her, making her stay alive.

I nod at her hands. "Your wounds have healed faster than I'd thought they would."

She nods and looks down, turning her now-scarred fingers this way and that. "The headman for the prison team I worked for took me off my shift early, after the Premier sent word halfway through the month that you'd been doing well." Her words turn careful as her eyes dart back to me. "I spent two weeks in the hospital there, doing nothing but listening to stories coming back from prisoners of war along the outer Karensan states."

I am careful not to react to my mother's words, careful to keep my mind calm so that even at this distance from the palace, I don't potentially alert Constantine to what I'm thinking. But my heart skips a beat.

This is the other reason my mother has decided to keep living. This is something that Constantine *didn't* anticipate. Few others in Cardinia move around as much as my mother, from prison district to mayor's estate in the span of a month. With each new place she's brought to, she listens. She searches for information that might be useful to me.

She is spying.

"I'm grateful you had those stories to listen to while you healed," I answer her, my fingers moving casually.

"They were nothing but rumors." My mother shrugs. "Just a few skirmishes and protests from citizens in Tanapeg. A few of the ones arrested were sent to the prison district I worked in. The mayor has put them to work on her estate."

Just a few skirmishes and protests. It is a careful phrasing. As she says it, she turns to give me a pointed, sidelong look, and I know immediately what my mother is really trying to tell me.

The mayor has put them to work on her estate. And I remember what the mayor said to me when I first arrived. *She's stronger than she should be after such a long captivity. Maybe we're treating our prisoners right, after all.*

Did my mother heal quickly because of the mayor's help? And if so . . . why would the mayor help her? The thought is so wild that I'm afraid to follow it. What else is the mayor helping?

"Oh?" I answer calmly, waiting for more. "I didn't think they had much to protest, now that they're under the Federation's fold."

My mother eases her horse into a slow trot, and I nudge my steed to do the same, until we're riding around the edge of the thicket of trees. "Does it really matter if the other states have the occasional group that wants to separate?" She glances back once at me. "It's only real trouble for the Federation if they bring it here."

At that, I look sharply at my mother. My fingers move rapidly, words that she can see but no one else can hear. "And have they brought it to Cardinia?"

She nods once. "Right into the heart," she signs back to me.

Then she prods her horse into a fast trot. I do the same. "And now I'm here, resting on this estate. Who knows where those prisoners have been shipped off to? Maybe they've already died in the prison district." She laughs a little. "Or maybe they've found themselves working in higher places."

Her statements are said lightly, with such little fanfare, that anyone who doesn't know her might think she's speaking sarcastically. But I catch the glint in her eye. *Maybe they've found themselves working in higher places.*

She knows some of those former prisoners. She knows some of these rebels hiding in plain sight. She knows where they've been placed.

Right here.

"What kind of higher places?" I sign.

"The National Laboratory," she signs back.

I trot alongside my mother as we fall into silence, but my hands are shaking now. Someone has found their way into the very birthplace of the Federation's war experiments.

She smiles a little at my expression and signs again: "Only rumors. But they say you should speak to someone there with a scar behind their ear."

All my thoughts swirl in a din in my head. I tamp it down, force myself to turn my mind back to riding with my mother.

But she has already told me what I need to know. The rebels that have been stirring unrest at the Federation's border states have brought it to Cardinia. They are *here*, in the capital. Working under the mayor.

Perhaps working *with* the mayor.

If Mayor Elland is actually involved, then that means the unrest could be much larger than I'd thought. It is a movement gathering steam. And if I can find out more about it, if I can find a way to help the cause . . . well. An old thought returns to me, one I'd clung to on the day Mara had been defeated.

The Federation has conquered us. But it has not annihilated us yet.

13

RED

THE LAST TIME I WALKED THROUGH CARDINIA freely, I was twelve.

Think back, and I remember it all. It was a warm, sticky day, and the summer exhibition was happening throughout the city, a festival showcasing a system of irrigation tunnels that children were allowed to slide down. I'd gone with two friends, and returned drenched and laughing, two frozen pops melting over our hands with their sticky sugar.

What a fun time I had. How little I thought about everything happening around me.

Back then, I'd looked at the guards standing on street corners and watching me play as my guardians, protecting me from falling or drowning or running into the streets in front of the horses and carriages. A year later, I'd return to the city as a disgraced soldier, accused of the indirect murder of my superior because I'd failed to shoot a girl. Talin.

Talin, the girl I can't stop worrying about. The girl I can't imagine not saving, not taking with us out of this place.

As I walk through Cardinia's streets with Jeran behind me, dressed in a flowing Karensan outfit and a reveler's mask over my face, I find myself tensing along every street with more than two guards standing watch.

Our train had finally arrived in Cardinia two evenings after we'd left Mara's borders, to a city fully immersed in the solstice celebrations. The first thing we'd done when we arrived in the city was trade several of our knives for money, acting as peddlers selling scraps of the newly conquered Mara, and then we bought ourselves new clothes. Cardinia had once been Togaia's capital, after all, before it became the Karensa Federation's, and that means it's a city where everyone is used to newly conquered visitors struggling to fit in. With so many different people in Cardinia, we've blended in with the crowds easily—but that doesn't mean General Caitoman doesn't have his soldiers on alert, possibly searching for anyone who resembles us.

The entire city has turned out for the solstice festival, and the crowds jostle beside us, giving us the protection of anonymity. As we go, I make a habit of noting the armbands on any passing guard's sleeve, each marked with a distinct symbol detailing which city patrol they belong to.

My eyes hitch each time I spot a guard who still looks like a boy, no older than I was when I became one.

The sight sends a current of unwelcome nostalgia through me. Suddenly, I feel like a young soldier again, little more than a child recruit, double-banding my insignia in order to make sure it doesn't slip down my boyish arm. I used to keep track of the other city patrols during my daily duties because it told me where I could find my friends that were assigned to other patrols. I push that memory away as I keep a mental tally of the symbols I see. The brand of my old patrol insignia, which had been burned into my chest, aches underneath my clothing.

Are any of those old friends still here, patrolling the city? They were only children then, like me. Would they recognize me now, even behind my reveler's mask? On instinct, I reach up and adjust the cloth I've looped loosely around my head.

Jeran walks beside me, his eyes wide behind his half mask as he takes in the sights. "I've read about this festival," he says in near-perfect Karenese, "but I didn't realize how big it was."

Thank you, Jeran, I think to myself, *for being so fluent*. "It's not ours," I reply. "It was a tradition from Carreal. When Karensa overtook that country decades ago, they found their solstice festival so enlightening that they decided to adopt it."

Jeran's lips tighten. He stares as we walk the main thoroughfare and pass the hundreds of stalls lining the wide avenue. "Was it always this contentious?"

At his words, I glance over to what he's looking at. Jeran's attention is fixed on a smear of black paint scrawled against the marble base of a sculpture along the thoroughfare.

It's the Premier's seal, consumed in flames.

Another sculpture nearby has been vandalized too, painted in scarlet and smudged with angry words.

KARENSA IS DEAD

I blink, stunned for a moment into silence. "No, that's new," I murmur.

The news of occasional unrest in the city is familiar to me; my superiors used to do plenty of rotations here, spying on potential rebels and arresting those who seemed suspicious. But this kind of open rebellion? I've never seen that.

Jeran stares for a moment longer, taking stock of which sculptures have been damaged. "Can you sense Talin at all here?" he asks.

The mention of Talin sends a wave of new fear through me. Her heartbeat had accompanied me for the entire train ride, but now it seems to flicker in and out, some of the vibrations lost among the noise and chaos of the festival. Whatever emotions she might be feeling right now, I can't sense them. She must be holding her thoughts tight.

I shake my head. "I don't know," I admit. "She's in the city. That's all I can tell."

The memory of her last night comes back to me now. Part of me still believes that our entire conversation had just been a dream, but it seemed so sharp, so unwavering even after sleep that it must have been real.

Jeran glances sidelong at me. "Do we know how long her mother has been in her current location?"

My mother, Talin had told me through our bond, and her voice had sounded so sharp, so desperate in its sadness and fury, that I can feel the stab of her pain even now. Talin works for the Premier solely because of her mother. I know the agony of that trap.

"Nearly a week," I answer in a low voice. "She'll stay there for another week. Then Constantine will order her moved again, depending on his pleasure or displeasure with Talin."

Jeran winces. Is he thinking about his own father? I wonder. But when he speaks, he just says, "Then we'll need to figure out where she is soon. How would we start a search like that?"

I look around at the festive scene. Where *could* we even begin? "Talin said the Premier decides the location on his own," I whisper as we slide past a crowd gathered around a street performer. "But without consulting anyone else, the day before her mother is moved. That means we have a slim window to find out ahead of time where her mother is going to be transferred. That window is our only shot at freeing her."

Jeran shakes his head. "But *someone* knows where her mother is. A guard at the future location, maybe, so they can prepare for a new, high-profile prisoner. After all, the Premier doesn't move her himself."

I snort at the mental image. "If he tried, he'd be unconscious and bleeding in the grass."

Jeran laughs a little, in spite of himself.

"Rumors of prisoner movement tend to spread among the guards," I tell Jeran as we near the lab complex. "I remember gambling on that when I was a young soldier here."

"Gambling?" Jeran asks.

I nod. "My friends and I would place bets on where we thought high-profile prisoners would end up, and which patrols would be assigned to them. I was once assigned as a junior guard to the patrol for a general arrested from Basea. We weren't to talk about his location, on penalty of death. But we still placed our bets anyway."

"Did you win?"

I look away, unwilling to meet his steady gaze. "Three hundred notes," I answer in a low voice, "yeah, I did."

"Where would we go if we wanted to catch conversations like that?"

I shrug. "Wherever the highest concentration of soldiers is right now—and seeing as how the new Maran prisoners have the most attention, wherever they're headed."

Jeran looks around. "Where do you think they would bring Striker prisoners during all this?"

"They'll either be at the National Laboratory," I reply, "or held in the rooms underneath the arena seats."

At that, Jeran glances sharply at me. "Arena seats?"

I nod once. "Karensans love sport," I tell him. "The Premier likes to hold the events to keep the people happy, and they especially like to do it with prisoners of war. The events are always a secret. The audience gathers in the arena each day without knowing what they've come to witness." My voice halts, and when I speak again, it sounds hoarse. "The Strikers will be either qualified for some experimental program at the lab complex or used to entertain the people."

Jeran's silent, but when I look at his eyes above his mask, they shine with a grave light. There is fury there for what Karensa will do to our friends—but there is also a twinge of guilty understanding. Mara did something similar with their prisoners, after all. I'd been one, hadn't I? It's never as entertaining when you are the one sent into the stadium to die.

We look away from each other, two soldiers from enemy nations, and the silence settles awkwardly between us.

When we pass by the lab complex, I can tell immediately that the Strikers aren't there. No crowd has gathered in front of its gates, peering curiously for a look at the new prisoners of war. So we move on in the direction of the arena at the center of the city.

All around us, people are dressed in the colors of Karensa. They're happy and laughing, hungry as they wait in lines at the food stalls, giddy to see what's going to happen in the arena on each day. I watch them go about their celebrations with a surreal sense of shame. I used to be that little boy, waiting in line for fried cheese. I used to be the one running into the arena, curious about what new entertainment they would have for the day. Now I'm here, heart in my throat, waiting to see if my friends will be the ones forced to amuse this crowd.

The masses thicken as we draw closer. The structure is a perfect circle. Through a dozen different gates embedded into its curved outer wall, there are a dozen different holding rooms that then lead into the main arena. With the sheer number of people here today, the Strikers must have already been ushered inside. They'll stay in there until the day they're selected to go into the arena.

Until the day they're scheduled to be killed.

We edge close enough to the first gate to see the details of the sliding metal door. The crowd moves around us in a swarm of festivity. No, too many people here. I glance ahead through the throngs to get a better look at the second gate.

That's when I notice the rectangular metal slabs on the sides of some of the pillars. Vents. Memories flash back to me as a child walking through the gates, feeling the draft from overhead. Long air ducts tunnel throughout the halls underneath the arena, under every seated row. And where there are vents, there are open spaces to hide.

The metal grilles over the vents are high, near the ceiling of the curved gates, too high for an average human to reach. But for Jeran and me, they're within reaching distance. If we worm our way inside them, we can travel undetected through the ducts to search the holding rooms.

I tap Jeran once and, without explaining, let the crowd sweep us toward one of the gates. Fewer people gather under these shaded entryways, which means Jeran and I can slip in behind the pillars on either side of the gate, partly hidden and forgotten as the rest of the crowd mills restlessly around the entrance doors to the holding rooms on the off chance of glimpsing the prisoners.

Jeran looks puzzled by what I'm doing, but he doesn't react. Instead, he watches me as I study the metal grille above us. Then, hidden in the shadows behind the pillar, I pull myself up stone by stone and then push off with my boots as hard as I can. It's enough for me to reach the edge of the grille. I take a knife from my belt and worm it between the grille and its frame, then push.

My wings may be damaged, but my strength is still intact. The force of my shove is enough to pop off the grille so it can swing open. I lift myself higher to peer into the dark tunnel it reveals. Sure enough, it's an air duct, its cool, circulating breeze combing through my hair.

I look down at Jeran, who has caught on. He climbs lightly up the pillar, his boots finding the tiniest footholds. I crawl into the vent, then move forward to give him room. A moment later, Jeran appears behind me. I hear the faint clink from him replacing the metal grille.

We exchange a brief smile. Then I turn forward and begin making my way through the duct.

It's cool inside the hall of holding rooms. The duct curves, following the arc of the wall, and we move with it. All along the way, thin slats in the side of the duct give us a faint view of the corridor below.

Two guards stand at each holding room's door. We stay quiet in the shadows of the rafters, looking through the slats as scarlet-clad soldiers march by in regular intervals. None of them bother to look up at the duct running along the ceiling—none of them seem concerned.

We listen for a while, catching bits of their conversations as they go. Their focus seems to be on the prisoners who've just arrived, but as they talk and laugh, I see them do what I used to do—passing bets on slips of paper between them. Likely on whom they think will win the games over the next few days. As they tease one another, I study the rest of the hall.

The number of soldiers at the arena is numerous—but not as much as I'd expect. That's a surprise. Back when I lived in this city, there'd be at least a dozen patrols of six, all assigned to this area of the arena alone. Now I count three. Where are the rest?

I wait carefully until there's a brief pause between clusters of soldiers, then continue without a sound along the tunnel. Jeran moves in a silent crouch as he glances inside each of the rooms across the hall below, looking past the grates for any sign of someone familiar. He has been the more careful one of us, but now his movements take on urgency that's rare in him. I have only ever seen it once. It was on the battlefield during our final stand, and it was to protect Aramin.

He stops abruptly. Everything in him freezes. Then he glances over his shoulder at me and nods once.

The door is a series of wide metal bars, and through them, I find myself looking into a dimly lit room at the shadowed faces of Adena and Aramin. No sign of Tomm or Pira, who must be kept in a different room. Both of them are so heavily chained that it looks ridiculous; shackles on their wrists and ankles, waists and neck, all of them connected to the wall, while half a dozen guards stand outside their door—three facing them, three facing the hall.

My heart sinks. Constantine fully intends for them to participate in the game tomorrow.

Being held here, they will be hard to get out. The keys that unlock these prison doors and their chains are not keys at all, but strings of numbers input as a code. The codes are kept at the palace itself, accessible likely only by the Premier's personal guard.

One of the soldiers is saying something to Adena, but she doesn't pay him any attention. Neither she nor Aramin looks up where we are crouched in the shadows, watching from our small opening. Instead, they sit across from each other in the room with their arms weighed down, leaning against their knees as they ignore the guard speaking to them.

A knot sits thick in my throat. I can only imagine the emotions coursing through Jeran, but even in the darkness, I can tell that he is trembling all over. He keeps his eyes fixed on Aramin, his gaze darting slightly about as if he is studying the chains and wondering whether there is any way we can break them free.

The thought crowds my mind too. But I know it will be impossible. The crowds today are too thick, and the focus on these prisoners too strong. Everyone is here to watch them perform. Too many eyes.

But what if you could cut through the guards, past those cell doors and their chains?

No. I can't fly. My wings are too far damaged, and without reliance on my flight, it will be too hard to force our way in, cause a commotion, and then try to get them out of the city without attracting the attention of every guard in the city. The Premier will know—he will probably send Talin to face us. Ghosts will be released from their pens around the city's military complexes and the lab.

I shake my head in silent frustration as two of the guards rotate out. Beside me, Jeran glances at me and seems to guess what I'm struggling with. His hands flicker in the dim light.

"Smaller shifts," he signs to me, pointing down at the moving soldiers below. "More frequent."

I nod grimly. There is a pattern to the soldiers they've positioned. And when I glance up to the corners of the ceiling, I notice curved rims of mirrors strategically placed. They are designed so that there is no inch of this floor unseen by the guards, no matter where the soldiers stand. They can see a reflection of every curve against this wall. We'll have to knock them out if we're to set foot outside this vent.

I do my best to sign this to Jeran. He shakes his head, frowning a few times, but eventually gets the gist of my efforts when he looks at the mirrors.

We settle back to study the soldiers again. No matter how we look at them, we both reach the same conclusion. There is nothing we can do to get them out right now. We are as helpless as if we were standing on opposite shores of an ocean.

Eventually one of the guards stops trying to talk to them and turns his back. Jeran moves slightly against the opening in the vent. One of the buttons at his collar gleams in the light.

A moment later, Aramin's eyes slide up the wall opposite him. His gaze travels to the soldiers standing outside, then go up to fixate on the slits in the ceiling vent, right where Jeran's button must have glinted.

At first, the Firstblade doesn't seem to see us.

But even as Aramin's gaze breaks away, he comes back again and again to look up in our direction. Jeran does the same each time, shifting just enough for a tiny bit of movement to be seen from outside the vent.

A small, sad smile appears on the edges of Aramin's lips. Maybe he knows it's us.

I look to Jeran. He does not utter a sound, is so still that even I think he has blended in with the shadows, but when I take in his face, I see tears streaming down his cheeks. His gaze stays locked on Aramin. Neither of them makes a single gesture, but something passes between them, a conversation I cannot understand.

As I look on, I see Aramin's fist clench tight. He looks back down at the floor, but in silence, he presses his fist to his chest in the Striker salute. The gesture is subtle and quiet. But, as with everything about the Strikers, the silence is not silence at all. He is telling us that he knows we are here. He is reminding us that they are alive, that we still have time.

Adena, too, catches the gesture. She knows better than to react, but I can see her recognition in the slight widening of her eyes. She follows the turn of Aramin's body to look at the vent. The ghost of a grin touches her lips.

"Jeran," I sign gently, until he glances at me with grief in his eyes. I nod once. "We'll come again."

Jeran nods, as if snapped out of a daze. We can't stay camped in these ducts forever, hoping to catch a whiff of soldiers' gossip. But Aramin and Adena can, at least until they're forced into the arena. They might hear something that will help us.

When Jeran can't tear his eyes away from Aramin, I touch his shoulder softly. "Tomorrow," I sign. "More time then."

Jeran's eyes are still locked on the prison door below. "What will happen to them?" he signs back.

I shake my head. "I don't know."

And I genuinely don't. Like many of Karensa's punishments, this is designed to be a game. A surprise. Something the crowds are forced to look forward to in morbid curiosity. What will happen in the arena tomorrow is anyone's guess, although rumors must have already begun to spread.

"I can tell you this." This time, I lean closer to Jeran so I can whisper in his ear. "Constantine will give them a fighting chance. No one goes through this much trouble to bring prisoners to the solstice games without making a sport of it." I nod down to where Aramin and Adena sit. "Mara's Strikers are legendary. People will be clamoring to see them. The Federation will stretch this out for longer than a day. They will still be here tomorrow night. And that means we'll still have a chance to rescue them."

"Rescue," Jeran signs as he forces his eyes away from the prison. He meets my gaze. "Is that possible?"

"Any other year? No. Their keys and any duplicates are too hard to get." I give him a small smile. "But this year?" I whisper. "We may know someone on the inside."

Talin. If the palace holds the key, then she might be able to get her hands on one for us. *If.*

The other voice in me perks up all of a sudden.

You hate using that word with her. As if she might choose to betray you instead. As if she isn't someone you can trust.

I don't know what Jeran sees on my face, or how this boy constantly notices everything said and unsaid, but something about my words must agree with him, because he nods numbly at my words. "Tomorrow night," he signs.

I cast a last look down at the holding room too. Now Adena is standing, snapping at the guards over something, and Aramin has turned his attention away from us. He doesn't dare look at us again, not with the guards' attention now fully on them. As they argue, I start to make my way back down the duct.

It is only then that I overhear something the guards say. It freezes my blood.

"If they're lucky enough to survive, they'll eventually face the Skyhunter."

Jeran hears it too. We halt, our eyes locked in a shared moment of horror.

I don't know what the games will ultimately be. But Constantine is going to force them to take on Talin.

14

TALIN

THE CELEBRATORY GAMES IN CARDINIA ARE set to begin tomorrow. For now, the streets are a whirlwind of red tissue raining from the balconies and street vendors filling the air with the smell of roasted meat and sticky sugar. The occasional scrawl still appears on sculptures here and there, but they are gone by the end of the day, hurriedly scrubbed clean, the damaged sculptures removed and replaced with others.

But I remember them. And that memory reminds me that all is not as it seems in the city.

This morning, I walk in the midst of the ongoing festivities with a small patrol of guards behind me. Here in the capital, I typically spend some of my days protecting Constantine during his official duties. Other days, I'll patrol the city, following leads about unrest or violence, ensuring everyone keeps the peace. My watches follow a pattern: I go through the streets; I check on specific shops; I attend some of the official announcements that happen weekly in the city square in order to observe the public's reactions. I report anything suspicious or arrest lawbreakers. Anyone stirring up trouble. I go to the National Laboratory at least once a week—sometimes to report on how the experiments are going, sometimes to meet with the Chief Architect myself in order to get enhancements for my ongoing transformation.

All it takes on most days is for people to simply see me coming down the street. It is in Constantine's best interest to show off his most fearsome weapon for his people. Everywhere I go, I can see people parting for me like a tide, followed by hushed murmurs and averted eyes, their heads bowed instinctively in fear. Their gazes linger on my black armor and the two flat stripes of metal along my back.

Skyhunter. I can hear their whispers in my wake. *That's the Skyhunter.*

Today, I'm assigned to visit the Laboratory. As we turn in the direction of the complex, my mother's signed words run repeatedly through my mind.

Someone there is working actively against the Federation.

Did my mother tell me this as instructed by Mayor Elland, or against her wishes? If a lab worker is secretly part of some rebellion, what are their plans? Are they one of the victims currently slated to be transformed into a Ghost—or a Skyhunter? One of the workers or an assistant? And how are they keeping themselves from the ever-watchful eyes of the Chief Architect?

I take in a deep breath. It's likely my mother would never tell me this directly—but maybe she is a part of the rebellion herself. She knows the slow torture I'm experiencing, doing the Premier's bidding. She has seen the results of my awful transformation. She is as angry as I am, probably feels the fire churning in her chest just like I do.

If my mother's in on it, then I am too.

So I turn my attention in the direction of the lab institute. To my guards, I just signal simple commands in Karenese sign language.

"You," I sign, pointing at one of them, then another. "You. Come with me." Then, to the others, I gesture to the multiple points around the estate's gates, indicating for them to take up their typical shifts at the gates while they wait for me.

The guards don't hesitate at all. They bow and move immediately toward their assigned positions, their obedience to me as unflinching as that of Ghosts.

One of the two guards chosen to stay with me bows her head and gives me a questioning look. "I'm not a scribe, Skyhunter," she says to me in Karenese. "Is that all right?"

Sometimes the guards are tasked to record the conversations I have with the Chief Architect, or write down notes of interest about how specific victims are doing in the lab institute.

I shake my head. "It's fine. No notes today."

The soldiers don't know Karenese sign language except the handful of commands they've been required to learn since I joined the Premier's side. But it's enough to convey our messages to each other. I think Constantine is also satisfied with how limited it keeps my control over them. There's only so much I can say.

The soldier bows her head. "Of course, Skyhunter," she replies.

During the celebrations, the lab institute's gates have been draped almost entirely in festive red cloth. Rains from the night before have left them soggy. I stare at the line of water left beneath them as we step through to the front gate, where the institute's guards bow low to me. Dread has begun a slow churn in the pit of my stomach. It doesn't matter how many times I set foot in this place. I always hate it.

The Chief Architect is already waiting for me at the entrance, shoulders perpetually tense. A young translator stands by her side.

The Chief Architect lowers her head at the sight of me, then pushes her glasses higher and smiles a smile that never reaches her eyes. "You're early this morning, Skyhunter," she says to me in Karenese. Beside her, the translator signs to me in Maran sign language.

As always, I wonder who this girl used to be. Whether she was once a Striker now taken from her old position and made a translator by Constantine. Where she used to live in Mara and how she ended up here.

Now, though, I have a new suspicion: whether or not she's actually a spy for a rebellion.

I look at the translator, searching for some clue in her eyes, but she just turns her gaze nervously down and follows the Chief Architect as she leads us inside. As we go, I manage to glance behind the translator's ears, searching for any telltale scar. But there's nothing.

My gut gives a nauseating lurch as we head through the entrance and deeper down the hall. It's the feeling I have every time I step in here. I'd spent months within these corridors, bearing torture as they transformed me. Every corner is full of terrors. I can feel those nightmares crowding in my mind now, threatening to overwhelm me, but I force myself to stay straight and unerring, to put one foot in front of the other. I'll be damned if I'm going to show weakness to the one who turned me into the weapon that I am.

"The Premier wants an update on how the other Skyhunters are progressing," I sign to her now, an order she's used to seeing from me. To my relief, my hands are steady, nothing like the turmoil in my mind.

"Since you're early, I'm afraid one of them is still resting," she tells me after the translator explains my words. "One of our Skyhunters-in-progress can't be disturbed right now. But you're welcome to see the second one."

I nod at her. "Show me."

The Chief Architect turns to the two guards trailing me. "Stay out of the room," she tells them in Karenese that I understand. "This is only for the Skyhunter to see."

They don't hesitate to do her bidding. One of them casts a nervous glance down the hallway, knowing that the vast rooms beyond contain a multitude of monsters.

They stop at the end of the hall while we continue on. The Chief Architect opens one of the doors and ushers me inside.

It's a dimly lit space, lighting that I remember from my time here, tailored specifically not to injure our new eyes when they're healing.

Before, my eyes had to adjust to the dark. Now, though, I can see everything immediately. My gaze goes straight to the figure sitting in a warm bath at one side of the room. It looks like it should be luxurious and relaxing, but he's hunched in the water and trembling slightly. His eyes are hidden behind a layer of bandages.

His head turns toward us at the sound of our arrival, and every muscle in his shoulders stiffens. His trembling worsens.

"Our second Skyhunter," the Chief Architect tells me, her hands folded behind her back. "As you can see, he has just had his eyes enhanced. A process you're familiar with, I'm sure."

I remember this procedure right away. It's a process that—for several weeks—leaves you feeling like you've been completely blinded, with a deep, aching pain behind your sockets. The procedure also makes you colder than you should be. When I'd undergone it, I'd shivered even in warm rooms, even when the windows were left open to the summer air.

The hot bath is necessary to stabilize his body's heat.

The nausea stirring in my stomach lurches, and I wince, fighting back the urge to retch. His pain suddenly seems to be mine, and for a moment, I feel as if I'm the one undergoing the transformation again. In the low light, his hair—already going gray with the metallic additives in his bloodstream—reminds me of Red.

I force myself to nod calmly. "His progress seems slower than before,"

I sign to the translator, dutifully asking the questions that Constantine wants.

"He had a close call earlier in the week," the Chief Architect explains as she wrings her hands unconsciously. "His heart stopped during his eye operation, and we had to postpone it in order to let his body rest. We think he's out of the danger zone."

Her words make me want to laugh. Out of the danger zone. As if they are at all concerned about our health.

"Where is this one from?" I ask her. This isn't one of Constantine's questions.

"Tanapeg," she replies.

One of the border states. I wonder if he might be who my mother is talking about.

"May I?" I ask the Architect, and she bows her head slightly to me, giving me permission.

I skirt my way around the room until I'm standing over the young man in the bath. He senses my presence. I see his skin prickle at my nearness, as if he knows somehow that something powerful and deadly is at his side. Then I lean down to take a better look at him.

No scars behind his ears. Nothing else to go off. But I still linger, taking in his face and his body. He nearly died during the eye procedure—he thinks this is torturous. But he hasn't yet begun the process of steel infusion, of installing the great black wings on his back. There is so much pain ahead of him, and no way for me to prepare him for the worst of it.

Did he leave a family behind? Who once called him *son*? Did they mourn him? Do they know where he ended up? Are they also imprisoned here, like Red's family had been, or are they perhaps—mercifully—dead? Trapped in this room, blinded and frightened, who does he think about? Does he weep for anyone in his sleep, as I wept for Red?

If the Early Ones had not destroyed themselves, what would they think of the way the Federation has used their knowledge? Would they shrink away in disgust? Or would they approve? Would they see an echo of themselves in this?

I have a sudden urge to kill him here. To slice out with my own steel wings and cut his throat, end his suffering. Destroy one of Constantine's Skyhunters before he can become like me, a weapon at the Premier's beck and call. Everything in me screams to do it. At the door, the Chief Architect watches me quietly. If she's afraid of what I might be thinking, she doesn't react.

Then I feel that familiar tug in the back of my mind. Constantine's presence, ever there. He says nothing. He probably isn't even paying attention to what my moods are or what I might be doing right now. But it's all the reminder I need.

I force myself to stand up and return to the Chief Architect's side. "He looks well," I sign to her. Beside her, the translator murmurs my answer.

The Architect gives me a practiced smile. "This one will join you someday, Skyhunter," she replies. "So I'm glad you approve."

She then turns to open the door, ushering us out. I'm glad she doesn't see the look of hatred on my face. I follow her out with my hands balled into fists.

As I go through my weekly inspection of the Ghosts' glass chambers and the Chief Architect's report on her experiments' progress, I feel the weight of my mother's words shift. The translator following us doesn't once glance up at me. She never errs in her steps around the Architect. The Ghosts in their chambers are all in various stages of their transformations. The ones that have completely changed are listless, standing at attention as if ready to be led out obediently in chains. A few other lab workers and engineers bow their heads at us as we pass by.

Nothing seems amiss. There are no clues that anyone here might have ulterior motives.

What am I searching for? What had my mother wanted me to find? Or—what if the things my mother had heard really were just rumors? What if she is mistaken after all? What if this, too, is another cruel game that Constantine has set up for me, giving me false hope that there might be some rebellion in the works—sending me on a desperate goose chase by using my mother as a hapless pawn?

The thought that this last shred of hope is nothing but a ruse is almost too much for me to bear. I've seen my friends jailed. I've had to beg my mother to stay alive. Is this the rest of my life that I have to look forward to? Watching helplessly as my loved ones suffer?

And then, just as my thoughts continue to spiral, I notice something about the Chief Architect as she turns in front of me. She steps under a bright sconce against the wall, and the shadows behind her head momentarily clear right as I catch a glimpse.

A scar behind her ear.

It isn't a big scar. I've certainly never noticed it before. Just a line of silver skin running behind her earlobe, fading into invisibility wherever shadows hit it. But it's unmistakable.

The Chief Architect is still talking, rapidly now, as she gestures at one glass chamber holding a Ghost that looks like it might be dying. "We are going to put this one down," she says as the creature shakes its broken jaw. "Its bones aren't setting right, for some reason, and it doesn't seem capable of keeping up with the others."

But her words sound muffled and distant in my ears. I listen numbly, my breath frozen in my chest.

How can the Chief Architect be the one behind a rebellion? She had personally overseen the mutilation of Red into a Skyhunter, then mine. She has torn thousands of families apart in her creation of her monstrosities, has been instrumental in the Federation's conquering of so many nations. She spends her days walking anxiously around her lab, always doing the Premier's bidding, always bowing to the horrors she inflicts.

She finishes talking now and turns to look at me. Something in my eyes must catch her attention—because for an instant, she hesitates, and some emotion flashes by on her face.

Then the Chief Architect nods at the young translator. "That will be all," she says. "I have a few checks I need to do with our Skyhunter."

The girl glances quickly at the woman's face, as if checking to make sure she is being given a proper dismissal. But the Chief Architect just nods again at her. "Go on."

We watch the girl leave. For a moment, we are alone here in the corner of the institute.

The Chief Architect turns away. "Follow me," she calls over her shoulder, glancing back briefly at me.

"Architect—" I start to sign at her, but she glimpses my movement and interrupts me.

"My name is Raina de Balman," she replies.

We move like a pair of shadows, with nothing but the sound of our boots echoing along the corridor. Finally, she leads me into one of the private rooms. In the weak light filtering in from outside, I see a sparsely furnished space, equipped only with a bed and dresser.

I tense immediately. I used to be sent into chambers like this one to recover from each round of experimentation during my Skyhunter transformation. They'd put me in a bed, and I'd lie still for an entire week at a time, waiting for the wounds in my back to slowly heal around my new wings or my skin to graft back together. An involuntary shudder courses through me at returning to this space, and I wonder what new experiment she'd brought me here for.

But she doesn't turn on any of the lights. Instead, she walks over to the side of the bed and presses her hand against a section of the wall there.

A slight groove in the wall materializes, then indents, as if a section of the wall has pushed inward. She waits without a word as the wall slides open by a couple of feet, then glances at me and nods for me to walk through the narrow darkness.

It opens abruptly into an illuminated space.

I find myself standing in a large chamber filled with what appears to be the same equipment used during my Skyhunter transformation.

We aren't alone in here. At the other end of the windowless space, seated calmly at a low table sprawled with what look like blueprints, is Mayor Elland.

She leans back in her seat and regards me with her penetrating look. "Ah," she says. "You all took your time out there."

My mother's quiet message to me at the mayor's estate. Her hint to me. Suddenly the words of the prisoner from Carreal return to me again.

I am not the rebel leader you think you have. I am just one of many.

The mayor had used my mother to communicate with me, had wanted me in on whatever this meeting is. I stare at her, unsure how to react or what to expect.

When I hesitate longer, the woman rolls her eyes and gestures to the seats beside her. "You don't have all day here," she says. "Constantine will expect you back eventually, so let's talk."

I feel uneasy as I settle into a seat across from the mayor and the Chief Architect shuffles to sit beside me.

The Chief Architect glances sidelong at me. "Panic room," she explains, gesturing around us at the enclosed space. "The lab complex is equipped with a small number of these. In the event that something goes wrong with one of our experiments, our scientists can escape to relative safety for a moment while sending out a distress signal to have guards sent in." She nods at me, her own tense nature in contrast to her words. "No one can hear us in here."

Mayor Elland folds her arms against the table. Unlike Raina, she looks as regal and self-assured as she did at her estate. "A good place for you to flee if Constantine ever discovers the real reason why he's ill all the time," she quips.

At that, my eyes dart from the mayor to the Chief Architect. Constantine's failing health. The fog in his mind. Then I think of the medicinal soup that Constantine drinks, that it was formulated by the Chief Architect to help him think. "Constantine's treatments," I sign to her, my hands faltering for a moment. "His illness. You—"

She greets my realization with a blink. "It's just an illness, Skyhunter," she says pointedly. "Or is it?"

An illness. Or a poisoned body, slowly dying.

"The tonic I gave you on the wall," she continues, pushing up her glasses in a nervous gesture, "was one I sometimes used on Red when we were still figuring out his limits. He was the first person I ever attempted a link upon. This tonic weakens the effects of your mind link so that the effects reduce to a trickle. It should prevent you from sharing with the Premier most visions of where you currently are. It is a suppression of one of the many threads that make up your bond with Constantine."

It is a suppression. Her words are so quiet I barely hear her. But there they are, hanging in the air.

Mayor Elland tucks a strand of silver-gray hair behind her ear and leans toward me. "You thought the war ended when you lost Mara. But this, Talin, can be our chance to truly end the war. This can be the real end. And I know you want to see the fall of the Karensa Federation. Don't you?"

I meet her eyes, hardly able to believe what I'm hearing. *I am just one of many.*

These are the many. I am sitting with leaders of the rebellion.

She gives me a grim nod. "Interested, eh? Good. Now let's get you caught up."

15

RED

THE EVENING IS SPLIT BY THE ECHOES OF horns blasting around the city, each of them harmonious with the next. The chorus resounds eagerly from every tower in the city as people flood into the streets, celebrating in anticipation of tomorrow's game.

I remember the sound of these horns. I'd sport bracelets on my arms and run alongside my father as we headed out to the festival grounds. Once, the festival had coincided with the conquering of the western nation of Larc.

What a little fool. How could I have enjoyed myself so much back then?

Tonight, Jeran and I try to keep a low profile in our Karenese wardrobe as we join the crowds teeming around the city. We sport yellow stripes tied around our wrists. Like the rest of the crowd, we know little about what will happen in the arena tomorrow—only that it will involve captive Strikers from Mara, and that they will each be sporting a different color so that the audience can distinguish easily between them. Already, I can overhear conversations around me from those taking bets on which colors will survive and which will perish, gambling on the lives of people none of them have even seen.

Beside me, I can sense Jeran's tension. Maybe Adena will be wearing the yellow bracelet. Maybe Aramin.

Maybe Talin will be the one ripping those bracelets from their wrists after taking their lives.

Clusters of soldiers stand at attention along the thoroughfare. I glance at them whenever I can, listening for snatches of conversations, bored chatter, clues. But the few that talk are only barking out orders, herding people in the right direction. As always, I search for the symbols on their sleeves, keeping track of the patrols I see.

Strange. There are fewer patrols here than there should be.

Up ahead, rising up in the center of the Solstice Circle, is Cardinia's arena, decked out entirely tonight in colorful banners.

We avoid the arena and end up walking along the path linking the surrounding festival grounds to the road leading to the lab complex. The guards cluster thickly around here. Immediately I know what it means; Ghosts must have been transported along this route earlier in the morning, ushered into the arena's holding rooms in anticipation of tomorrow's events.

With the realization comes a wave of sickness. Whatever's happening to the captive Strikers tomorrow, it'll involve them facing Ghosts. Except Constantine's not going to make it a fair fight for them.

Soon we find ourselves lost in the crowds milling around the edges of the complex's ivy-strewn walls, the people browsing solstice gifts and trinkets laid out for sale by small vendors along the gates. None of these little stalls are legal businesses, but the guards don't seem to care. Now and then, I see a few of them accepting bribes from the stall owners, pocketing handfuls of coins and paper in exchange for looking the other way. Some of them hold up solstice bracelets to the light, admiring the jewelry.

Jeran and I listen for snippets of conversation as we go, gradually letting ourselves take in the chatter of the soldiers. Most of them seem to be wondering what will happen in the arena.

"Don't believe for a second that those Marans can make it to the end of tomorrow," one soldier scoffs to another as we pass them by a side gate of the complex.

"They managed to hold off our troops for long enough at their warfront, didn't they?" the other replies.

"So? And now they're here, sport in the stadium." The first snorts. "You and Taran can place a bet. I'm not wasting my money."

"Aye, Taran would, if he weren't sick tonight."

"Again?"

We pretend to browse the wares nearby as they return to their guard posts. I glance at Jeran, who shakes his head in response. No mention of other prisoners from the train. No mention of the prison district or anything that would hint remotely at where Talin's mother might be.

"A double shift tonight for you too?" another soldier complains at yet another gate.

Her friend nods. "For most of us. I think the General expects folks to be rowdy after the festivities tonight. He's pulling some of us off duty in the seventh district."

The first sighs. "Ah, they always think that. Just let them run loose a bit."

They both laugh. We move on.

"What's in the seventh district?" Jeran asks me in a low voice as we go.

"Prisons," I answer, "and factories. It's the walled district circling against the inside of the city's wall."

"Is it normal for them to pull patrols from there for the solstice?"

I nod. "Normal enough." Then I frown. "But something about the patrols here aren't adding up."

"What do you mean?"

I nod at the soldiers at the gates. "Ever since we arrived in the city, I've been tracking the symbols of the patrols wandering the streets. There are several patrols fewer than I remember them having during past festivities." I glance down a thoroughfare. "Cardinia's east city patrols should be down that street, but they aren't. Neither are the southeast patrols, though they're usually responsible for the area we're walking through."

"Does that mean the General's spreading them thin?"

"It could." I give Jeran a pointed look. "*That's* not normal. This is the biggest celebration of the year, especially now that Karensa stretches from sea to sea. It means Caitoman needs them somewhere else, for something just as important as the solstice."

At that, Jeran nods. "Perhaps they're watching Talin's mother."

I'm silent for a while, but my head spins as I make a mental list of those patrols that seem to be missing from the festival. *Someone* must be guarding Talin's mother. If I can find out where those patrols are stationed, I might be able to figure out where Talin's mother is being kept.

We go on around the edge of the complex. Each time we run into a group of soldiers, we listen as intently as we can. They talk about the arena. Their posts. Some complain of hunger, wanting supper. Others talk about news of more unrest at the border states. No more clues on Talin's mother or her whereabouts.

We've almost made our way around the entire lab complex when a crowd of people gathered by one of the complex's side gates halts us in our tracks.

The cluster seems to be lining either side of the path leading up to the gate, craning their necks in curiosity as a team of soldiers walk along. Even as we approach the scene, I can hear some of the soldiers shouting.

"Back away! Back away!"

As Jeran and I make it to an open pocket in the crowd, I see several soldiers calling for someone to open the gate while two others rush back up along the path to help the patrol heading toward it. As the gate opens, the rest of the patrol down the path comes into view.

And that's when I hear an anguished moan that raises every hair on the back of my neck. My other voice springs to life in my mind, shaking, as if I'm back on the defensive in the Laboratory. It's the kind of sound made by a throat filled with blood, something you recognize from the battlefield. It's the kind of sound you've heard in glass chambers around you, moans that filled your sleep with nightmares.

A small team of soldiers and lab workers are hoisting a stretcher down the path, and lying on that stretcher is a struggling patient. The source of the moan.

Though the victim has bandages over his eyes, I recognize him immediately. He's one of the workers from the dig team that had been on our train to Cardinia, the man in charge of securing the cylindrical artifact to the train car. I'd woken on the top of the train that night, freshly disoriented from my dream about Talin, to see this man retching violently over the side of their moving carriage.

Something has burned this man so badly that his skin is a mottled red, blistered and angry. The bandages around his eyes are stained with blood.

"What happened to him?" someone beside us asks.

Their friend just shrugs. "Nothing, I heard."

"What do you mean?"

"I mean exactly that. *Nothing happened.* He was on the train from Mara back here to Cardinia."

The stretcher rushes past us and into the lab complex. Scarcely has it disappeared from view when another comes in its wake. Another person with the same injuries—a bloodied bandage over the eyes, angry red sores all over his body. The same skin-crawling moan. His head is turned weakly toward the crowd, his breathing laborious as he heaves a wet cough. Flecks of blood dot his shirt. It's as if he's bleeding from the inside out.

How the hell had these workers gone from being strong enough to haul the artifact onto the train, to lying there in a gurgling mess? Instantly, the memory of that enormous metal cylinder comes back to me, its unnatural silver surface glinting under the moonlight. The strange weight of it. A chill builds inside me and seeps down my limbs.

The hurried voice of another soldier comes to us as she rushes past. "They were still out in the square during the blessing of the new sculptures from Mara. Already saw some blisters on their faces then, but this . . ."

"That's impossible," says a lab worker who meets them at the gate to usher them inside. Then he glances at the crowd gathered around and seems to temper the rest of his words. He raises his voice. "Hey—get back, back! State business. *Back!*" He waves a hand impatiently at the rest of the patrol, and guards begin to physically nudge the crowd in either direction.

"We should go," Jeran whispers beside me. His eyes linger on the two men on the stretchers, then flick up to me. "Something tells me it'd be best if we aren't too near them."

I nod, and in one motion, the two of us turn away from the scene. But the last image of the victims disappearing inside the complex stays seared in my mind. The chill in my body lingers.

"Do we know where they're keeping that artifact from the train?" I reply as we go.

"Didn't they unload it from the train with those enormous platforms?" Jeran says. "Where would they bring equipment like that in the city?"

I frown as I think through Cardinia's locations. "There's a military district near the central palace," I finally murmur. Around us, people blur past, oblivious to what had happened near the lab gate and excited about the upcoming game. "Those platforms are typically for transporting larger weapons like catapults and cannons. Maybe that artifact had been moved with them to that district."

Jeran nods once. He looks pale too, even under the evening light. "We don't have much time," he says quietly. And he doesn't even have to explain his words for me to know what he means.

The Federation has sunk its teeth into the land of Mara, churning up its earth in an attempt to find something of value left over from the Early Ones. But the cylinder we'd seen them pull out . . . it can't just be a relic. I'd seen with my own eyes how those workers looked before they loaded the object and after, bleeding everywhere. There is something happening here that I don't understand, but I can feel the darkness of it hanging in the air, a foreboding of things to come.

It has come before, after all. The Early Ones were once mighty, and now they are gone.

If Karensa figures out how to weaponize what they found in Mara, whatever it is that has hurt those men, then soon it may no longer be just the Federation that we need to stop. Soon, all of us may become like the Early Ones—annihilated by something we couldn't control.

16

TALIN

I'VE ONLY EVER KNOWN THE CHIEF ARCHITECT of the Karensa Federation as a monster and a coward, a scientist who enabled all the anguish that Constantine has wrought.

It's an astonishing experience to sit here beside her and the mayor of Cardinia and hear her speak against the Premier.

"Karensa values their premiers because of their perceived strength," Raina says. "Their invincibility. Constantine's father was a ferocious man who instilled fear in everyone he met. Constantine does the same. The people of Karensa who support the Tyrus family think of them as the ones chosen to inherit the power of the Early Ones." She gives me a pointed look over her shining glasses. "But the Federation's borders have become unstable. Conquered people can only tolerate so much. Now is the time to make our move."

"Our plan is to weaken Constantine before his public," Mayor Elland continues. "Ensure their—as well as the military's—support of our move." She holds a hand out at Raina. "Fortunately, our Chief Architect has quite a way with manipulating the human body. Don't you, Raina?"

Raina winces at the mayor, but doesn't disagree.

The mayor winks at me. "She's so humble, isn't she? That's Raina's job in our rebellion—to make sure Constantine's health is where we want it to be."

Throughout all the time I've been with Raina—while she's been ordering wings grafted onto my back and steel infused into my bones—she's been quietly working with the rebellion.

Raina now coughs nervously. "The medication I've been giving Constantine has been sickening him for over a year. Gradually enough that he thinks it is a real illness, and looks to me to help cure him of it."

"And the military is primed for this?" I sign, skeptical.

She must sense my lingering dislike for her, because she shifts in her seat and looks away from me.

Mayor Elland looks questioningly to the Chief Architect to translate what I've said. Raina does, then answers, "The games that are about to happen are the right time to act. I will be increasing Constantine's doses over the next week. It should cause him enough pain to make him visibly weak and thus unfit for rule. There are enough in the military ready to act against the Premier when we give the signal at the end of the games."

"All of our rebels will be in place at the arena, ready to ignite the overthrow," the mayor adds. "The appropriate members of the military are prepped."

"And what happens afterward?" I sign. "Constantine is overthrown. Then what? What about General Caitoman? How will he react when you topple his brother?"

"We have a council ready to decide on the next ruler," Mayor Elland says.

"We will handle the General when the time comes," Raina says at the same time.

Then she pauses abruptly, as if ceding way for the mayor to speak again. But the mayor just shrugs her agreement. After a while, the Chief Architect says, "At any rate, that's not what you need to worry about. The coup is our main priority."

The mayor smiles thinly at me. "You, dear Skyhunter, will be the catalyst that flips the public to our side." She taps at one of the papers in front of us. It's a detailed blueprint of the arena where the games will be happening. "During the end of the games, we will call for the military to turn against Constantine. You, as the most visible symbol of his power, are to step forward with us. You will be the one to arrest Constantine and take him away."

Something in me bristles at the idea of taking more orders from these Karensan nobles, but then the impossible appears in my mind—turning to face Constantine and forcing him down from his throne, to twist his hands behind his back and lead him out of a screaming arena. The ability to strip him of his power just by turning away from him.

I remember the way the people looked to me in awe during our arrival into Cardinia. The mayor is right. I'm the most visible example of his power. If the people see me turn away, they will know that Constantine has lost.

"Why not kill him?" I sign.

Raina looks away with a grimace. "That's what I'd wish," she mutters sullenly.

But the mayor gives Raina a stern look and shakes her head. "Assassinate him, and risk a civil war among the people along with poisonous conspiracy theories," she says. "Turn the public against the Premier, though, and it will work even better than death. His ferocious demeanor is meant to hide his deteriorating condition. But the whispers are already out there. All we need now is a moment in front of the entire public where we can stage a proper coup. And you are the trigger for that."

Raina shakes her head, as if in disgust, but doesn't voice her objections. Again, I feel the hint of an old argument between the two women. "The mayor has a soft spot for Constantine," she tells me with a sidelong glance.

To my surprise, the mayor doesn't deny it. Her voice softens slightly. "I knew Constantine's mother," she replies.

The woman hesitates a little. In that hesitation, I hear something more than friendship. I hear an entire history that must have existed between this woman and the late queen. I hear an old, broken love.

"Mother?" I sign, and Raina translates.

"She died a long time ago," the mayor says quietly. Then her gaze steels again, and she looks at both of us. "Constantine is a monster, just like his father. We follow the plan."

Raina nods. "We follow the plan," she agrees.

The walls I've put up around my heart lurch and threaten to topple. If all that I'm hearing is true—if there really is a chance for us to destroy Constantine and the Federation as it currently stands . . .

But then I remember why I've pushed away all thoughts of my old friends. Why I'm terrified when Red and I connect in our dreams. I remember my mother, riding in those borrowed luxury silks.

"There's one problem," I sign to Raina. "You can break down my link to Constantine all you want—but if Constantine has my mother under his control, I won't make a move against him. I can't." I glance at the mayor. "Can you get to her? Can you hide her away on your estate?"

The mayor tightens her lips. "I can't do that, I'm afraid," she replies. "All our plans work under the assumption that Constantine trusts Raina and me. He's known me all his life, and sees me as something of an aunt. Raina de Balman has overseen his entire scientific campaign for his military conquests. We are two of his closest advisors. But if I suddenly request to keep your mother on my estate, he will immediately suspect us. We can't risk it. I can't keep your mother longer than Constantine wants her there."

I narrow my eyes at them. "If you don't help her, I won't help you."

"All of us have something significant to lose in this," the mayor tells me, her gaze piercing mine.

Raina holds up her hands. "We didn't say we wouldn't help her." Then she leans over the table and touches one of my hands with hers.

The walls in me go up, hiding my emotions behind their steel, and I pull my hand firmly away.

Raina fixes a steady gaze on me, unfazed. "I know how you feel. My husband and son need to escape the capital before Constantine's toppling too. I give you my word, Talin Kanami—if you promise to aid us in this, I promise we will get your mother to safety."

"Swear it," I sign, my movements slow and deliberate.

"I swear it."

My eyes go to the mayor. She nods once at me, and I recall the sympathy she'd had in her eyes when she'd told me to go see my mother yesterday morning.

"I swear it," the mayor repeats.

Something is shifting under the sands of the Federation, weakening its foundations, and when it falls, it might take us all down with it. It's likely that none of us will survive any of this. It's even likely that somehow, in spite of Raina's best efforts, Constantine has sensed the lurch of my feelings during this meeting and has already sent guards for me. We will be operating under constant fear of discovery. Of death.

And yet, here we are. We may all have something to lose, but we have everything to gain. For Raina, it's freedom for herself and her family. For Mayor Elland, perhaps it's revenge for the loss of a love.

And for me? Justice. For Basea, for Mara, for my mother. For myself.

I find myself looking back and forth between these two powerful women, united in spite of the tensions between them, in spite of everything they could lose.

And I find myself nodding at them.

17

RED

THE CELEBRATIONS IN THE CITY GO LATE, BUT some hours after midnight, everything finally settles down, and Jeran and I find ourselves squeezing into a space under a bridge not far from the arena. Along the horizon, I can see a little sliver of the National Museum's silhouette, stark and abrupt against the sky.

I used to cross this bridge every week with my sister and father to go to that museum. Laeni would probably wrinkle her nose if she could see me crouched down here right now.

But it's as safe a spot as any we can find. Patrols hate checking under these bridges because of the dampness and the stench of sewage bubbling up. When I was a boy, I used to gamble with the other new recruits for who had to keep the bridges free of people camping underneath them. Whenever I lost, I'd just take a reluctant peek under the arches, looking for people shivering among the wet weeds, before hurrying off to more interesting tasks. What a thankless, miserable job.

Well, I'm one of those shivering silhouettes now.

We stoop in knee-deep water. The quiet, sparsely populated night and our exhaustion have softened our fears, so we talk in low voices to distract each other from the wet chill of everything. Beside me, Jeran's fingers run idly along his belt, as if he's looking for all the weapons he used to have. I've learned over time what the idle gesture means.

"You're thinking about Aramin right now, aren't you?" I ask him as I chew reluctantly on one of our last sticks of dried seaweed and fish jerky.

Jeran glances at me and looks down. His fingers stop. "How'd you guess?"

"I've only been by your side for months," I say, scowling at the jerky. How do people stand the taste of fish? It's a crime. "I think I've picked up a few things."

Jeran smiles briefly, then falls silent. After a while, he says, "I'm thinking about what Aramin would do if our situations were reversed."

"I imagine he'd fly into a rage." I wave a hand out at the world beyond our bridge. "Killing everyone in sight in order to get to you."

At that, Jeran chuckles once. His cheeks look pink in the night. "Believe it or not, he'd probably still be back in Newage, gathering forces, crafting a less desperate plan than ours. Aramin is calculating like that."

"Are you saying he'd leave you behind to be slaughtered in the arena?" I shake my head. "I don't believe that for a second."

"Of course not," Jeran sniffs. "But Aramin became the Firstblade for a reason. He likes to gather all the information he can before he makes a move. He acts for the benefit of the greatest good." He smiles a little. "And he's usually cranky about it."

I fix my gaze on Jeran. Somehow, underneath all he's saying, I sense that he's afraid to believe that Aramin would come to rescue him. It makes me want to shake the boy. Does he have no idea how much the Firstblade cares about him? Does he not notice what the rest of us do, the way Aramin's eyes linger on him?

"Maybe," I answer. "But not when it's about you."

Jeran's blush deepens. Maybe he does know, then, and he's just shy to admit it.

When I speak again, I ask, "Was Aramin always so prickly?"

He shrugs. "As long as I've known him."

"Oh?" I smile and lean back against the cool stone. "Tell me a story and distract me from the misery of our surroundings."

Jeran's smile turns wistful. His hands toy with a bit of the wild stalks growing around us. There he goes again, fiddling unconsciously as his thoughts turn to the Firstblade. "I first met him because he needed a translator."

I laugh. "Naturally."

"This was long before he became the Firstblade. He and a few others needed to interrogate a Karensan soldier they'd captured. They couldn't understand a word of what the soldier was saying, of course, so he came to fetch me." Jeran drops the rest of the wild stalks into the water. "'I heard you're the only one in the east patrols who can speak Karenese.' That was the first thing he ever said to me."

"He's so romantic."

That makes Jeran genuinely chuckle, and his eyes dart up to the underside of the bridge, as if the rest of the city could have heard him. "He looked so annoyed to be asking me that I was genuinely offended," he says, barely above a whisper.

"And what did an offended Jeran say in return?" I whisper back.

He smiles, and for an instant, a mischievous glint appears in his eyes. "'How much?'"

I stifle a burst of laughter, and it makes me cough instead. I lean forward and shove his shoulder. "Somehow, I get the sense this is a rare thing coming from you."

"I wasn't being sarcastic. He paid me fifty of his mess hall credits for that translation."

I lean my arm on one knee and regard him in amusement. "Jeran Min Terra, I never took you for a mercenary."

"Aramin brings it out in me." He winks. "He didn't speak to me again for months afterward. It took our mutual friends Adena and Corian to force us to start hanging out together in the mess hall."

I try to imagine all these young soldiers, still recruits who hadn't witnessed the harshness of the warfront, laughing and joking and pranking one another in the warmth of a shared hall. Hadn't I once been like that too? Gambling with bored guards, betting on games, covering one another on our watches to sneak to food stands during the solstice?

And then you see the world for what it really is. You're forced to participate in all the ugliness it can offer. And things change.

If Talin and I can survive all this, what comes next? Can things ever be soft and silly and gentle between us?

"It's my turn to guess your thoughts," Jeran says, and I glance over to see him giving me a sad nod. "You're thinking of Talin, aren't you?"

Do I make unconscious gestures when I think of her too? I nod, quiet for a while. I'm not ready to talk about the way she'd pulled away during our last dream.

"You really love her," Jeran says quietly.

To my embarrassment, I feel the blush rising on my cheeks. Maybe I'll stop teasing Jeran so much. "I don't know," I admit. "I don't think I've ever been in love before."

He looks unfazed. "You've never had the chance to be with anyone before?"

"No." My blush deepens and I curse the warmth of it. "Not . . . like that."

He smiles gently at me. "It's always easier for someone else to tell than for you to see it."

"And you see it?" I hesitate. "That I'm in love?"

He nods. "I see it."

"I'm disappointed to be so easily read."

Jeran's lips twitch in good humor. "If it makes you feel any better," he replies, "I'm just good at reading people."

"I like this confident Jeran. He should hang out with us more often."

We pause for a moment. And for some reason, I find my thoughts turning again to my father and sister. To little Laeni. That kind of love, I understand. I look off into the night, back to where the National Museum looms in the distance. Laeni and I used to compete with each other as we raced around in there, rattling off as many of the Early Ones' sculptures we knew by name. We'd hurry from one exhibit to another until my father would call us back to him. Laeni was too short to see some of the plaques, so I'd always lift her onto my shoulders. I can still feel her weight shifting as she'd lean forward, reading out each description.

When my father looked at his children running around the museum, did he see our mother in us? Did his love hurt him, on nights when we were asleep and he stayed up alone?

"How did you know?" I ask Jeran after a while.

"Know what?"

"When you first fell in love with Aramin?"

He hesitates, then answers, "When he visited me after my first kill on the warfront."

I'm silent, waiting for him to continue.

"I'm usually the one cooking for our patrol, you see. But that night, I didn't show up around our campfire. Adena was already out searching for me, but Aramin was the one who found me. He knew, somehow, where I'd be." Jeran looks up at the bridge. "I'd gone behind the bushes that grew thick around our defense compound, and wedged myself deep in there so that I couldn't be seen. I'm still not sure how he saw me."

He shakes his head. "I couldn't breathe. I was covered in sweat. I just remember sitting there, my hands clinging as hard to my knees as I could, trying to take in gasp after gasp of air but feeling like I wasn't getting anything. I have a blurry memory of Aramin bending down toward me and taking my hand. He squeezed it hard enough for me to feel it through my panic. And all I can remember is that steady voice of his. *Breathe with me. One. Two. Three.* He would count and count, and I remember the hypnosis of those numbers as I struggled to keep pace with his measured breaths." His voice turned into a whisper. "He kept telling me, '*It's just your thoughts. It's only your thoughts. They can't hurt you.*' How did he know what I was thinking?" Jeran shakes his head. "And somehow, I came out of it."

He stretches his legs out, grimacing at the water soaking his pants. "When I finally managed to contain myself enough to come out of the thickets, he guided me back to the others without a word. He had a hand on my shoulder and a hand holding my own, and I just remember . . . how warm he felt. He told the others I'd gone off to pay my respects to the dead. He never mentioned it again."

In the silence that follows, I nod at him. "We're going to get him out of there," I say. "Just like how we're going to save Talin. I don't know how, but we will."

He nods back. "I know how love can power you," Jeran says softly.

Love. I think of the ways it can trap us, make us do things that can destroy us. And how we do it anyway.

That is why I'm here. To save the other Strikers, to rescue Talin. And somehow, that's how I know I love her.

My eyes return to the museum in the distance.

This time, when I stare at it, I remember something different. In one of the displays that Laeni and I used to run past was a small object that looked like a steel cylinder.

Something that looked remarkably like what we'd seen loaded onto the train.

That's why I'd thought the artifacts in Mara looked oddly familiar. That's where I'd seen them before.

That's where we might be able to uncover some clues about why Constantine is so interested in these artifacts, and what they might be capable of.

I must have sucked in my breath, because Jeran glances at me. "What?" he asks.

I look at him. "Care to tour the National Museum with me?"

18

TALIN

THE FIRST MORNING OF THE GAMES DAWNS A bloody red.

The center of the arena today has been transformed into an intricate maze of walls. They stretch tall enough that the spectators can see everything happening within the walls, but anyone wandering through the maze itself is unable to see much aside from the sky.

Today, I soar high above the arena in a visible sweep of the city, looking for signs of unrest in the crowds below. As I angle my wings and swoop in an arc following the curve of the arena, my shadow stretches wide below. People along the thoroughfare duck instinctively when the darkness glides over them. I can see their eyes following the lethal grace of my movements. Constantine wants them to remember what kind of power he has at his side.

He also wants me to see the entirety of the arena. To remind me that this is where my lifelong friends and companions might die. All part of his own secret game.

Well, I'm playing one too.

A part of me yearns to reach out to Red. Wherever he is, he must not be far from the city center if we were able to connect in our dreams. But the instant I think it, I recoil as if struck by a whip. The walls go up again, and I cringe, forcing him from my thoughts. His hands, touching mine in my dream. His eyes, searching mine. His presence, so clear I was almost fooled into thinking he was there.

I can't let myself get close to him like that. It could cost him his life.

As I finish my surveillance of the festivities and rejoin the Premier, we head onto his balcony at the arena. He doesn't address me at all. Through our bond, I search for any hints that he might know about the meeting I had with the Chief Architect and Mayor Elland—but there's nothing today. Instead, I sense the weight of exhaustion in him, hidden under his usual blanket of false strength.

Today it feels especially heavy. When I glance at him through my lashes, I notice his shoulders hunched more than usual, the uneven labor of his breathing, the hesitation in his steps. Raina's words from the meeting come back to me. She has increased his doses of medication this week.

I continue observing him as we arrive at the balcony and take our seats. Behind the paint on the Premier's face—the stripe, the black around his eyes—he looks visibly weak. Constantine can see me studying him, even though he ignores it.

Good. Let him think I'm puzzled by his agony today, that this is me confused and concerned.

I finally look away from him and down at the arena. Here, I get a clear view of the awful space—and an idea of what they'll be forcing the Strikers to do.

One end of the maze leads into a series of large, metal sliding doors that remind me of the gate design at the lab complex. I can see thin grooves on the sides of each stone wall, as if they might move at any given moment. They are going to keep the Strikers guessing, to change the maze to suit the game and keep the players from winning or dying too easily.

At the other end of the maze stands a line of Ghosts, all chained in their cages and pacing restlessly.

"You're willing to lose ten silver notes?"

Two soldiers behind me laugh, shoving each other, as we settle into the space.

"Ten on the inventor," the second soldier retorts, "and you'll be the one handing it to me."

"But I heard one was their Firstblade."

Their words make my heart twist in helpless fury. Strikers, the strength of Mara, forced to fight for their lives all to entertain these Karensans. I glance over my shoulder at them and lock my stare on theirs. The first one catches sight of me and pales, his confident jests suddenly turning into stammers. His eyes dart to the floor. His companion notices me too and hurriedly bows his head.

"Skyhunter," he murmurs.

I stare at them a moment longer, my eyes glowing, before turning back around. Behind me, their silence lingers.

Constantine has his attention fixed on the crowd around us, his hand up in a wave as they cheer for him. On his other side, Caitoman exchanges a few words with the rest of their guards. The expression on his face is one of dark interest. With a sickening feeling, I realize that he's making bets with them too. Telling them how he hopes each of the Strikers will go.

Finally, far at the end sits the Chief Architect, who stares down at the maze with an expressionless face.

I stare at her for a moment. As her head turns in my direction, her deep-set eyes flicker to mine, holding my gaze for a heartbeat. Then she looks away again.

The arena is rowdy and restless, eager for the game to begin. Everyone wants to see for themselves just how good Strikers are at killing monsters. My stomach turns as I look at the people chanting for the event to begin. But even as I do, I can see unsettled glances passing between some of the people, whispers that are drowned out behind a chorus of cheers. Not everyone is here to enjoy it.

How many here are a part of the rebellion?

My eyes shift toward the gates leading to where the Strikers are being kept. I think I see a glimpse of sapphire coats. Have they been given back some of their gear too? Has the Premier seen to it that the audience will get to see a show as authentic as if they were all out on the warfront?

As if he felt the shift of my emotions at the sight of the gates, Constantine tilts his head slightly at me. "Don't despair, Talin," he says. "Your friends will get a fighting chance. That's the point of it, after all."

The point of it. The sickening fear roiling in my stomach makes way for my usual anger, and I scowl back at him. Maybe the tonic that Raina had given me has already done its work, because I don't feel the strength of his satisfaction in return.

You're one to talk about fairness, I answer.

Fairness? He shakes his head. *You think any of this is fair?*

It's not quite the answer I'd expected from him.

At my pause, a small smile drifts across Constantine's lips. The dark stripe down his face is freshly black and shines under the light—and in spite of Raina's continued efforts to weaken him, he still cuts a terrifying figure. *They have a chance because this is meant to entertain. But it isn't fair, Talin. If it were fair, I would give them an opportunity to escape.*

I narrow my eyes at him. *You could, of course. You just won't.*

If only the world were fair, Constantine replies. *But no one wants that. They just want it to be fair for* them.

There is a note of some bitterness in those words, an old wound from somewhere long ago.

And there, beyond the steady link I have with Constantine, is a tug I know all too well.

I know better than to react, immediately tampering down my emotions in an attempt to keep my realization from the Premier. Raina's tonic must have helped too. As I do, I look out into the audience of the arena, my eyes resting instinctively on where I think the pull is coming from.

Red is here.

I can't see him in this crowd, but I can feel him. The elation in my chest mixes with terror. He is *here*, in the capital, surrounded by enemies who want him dead.

It can't be. It's impossible.

And yet, even as I struggle with this realization, I can feel the clear beat of his heart through our link, can sense his presence out in the crowd as surely as I can feel the breeze in the air.

No, Red, I want to scream to him. *You can't be here. It's too dangerous.*

Down below, in the center of the arena, an announcer raises his voice to address the audience. In a daze, I turn to look at him.

"Welcome to the solstice festival!" he shouts. The answering cheers are deafening. The announcer smiles before pointing one hand in the direction of the Strikers' gates. "The Strikers of Mara are famed for their ability to fight our Federation's fearsome Ghosts. You've heard these stories for years, I'm sure—but today, you will get to see the legend in action!"

That's all he needs to say. The people are on their feet now, jumping with anticipation in their seats as everyone cranes their necks in the direction of the gates. On the other end of the maze, guards undo the chains holding back the Ghosts, and they snarl against the bars of their cages.

My muscles tense until I feel as if I might shatter.

Constantine nods once. On the other side of the arena, two bannermen wave scarlet flags.

The Striker gates slide open at the same time the guards unleash the Ghosts from their cages.

The first person to step out into the light is Aramin.

I can't help sucking in my breath. He has been given a full Striker uniform, with his double blades strapped to his hips and his arrows and guns completely equipped. They have trimmed his hair and let him tie it up into the traditional Maran knot. The only telltale change that sticks out is the bright yellow band around his wrist.

I stare at him, hardly able to believe the sight of the Firstblade stepping out of Cardinia's central arena in his full glory. Such cruelty, letting him play at his former role in a game. Where did they get the uniform? From a fallen Striker? The thought makes my stomach turn.

He turns his gaze up to the sky, hearing the roar of the crowd but unable to see them. The only thing he can make out is the edge of the balcony where we now stand, our faces turned in his direction.

He meets my gaze, if only for the briefest moment. In it, I see a world of fury and grief. I want to pour my heart out to him, tell him I will save him and the others—except I can't, and he knows it. So all we can do is stare at each other until he finally breaks away.

Behind him, Adena steps smoothly out into the arena, dressed in similar Striker finery, her wrist banded in red. Then there is Tomm and Pira, banded with blue and green. Adena focuses on the multiple routes before them that lead into the maze. She and Aramin pull out their blades in a uniform flourish. Their movements are so graceful and synced that the audience murmurs in excitement. So these are the legendary pairs of Maran warriors, they're probably thinking, bonded until death to each other.

I don't know why I feel compelled to do it now—they might not even be able to see my hands from here. But I still find myself signing to them, then pressing a fist gently to my chest. It's subtle enough that the Premier doesn't seem to notice, nor do the audience. But down in the maze, Aramin, Adena, Tomm, and Pira see me.

"May there be future dawns."

They see the signs; they understand my words. And each of them lifts their fist in return and presses it once to their chest.

They are breathtaking, and in this moment, I want to cry for them. Each of us had pledged our lives to Mara when we became Strikers, and each of us prepared in some way for death to claim us—but not like this. Not in an arena full of screaming people, competing for our lives.

On the other side of the maze, the Ghosts let out a shriek as they're given their freedom. They charge blindly into the maze. My eyes dart back to the Strikers. Every single one of them turns in the direction of the Ghosts' screams and shifts into a fighting stance. I see Aramin sign to the others. He's telling them to stay together.

Then they move forward as a unit.

It is the wisest strategy—together, they can take out the Ghosts heading down one path while avoiding those in the others. But barely a minute after they make their way down one of the maze's paths, the maze moves for the first time, sliding along those grooves I'd seen in the way that I'd feared. One moment, the four of them are traveling together—the next, a wall suddenly turns after Aramin and Adena have made their way down the front of the path.

Tomm and Pira get caught behind the moving stone. Tomm leaps out of the way in time to keep from being swept and crushed against the side of another wall, but they are now separated from the other two, forced down a new path in the maze. In the audience, people shout out in delighted surprise and try to call down advice. My gaze skids to the other end of the maze, to where the first pack of Ghosts is well on its way toward where Aramin walks.

Adena pauses first, holding up a fist as she tilts her head in the direction of the Ghosts. The beasts aren't loud, but a lifetime of training has alerted her to some telltale hint of their gnashing teeth and rasping breath. She signs at Aramin. Aramin nods and points, and Adena moves without a sound to where he indicates. She kneels a short distance in front of him.

As the first Ghost lurches around the corner and into view, Aramin sprints forward and kicks off Adena's shoulders, launching himself into the air. He's on the Ghost's shoulders before the creature can react, and stabs it three times in the neck before he leaps up and grabs the top edge of the maze wall with both gloved hands.

He's going to try to get to the top of the wall. Of course.

The people in the stands roar, excited by Aramin's deadly grace. Aramin pulls himself onto the top of the wall, and for the first time, he gets a clear view of the entire game space. Down below, Adena spins and delivers a fatal arrow to the injured Ghost's neck, while Aramin darts forward down the path toward the second Ghost.

I realize I'm leaning forward, my heart in my throat as I will Aramin to break down the game and sprint along the top of the maze wall to the end. But as soon as he begins running, the maze shifts again. The wall he's on begins to move—at the same time, spikes embedded in the top of the maze wall shoot up, anticipating his plan.

Aramin flips off just in time. He sails through the air in an arc as the spikes make it impossible to travel on the top. He kicks off against the wall's side on his way down, then lands next to Adena with a light flourish.

The two of them press their backs to each other as more Ghosts reach them. They draw their weapons at the same time, then dart forward, slicing at the beasts that snap at their limbs. The largest Ghost, a creature taller than the maze's walls, manages to cut between them—Adena dodges its swipes, but the move separates her from Aramin. Aramin slides under the Ghost's legs, but the creature twists, snapping for him, and he's forced to retreat again with his back to the wall.

Behind him, Adena creeps like a shadow, her movements so silent and smooth that none of the beasts realize she's made her way around the fight. She pulls out her gun and fires twice at one of the Ghosts. It whirls, confused by the direction of the attack, but by the time it turns, Adena has moved again—she skips up the side of its back. As she does, she swings off her Striker coat and flings it up at the wall. The cloth catches against the spikes still jutting out from the top, and for an instant, her coat becomes a swing. She spins in a sharp arc and releases the coat, launching herself on top of the largest Ghost that has backed Aramin into a corner. She takes her blade and jabs it deep into the Ghost's neck, hitting its vulnerable vein.

The people in the stands scream as the Ghost stumbles and falls. As it does, Aramin and Adena scatter again, soundless, Adena's coat left to hang on top of the wall. The other Ghosts whirl around and lunge for them again, but Aramin has taken advantage of a shadow in one corner to vanish completely into, and the beast is momentarily thrown off. It sniffs angrily around for its prey.

Suddenly the maze shifts again. Adena is caught this time, forced to jump backward to avoid the moving wall. Aramin races toward her, trying to pull her back so that it doesn't separate them—but the shift happens too quickly. Suddenly, he is torn between darting through the narrowing shift with Adena, or staying in his path.

Adena is the one who shoves Aramin back. It's a single, sharp gesture, and even from here, I know she's giving Aramin the firm stare

I've often seen her give on the warfront. This is her silently begging for Aramin to stay on his path. Then she disappears from Aramin's view as the wall finishes turning, sealing her away from the others.

My gaze goes farther down the maze. Adena has an entire pack of Ghosts to face up ahead, while a second pack is heading down the altered corridor where Aramin is now trapped.

They are all going to die. And even as I still try to temper my emotions, I feel the fear of that thought coursing cold through my bones.

Down a separate path, Tomm and Pira hit a new pocket of Ghosts. The audience roars as they sync their movements and cut the beasts down. Each group of Strikers has survived half of the maze, but there is still so much left.

The roar of the audience forces me to look elsewhere. It's Adena, who has somehow used a strip of her old coat to tie together her daggers into a serrated whip. She swings it at one of the Ghost's neck and it wraps all the way around, the blades all digging in. Down on his own path, Aramin leaps out of the way as a Ghost lunges forward at him, then sweeps into a ferocious attack.

But their movements are beginning to become more labored, the gaps between each attack slightly longer than the last.

And they are all tiring.

Abruptly, the audience gasps as one. The sound is so terrible that I jerk my head toward what has caught everyone's attention.

A Ghost has managed to bite deeply into Tomm's leg.

It drags him down the path as he scrambles desperately against the ground, reaching in vain for his blade. Even now, in the throes of unimaginable pain, he doesn't make a sound.

Out in the arena, I feel Red's emotions twist. He has witnessed the same thing.

Pira rushes at the Ghost. She arcs underneath it and shoots at its knees. It stumbles, hobbled and screaming, but behind it come three others.

She and Tomm meet each other's eyes for just an instant. The audience doesn't know yet, but I recognize their expression immediately. It is a look I know all too well from the old warfront. Then Pira turns her blade down—not at the Ghost, but at him. She skids next to him, then pulls him to her in a sudden hug.

I don't see the dagger go in, but I know she has stabbed him in the heart.

I wince and jerk my gaze away from the scene so suddenly that Constantine looks at me. *Corian.* Corian, Corian. The memory flashes through me like a bolt of lightning—the Ghost opening its jaws behind him as he crouched there on the forest floor, paying his respects to the creatures he had just killed. Me, rushing forward too late. His bright blue eyes looking up at me, filled with tears, knowing what I have to do.

Me, slashing down with my blade. Ending his life.

I am Pira. Tomm is Corian. And I am witnessing the agony of my memory again, live, right before my eyes. I am her, tugging her Shield to herself in order to bury her own dagger in his chest, ending his suffering. And despite our stormy past, despite all the times Tomm had ever tormented me or Pira had lashed out, I can feel nothing but anguish for them.

Relax a little, Talin.

At Constantine's voice in my head, I look at him through a veil of tears. He nods down at my hands. They are clenched so tight against the stone of the balcony that I've scraped my fingers bloody.

I release my grip, but the tide of my fury at Constantine rises in a wave. Corian, dead because of this young Premier. Because of his monsters.

With every ounce of strength I can muster, I push down the swell of anguish. I force my gaze back to where Pira is crouched beside Tomm's now-still body. And I watch.

Pira doesn't even have time to mourn her Shield. Instead, she leaves her dagger where it is, embedded in his chest, and runs down the path as the other Ghosts come for her. Up in the stands, the audience rewards her quick thinking with a thunderous cheer. Behind Pira, Tomm's body collapses to the floor as the Ghosts finish with him.

She doesn't get far. The other Ghosts finally catch up with her. She whirls on them, teeth bared, a ferocious whirlwind, and in this moment, she looks so powerful that I think maybe she really can fend them all off. But then she stumbles against one of them as it grabs her, then shoves her hard against the wall. She hits her head. Her movements become slow and unsteady.

I look away again, but the crowd screams, and I know what has happened.

Pira is dead.

My hands stay steady at my side, but my jaw has clenched so tightly now that I'm afraid I may break my teeth. Tomm and Pira had not been my friends on the warfront, but we had been allies. We had both fought against the Federation in Mara's last stand. Now they're gone, not from fighting Ghosts on the front, but from holding them back in an arena, where they gave their lives entertaining a crowd of fifty thousand.

I close my eyes. Beside me, Constantine shifts, but this time, his voice doesn't appear in my thoughts. I'm grateful for the silence.

When my eyes open, I see down below that Aramin has reached the yellow flag at the end of his maze path. He nods silently as he faces a final Ghost, who snarls at him from underneath where the flag hangs. He doesn't even bother pulling the blade out as he launches up from the Ghost's back to grab the flag.

His steel gate slides shut, sealing him off from the rest of the Ghosts in the maze.

Adena is last, having fought the entire path alone. Miraculously, she leaps off the back of a dying Ghost—the creature still clutching its ruined throat—and grabs the scarlet flag hanging over the path. Immediately, as if her movement had triggered an action, a steel gate slides shut between her and the rest of the path. Two Ghosts hurl themselves at the closed wall, shrieking their rage at being unable to reach her. Adena stands there, her bloody makeshift weapon still in one hand, a sword in the other, breathing heavily.

She has survived. My heart leaps with hope. My limbs weaken in relief.

She looks automatically up toward the Premier. Then, before anyone can stop her, she points her gun at his balcony and shoots straight in the direction of Constantine.

No. I can't be seeing this. What is she doing?

Adena is much too far away for the bullet to hit, let alone accurately, but she shoots anyway, again and again. Her eyes are narrowed to slits, and her face is a picture of rage that I've never seen on her.

My breath hisses through my teeth. Fool! I want to scream at her. Constantine will punish her for such an offense. She has just survived an entire maze only to die because she can't contain her anger.

And yet, deep down, I know I'm furious because Adena has never, ever hesitated to take a stand for what she believes in. While I stay up here beside the Premier that destroyed my homeland, she is down there, pointing her gun at him, unwilling to give him anything. I'm furious because I wish I could be her.

Constantine doesn't flinch at her threat, but his posture stiffens in anger. In the stadium, the audience seems to inhale as a single entity, excited by this brazen show of rebellion, awed and eager to witness the consequence of this Maran Striker's threat against the Premier.

No. *No.* I swear at Adena in my thoughts, screaming silently at her to stop. *You idiot! You could save yourself and live to fight another day!* But she doesn't care anymore. I can tell that any semblance of self-preservation has vanished from her. She fires again. The bullets hit too low, unable to reach us, but they arc instead to ping against the stone below the balcony.

Talin.

Constantine's voice in my head makes me run cold. I turn to see him staring down at Adena, his face a mask of calm.

Kill her, he tells me.

There is no emotion in his voice. No amusement, no anger. Just . . . nothing. It's as if he's telling me to fetch him his slippers.

Adena is threatening him publicly in this arena, an open rebellion—he would never let such a public threat against himself pass.

I was expecting his command. But it still takes me off guard.

Out in the arena, Red's emotions surge. He knows what Constantine must be asking me to do. The furious anguish in him crashes through me like a tide, and I want desperately to answer it. To tell him to stay put, to not make a move. To warn him to get out of here.

But despite Raina's tonic, there's still no real telling how much Constantine can sense. What will happen if he learns that Red is in this audience?

I turn to Constantine, hating how pathetic I look—tears glinting in my eyes, my hands clenched. But he doesn't even bother turning to me. Instead, he's looking around the arena itself, at the screaming audience. At those cheering for blood, cheering for him. Then, at the sound of those who are shouting their disapproval at punishing Adena. The ones who stay quiet, watching with thoughtful expressions. He knows there are rebels out there, enough of them that General Caitoman has called them a real threat. He knows that they represent the crumbling edges of the Federation, this unsteady empire he is fighting to hold on to.

Beside him, General Caitoman watches the display with approval. This is the spectacle he's come to see.

Go, Skyhunter, Constantine says, and this time, his voice in my mind is firm.

He knows I have no choice. He can feel the hatred boiling through me at him. Here I am, the most powerful creation in the world, trapped into doing his bidding. Forced to use that power to end the life of her friend.

As if in a daze, I spread my steel wings. I sense the warmth of my glowing eyes. My feet lift off the floor, and the arena gasps audibly as they witness me launch into the air in Adena's direction. I see the world sprawl below me, feel myself fly through the air as if I'm watching from somewhere far away. As if I'm no longer in my body at all.

Down below, Adena looks up to meet my gaze, and I find myself barely able to return it. She doesn't flinch. Even when the audience shrinks back as I hurtle down toward the maze and come to a landing on top of the structure, Adena stands her ground with a straight back and level stare.

I crouch above her, my wings spread to their full expanse, blocking out the sun.

But Adena just stares at me with a resigned expression. "Come get it over with," she signs. It's a message meant only for me.

The entire arena seems to be holding its breath, waiting for me. I just stay where I am. The threat of what could happen to my mother hovers over me, the ever-persistent cloud, and yet I cannot bring myself to go down there and cut her throat. I can't bear the thought of my weapons drawing her blood.

Even though I don't know where Red is, I can feel him watching this moment. Fearing what I'll be forced to do.

When I lift my eyes, I can see Constantine sitting at his balcony, observing me with that steady expression.

I utter my answer to Constantine through our bond. It is steady, resolute, unshakable.

I won't do it. I won't kill her.

There's a mild current of surprise that comes through the link, followed by a bit of amusement. Constantine is *humored* by my answer. I glare up at him, but he just studies me, testing me.

What about your mother, Talin? he asks me.

I shake my head, not knowing what to do. But I do know this. The certainty of it sears through me in a wave of heat. Constantine's control of my mother is the only thing he currently has with which to subdue me. But that means, with her, I can also control him. He can't afford to kill my mother. Without her, his command over me breaks. So this moment is a bet between us. It is us pitted against each other, the Premier and his Skyhunter, each daring the other to back down first.

I don't dare look directly at the Chief Architect beside him. But even from my peripheral view, I can see her figure turned fully toward me, her focus on what I'll do.

Adena stares up at me, waiting in the wake of my hesitation. In her gaze, I see the Striker with whom I've fought side by side, who had brought me baskets of pies after Corian's death. Who would fashion endless gadgets to help me stay alive at the warfront. For a moment, we are no longer standing on opposite sides of the divide. We're companions again.

The crowd around us stirs restlessly, then begins chanting again.

Some are chanting for her death; others are chanting something that takes me aback.

Mercy. Mercy.

Constantine rises, then lifts his arms. He raises his voice.

"My Skyhunter moves to defend me," he calls out, "but for this good performance, this excellent entertainment, I order the life of this Striker spared." His eyes meet mine again. "May she entertain us again on another day."

Constantine is sparing Adena's life.

I don't know if it's because he wants to appease the restless crowds, or if he's sending a message to his people that he can be a merciful ruler. I don't know if this is his way of reasserting authority, a way to soothe the fraying nerves at the edges of his Federation, or a way to disguise my defiance to the public, that he is actually capitulating to my demand. But I don't care.

I drop to my knees before him anyway, on top of the maze structure, and bow my head in his direction. My subservience. My obedience to the Premier, on full display.

Mercy granted.

For a terrible moment, I think he will order his soldiers to kill Adena anyway.

But he doesn't. Instead, he nods at me and folds his arms, as if he expected my reaction all along.

Nearby in the balcony, General Caitoman looks away in disgusted disappointment. The Chief Architect merely folds her arms.

I'm shaking. I don't know what this will mean for my mother. But if I continue to head down this path, I'll reach a point of no return. Where I will do something I'll regret for the rest of my life. Where my own mother would shake her head in grief at my action.

Adena and I lock eyes a final time. She gives me a faint nod before the guards come. Then they grab her, and she's escorted down the remaining path to the holding room at the end of the maze. The arena roars in delight over a stunningly entertaining game.

Somewhere in the audience, Red is watching. I can feel the pity in him, the deep understanding of why I'd done what I did. He is proud of me. He is afraid for me.

Fury simmers low in my stomach. *Thank you*, I force myself to say to Constantine through our bond.

But his eyes remain cold, and his voice chills me to the bone.

I wouldn't, he answers.

19

RED

AS A CHILD, I'D STAND IN THIS ARENA WITH MY father at my side, Laeni sitting on his shoulders, and cheer as horses would thunder around the track. Or as prisoners were brought in to fight one another to the death. Or as traitors were executed.

You'd always cheered. What else do you do? It's supposed to be fun, isn't it?

Sometimes you're the happiest when you're most ignorant. Better not to know the truth and enjoy life as you know it. That you're not witnessing a horror.

But now I know, and the knowing is agony.

For once, the walls that Talin has put up around her emotions crumble in this arena. Being this close to her again puts everything about her in greater clarity, and I feel the flood of her anguish and desperation and sadness. All I want is to reach out to her. I want to take her hand and lead her out of this place.

As I focus on my bond with Talin, Jeran watches the maze with his hands balled into white-knuckled fists, his eyes fixed on Aramin. We look on helplessly as Tomm falls, then Pira. Jeran lets out a shuddering breath as Aramin reaches the safety of his gate, followed by Adena.

And then we see Adena raise her gun toward Constantine.

I see Constantine gesture for Talin to fly down to where Adena is making her stand.

And I see Talin stand her ground, refusing to strike down her friend.

Everything feels like a blur. I can't believe what I'm seeing.

Then Jeran leans toward me. His voice is hoarse and soft, but clear. "The Premier is ill today."

It's only then that I notice he's right. Constantine is leaning visibly against the edge of the balcony today, and his figure looks hunched, exhausted. Even the paint on his face can't hide the hollows of his cheeks. We can see his weariness from here.

Talin lifts into the air and soars back to the balcony amid a cacophony of cheers and boos from the crowd. Beside her, the seemingly invincible Skyhunter, Constantine looks even weaker.

And if we can see it, surely the rest of the arena can too.

I narrow my eyes at him. I can feel that Skyhunter rage tingling in my limbs, feel it stretching against the boundaries of my body, wanting to set my blood alight and unfurl my bladed wings.

With a mighty effort, I pull myself back. Down below, soldiers emerge and pull Adena into the shadows behind the gates. The games are over, at least for today. I turn my focus on Talin as she stands beside Constantine. To my surprise, she is dry-eyed.

And looking straight in our direction.

I don't know if she can see us here; her Skyhunter eyesight is keener than it should possibly be. But I return her stare anyway, willing her to hear me. My hands clench and unclench.

I'm going to find a way back to your side. I'm going to free you.

I swear everything on it.

20

TALIN

I CAN'T STOP THINKING ABOUT RED.

Long after the horrors of the arena have been left behind, long after the streets of the capital have quieted, I sit up in my bed with the moonlight slanting into my room, my arms wrapped around my legs. My eyes are closed. Constantine has fallen into an uneasy sleep, his dream state shallow and rhythmic in the way I'm used to sensing through our bond. I concentrate on keeping my emotions even, but my mind keeps replaying the feeling of Red's heartbeat.

Red is here in Cardinia. *Here!*

My heart lurches even now, hours later, at the thought, and it takes all my effort to keep myself steady. I always feel Red's heartbeat, of course, but the pulse of it had been so strong in the arena that I could look in the direction it came from and imagine him there in the stands. Even though he was far enough away that I couldn't pinpoint exactly where he was, I knew it was him.

It was *him*.

I draw in a slow, shaky breath and let it out through my mouth, again and again.

Maybe his presence had given me the courage to rage against

the Premier, to stand there and refuse to kill Adena. Maybe I would have felt compelled to do it without him. I don't know. I don't know. All I remember is Adena's eyes locked on mine, unrelenting and furious.

She was ready to die at my hands. I could see that in her, the familiar look she used to get on the warfront whenever it looked like we might lose our lives at the hands of Ghosts.

But I couldn't. I wouldn't. And her eyes had widened instead in disbelief. Not only had I rebelled against the Premier's command in my mind, but Adena had sensed it. Seen it for herself. So had Red. I'd looked back at Constantine and dared him to punish me in front of that crowd by ordering his guards to kill Adena anyway.

But he hadn't. I knew he wouldn't. If he did, the entire audience would have known that he'd been forced to make his other guards do something that I'd refused to do. They would have realized that his hold on his Skyhunter isn't as solid as he's promised and—worse—that I can act independently of his authority.

Better to play along instead. Let the crowd think that Constantine had planned to pardon Adena of her actions all along, that she had performed so well in the maze the Premier himself felt generous and wanted her to live.

But how *long* is he going to let her live? I know, deep in my bones, that he will make sure Adena and Aramin die in the next games. He'll never let them survive and give me that satisfaction. This time I'm going to be forced to stand by, forced to watch the warfront family I've had since childhood be slaughtered for sport.

The thought sends me shaking again. No, no, no. I can't let this happen. But how can I possibly stop it by myself, when I'm trapped by the Premier's side?

I wince and clutch my head in my hands. This is going to hurt my mother. What was I thinking? But what else *could* I have done?

My mother's safety or Adena's life. It is not a choice.

Red, I call through our bond. I feel my voice echoing futilely, like sound through a tunnel with no end. *Look what is happening to everyone I love. Why can't you just stay away and protect yourself?*

I sit with my head in my hands and count the minutes. In the morning, I will have to walk back out there with Constantine. Stand ready at the Premier's beck and call. Shadow General Caitoman on tours of the city. Dole out punishments as they see fit. The solstice celebrations will continue. There will be banquets and dancing. There will be another game, and this time I will see Adena and Aramin murdered, I know it. And I'll have to attend all of it.

Someday, I remind myself again and again. Someday, this will be over. The rebellion will unfurl, Raina and Mayor Elland will turn the country against Constantine, and the unrest stirring in all corners of the Federation will finally crack open. And I will be at the heart of it, taking him down.

The thought of it is so clear and sharp that I immediately force my feelings back into line. Push all images of Raina out of my head. Stop thinking about Red. Stop thinking about Adena and Aramin. I focus on stilling my emotions until my heart beats at a normal pace again, slow and steady.

I don't know when I drift off. I'm only aware I've fallen asleep because when I suddenly stir, I am heading down a rope bridge suspended in a fog of darkness. Down below is an endless chasm. And somewhere ahead is a land of pale mist, its air pulsing with the slight, steady rhythm of Red's heart.

I must have opened myself up again, enough to let my link with Red come through. Our dreams have bound us together, letting us meet once more in this singular state of unconsciousness.

The realization sends me into a new panic. *No, Red. Go away.*

But in this state, I'm helpless. Gradually, Red's mind responds to mine. Fragments of his surroundings materialize around me.

He's somewhere on the outskirts of Cardinia, outside of the city and beyond the bridges that stretch over the river encircling the capital. Out here, there are cheaper installations displayed in the same pattern as those inside the city—narrower thoroughfares radiating out from the city walls, with old bits of twisted steel taken from stolen fields and razed forests arching along their paths. Messier apartment towers sprawl outward. Many of them are worn down, some of them painted on. One of these towers casts its shadow into the alley where Red's camped for the night.

He's curled on the ground in some quiet, abandoned corner. And beside him is a companion—a Striker with a distinct, graceful presence.

Jeran? *Jeran!* All the breath leaves me in a rush.

In my dream, I feel as if I'm standing right at his side. The moonlight cuts blue and gray across the narrow alley, slanting an arc of light against his face.

Red opens his eyes and sits up. Then he stares directly at me. Is he really awake? At first, his stare looks wild, like he can't quite be sure where he is. Strands of his metallic hair cling to the side of his face.

"Talin?" he whispers aloud. Then he blinks and really sees me for the first time. He realizes we have linked in our dreams. And his entire face changes.

He reaches for me before I can say anything more, then pauses, his hands stopping before they touch me as if he's afraid.

Why are you here? I whisper in our dream this time, and the sound seems to come out like a sob. *I told you to stay in the wilds outside Newage.*

He doesn't speak right away. Instead, he bows his head. I am next to him, but not. I can feel the stir of his breath against me, but *he* feels far away, the warmth of him dampened. I can feel every painful edge of his emotions, but I cannot see the finer details of his face. He looks like I'm gazing at him through a fine, translucent cloth, his features softened. I am keenly aware of the way the moonlight outlines the edge of his arm and neck and shoulder in silver.

I turn away in my dream, in a desperate attempt to escape this meeting. I've caused enough pain in one day. If I hurt Red now . . .

Then Red lifts his eyes and looks directly at me. *Wait*, he says.

I stop, listening for more.

You fear Constantine sensing the tide of your emotions, he says. *But there's nothing we can do to stop ourselves from seeing each other in our dreams like this. It's inevitable.*

I shake my head.

But maybe we can *control what he senses from you during these dreams*, he continues softly. *Maybe we can alter these meetings somehow, manipulate our emotions so he can't suspect anything is amiss.*

I start to shake my head again. Even with Raina's tonic, the thought of hurting the Strikers and Red again is terrifying. How can I feel anything but anguish and yearning and fear? How can I—

But as I think this, Red takes a deep breath and closes his eyes.

The dark alleyway, the scene of Cardinia at night.

It all shifts abruptly, like a ripple on a pond. Red opens his eyes and then looks around us. He glances back at me.

Think of the warmest memory you have, he tells me. *Think of a place that brings you peace.*

Peace. It's such a foreign, distant thought that I want to laugh through my tears. But instead, I find my thoughts going immediately to a tree-lined street.

The tree-lined street of my childhood.

Their branches once arched so low that I could simply pull myself up into their crooks and idle away. Those trees are long gone now, burned away when the Federation had first conquered Basea. But I imagine it regardless, painting in my mind the picture of their wide leaves and the sun-dappled ground beneath them. Flowering bushes grow thick on either side of the small street leading to my family's home.

And as I imagine it, it appears around us. Those beautiful, curving trees. The little stall on the side of the street that I used to visit, selling frozen cubes of sweet strawberry juice and ice-cold watermelon slices. The houses of our neighbors, each of their doors unlocked and some of them open, because there was simply no need to worry about thieves. And instead of me crouched in front of Red in the dank alley, we are instead both swinging our legs as we sit on the branches of the largest, oldest tree, savoring a breeze between the shady leaves, watermelon juice sticky on our lips.

It is so real that, in this dream, I believe it. My terror melts away, replaced by the deepest serenity I've felt in a long time, a sense of security and belonging and home. My emotions settle into a still lake. Peace hangs over the surface.

I let out a breath. *Oh.*

Red smiles as he looks around us in wonder. *Now this is much nicer,* he says gently.

If Constantine feels anything coming from me now, he will sense only my nostalgia, my contentment. And with any luck, Raina's work in weakening my bond with Constantine should only help.

The warmth of having Red nearby seems so real that I lean into it, letting myself believe that if I wanted to, I could . . .

Touch his hand.

Touch his face.

Pull him to me.

Feel him whisper against my neck.

With all my effort, I hold back and keep my distance. *Where are you in the city?* I ask him instead.

Near the National Museum, he replies. He hesitates. *We're trying to gather more information on the artifacts that Constantine brought back from Mara.*

An image flickers between us of the lab institute on the day before the first game. I catch a glimpse of him standing with a crowd as two soldiers rush a bleeding man to the institute on a gurney.

I frown. *Why?*

He shakes his head. *I don't know. But there's something more to those artifacts—they must be more than a potential energy source for the Federation.*

I nod, looking around at the serene street of my childhood. *There is always another reason with this Premier.*

Always, Red agrees.

We're quiet for a moment as we soak in the peace around us. The metallic sheen of his hair shines under the dappled light. Even in a dream, he is so beautiful.

I wish this were real, I say. *I wish I could erase everything that had happened in the arena with this.*

Red searches my gaze. *There was nothing you could have done differently*, he tells me.

He saw what happened. He knows what it's like. I turn my face down, determined to keep the peace in my mind.

I'm a Striker, I finally whisper to him. *I'm supposed to know what it's like to lose those we love out on the warfront. I take the hit and I don't make a sound, so I can live to fight another day. But I just . . . couldn't take this hit. I couldn't do it. Not after I put them there in the first place. Not when I was the one standing by and allowing soldiers to shackle them.*

I swallow, the guilt lodging thick in my throat. What if Constantine hadn't taken my bait today? What if he had ordered me to go ahead and kill Adena anyway, or told his soldiers to do so? How would I have lived with it if he had?

Red doesn't answer, but I can feel the pulse of his emotions through our link, his answering pain. He has been down this road before, countless times. What's the point of taking the hit if there is no hope left? What's the point if you lose either way?

You shouldn't have to, he finally answers.

I tighten my lips. *I have to get them out of there*, I say. *I have to get them out, Red. I just . . . have to.*

I finally look up at him to meet his gaze. His eyes are steady and somber, the deep blue that makes me think of open seas and evening skies. Somehow, all I can think of is the afternoon in Mara when we'd both been down in the baths, each of us in a separate bath but the same house, able to sense the other through our new link as steam shrouded everything around us. I had not been able to see anything of him through our link that day, other than the glimpse through his eyes of locks of his hair floating serenely in the water. It hadn't mattered. Some of our closest moments were when we aren't close at all.

I suck in my breath, and for an instant, our surroundings flicker again—this time to those baths. I can feel the warm pool suddenly lapping against my skin, can look over to see Red there beside me, water beading on his bare chest. Steam floats between us, softening his features behind it. The surface of the bath ripples between us, colliding in the middle.

The memory shivers and fades again as I hastily pull it back, embarrassed. The tree branches return around us. But Red doesn't tease me. His blue eyes remain steady, searching my gaze, and I realize that perhaps he was thinking about those baths too.

He hesitates again, his hand in midair. Then he closes the gap between us, reaching out in the dream to smooth the strands of my hair away from my face.

I almost expect his touch to pass through me—but when his hand brushes my face, I *feel* him. I can sense his skin against mine.

He feels me too, and jerks his hand back in surprise. His eyes dart abruptly to mine.

I didn't know we could do that, he whispers.

He's scarcely uttered his words before I lean forward and kiss him.

I have wondered about what it might be like to kiss him since that day in the bathhouse. It's hard to imagine that we would embrace in our dream, through our bond—but I startle just the same. His lips are full and warm, his body yearning toward mine. He's kissing me back before I can comprehend what I'm doing. I wrap my arms around his neck—can I do this? He loops his arms around my waist—can he do this?

Talin, he whispers, my name hoarse on his tongue. Moments from our past flash through me—the night after our first battle together, when he'd touched my hand and begged feverishly for me to stay at his side; the way we'd sat side by side at my mother's table, enjoying the quiet of each other's company; the last time I'd seen him before Mara fell. Then I think of today, of sensing him out there in the audience while I hovered over Adena, trying to decide between killing my friend and sparing my mother any more pain.

The sun-soaked trees and the street of my childhood waver around us, my peace threatening to topple. Will Constantine find a way to dig into my mind and unearth everything? Will I accidentally utter something that gives Red away, as I did outside Newage? If I did, would I ever be able to forgive myself? Could I ever undo the harm that would cause?

I could be the weak link again.

This is the thought that finally forces me to tear away from Red. My arms leave him, my body draws back from his. The air between us cools. He opens his eyes and stares at me as we both breathe heavily, dizzy with the presence of each other.

We're going to free you, he whispers to me. *And we're going to free the others. I swear it.*

I shake my head. *Save yourself and save Jeran. Get him away from here.*

He narrows his eyes at me. *You can't be willing to sacrifice yourself for the others and then tell us to save ourselves.*

Everything in me wants to tell him about Raina, that he and Jeran aren't operating alone out there, that there are so many other forces at work in this city. But I find myself holding back, afraid. My hands chained once again by fear.

Yes I can, I reply. *Because this is no way for us to keep meeting. I'm sorry, Red.*

We can find a way to work together, he starts to say.

No, we can't! The peace in me trembles, and with a great effort, I pull the world around us back together. The wind makes the leaves flutter in the trees. A cloud covers the sun overhead.

No, I say again, calmer. *We can't.*

Talk to me, he insists. *Talk to me when you're awake, not when we're dreaming. At least we can then have better control. Maybe our link is just aching for our connection. Maybe it'll stop in our dreams if we just connect when we're awake.*

I shake my head. I'm too afraid to hurt them again.

We can't win if we don't help each other, he says, and through our bond, I can feel his heart breaking. *Talin, please.*

You can't help me, I answer.

He reaches for me, then stops short. The street of my childhood finally fades around me. At my back, the dark tunnel yawns. The feeling of his lips against mine has become a faint memory. I'm suddenly unsure it ever happened.

I'm sorry, I tell him as I feel the dream pulling to an end. I'm not entirely sure what I'm sorry for. Everything, maybe.

Then he's gone, and I'm back in my bed, lying on my side with my blankets sprawled around me. I can tell that the Premier is still asleep, lost in his own dream. My emotions must have calmed enough with the peaceful memory of my childhood home to keep from stirring him awake.

Red and Jeran are out there. They are on the move. I hang on to this belief, feverishly hoping it to be true.

I should tell them everything. I should keep reaching out to Red.

We can't win if we don't help each other, Red had said to me.

But how can we win if I am the tool Constantine uses to hurt everyone I love? How can I help them, even with Raina's tonic weakening my link with the Premier? I have already put my friends in the arena and nearly gotten Red recaptured.

Next time, they may die. The only way I can help them is to keep my distance.

The image of Adena facing me in the arena hovers over my heart. How brave I'd been then, thinking I could turn Constantine's own game against him. And yet, here I am again, sick to my stomach about what that moment might do to my mother. What good am I to Red and Jeran now, anyway? Will I help them best by simply staying away?

Someday, maybe, I will be free too. Then I will show everyone what I'm capable of doing against this Federation.

But I may have to do it alone.

21

RED

IF THERE'S ONE PLACE IN THE CAPITAL THAT no one is interested in tonight, it's the National Museum.

As the celebrations go deep into the night, fireworks whistling and sparking through the evening air, Jeran and I head to the quiet paths around the museum.

There are no soldiers here. Why should there be? No one is thinking about the relics on display in these halls, and every guard is busy with the rowdy crowds swarming elsewhere in the capital. Only a single sentry is posted at the front and one at the back of the museum, watching halfheartedly for petty thieves. One look at their faces tells me that they're just biding their time, grouchy for having to spend a solstice celebration night stuck at the museum's steps.

I'm quiet, but my mind is a storm. I can't stop thinking about the dream I'd had with Talin earlier in the night, that half kiss. I can still feel the heat of her touch, however phantom it might've been. I can still feel myself pleading with her not to go, to reach out to me when she wakes. I can still feel the agony of her pulling away again, her fear returning. Her pain had washed over me in waves.

Constantine is certainly pressuring her will at every turn, and I can feel her cracking under the strain of it all. They are breaking her as surely as they'd wanted to break me, to turn her into the perfect Skyhunter—obedient, efficient, cruel.

If you don't find a way to take this whole damn system down, they just might succeed.

My fists clench. No. No way I'm going to lose Talin too.

My focus turns back on the museum. If we can uncover what exactly the artifacts from Mara are—and why Constantine is so hell-bent on retrieving them—then maybe we can figure out how to use them against him. How to destroy them.

The benefits of Striker training never cease. Jeran moves so quietly within the shadows of the museum that even I lose him now and then as we go. I head to the opposite side of the building. We take note of each other at either end of the museum's looming steps, above where a sentry stands guard. As we do, I remove some of the wristbands from my arm and untie the ceremonial sash around my sleeve. Then I make my way to the thickets that line the edge of the museum's raised foundation.

There, I purse my lips and make a whistle that imitates one of the fireworks launching along the thoroughfares.

The sentry turns in my direction. He sighs, then heads down the steps while grumbling to himself. I press against the side of the rising stone stairs, melting into the shadows. He passes by without noticing me at all.

From the other side of the building, Jeran steals into the museum without a sound.

As the sentry goes to investigate, I pull myself up the side of the entrance steps and rush toward the entrance. As I move, I hear the sentry again make his annoyed huff as he finds my abandoned wristbands and sash.

"Bunch of wild children," I hear him mutter out loud.

Before he can turn back around and return to his post, I disappear inside the darkness of the museum.

Skylights up above us shed squares of blue light against the marble floors, where objects stolen from every corner of the Federation's conquered lands stand in beautiful, curated rows. Graceful statues, jewels that sparkle in the night, enormous vases and carved plaques. Pillars and pieces of monuments. Tapestries hang on the pale stone walls. It's so quiet I can hear my heartbeat thumping in my ears.

I've never been in here at night before. The daylight cast the entire space in a dreamy fog. In this midnight air, though, the museum feels haunted. There are spirits in here, whispering stories ripped away from their roots.

Jeran materializes from the shadows beside me. The light halos him in silver. He looks questioningly at me, waiting for my cue on where to go.

I nod, then close my eyes, trying to remember the paths I used to take. Then I turn down a hall, and he follows.

We make our way past old doors salvaged from early Karensa and conquered Reo, plates and dishes and silverware taken from the rubble of destroyed homes in Benton, rugs depicting Azaran folk tales that must have once decorated the walls of their libraries. As we go, I can feel a flicker of my boyish self in here, taking these same steps, walking these same corridors. I'd seen these same displays back then. I'd lift my sister so she could get a better look at paintings and artwork on the walls. Laeni would let out purposefully loud laughs just to hear the way it echoed down the corridors. I can almost hear her now, some memory of her voice still preserved in this space.

I nod at a table set that we pass by. "See that?" I whisper so quietly that my voice seems to dissolve into the air. "I remember the soldiers bringing that into the museum for the caretakers to polish. They'd brought it back on a train from Carreal."

"Did you have happy memories here?" Jeran asks.

We reach the bottom of the stairs leading up to the second floor. "So many," I whisper.

Jeran gives me an understanding smile. "It's okay to keep those memories, you know," he whispers. "Even here."

"I know," I murmur back as I look up. Then I make my way up the same steps I used to take as a child.

We emerge onto a second floor dedicated entirely to relics from the Early Ones.

Jeran sucks in his breath. Rows and rows of artifacts are on display—archways from ancient halls, shards of twisted metal, gadgets that must have once worked, old engines and intricate gears, metal and glass polished to such a fine sheen that they look like nothing that exists today. One display is a series of charts drawn inside an old notebook, meticulously spelling out the life spans of various persons. They seem impossibly long: 140 years, 151 years, 160 years. Another is a line of glass jars containing curiosities preserved inside murky liquid, pieces of something organic that must have been alive a long time ago.

Goose bumps rise on my arms. No matter how many times I see these objects, I'm always haunted by them.

"I've never seen anything like this," Jeran whispers as he stops in front of a glass display case showing what looks like a rectangle covered with rows of slim, shiny metal. "Does the Federation know what it's for?"

I glance at the placard with it. Another long-lost memory returns: I was a little boy standing beside my father, pointing at this exact object, and asking him what it does. He stooped down to my height, his hands warm on my shoulders, and said, *We think it was an engine of sorts, something that could power a metal machine and tell it what to do.*

I stared in fascination at the slim, neat rows of metal. *How can this tell something what to do?*

My father shrugged. *Well, how does an engine tell a train to move?* He glanced at me. *How do we tell the Ghosts to attack or to stay? The Early Ones were always searching for that.*

For what?

Control.

Why'd they want that so badly?

He stood back up, patted my shoulder, and fell silent. *If you could control the entire world, all of life, with a touch of your hand, you would.* In his expression, I could see a glimmer of my mother and the sadness that always accompanied it.

I looked away from him and across the room, my eyes finding Laeni as she stood on tiptoe to peer at a mechanical doll on display in a glass case. Whenever my father got quiet like this, I found myself shying away, wanting to give him his space.

Looking back, I realize that maybe I was trying to control my own narrative.

The memory fades. I am looking straight across the same room and seeing the same mechanical doll on display against the opposite wall. Except now there's no Laeni standing in front of it.

"Control," I whisper.

Jeran looks at me.

"Everything the Early Ones created was about seeking control," I explain, leading us around the room, relying on the muscle memory of a hundred trips in here. "The philosophy behind Ghosts was to reduce a human down to something you could control. Electricity, to control when you could have light. Trains, to control a massive machine that could take you where you wanted to go."

I finally stop before a series of small objects in three separate glass cases.

"I guess the question is what the Early Ones wanted to control with those artifacts," Jeran murmurs.

I look down at the objects. All three are identical, and all three look exactly like miniature versions of the cylinders that I'd seen dug up in Mara. The rush of familiarity comes back to me. No wonder I watched those things loaded onto the train cars and thought I'd seen them somewhere before. They were here, all along.

"'Purpose unknown,'" Jeran reads from the placards alongside them. "It's all that's written about them."

I shake my head, then bend closer to the objects. "These look like models of those artifacts, except these have their ends opened up." I point to the insides of each miniature cylinder, which was loaded with thinner rods structured around a hollow center.

"Now, come take a look at this."

I gesture for Jeran to follow me to the other side of the room, then point at several engravings on display against the wall. "Maybe there's a reason they buried those artifacts so deep underground."

"Energy source?" Jeran asks.

"Maybe," I reply, nodding up at the engravings. "But to power what?"

It's a series of paintings long faded by time, but the grooves are deep enough to reveal what must once have been on the wood panels. "A depiction of life as it unraveled during the end of the Early Ones' reign," I say.

The images show the massive height of the walls being built around various cities. Down below, an image depicts a cross section showing layers of earth beneath the walls, where bodies of people deemed infected were buried deep, deeper than any body should need to go. As if the survivors were terrified of them.

"It's believed that whatever they created and unleashed upon themselves had something to do with lengthening their lives," I tell Jeran.

He nods. "Infinite Destiny," he murmurs. "Their words engraved on ruins in Mara. They would live as long as the stars."

"Now, do you see this?" I lean closer to the wood panels and point out some of the items installed on the tops of the walls.

Jeran frowns. The engraving is rough and hard to make out. But when I look closely enough at it, I can see the subtle signs of an image once there, with blocks of text below. The image appears to depict a small crowd of people gathered in a loose circle around something. As a boy, I'd get as close to this engraving as I could, attempting to make out the faces of the Early Ones, marveling at their strange clothes, wondering if they acted like us as much as they looked like us.

"This is a wood print of some old papers written by the Early Ones," I explain in a low voice, nodding at the accompanying placard. "They used to release regular, written reports of events happening in their society to their people. This one discusses an accidental explosion that consumed one of their towns."

Jeran and I stare for a moment at the engraved image. The loose crowd of people seems to be standing around crumpled, rodlike canisters strewn across the ground.

"What if those artifacts aren't an energy source, but a weapon that failed?" I whisper, looking at Jeran.

"A weapon they couldn't control?" Jeran adds.

I nod. "What if those cylinders were made in an attempt to create a weapon, then buried because they realized how dangerous they were?"

Jeran looks at me. "Then they should never have been dug back out."

"Look at what they've done to the workers that rode the train with them."

"What if they're unstable in the open air?"

"Bombs?"

If those artifacts are sitting out and are truly unstable, then we have even less time than we thought. Surely the Karensans don't realize what they've gotten their hands on. They think it's an object that has the potential to power their cities. But it may be the most dangerous thing that's ever been brought back to Cardinia, an object that, once exposed aboveground, could unleash destruction on the entire city. Could kill us all at any moment.

You don't know what it might do. And it's this unknown that chills you straight to your core.

"Do you think Constantine suspects the danger of those artifacts?" Jeran asks.

I frown. "Yes. But he has always been willing to overlook the danger of something if it can offer what he considers to be worthy rewards."

"What's the worthy reward in this case?" Jeran says. "Why does he want it so badly?"

Talin had told us that the Premier was searching for those artifacts because they are a potential energy source. But the Federation has plenty of resources. There has to be another reason. Something deeper, something that has him digging obsessively for these relics.

"I don't know," I whisper. "But if it's all that valuable to him, then it can also be his weakness. We have to figure out what he wants with it."

22

TALIN

THE FOLLOWING DAY, AS EVENING CASTS PURPLE across the sky, I join Constantine as his carriage heads out of the palace and toward the exhibition building known as the Sun Dial, where he will have a public feast with the crowds of Cardinia.

The main thoroughfares are lit with torches, and red paper hangs from each stall. Music prompts spontaneous dancing in the streets. Ahead looms the massive glass-and-steel structure. The Sun Dial is the same building that had acted as the exhibition hall for the National Fair in Cardinia, the festivity I'd witnessed with Adena and Jeran over a year ago, where the Chief Architect had paraded a train of caged Ghosts in the middle of their transformations. Now the exhibitions have been cleared from the Sun Dial, replaced with an enormous, curved banquet table that follows the arc of the dais in the center of the building's glass atrium.

Tonight's banquet is meant for the Karensan people to see their Premier celebrating the solstice festival with them, culminating in dancing and more reveling. Privately, I know it's meant as a show of Constantine's strength and popularity, a bribe of free food and drink for the people to see that he's strong and unafraid of the growing unrest in the city.

As we enter the hall and approach the circular, central dais, I see a memory of myself standing here alongside Adena and Jeran as we watched the cages of the transforming Ghosts being paraded before the public. Back then I'd hidden among the crowd with my fellow Strikers, afraid to be seen. Now I see people ripple away from our procession, their eyes both following my steps and averting in fear. My wings are partially extended, casting a shadow against the ground.

I ball my fists, satisfied to see these Karensans cowering in my presence, angry to allow myself that satisfaction at the monstrosity I've become.

Right as the sun dips low against the horizon, dancers in shimmering gold outfits emerge, twirling around the dais in rows. Food stands stretch off in every direction. By the time we reach the center of the atrium, a crowd has gathered around the low barriers put up around the dais, each of them eager to get a glimpse of the Tyrus brothers and the Premier's Skyhunter.

For once, I'm not dressed in my black Skyhunter uniform, but a set of white-and-gold top and pants wide enough to look like a dress. Circlets adorn my arms. Knives and a sword still hang on my belt. Constantine takes the steps up to his position on the dais, where tables have been set up for the Premier and his entourage.

He looks even paler today than he did at the game. His movements are slow, and through our bond, I feel a rush of nausea roiling through him.

Raina's work, no doubt, and done purposefully for an evening when she knows he must put on a show of strength. I force myself to keep my emotions even, my heartbeat steady. As always, I'm exhausted. After I stirred awake from my dream with Red, I never fell back asleep. I paced and paced until morning finally arrived, our kiss still burning on my lips.

As I take a seat beside Constantine, I expect him to cast me a brief glance, but he doesn't. He knows I'm waiting for his reaction to the events in the arena, dreading his orders to his soldiers to hurt my mother, but to punish me, he stays quiet. Nothing I did yesterday seems to have troubled him. So I tighten my lips and look away, unwilling to let him feel my unease.

Beside me is seated Raina, the Chief Architect. I look at her occasionally, but she doesn't seem to mind my presence, sipping instead on her wine and searching the audience with her careful gaze. Down below, Mayor Elland is mingling with some people who must be Karensan nobles, her head thrown back in a laugh. She seems comfortable, with a beautiful young woman on her arm, and chats away as if she'd had the most wonderful day yesterday at the games.

Finally, as the sky turns into shades of deeper purple and blue and the public gets louder, I see the Chief Architect turn her face slightly toward mine. On my left, Constantine laughs at something Caitoman tells him.

His brother smiles back, then lifts his glass. He raises his voice. "A toast," he calls out.

I don't actually understand the Karenese word he uses, but his gesture lets me infer it. He rises to his feet, and as I stare up at him, he holds the glass out to the gathered audience and then toward the Premier. Everyone quiets to hear his words.

"To my brother's successes," he says, "on the first eve of the summer solstice and every eve after, and for carrying forward our Infinite Destiny for all the years you'll live."

The crowd cheers, following him in chanting a mantra for the Premier's long life. But when I look out at the people gathered, I notice that not all of them repeat the chant. Some don't glance our way.

At the table, the Architect bows her head and sips her wine. Constantine drinks. So does Caitoman.

Everything in me wants to defy the toast, but I lift my glass too, then tilt my head back and take a quick swig. The liquid runs through me, warm and tingling.

The meal begins. I glance toward Constantine, but he seems unconcerned as he listens to Caitoman talk about the border states.

Something about my expression must catch Caitoman's interest, because abruptly the General pauses in his conversation to give me a barbed smile. "Your Skyhunter looks ill today," he says to his brother. He pushes his chair slightly back, then leans toward me. "Does such rich food not sit well with you?"

I stiffen. He must know I'm shaken by what happened in the arena, and the thought of it sparks him with delight.

"Oh, brother," Caitoman says, studying my face with satisfaction. "Look at her face. You've really outdone yourself, destroying this one." He raises his glass to me for a toast. "To you then, Skyhunter, and your merciful heart."

Trapped, I raise my wine to his, but the taunt in his voice makes me stop short of clinking glasses with him.

Caitoman sees the defiance on my face. Without warning, his other hand shoots out to seize my wrist, closing around it like a vise. The General cannot physically hurt me, but he knows he can still force me to do things against my will. His smile sharpens.

"When I offer you a toast, you take it," he tells me in a low voice.

Constantine glances once at his brother. "She is my Skyhunter," he says smoothly. "Not yours."

Caitoman doesn't look at his brother. Instead, he keeps his stare on me, gauging my will, before he releases me and leans back in his chair. I do the same, relieved to be free of the General, disgusted that it was Constantine who came to my rescue.

The General smiles at his brother. "Of course, Premier," he says mildly.

Constantine says nothing through our link as he returns to his conversation with his brother. But I go back to staring at my plate, any semblance of an appetite gone. The Premier may torment me for a purpose—but the General does it for pleasure. Even though I have the physical advantage over him, I do not have the political power to touch him, and the reminder tightens around my heart.

When the meal has gone on long enough, dancing breaks out in clusters in the ringed streets below. Caitoman heads down to join the festivities. I let out a small breath of relief at his absence, then watch the twirling bodies for a while before Constantine rises, holding his hand out to me to join him in the dance.

At first, I feel myself recoil at the thought of having to dance with him.

Then, I realize that's not the real reason why Constantine is calling for me to accompany him. Through our bond, I sense his nausea and exhaustion gain in intensity, wracking his body. But even without sensing his emotions, I can see him sway slightly in place, as if crumbling under the pressure of his weakness. His eyes look bloodshot, and his breathing seems labored.

He's holding his hand out to me because he needs help going down the steps.

I go to him. Beside me, the Chief Architect watches us before she rises and heads down into the festivities herself. I watch her embrace her husband and join him in the dances while a boy who must be her young son twirls with his maid nearby.

I loop my hand through Constantine's outstretched arm. His long, thin fingers wrap around my wrist. Immediately, I feel him lean heavily against me, his body shaking slightly.

Premier? I say through our bond.

His expression doesn't change. Instead, he tightens his jaw and takes a step down from the dais with me. *Just go*, he replies.

We take a few steps down toward the whirling dancers.

He pauses for a moment, my arm still in his tight grip. His trembling quickens. When I look over at him, his eyes are closed and his face sickly pale, as if he's steadying himself for the next step.

I glance out at the crowd. People have noticed us now—a few murmurs come from the gathered nobles.

Down below, Caitoman's smile fades a little at the sight of his brother's face.

Constantine, I say, this time daring to use his name.

His eyes snap open—bloodshot, unforgiving. He fixes his hard stare on me. *I'm fine,* he replies through the link, his voice almost a snarl. Then he forces himself down another step.

He falters.

A louder gasp sweeps through the crowd as Constantine stumbles and kneels right on the steps, his robes draping across the terraced stone. In the blink of an eye, Caitoman is at his brother's side, taking a knee beside him to offer him his arm. The guards around us shift their stances. And instinctively, I turn toward the Premier, as if I genuinely believe in my role to protect him. My wings spread.

Constantine stays where he is for what seems like a long moment. I kneel on his other side, meeting Caitoman's gaze briefly before looking back at the young Premier.

"Can you walk, brother?" Caitoman asks him in a low voice.

Constantine grits his teeth and tightens his grip on his brother's arm. "I can," he replies. "Step away."

Caitoman just shakes his head, then stands up to motion at the nearest guards. "Take the Premier back to the palace," he says. "He's unwell."

At that, though, Constantine forces himself to his feet with every ounce of strength he has. His strain pulls our link taut. He straightens, turns his piercing gaze on his brother, then sweeps his stare out at the crowd. Everyone has stopped to watch him.

Take my hand, Constantine snaps through our link.

I take his outstretched arm and pull him to his feet in one move. He sways again, leaning against me, before gathering his strength and stepping down past his brother. Caitoman watches him with a wary gaze.

Down below, I can see that small pockets of the crowd who had looked away during the toast are now murmuring among one another. Still others crane their necks, eager for another look at the Premier's pale face. Most look stunned into silence. Even the music has stopped.

No one has ever seen Constantine falter before.

Constantine lifts his chin high and nods at the crowd, then smiles, holding his hand out at them in greeting. There's a nervous wave of smiles in return. The musicians remember their place and begin to play again. Gradually, the dance starts where it left off, and by the time we reach the bottom step, they've all begun spinning around the dais again.

Caitoman heads down to the dances too. He takes up a position on the opposite side of the dancing ring from his brother. As I look on, the General stops beside Raina and pulls her briefly aside to say something in her ear. Caitoman's gaze looks as lethal as ever. Raina stays calm—but as she turns to reply, I can't help wondering what he said to her. Whether he's taunting her too.

Whether he's suspicious of her plans.

Constantine leads me with a small turn into the dance circle, and I push the brief exchange out of my thoughts. I can feel his exhaustion reaching the breaking point tonight, but he forces himself into the steps along with everyone else, one of his hands gripping mine tightly and the other pressed against the small of my back. I can tell from the way he moves that he's relying heavily on my strength to keep him upright and moving with everyone else.

And even though I now know exactly why this is happening, that this is what we want to happen, I still cringe at how weak he is. Why do I care at all? Maybe it's the bond between us, giving me the illusion that I should care for someone who shares his emotions with me. Then I realize that I'm scared of his faltering because it means the plan *is* working. Which means soon, in a few days, I will need to stand in the arena and make my move against him.

Which means I'll need to trust that Raina and Mayor Elland will protect my mother as they've promised.

If everything continues to go according to plan.

Well, Talin, Constantine says to me as we turn. I meet his eyes to see a slight, sinister smile on his lips. *You must be thrilled to have seen me like that.*

I keep my gaze steady. *I'm only frightened*, I answer, and am relieved at how truthful it must feel through our bond.

And why is that?

My mother's life is in your hands. What happens to her if something happens to you?

Constantine laughs a little at my words as he steps in time to the music. Somehow, even in his condition, he manages to keep up with the nobles dancing around us. I can still see other people glancing in our direction, staring at the Premier, wondering when he'll falter next.

You're wise to worry, Constantine answers. His weight presses against me as he fights to keep himself going.

I harden my heart and tighten my hand in his. As we go, I glimpse Raina dancing with her husband a few couples in front of us. When she catches my gaze, she holds it for a second. If she's shaken after her encounter with Caitoman, she doesn't show it.

Elsewhere in the circle, I see Mayor Elland in the crowd too, dancing with her partner. The crowd is heavy with tension, the cheers and laughter now seemingly more forced, the pockets of unhappy people murmuring louder.

I keep a grip on the walls around my heart and continue to spin with the Premier.

The song crests, and the dance shifts. I find myself staring at the rings glinting on the Chief Architect's fingers a short distance away. There is a plain band, a silver swirl, a sun with radiating lines.

We turn again, and the world blurs around me. The air, crisp and cool, stings my cheeks.

The tension in the air thickens. My muscles are tensing. Something feels like it's going to happen.

As I think it, Constantine looks at me. He notices my unease.

That's when I hear a tiny *pop* come from somewhere in the audience. Something sparks in the air.

Ironically, the part of me that catches this is not the Skyhunter enhancements made to me by the Chief Architect, but all my years of training as a Striker.

The *pop* is from a gun. The spark is gunpowder.

At the same time, I hear a resounding shout, the words ringing clear in the air.

"He is not ordained to rule us!"

I move without thinking. One of my steel wings curves protectively around Constantine, forming an impenetrable shell of steel. I feel the reverberation of the bullet against the blades of my wings. Every movement is so inhumanly fast that I find myself taken aback by the sheer force of my response. It is like watching someone else command my body.

In reality, the entire moment must have happened inside a fraction of a second, and I must have moved so quickly that others barely saw it. Constantine doesn't even turn toward the sound until I've covered him.

Get down! I scream through our bond before my wings close around him. And as the world around us explodes in chaos.

Someone has just attempted to assassinate the Premier. The game against Constantine has begun.

23

TALIN

THE MOMENT IS ALL A BLUR.

The shot misses Constantine, pinging harmlessly off my wings, but he collapses against me from the shock of our sudden movement. My arms loop through his in a second.

Somewhere near me, Caitoman is shouting for the carriage as he swoops to his brother's side and starts to lead him down the path out of the building. People are running everywhere, some crouching in place in terror, others riled up by the incident and shouting at the guards. Soldiers seem to multiply from nowhere, forming scarlet lines as they push the people back to give us room.

Caitoman reaches me first. "Take him to the carriage," he snaps at me, nodding down toward the horses waiting along the front of the building.

I don't hesitate. We guide Constantine into the carriage waiting for him. Revelers crowd around the carriage; people scream in the streets; the news of an attempted assassination spreads like wildfire.

Raina and Mayor Elland were right. Make Constantine look vulnerable. And kick the hornet's nest.

The last thing I see as the carriage pulls away is the body of the would-be assassin in the distance. Beyond the parted path the soldiers made for us, her figure lies in the middle of the now-empty dance ring before the dais, her blood pooling on the stone ground.

She doesn't look like some seasoned mercenary or cunning soldier. She's just a girl.

A girl—perhaps younger than me—had seized the moment of Constantine's weakness and dared aim a gun at him.

She had done it knowing that it would mean certain death, that she would be giving up everything. I stare and stare at her body until we turn and she vanishes from view. Then I sit in silence, the image of her seared into my mind.

Just a girl, with no Skyhunter powers or Striker training.

She had still been braver than me.

• • •

At the palace, soldiers swarm furiously around the grounds. There are shouts in the streets and people clustered around the outer gates, onlookers trying to peek over the guards' heads to catch sight of anything interesting happening within. As if they could get a glimpse of Constantine or any clue as to what his reaction to the attempted assassination was.

Inside, Constantine has been taken to his chambers, and a flurry of doctors surrounds him, along with the Chief Architect and Mayor Elland.

I'm careful to avoid them, my attention fixated on him as he snaps at a doctor administering a poultice to a cut he'd suffered on his arm during our escape from the Sun Dial. Elsewhere, the Chief Architect speaks softly to another of the Premier's doctors, and Mayor Elland stands in a tight circle with his advisors, her face tight with concern.

For once, I wish I had a bond with more people. What are they thinking right now? Was this supposed to happen today?

Even if I hadn't been there, it would have been a hopeless gamble. The would-be assassin was never close enough to get a good aim, and by the time she was, General Caitoman had been able to pull Constantine from behind my wings and away from immediate harm.

The girl was shot at least a dozen times. I heard one of the soldiers say it breathlessly as we arrived here. She'd been dead before she even hit the ground.

Again, I find myself dwelling on her still body. On how she threw herself so willingly into death.

"Cancel the rest of the games," Caitoman is saying to him right now. He shakes his head at the Premier. "You're in no condition to continue greeting the public, brother. You need rest, sleep, some nutrition to bring blood back through your body. You—"

"Tell me again to cancel my appearances," Constantine says in a warning voice to his brother.

He hesitates, catching the dangerous quiet in the Premier's voice. "Brother," he begins again. It's strange to hear this man, with all his cruel nature, try to sound concerned. "You know I'm right. You're weak."

"The games go on," Constantine says.

The tone of his voice makes the entire room go quiet. Raina looks at him warily. The mayor stares at him from across the room, her lips tight. Constantine meets their gazes with his own fiery one before settling back on his brother.

Caitoman gives him a grim smile. "You've never liked taking orders from me, have you?" he says.

"I don't take orders from my subordinates," Constantine answers. He ignores his brother's look and scans the rest of the room. When I reach out through our link to him, I hit a wall. He has pulled his defenses around himself so tightly that I can sense nothing except a veil of rage.

Caitoman just raises his hands and shrugs once. Then he looks around the room. "Leave him," he says, nodding at his guards to open the chamber doors. "Let my brother rest."

As I watch advisors file out, I can't help the satisfaction that rises in me. Constantine looks fearsome on the surface—I can see the way his council members duck their heads as they leave, as if they're terrified that the Premier will suddenly order their arrest and execution. They almost trip over their own feet in their rush to get out.

But I can feel the fear running through his bones, now leaking through the walls he's attempted to put up. The assassination attempt surprised him. But most of all, his weakness on the steps today had taken him off guard. He knows that he'd betrayed himself before his entire public. He knows the word has already spread.

I can see his bloodshot eyes roaming the emptying room before settling on me.

Talin, he says through our bond.

Premier? I answer calmly.

Send in my captain of the arenas, he tells me. *Tell him we're moving up the next game to tomorrow.*

My heart seizes at that. *Tomorrow?*

He has no patience for our teasing tonight. *I know you heard me, Skyhunter*, he says. His lip curls into a dark snarl. *Tomorrow.*

Adena and Aramin. I don't have to say it aloud to know, without a doubt, that Constantine will unleash his rage on them tomorrow. By the end of the day, my Striker friends will be dead. He won't be sparing any lives after an attempted assassination.

I bow my head. *Yes, Premier*, I say.

As I turn to leave, I see Constantine's eyes roaming the abandoned chamber. I can sense the fear in him lingering in the air—it permeates everything.

Who are your friends, Premier? And who are your enemies?

Good. Let Constantine feel the unraveling of his own mind. Let Raina's poisons course through his body. Let this city's unrest and his people's hatred for him eat him alive.

And as I sense this, I feel the resurgence of some part of me that I'd feared I'd lost. It's the part of me that had flickered out when Constantine first captured me, the part that had let myself open my heart to others, to accept help, to trust my life to a Shield, to be a part of team willing to give their lives for one another. It's the girl who had been brave enough to flee Basea with her mother. The girl who had lingered as a child near the Striker arena with grand dreams of joining the Strikers. It's the girl who was willing to step into the woods at the warfront because she knew she had allies at her side. It's the girl who could so easily distinguish right from wrong, who could make decisions she believed in even when they were hard.

It is the part of me that had once helped a boy prisoner in the Striker arena, for no reason other than I believed he deserved better. It is the part of me that wants so badly to open itself up to Red's call through our link. The part of me that is like that young, would-be assassin willing to lay down her life for what is right.

I think back to the night when Constantine had leaned back against his pillow and told me, *Everyone wants someone to believe them*. How lonely he'd seemed in that moment, in spite of all his power. How I pitied him. Now I know why. I pitied him because I knew, even then, that I am not like him.

I am not alone. Not if I let myself reach out to the world beyond me. And perhaps I'm not protecting anyone by walling myself away like this.

We can't win if we don't help each other, Red told me in our dream.

Maybe he's right, after all. Maybe I need to be braver.

As I step out of the room, I let down the walls of my emotions for the first time in a long time. Then I close my eyes and reach tentatively out for Red, seeking our bond.

If we're going to take down this Federation, we're going to use all the help we can get. And another Skyhunter might be exactly what we need.

24

RED

WE DON'T EVEN NEED TO HEAR ABOUT CON- stantine's attempted assassination to know that something has happened at the solstice festival. No one tries to shoot the Premier and not cause a scene, you know?

From our vantage point near the lab complex, we can hear the commotion, see the guards rushing toward the Sun Dial building. I lower myself among the tree branches surrounding the lab complex and exchange a quiet stare with Jeran crouched in the next tree. We'd come here in the hopes of hearing some updates about the two victims that had arrived at the complex, but we've heard nothing.

Now, with the guards running through the streets, we'll have to wait until later in the night to move securely away from the area.

But that doesn't mean we don't get to witness the spectacle caused by an attempted assassination. The shouts are everywhere in the streets. The news reaches us, fragmented and fleeting, from citizens hurrying by.

"—the Premier is shot!—"

"—a girl—"

"—taking him back to his estate—"

"—had collapsed on the steps of the dais—"

"—rebels right in the center of the city!—"

"—he's weak—"

"—he's injured—"

"—he's dying—"

Not until hours later do we finally move from our cramped spots. In the distance looms the arena, its lights illuminating the street encircling it. I wonder if they've done anything differently with Adena and Aramin since the assassination attempt. If they've secured them more, our plans just became more complicated.

That's when the impossible happens. I feel a sudden tug through my bond with Talin. It's not the tenuous connection we have in our sleep, in that unreal dream world, where we seem to have little control over when we get to speak. No, this is conscious and deliberate.

It's Talin reaching out directly to me.

Red.

It's such a shock that at first I don't answer. Must be dreaming. Talin should be at the Premier's side right now, following his orders and making sure he's safe. Why would she reach out to me now, when she insisted I go away?

But her voice comes through unmistakably.

Red, I need your help.

I close my eyes. Now I really must be dreaming. But when I open my eyes, I see Jeran looking at me in bemusement, his gaze focused on the small smile that's emerged on my face.

What do you need? I ask her.

Adena and Aramin, she responds. *Constantine is in a fury, and he's going to take it out on them. He's moving up the games to tomorrow. Adena and Aramin aren't going to survive another round. I know it. But I can't free them. My hands are tied.*

Talin must truly be afraid for them, if she's finally reaching out to me. My relief and fear clash at the thought.

We can get to them, I tell her. I look over again at the arena. *We just have no code for the keys they keep. Jeran says the guards at the arena don't have them.*

I can get the code to you.

Across from me, Jeran's eyes widen as he searches my face. Even though he doesn't know what we're saying through our bond, he can see the light sparking in my expression, the possibility of something.

How? I ask Talin. *When?*

Tonight. Her voice sounds hurried and tense. *Midnight, at the northern thoroughfare.*

My heart starts pounding. *Will I see you in person?*

She doesn't answer right away, but I can sense her answer in the careful emotions that leak to me.

Not for long, she finally replies. *But I'll be there.*

My smile widens. My hand curls into a fist. I can sense the old Talin sparking to life, the Striker, the Basean, the survivor, her ferocious light breaking through the cracks in the walls. The strength of her permeates our link, and all I see in this moment is the same girl who once stood before me and defended me, eyes flashing.

She is back.

Then we'll be there, I say. *No matter what.*

25

TALIN

THE REST OF THE NIGHT SETTLES INTO AN uneasy calm as Constantine remains in his chamber. The number of guards posted around the palace stays high, and as I head into my room in the same hall, my keen ears can pick up their added footsteps echoing down the halls. Outside in the city, unrest roils. Extra troops are called to quell pockets of violence, but even from this far inside the palace grounds, I can hear the distant roar of potential rebels protesting against the soldiers. Of shots being fired.

As soon as I close my door, I bolt for the bathroom. There, everything in my stomach comes up, and I hurl over and over into the bathtub until there is nothing left in me. The sourness in my mouth reminds me too much of the tang of blood in the air. When I close my eyes, all I can see is the dead girl's limp figure lying near the dais of the Sun Dial. It morphs into the corpses of Tomm and Pira.

The events of the past two days are all too much.

Through the sickness that swirls inside me, I feel Red's energy stir. There is fear laced through the thread linking us.

And a new warmth, too. Because in spite of everything, at least he is here with me again. At least the thrum of his presence in my mind is a reminder that I'm not alone.

I take a deep breath and remind myself that he and Jeran are out there. They are at my side, in spirit if not in person, and I am at theirs. And someday, we will be on the other side of this. I have to believe it.

The code for the arena's holding room keys. Constantine keeps those keys with him now. But if he's in his chambers sleeping, can I really get in there tonight, on a night when he's restless from the drama of his own day? Can I really meet Red and Jeran tonight? What if I can't get the code for the Strikers' key? What if Constantine finds out?

I close my eyes. Count. Minutes drag on, turn into hours. I don't know how long. I push myself up off my knees and go to the sink, where I splash water on my face and rinse out my mouth. The sour aftertaste fades from my tongue, and my head clears a bit.

Only then do I realize that the spike of fear I'm feeling isn't coming from Red at all—but from Constantine.

My headspace had been so muddled that for a second I couldn't tell. Now it's unmistakable—a jaggedness that is distinctly his, followed by a tide of darkness. At first I think that maybe this is coming from a nightmare, but then the emotions crest and dip in an uneven pattern, not like the even waves that come with his sleep.

Curiosity momentarily cuts through my anguish. I look up from the sink and back toward my bedchamber, to the wall where Constantine rests on the other side. The moonlight spilling against the floor stretches all the way across the room.

He's not in his bed. He's not anywhere in the room. And when I sense the emotions cresting over him, I realize that they're coming from somewhere else.

After the assassination attempt earlier in the evening, some ominous premonition stirs in me. Did they catch someone else who was involved in the plot? Do the guards standing outside his door know that the Premier has left his chamber? Are Raina and Mayor Elland doing something else I don't know about?

I find myself walking back into my bedroom and toward the door. I step out quietly into the hall.

Two guards posted in front of his bedroom stand straighter at the sight of me, blinking nervously. I give them a silent nod, then turn away and head down the hall, following the tug of our link.

Just because we are bonded doesn't mean I always know exactly where he is. But unlike earlier—when he shielded all his emotions from me—now he is holding nothing back. His emotions are so strong, I find myself crossing the palace hall in confidence, following him as if he were a beacon. Light and darkness stripe past me as I make my way to the other end of the second floor, then down the flight of stairs. Guards posted around the palace note me as I pass them in silence, but they don't dare make a move to question where I'm going.

I step into the atrium and follow a glass hallway into the greenhouse branching off from the palace.

Constantine's pulse grows stronger. He's in here somewhere.

Warm air greets me as I step in. Lush plants nod their heads down at me, and the scent of flowers from all parts of the world hit my senses. Overhead, the glass dome reflects a cool blue hue from the night sky. Like the sculptures that decorate the city's thoroughfares, this greenhouse comprises plants taken from the Federation's conquered territories. I catch sight of the broad-leaved trees I remember growing around Basea. Soon, there will probably be a pond here featuring the hardy camifera seaweed that grows along Mara's sea cliffs.

My attention shifts to the greenhouse's back wall, which connects it to the palace, the only wall made of stone instead of glass. As I walk toward it, I realize that there is a slight opening in the wall, and within that slit flickers a faint light.

I walk up to the opening and find that it slides open.

It gives way to a dark, narrow corridor wide enough only for a single person.

I hesitate. I've been in this greenhouse multiple times, shadowing Constantine as he enjoys his manicured garden, but this is the first time I've noticed this hidden space. There's a corridor that runs behind this back wall, with a rectangle of weak light illuminating the very end of it. In the darkness, I can see the faint glow coming from my eyes, lighting the way. The farther down the corridor I go, the more distinct the outline at the end becomes, until I finally reach it. I give the door the gentlest push. At first it doesn't budge, but with a little more pressure, it slides open to reveal a small, dimly lit room with no windows.

I find myself staring at Constantine's back, lantern light illuminating him as he leans hunched over a table.

His headpiece, no longer on his bare head, lies untouched on the edge of the desk, and the wide black mark running down his eye is smudged, as if he's run his hands repeatedly across his face.

The smell of wine hangs heavy in the air. His emotions, jagged before through our bond, are now overwhelming, a bleak, black ocean that swells against my mind, threatening to drown out anything and everything else.

The room itself borders on madness. Every wall is covered with maps and outlines. Beautifully detailed drawings of each former nation conquered by the Karensa Federation are nailed one on top of another, the intricate sketches of the towns and cities marred by raw lines of rough ink and pencil scribbled over them. The writing is jagged, the handwriting so messy it's illegible. The maps look old, the paper sepia red and curling at the edges with age. Underneath these stacks of individual maps is an enormous tapestry stretching across the entire side of one wall, depicting the Federation as it stood before Mara's fall. My eyes jump instinctively up to where Mara is, and there I see a new map nailed above all the others—an exquisite drawing of every territory in my former nation. This, too, has been scribbled on, circling each of Mara's cities in deep graphite.

No surface remains uncovered. Without any windows in here to let in light, it's as if I've literally stepped into a chamber of the Premier's mind.

My eyes widen as I scan the walls. It takes me another moment to realize that every place he's circled in Mara is a location where he has been digging for artifacts. This is where he goes to study the artifacts that have become his obsession.

There are sketches of the relics that his teams have already dug up near Newage, alongside blueprints scribbled with notes from the pages of documents by the Early Ones. The papers are everywhere. A small stack of them lies on a table nearest the entrance of the tiny room.

Then I spot it. His small loop of keys, lying on the same table. The thin rectangle of metal, its holes punched in an elaborate sequence of patterns.

The key to Adena and Aramin's cell and shackles, imprinted with a series of numbers. Immediately I remember the code that had gotten us inside the lab institute during my failed attempt with my fellow Strikers at destroying the complex.

The Premier stays curled over his table. From here, I can tell that this surface is covered with maps and drawings too, but of lands I don't recognize, places on the other side of the sea. He has drawn haphazardly over them, and now stares blankly at the maps as if he can see something on the other side.

I take a step forward, conscious of exactly how far I am from those keys.

Constantine stirs for the first time. He glances at me over his shoulder. He's deeply drunk, and his gaze is lost, leaving him looking, for the first time, as young as he actually is.

Constantine stares at me for a long moment. Then he narrows his eyes, and in that gaze is a cold anger I've never seen. Now I can tell that the paint on his face is smudged because he's been crying. Through the bond between us, his rage spikes.

What are you doing here? he says, his voice snarling. He must be even drunker than I thought, if he has only now noticd me.

I didn't see you in your bed, I tell him. *So I came in to investigate. Seemed reasonable, after your eventful night. Why aren't you back in the palace?*

Am I obliged to tell you everything, my little Skyhunter? Even in my mind, his voice sounds slurred and careless.

How can I protect you if I don't know where you are?

So interested in protecting me today. He laughs once and turns his back to me again. *Get out.*

I hesitate, my curiosity locking me in place as my eyes dart up to the maps, then to the keys again, then back to this unsteady Premier. The assassination attempt really did get to him, after all.

A tempting thought emerges: I could kill him here. No windows, no one else here to protect him. It's likely that no one knows this room exists except for the Premier. Everyone trusts me with him, given the very public way I just saved his life. But here he is alone and weak, a dying young man left to face the Skyhunter, the near-indestructible weapon he has created. I could cut his throat and flee in the middle of the night. Grab the keys and free my Striker friends. By the time anyone else finds him, we'll all be long gone. What delicious irony it would be. The urge that fills me is so strong that my fists tighten, every bit of my body wanting to move forward.

When I don't leave, Constantine looks skeptically at me. *You want to kill me*, he says through our bond.

I say nothing.

Of course you do. Everyone does. He gives me a bitter smile. *You should have just done it during the dance. You would've gotten to me faster than that girl.* He turns his back again. *Go ahead, then. Do it, and flee this hall. Just remember—if you can't find your mother by the time I'm reported missing, my soldiers will slice her throat. So risk her if you like.*

Constantine's words cut me like knife after knife. Again and again, this is the damn truth that keeps me captive. If I kill Constantine now, my mother will almost certainly die. Caitoman will look for his brother in the morning, as will the rest of his advisors. I can try to get to my mother before then. Maybe Red and Jeran will. But the risk is far too great.

You know I can't, I say.

He stares at me, his eyes reflecting the fire of the lanterns, before turning back to his maps. My gaze follows his.

These are the artifacts you've ordered to be uncovered, I tell him. *You've been studying them for a long time.*

I half expect Constantine to command me out of the room again. But he seems lost in thought, his hands running idly over the papers on the table.

My father first discovered mentions of those relics in the Early Ones' writing, he finally replies, as if talking to himself.

His father. I was only a child when the late Premier swept the Federation's armies across the middle of our continent—but even as a little girl, I could remember the adults around me talking in hushed, worried tones about the Federation's advancing armies. I could recall my mother saying to my father, *And what happens if that man turns his sights on Basea?* on evenings when they thought I was just playing with my wooden toys.

Why so much interest? I ask Constantine now. I've moved closer to the keys. My hand clenches and unclenches at my side. *Is this truly about powering your Federation with their energy?*

He turns his face up to the large map tapestry covering one of the walls.

In the brief silence between us, I think the Premier has forgotten that I'm here. The emotions flowing through our bond are a confusing jumble, a storm where before there was only his coldness and cruelty.

I'm finally close enough to the keys. I hesitate for just a moment, letting myself quietly memorize the pattern imprinted on the metal.

Constantine doesn't answer right away. But when he speaks again, he says, *I loved my mother.*

And in a sudden rush, one of his memories sears bright in my mind, drowning out the dark tide that had threatened to consume us both. For an instant, I pause in my memorization.

I wince, blinking, as the tiny room vanishes. When I open my eyes, I find myself in the body of a young boy squealing with laughter as he runs with his younger brother, still a small thing toddling about. I recognize Caitoman immediately in the memory—already stockier than Constantine, even as a tiny child. The boys chase each other down the hall, shouts echoing, until they reach a corridor where they see their father standing at the end of it. The old Premier looks in his prime, strong and formidably built, the figure that Caitoman inherited but Constantine failed to. He's talking in low voices with his advisors. From this distance, I can hear one of the advisors murmuring to the Premier.

"I'm sure your wife and new son will be fine. It is written in the stars."

New son?

Caitoman halts, his gaze shy at the sight of his father. Constantine stops too, then gestures for his brother to follow him down a different hall. They chase each other through the maze of the palace; the farther they get from their father, the more at ease they seem to be.

Eventually, the boys double back and find themselves heading down a dimmer corridor. Constantine has pulled ahead, alone for a few minutes while his brother chases after him.

Here he slows, then stops as he wanders to a slightly ajar bedroom door. He peers into its darkness, where he catches a glimpse of his mother lying in the bed, midwives buzzing around her.

He listens, waiting for the screams of his mother to echo again through the palace halls, as they have been for hours.

But this time, he hears nothing.

He presses his ear against the door a little longer, then puts his face against the slit in the ajar door again.

One of the midwives carries bundles of cloth soaked in blood.

His eyes settle on the shape lying on the bed. His mother. All he can see is her outline, her hand being held by the hand of a richly dressed noblewoman. He can't hear her voice.

"What are we going to tell the Premier?" one of the midwives says.

The other shakes her head. "Fetch him right away."

Constantine's hands start to tremble. Somehow, he knows the worst has happened.

"Santine?" the young Caitoman says, doing his best to pronounce his brother's name, then shuffles up to Constantine and peers curiously into the room.

Constantine puts a hand on his little brother's shoulder and guides him away. "It's nothing," he tells the smaller child. "Come on. Let's go to the east wing."

As they turn the corner, they bump into their father, headed down the hall from where they'd just come. Constantine jumps back—Caitoman lets out a small squeak.

The Premier gives Constantine a stern glare, then glances briefly at Caitoman. The glare turns into a sneer.

"Get this thing out of my halls," he mutters at Constantine as he brushes past the boys. "I told you not to bring him into the palace."

It takes me another second to realize that he meant Caitoman. Caitoman was the *thing* to be rid of. A glimmer of realization hits me. Did Caitoman not grow up in the palace with Constantine?

The memory shifts. I see young Constantine again, this time dressed in somber blacks, going up to his father at night as the man leans back in his chair. The boy's eyes look pink, as if he's been crying. A fire crackles at one end of the meeting room.

"Look," his father says to him, without looking at him at all. Instead, he points the wineglass at a tapestry on the wall.

Constantine obeys and looks. On the tapestry, Karensa had not yet conquered the northernmost and southernmost states. The Federation's borders extend like a gash through the center of the continent, bleeding ever wider.

When Constantine looks up at the man, he sees the face of someone dissatisfied with how slowly his campaign is moving. A ruler who wants more. Someone with something missing. Someone . . . disgusted.

The young Constantine swallows and looks at his father. "Do you miss Mother?" he asks.

The Premier takes a sip from his glass before he shakes his head. "Why?" he mutters. "The dead are useless."

The memory ends. I return to the room as it is now, with Constantine the Premier leaning against the table, disheveled, the sleeves of his robe pushed up and wrinkled, my hand near the keys. If he is uncomfortable with me having seen a glimpse of his past, he doesn't show it. Perhaps the wine has dampened how much he cares.

Did your mother die in childbirth? I ask him.

Yes. I was meant to have a third brother. Constantine lets out a scornful chuckle. *My father's hopes and dreams.*

When I don't respond, he continues. *The older my father got, the more he realized he wouldn't live to see Karensa's borders stretch from sea to sea. He wouldn't finish what he started. Worst of all, he thought I—his poor, fragile firstborn—didn't have the ability to carry on his legacy.*

Another memory sears through our bond, and suddenly I glimpse a young Constantine pounding on the door of a small closet, screaming to be let out, while his father snaps at him from the other side. About some failed lesson. Some poor performance on horseback. Some weakness. I see Constantine curled on the floor of the closet as the light under the slit changes, until finally Caitoman lets him out. I see Constantine facing another boy in a courtyard. The old Premier kneels beside Constantine, telling him how to strike the other boy. Constantine ends up bloodied and bruised and the loser. The Premier leaves in disgust.

And what about your brother? I ask.

Constantine glances at me. *Caitoman is my half brother.*

Caitoman is a bastard.

Of course he is. He and Constantine look so little alike; the old Premier had reacted to the young Caitoman with such dismissive disgust.

Who is his mother? I ask.

Constantine looks away again. *Who knows?*

Caitoman cannot inherit the throne without a proper lineage, and Constantine was considered incapable. The old Premier had been counting on his wife's second child before she died in childbirth. The Tyrus line was in danger of disappearing, erasing any hope for the Federation's Infinite Destiny.

Your father was cruel to you, then, I say. *And to Caitoman.*

He says nothing for a moment. *I just felt sorry for my brother*, Constantine replies softly.

The memory cuts off abruptly and I'm left to stare at the young Premier's thin back, his wiry frame still bent over the desk. It's no wonder he fears death as he does, why today's assassination attempt has shaken him to his core. His mother had died young, managing only to touch her eldest son's life briefly before leaving him. His father had died with unfinished business, tormented by the thought that no one could carry on his legacy.

And Constantine?

The meaning of his entire life has hinged upon Infinite Destiny—his driving need to finish what his father started, to prove that he is worthy. Today must have felt like an omen of his mortality, the truth in his father's words. That his father was right about him, after all.

He is going to die young, die soon, and that no number of accomplishments will change that.

My attention goes back to all the sketches on the walls. *Why do you really want those Maran artifacts?* I ask him again.

He doesn't answer, but I see his hands skimming repeatedly over the papers scattered on his desk. The symbols scrawled across those pages are in the language of the Early Ones, but I can see notes along their edges written in Constantine's hand, along with drawings of the sun and the moon.

I look back again at the table closest to me, where the keys lie. Beside them is the stack of papers, sketches and blueprints. On impulse, I slip the top paper off the stack and roll it silently up, sliding it into my pocket.

As I do, Constantine keeps his head down and stops his hand over a paper with Mara on the map before him.

If I could only unlock them, he finally mutters through our link. *It could solve everything.*

Unlock what? I ask.

I'll know it when I see it, he answers.

Maybe you're just scared to die, I tell him, my voice soft and steady.

He turns his profile toward me. His eyes search me with a spark of life, a sober moment through his drunken tirade. When he finally speaks, the warning in his voice is frighteningly still. It is the air before the lightning strikes.

Get out, Talin, or I will order my soldiers to tear your mother limb from limb and hang her from the walls. He turns his back again. *Get out.*

I walk away. My last image of him tonight is his hunched silhouette outlined by candlelight, his head bowed before all the tapestries on the wall—the conquests that insist he has won.

When I reach the hidden door, I cast one final look at him over my shoulder. He doesn't bother glancing my way again. Instead, he looks like how he did before I came in.

Not a Premier.

Not a leader.

Just a young man willing to destroy nations in a quest for more time, while death waits inevitably for him in its corner.

26

RED

I'VE ALWAYS THOUGHT THAT CARDINIA TRANS-forms at night.

During the day, the streets are a riot of color and sound, the rivers filled with boats and the walls draped with banners and flowers. The sculptures lining the thoroughfares fill the city with the flavor of art, and people dine outside with them in the backdrop, while children run by with honeyed sweets on sticks. It looks like what the Federation thinks it is.

At night, though, when the wide avenues empty and revelers retreat to their beds, the chairs and tables sit empty along the streets. The banners look somber, ominous against the walls. The ground is littered with confetti. And the sculptures, carefully chosen to be works of art beautifying the city, look in the darkness like the truth: skeletons stolen from other places, like bleached bone and teeth, their silhouettes carving up the night sky.

They seem to be watching us now as Jeran and I hide in silence within the enormous, arching ribs of the Seven Sisters. According to its plaque, this distinctive sculpture had once been part of the structural support of Senate Hill in Tanapeg's capital. The shadows it casts are so wide that we are able to melt entirely into the darkness—but even then, I can almost feel the ragged breaths of this building fragment, the sound frothy with blood, mingling eventually with the awakened other voice in my mind.

In reality, Tanapeg's collapse had been one of the most gruesome massacres in history. They don't teach you that in school though. Your textbook had made it sound romantic, of their citizens waving Karensan flags from bridges as your soldiers marched through the gates of their capital. That is not what happened.

It is easy to bend the truth when you *are* the truth.

The bloody history of these sculptures stretches particularly long across the thoroughfare tonight. Even without the surge of Talin's emotions, I would have known about today's attempt on the Premier's life. People flooded major intersections in the city. Jeran and I had been forced to lie low, hiding in alleys as extra troops flooded the streets to clear out the people. Even as a young soldier doing simple assignments throughout the city, I'd never seen unrest as sharp as that.

From where we hide, I can see the broken limbs. When Talin and I agreed to meet here, we had no idea the city would be thrown into this kind of chaos. A pang of worry pierces through me as I wonder if she can still show up.

I've almost given up on her appearing when I sense her coming down the thoroughfare. Her heartbeat pulsing through our bond strengthens, a gradual, familiar pattern that conjures in my mind the image of Talin's figure.

Jeran is the first to signal. From his post high up on the sculpture, I see his silhouette ripple—almost invisible—within the ribs' shadows. He straightens from his crouch and looks down at me, then lifts two fingers east.

I turn and see her coming.

Talin has always been graceful, in the deadly way that all Strikers I've known are, but now her movements have an eerie, superhuman quality to them. Her walk is just a little too fast to seem natural, and her gait is a little too smooth to match it. The way she watches the world around her is a little too keen. I stare at her as she cuts her way through the shadows darkening the thoroughfare, inconspicuous to anyone except those who know she's coming.

The unsettling way she moves is like staring back at yourself. *You're the same kind of monster now.*

Through our bond, the faint trickle of her emotions is tense, held so tightly around her that I can barely tell what they are.

It suddenly occurs to me that this must be how she's been for the past six months—holding her emotions close in an attempt to keep Constantine from sensing them, hiding her feelings so that the Federation can't use them against her, hiding herself from me in an attempt to protect us.

A tide of yearning fills me—the ache of missing her, the agony of watching her go through the same torment that I did, the pain of facing off against her as enemies. I let my heart fill my mind.

Let her know that there's someone here who loves her fiercely.

Let her remember that she's not alone.

Talin pauses for the briefest moment and turns her head to where I'm crouched in the shadows of the sculpture. The tight hold she has over her feelings wavers slightly, but she immediately clutches it close again. Then she picks up her pace and draws near to us.

Jeran jumps down from his vantage point as Talin steps into the wide shadow under the sculpture. We stare at her as she stands mere feet from us. Her body is slender but strong, fortified with steel, the image of a killer. There is a threat in the way she stands, as if she is ready to lunge.

And for a second, I'm afraid she might attack us right here.

Then her eyes widen in the dark, and as they meet mine, they well with tears.

You're a traitor and a fool. Of course she saw the fear in your eyes. You can see the hurt of it reflected on her face.

Everything in me wants to pull her close. Still, I can sense her hesitation. It makes me hold back too. She looks like she's caught in a web, too terrified to touch me in case her emotions come loose.

But Jeran doesn't wait. He sees her expression and steps forward as if driven by some desperation in him. In an instant, Jeran wraps an arm around Talin's neck and hugs her to him. In the quiet night, I hear the faintest whisper of a sob escape his lips.

At Jeran's embrace, something inside Talin seems to crumple. I feel her grip loosen on her emotions, and a spike of pain and joy rush through her. She hugs Jeran back and squeezes her eyes shut as if to hold back her tears. Her hands clutch his clothes tightly. Then her eyes open again, turned toward me. A small smile trembles on her lips.

Should've been you. You should've stepped up in Jeran's place and comforted her. Instead you're standing here, awkward as hell, caught between loving her and remembering the man watching from the other end of her mind.

Finally, I settle on a stiff nod at her before smiling back.

Talin finally pulls away and fixes a steady stare on us. *The key to their holding room*, she says through our bond. At the same time, she signs the words to Jeran so he can understand it. *I have the code.*

She reads the numbers to us slowly, several times, giving us both a moment to take them in. Jeran scratches them into a bit of cloth behind his sleeve.

You will have to move fast, she tells us. *They change the lock to the doors every day.*

"Will Constantine think you did it?" I whisper.

She shakes her head. *Let me deal with him*, she answers. *He doesn't know you're in the city. I have my alibi, watching him in the room beside his chambers.*

For a second, her shoulders loosen slightly, as if casting off a weight. There's such deep sadness in her that all I want to do is leave with her—take off into the sky together, this world be damned.

The other voice begins to sound skeptical in my head.

She isn't telling you everything. She's afraid to betray you again.

We should be afraid too. And a part of me still is. Everything in me yearns to tell her about our plans, but all I can think about is the moment in the train yard outside Newage when we realized we were stepping into a trap. All I can see is the memory of Talin's regret in her eyes, and the way she had been forced to give us away.

No. Too risky.

Talin looks down and produces something else from her pocket. "I have something else for you both," she signs, repeating the same through our link. "I know you've been searching for answers on the artifacts."

She unrolls a slip of paper covered in sketches and scribbled notes.

I recognize Constantine's hand immediately; it's the same curving script I've seen sign declarations hung around the city. Jeran leans over as we unfurl the page and study it. Then I utter a soft gasp.

This looks like one page of many, a partial blueprint of a cylindrical object that looks like the Early Ones' artifact.

That *is* the artifact.

It's a schematic drawn of the interior of the cylinder, with the same inner ring of smaller metal rods and a hollow center. But in this drawing, there is something inside the hollow center.

A drawing of a human.

It's a person lying within the cylinder, hands folded across the chest.

I can't read the Karenese, Talin says as we read. *What does it say?*

I look up at her. "Where did you get this?" I whisper.

She shakes her head. "Constantine has hidden himself away in a private chamber," she signs. "A room filled with these kinds of schematics. He's in bad shape."

Jeran points to a block of text scribbled along the side of the cylinder. "This is a translation of some text from the Early Ones," he murmurs. "An experimental machine of theirs."

I scan the entire paper before my gaze hitches on the bottom of the paper.

"'In this mechanism,'" I read slowly, "'we find probable cause to believe that a human subjected properly to this energy may find aging slowed. Evidence toward this theory. Evidence contrary.'" The text cuts off abruptly at the bottom of the page, pencil drawings of arrows sliding off the page and presumably onto another sheet.

"Aging slowed," Jeran whispers.

And then I understand, at last, the true source of Constantine's obsession with these artifacts.

I suck in my breath at the same time Talin does.

"Immortality," I whisper in unison with Jeran.

Immortality, Talin confirms through our link.

His search for the artifacts was never about harnessing the Early Ones' energy to power all of the Karensa Federation, nor was it about learning their weaponry. It was always about one thing and one thing only: Infinite Destiny. The belief that Karensa can accomplish what the Early Ones couldn't—and in doing so, rule forever.

Constantine has hunted for them because he believes the power within those artifacts might be what can cure his weaknesses, grant him eternal life.

"Does it work, then?" Jeran whispers as he scans the rest of the page.

I shake my head. "If it did, the Early Ones would still be here."

But Constantine won't give up. He believes he can figure out those artifacts, Talin adds. *He has been searching for immortality for so long. The research I saw in his private chamber proves it. He genuinely believes he can harness this energy and achieve the impossible.*

I narrow my eyes as I tap on the paper. "And in the process, he'll kill everyone here."

What do you mean?

"Here." I point to a small cluster of Karenese words scribbled in the center of the mechanism.

Talin looks at us. *What does it say?*

"Translated directly?" Jeran says. "'Fire.'"

I nod, but it means so much more than that. Karensa may not have a word for *restitution*, but we have many different words for *destruction*.

"It means the center of the cylinder is deeply unstable," I add. "The Early Ones never figured out how to stabilize it. If tampered with incorrectly, it will set off a chain reaction. We saw what it can do to people just by being out in the open air—it can burn their skin off, make them bleed from the inside out. Whatever the Early Ones created, it isn't a machine of eternal life. It's a toxic energy. It's poisonous."

"And a weapon," Jeran replies.

I nod. "Fire, but no ordinary fire. Fire, as if sent from the sun. Fire that will destroy everything around it."

The color drains from Jeran's face. Talin sucks in her breath in a soft gasp.

"There are past relics from the Early Ones showing similar designs that have been used as weapons," I explain. "Why else would the Early Ones bury them so deep underground?"

"They've already brought back two to the capital. There are possibly more underground out there."

"We need to destroy them," Jeran affirms.

Talin looks at Jeran as she signs, while repeating the same phrases to me through our link. "If you do, do it quickly. There are big things happening in Cardinia soon—and too many threats. Those weapons can't fall into the wrong hands."

"We all have to get out of this city," I say.

"What about your mother?" Jeran asks Talin.

Through our bond, I can feel the tension in Talin's words. *I have to get to her somehow.*

Something is happening that she knows about, something big—but whatever it is, she keeps it behind the walls around her heart.

Everything in me rages to break past those walls to get back to the Talin I know. And when I look at her, I can tell that she sees my desperation. She gives me a small, sad smile.

I'm going to be okay, she tells me through our bond.

Jeran clears his throat beside us. "I'll leave you two for a moment," he whispers. And in the span of a breath, he's gone, vanished into the darkness as if he belongs there, off to watch for soldiers from a higher vantage point.

We don't have much time. I reach out for Talin's hand and squeeze it. She feels different in person now, and even her hand seems hard and harsh, metal where there used to be muscle. She squeezes back.

I make a show of wincing. "Ouch," I whisper out loud.

She lets out the hush of a laugh. *You're the worst.*

I shrug. *Not used to someone as strong as I am.*

At that, she looks down at our hands and runs her fingers against mine, lacing them together before untangling them again. Her touch sends a shiver through me, and I close my eyes for a second, relishing the feeling. Through our bond, her heart is beating rapidly, and when I open my eyes again, I realize she's smiling a little.

What? I ask her through our link.

There's moonlight in your eyes, she answers.

I lean close enough to her for our noses to touch. *I must look amazing.*

You remind me of the day I first visited you in Newage's prisons.

At that, I pull back from her. *Ah yes, back when I was a disgusting heap of old clothes.*

You were sitting under a pool of light. Your eyes had the same reflection.

I hesitate, silent for a moment. *Did I look good then?*

No.

But you thought I did.

Is that what you think?

I laugh a little. *That's what I think*, I answer. It's been so long since I've been able to tease her, to feel even a spark of amusement, that I breathe deep, as if I can savor it in the air.

She studies me with a bemused look, the weight in her eyes a little lighter. *And what else are you thinking?* she asks.

I smile, then turn quiet. *I'm thinking about the future*, I finally reply.

She doesn't answer.

I'm thinking about if we win, I go on. *If the Federation can be stopped. I'm wondering where we'd be, what we'd be doing.*

Talin turns her gaze briefly away to peer down the thoroughfare, her eyes hitching on each monument along the way, each piece of some lost society.

I'd be on a farm with my mother, she says at last. *She's growing something green and lush. I'm walking down a street lined with broad-leafed trees.* Her eyes return to me. *With you.*

My heart is so still, it feels as if it's stopped breathing. *I'd be riding in a carriage alongside you*, I tell her. *To that future home.*

She smiles, and through our bond, I can feel her cherishing that dream.

Dancing with you after dinner, she adds.

I glance up at the sky. *Lying in the middle of the road at night, pointing out the moon with you.*

I'd be doing this. Talin reaches toward me, and I feel the cool smoothness of her palm touching my cheek.

And I'd be doing this, I answer. And I lean forward to touch my lips to hers.

I pull back anxiously, suddenly embarrassed that perhaps I've done it wrong.

Talin smiles at my hesitation, her eyes softening. Then she kisses me, longer this time, her guiding us. My emotions are heat and light, searing through our bond. She feels like everything that has gone missing in my life, joy and love and laughter and companionship, all flooding back into me at once.

This is home. This is what I've been searching for. What I stayed alive for.

I have no idea how long we linger like this. All I know is that when we finally pull away from each other, I can see the faint mist of our breaths curling together in the dark.

Well, she says through our bond. *I didn't think it'd be like* that.

I tried my best, I protest, and her whisper of a laugh comes out again.

Don't die, Red, she says, and her tone is so sad that it breaks my heart. *Keep the others alive. You hear? Because when I go*—She pauses abruptly, as if realizing she's about to say more than she's comfortable with. *Because when I walk into that future, I want to make sure you're in it.*

I look at her and realize that I'm willing to do anything in the world to protect her. That if everything fails, if this city burns down, if Constantine has us all imprisoned, I will still stand between her and the Premier. I will die before she does.

We'll all be in it, I tell her. *I promise.*

How?

Because I love you, I answer. My words echo through our link, resolute. *And this Federation is not going to make me lose another loved one.*

She meets my gaze. Whatever it is that she can't tell me, I can see the fire of it dancing in her eyes. *Then let's go make sure of it*, she answers.

27

RED

WE ONLY HAVE A FEW HOURS LEFT BEFORE dawn. Better hurry.

The arena is still dotted with guards, but in this deepest part of the night, their numbers look sparse, and the part of me still keeping count of each city patrol we've come across roars back to life. The east patrols are noticeably missing.

As we approach the arena's gates, I can tell immediately that many of them have been drinking. Maybe all the chaos from the game and assassination attempt has been too stressful. They laugh and jostle one another, some of them arguing among themselves about who they think fought most impressively and whether or not they will appear in a future game.

I narrow my eyes at that. The key code that Talin had risked everything to give us now burns in my mind. Future game? Not a chance.

Jeran listens quietly as they crack jokes about how Tomm died and whether Pira needed to. I marvel at how he manages to keep his emotions in check; he doesn't flinch, even when they complain that Aramin moved too slowly when the maze separated him from Adena. I scan the grounds as we walk around the arena, pretending to be lost in our own drinks and arguments. Some of the soldiers are quieter than others, looking uneasy as their comrades laugh uproariously. As I watch them, they stir awake my other voice.

Maybe they're like how you once were. Silent. Knowing there is something sickening about the game you'd witnessed. Not strong enough to stop it.

Finally, Jeran nudges me quietly and tilts his head toward one of the arena gates. "Looks like those two patrols have merged into one," he signs to me in the night.

I look in the same direction as Jeran, and there, I see what he means. Some of the soldiers from one of the gates have left their post to throw bets with the others, all of them sharing food and drink in a small circle as they take a break from their watch.

We wait patiently until it seems like they're truly lost in their conversation. At the next peal of laughter, we move through the shadows and steal into the cool recesses of the gate's archway, then into the inner corridor behind the archway and make our way up the pillar again, aiming for the vent.

The halls inside the arena's prison are quiet, a startling contrast compared with the chaos we witnessed yesterday in the stands. Now there are only the soldiers patrolling the hall, rotating in and out every hour.

From within the air duct, I glance up and down the hall at the tiny mirrors that have been placed at regular intervals along the ceiling, each of them tilted just so in order for the guards to see the entirety of the space.

Jeran and I exchange a short nod in the darkness.

As the guards rotate, the hall falls into a brief silence. We waste no time. When the soldiers leave, Jeran pokes his head out briefly through the vent, then aims a slingshot at one of the mirrors. He shoots.

There's the faint breaking of glass. He whirls around and does the same to the mirror at the other end of the curving hall.

As he shoots, I break open a filter beside the vent. Weak light illuminates part of the duct. I lower myself down and land with a quiet thud into the hall. Jeran leaps down behind me, so silent I have to glance over my shoulder to make sure he's escaped.

We don't have much time before the guards rotate in again. Jeran goes first, stealing close to the holding room where Aramin and Adena had first been kept.

Now we see the lock on the door. At first, it's unrecognizable to me: a solid, rectangular grid that encircles the door handle and connects to the rest of the wall.

A chill surges down my spine. Is this a different lock? Had they changed it? Did the Federation know we were coming tonight?

But I see a slim line alongside the lock, where a series of small knobs can slide into a pattern. This is where we insert the code that Talin gave us.

The first figure to approach us from inside is Adena. Her dark eyes glint like stone in the night, and despite all she's been through, all the agony she endured in the arena, I can see the faintest hint of a smile on her lips. She doesn't speak, of course, not with the guards farther down the hall—but she does lift her hands to sign to me.

"What took you so long?"

I scowl affectionately at her. "We got lost."

Adena winks at me before turning her gaze to Jeran. The Shields nod at each other, an understanding born from a lifetime sworn to protecting each other blazing in their gazes. Jeran lifts his eyebrows slightly at her, and she shakes her head.

"I'm okay," she signs to him.

Then Jeran meets Aramin's gaze inside the cell. I expect to see Jeran's fingers dance unconsciously to where the weapons are typically strapped at his belt, the gesture he makes whenever he's thinking about Aramin. But he just stays frozen.

For once, Aramin's expression is not steel. He looks almost hesitant, as if he's not sure what to say or how to act. The Firstblade to the Strikers, at a loss for words.

Maybe it's for the best, because there's no time for greetings now. As they exchange a silent look, I kneel to the lock and start sliding the knobs carefully.

As I go, I think of my early days as a soldier. The number of prisoners I'd had to keep in their cells. I remember being on the warfront of Basea the day before we invaded Sur Kama, doing a round through a row of makeshift cages where we were keeping several captured Basean soldiers. One of them had been so young, a wide-eyed boy watching me through the bars. I'd stopped to look at him before Danna Wendrove nudged me away. *Don't touch them*, he'd said to me. *They're dirty.*

I'd listened to him. I'd stepped back from his cage and hurried away, my stomach roiling in shame.

Now I focus on inputting the code. On freeing them.

"Hurry," Jeran signs to me.

My fingers slip on one of the knobs as I go. It resets a few of the others. I curse under my breath as I start over again.

Jeran glances down the hall, listening carefully for the sounds of the guards returning. Their laughs come from farther down the corridor, but they won't stay away for long.

"You try it," I sign to Jeran in irritation as the knobs slip again.

Jeran bends down to the lock and begins again, his slender fingers working as rapidly as he can. But he's less familiar with the way Karensan locks work, and I can see the frustration on him as he puzzles out how to slide one knob after another.

Inside the door, Adena shifts restlessly. "Can we cut this open?" she signs, glancing at me. Jeran looks up briefly from his work to read her hands. "Your wings work, don't they?"

But I shake my head. "Too loud," I sign back. My blades hitting this kind of steel on the bars would send echoes screaming down the corridor.

"We can fight the soldiers off," she signs.

"Word will get back to Constantine that we were inputting a code," Jeran signs before looking back down at the lock. "He'll guess that Talin helped us."

At that, Adena's eyes widen slightly. "Talin helped you get the code?"

I nod.

Adena's hands tighten on the bars. Beside her, Aramin turns to look down the hallway. "The direction of their chatter's changed," he signs.

Aramin's right; I can hear the shift of their boots on the floor in the distance, know that they're starting to make their way back here.

Jeran stands up. "Help me with the last one," he signs.

I stoop to look. Damn these confounded designs. I watch as the last knob slips again, resetting the few before it. Jeran grits his teeth.

I try again. We're so close. Talin delivered this to us on pain of death, risking her mother for us. We have to get it open.

And then, at last, the final knob slides into place. There's a tiny, satisfying click before the lock falls open into my hand. I look up to give Jeran a triumphant grin.

And that's when I hear a voice behind us.

"Red? Is that you?"

I whirl around to see the wide eyes of a young Karensan guard, his gun in his hand, pointed straight at me. He blinks as he meets my gaze.

"I—I thought I saw you walking by," he stammers out.

Danna. I know him immediately. The boy I'd been on the same patrols with, had been friends with, had served together in Basea right up until the night I'd failed to shoot Talin. The boy who stayed silent when I needed him to speak up for me.

All this time, I'd been looking out for soldiers who might recognize me, who had served with me—how could I have missed Danna?

He opens his mouth, sucking in a breath in order to raise the alarm. That's when I bolt toward him and before he can yell, I clamp a hand hard against his mouth and shove him against the bars of the holding room. He lets out a grunt, his entire body contorting in agony.

I glance down the hall, momentarily at a loss. The other soldiers may be drunk and listless tonight, but they won't stay away from their posts forever.

"Yell," I hiss at him, "and I will break every bone in your body. I swear it. What are you doing here alone, without the rest of your patrol?"

He shakes his head, his eyes wide with terror. I stare at him until he looks like he's calmed down, and then move my fingers slightly so he can choke out a whisper.

"I just—thought I saw you," he croaks. "My patrol's not on rotation yet. I came down here on my own. I—I—"

I shake my head, furious.

I can't set him free. He'll simply alert everyone else.

"You know him?" Jeran asks.

I nod. "I do."

Adena slips out from the shadows as she and Aramin step through the open holding room door. She scowls at the soldier before something at his belt catches her eye. Then she stoops down and unhooks a satchel from his side.

"What is it?" Aramin whispers to her in Maran.

She opens the sack. "Explosives," she whispers, nodding at the tiny sticks. "Probably to light the way in the dark. Look at the fuse triggers on them."

Then she nods at Jeran. "Give me that lock. If we're going to get out of here without putting Talin in danger, make them think we did it some other way than using a code."

There's no time to hesitate. Jeran hands the device to Adena, who begins working it into the lock. Farther down the hall come peals of laughter from a group of soldiers. They are slowly making their way over here.

I look back at Danna. What am I going to do with him? He's crying now, his sobs muffled behind my hand, tears streaming silently down his cheeks. All I see is him as a young boy, with those gangly limbs and comically large ears, asking me if I'd ever visited Basea before.

But I'd also seen him drag a Basean boy out of his home during that invasion and shoot him dead. I'd followed after him when he told me to leave that other boy in his cage.

The other voice in me rises.

You know he can't live. You have to kill him.

Beside us, Adena finishes inserting the device and pulls the fuse trigger. A blinding light glows red and white inside the lock, and even half a dozen feet away, I feel the heat of it. Jeran backs away too. Beside us, Aramin shifts to a fighting stance.

Then a new thought occurs to me.

I turn back to Danna. "The east and southeast city patrols have been missing from the festivities," I whisper to him. "Do you know where they are?"

At that, Danna's eyes widen and he shakes his head vigorously.

I grit my teeth. Talin's tortured expression comes back to me now. I remember our stolen kiss, the desperate need I have to see her again. "Tell me again," I snap, my voice a low growl. "That you don't know." My hand tightens against his mouth, and I know with a terrible certainty that, if I wanted to, I could break off his entire jaw with my unnatural strength.

Danna trembles under my grip. Finally, the shake of his head changes to a nod. I move my hand slightly for him to gasp out, "Lei works on the east patrol now. Remember Lei?" Another fellow soldier, shipped to Tanapeg instead of Basea last I heard. "She said they've been sent to the prison district's water turbines. She's been complaining about her double shifts there for the past couple of days."

The water turbines. My heart skips. I have a vague recollection of that area inside the prison district, where much of the city's water power is generated.

"Why are they there instead of guarding the festival?" I demand. Beside us, the flare burns through the insides of the lock. Jeran looks down the hall in alarm as the sound of soldiers draws nearer.

Danna starts to cry again. "Please, Red, I didn't mean anything back when they took you—"

I don't have time for this. I tighten my grip against his face again until he squirms in discomfort. "Why are they *there*?" I repeat.

"A prisoner," he gasps out through his sobs as I loosen my fingers slightly. "A prisoner—a new prisoner."

"Who?"

"I don't know! The Premier commanded it himself."

The Premier commanded it himself.

That can only mean one person. The Premier must be moving Talin's mother early.

"We have to go," Jeran hisses at me. *"Now."*

I seize Danna by the throat, then unfurl one of my wings with an agonizing scrape. The other voice rises to a fever pitch in my head.

You have to kill Danna now.

But I stare at him and cannot bring myself to do it. Every muscle in me screams in protest, and yet all I can see before me is my former patrol mate. I see his parents, with whom I'd shared plenty of dinners. His mother, smiling at me and offering me more food. His father, praising the crisp edges of my ironed uniform while he converses with my own father. His sister, hair braided, running around the table with my own sister.

The other voice hisses at me.

He had known your family so well, and yet he knew that when he didn't speak for you, he would condemn them to punishment.

Does he remember all of that? Does it haunt him?

My hand loosens from his mouth in pity. Freed of my grip, he hesitates there like a trapped mouse.

Then he moves. A dagger is in his hand in an instant. I see it flash in the darkness. My hand comes up as he strikes at me, aiming for my throat.

But I don't have to attack him. Without warning, someone's hands close tight around Danna's weapon-wielding fist and twists it sharply down. I hear the snap of bone, then the dagger is shoved hard into Danna's own chest, all the way up to the hilt.

I look up and find myself staring into Aramin's dark, glittering eyes as he lets Danna's limp body slip to the floor.

"Live a little longer, Red," Aramin mutters at me, "and you won't hesitate so long." He grabs the dagger from Danna's chest and wipes it against the dead soldier's clothes, then tucks it securely at his own belt.

"Better they find him with a stab wound than a cut from a steel wing, anyway. No one needs to know you're in the city."

I nod silently, but all I can hear is the roar of my own heartbeat in my ears. All I can see is Danna's vacant gaze, frozen in fear. All I feel is the shame that I couldn't do it, that Aramin had to do it for me.

No time for regrets here. No time to mourn.

So I tear my eyes away from the lifeless face of my former comrade and hurry down the hall with the Strikers.

28

TALIN

THE FIRST THING I HEAR THE NEXT DAY IS THAT General Caitoman has ordered a complete rotation of the Premier's personal guard. Every soldier is to be replaced.

The second thing I hear is that they've identified the would-be assassin. She turned out to be Maran, a prisoner working on the mayor's estate. Someone who lost her entire family during the Federation's final push over our warfront. She had gotten her hands on some ill-fitting Karensan military gear and made it as far as the dance ring before firing her shots toward the Premier.

"She was never a part of our plans," Mayor Elland snaps as she paces the lab complex's panic room in the early morning. Raina and I sit watching her. I am supposedly getting enhancements done here, but instead I continue to take a liquid that will chip away at my link with the Premier. The mayor folds her arms across her chest and turns back to us, her brows furrowed. "That girl's going to force heightened security around the Premier."

Raina shakes her head. "We can work around it. It's a good thing she isn't connected officially to the rebellion. Constantine won't tie her back to us."

"Won't he?" The mayor sits down beside us with a frustrated flourish. She points a finger down on the table. "That girl worked on my estate. Because of her, I'm going to have to allow a full investigation of everyone in my employment. Constantine will expect to see some executions. She will cost several lives by the time we're through."

"And what did we expect?" Raina snaps, her usual anxiety giving way to anger. "This isn't a game. The entire city is ripe for chaos—all the work done by the official rebellion to stir up unrest among the people was bound to result in several taking things into their own hands. We can't control everyone. This is a good sign. We've lit sparks in others outside of our movement."

The mayor tightens her lips. "Are you so careless with the lives of those in our rebellion, Raina? Do you not worry that General Caitoman's prying eyes might ultimately land on us as they investigate?"

Raina folds her arms. "I'm only practical. The greater good should triumph over our individual concerns. And I have no time to waste on things that will slow this down."

Mayor Elland leans forward. "Is that so? And would you be equally willing to sacrifice your husband and son?"

The Chief Architect looks away at that. I think of the way she had pressed close to her husband during the dances at the Sun Dial, the image of her son and his hired maid in the crowd.

"The lives that may be sacrificed are also lives that have families," the mayor says quietly. "Mothers. Sons. Daughters. Fathers. Take care with the lives of our allies, Raina, or you may find yourself losing everything that matters to you."

Raina rises, refusing to meet the mayor's eyes. "We do what we have to do," she says, pushing her glasses up. "Nothing changes. We move forward."

Then she leaves us alone in the room.

I watch as the door slides shut behind her. Her words leave me uneasy, and I find myself hanging tighter to the walls around my emotions, lest Constantine sense me.

If Raina is so willing to sacrifice the lives of others, what's to keep her from being willing to sacrifice my mother?

The mayor meets my questioning gaze. "We've long been at odds," she finally says in a low voice. "I admit the Chief Architect wouldn't have survived this long without a few losses. But it's still a game I don't like to play."

I study the weary lines around the mayor's eyes. Today, her usual bravado and cheek are muted, burdened by the weight of what must be coming. There's grief beneath this woman's steel, and I find myself thinking back to what Raina had once dismissively said, that the mayor has a soft spot for Constantine.

I nod, and point a finger at her, then touch my hand to my heart.

Mayor Elland shakes her head at me, indicating she can't understand, and I swallow my frustration, wishing she could read my hands. I take a pen from the table and start to draw on one of the papers before us. A rough sketch of Constantine's crown, then a woman's figure beside it. I point at her questioningly again, then touch my hand to my heart.

This time, she seems to understand. "You want to know my past connections with the Premier," she says. "With his mother."

I nod.

She sighs and looks away. There's a distant memory in her eyes. Finally, she says, "I remember Constantine as a little boy. I used to walk with his mother, Darea, in the greenhouse on summer afternoons, and Constantine would sprint ahead as fast as his little legs would allow. That was before the whole scandal of Caitoman's birth, you know. Darea was happier back then."

I listen carefully to the way the lilt in her voice changes at the mention of Constantine's mother.

"I loved her," the mayor says quietly after a while. She looks sidelong at me. "Darea. She was a young bride that the old Premier had chosen from Carreal, then the latest conquest. Her entire family perished during that siege." She lets out a humorless laugh. "And what did the Premier do? Decide she was beautiful enough to make her his official queen." She shook her head. "At the time, I was just a young noblewoman waiting around for a wealthy young husband. Darea made a good companion. We'd walk the grounds of my manor, make up imaginary future lives together." She looks down at the table and furrows her brows, and in that gesture, I sense a grief borne from a lover's broken heart.

Mayor Elland had loved Constantine's mother. Had been *in* love. And then she had seen Queen Darea die in childbirth.

"She loved Constantine, as any mother would," she went on. "But there was a deep sadness in her. She knew that Constantine would become his father, take his place." She took a deep breath. "On her deathbed, as I sat by her side, she asked me to promise her that I would find a way to take this all down. All the things that had destroyed her world. Her past. Her family. Her childhood."

Promise me. I can almost hear the whisper suspended in the air. I think of the flash of memory I'd seen from Constantine in the greenhouse, of him as a child, peeking into the chamber at his dying mother holding the hand of a richly dressed woman. That had been the young Mayor Elland.

This is why the mayor spares a bit of pity for Constantine. For the boy that is no longer.

I suppose even monsters were children once.

"That's why I'm here," she says to me now. "Because I have a heart. Because action without heart is meaningless." She leans toward me.

"Protect your heart, Talin. It is good to grieve, to hurt for others, to care. If we don't, then all is lost anyway."

• • •

The third bit of news that arrives today comes shortly after I return to the palace. When a guard peeks in to escort me to the Premier, I can already sense that something has gone wrong. The guard murmurs the update to me.

Two Strikers have escaped from the arena and a lone soldier has been found dead, curiously separated from the rest of his patrol when he shouldn't have been. Today's game has been canceled.

So Red and Jeran made their move. And Adena and Aramin are free.

The four of them are now somewhere in the city. Unshackled and poised to strike.

The mix of emotions this brings threatens to shatter my defenses—relief, fear, disbelief. I want to reach out to Red, to make sure they're all okay, but the worry that Constantine will know keeps me in check. At least I can still feel the distant rhythm of Red's heartbeat. He's alive. Maybe that means the others are too.

I clamp down my emotions as best as I can as I head to the main atrium to meet Constantine, but today my protective walls are shaky. My fear is channeling through our link, strengthening the bond between us with its ruthless and insidious tendrils, forcing me to open my heart to him.

He might have been in a bad state last night, but today his mood is calm again. However, it's the kind of mood that I fear the most from him—the still surface over a deep anger. Dark circles rim the bottom of his eyes. He must not have slept at all after our confrontation, and even behind the security of his vicious black band of paint, exhaustion highlights the sickly paleness of his face this morning.

Patrols of guards swarm the palace's courtyards, sealing the gates and inspecting every inch of the grounds. More soldiers line the halls and the building's rooftops. Beside me, Constantine says nothing. His jaw is tight, set. He doesn't mention a word about what happened last night. He doesn't talk about the Strikers' escape.

Does he think I'm involved in it? He knows I was in my chamber during the time when they supposedly escaped. His guards can attest to it.

But it doesn't mean he believes it.

As we make it down to the main atrium, I hear a female voice that I recognize. Then we see them. There, at the bottom of the stairs with a team of her personal guard, is Mayor Elland. The weight on her is as heavy as it was during our last meeting, but she stands straighter now, her eyes hard and her chin high. There's no sign of the affection I'd seen in her earlier in the day.

Kneeling in a row before them, bands across their eyes and hands tied behind their backs, are three prisoners the mayor had ordered arrested from her estate.

Curiously, General Caitoman is nowhere to be seen.

One is elderly, while another is young. Too young. I think of the first time I'd ever seen Red, that scrawny, young boy soldier standing poised over me with his gun, reluctant to shoot. This child can't be much older than he was, but the defiance in his eyes is still bright.

I think of Raina and her dismissal of the consequence of the unplanned assassination.

They pause at the sight of us. As we reach the bottom of the stairs and approach them, the mayor casts me a sidelong glance before addressing the Premier.

"Premier," she says. "These are the workers I mentioned to you. After questioning, we discovered their ties with the girl who attacked you yesterday."

"Just three?" Constantine says mildly. The tone of his voice doesn't match the dark emotions welling in his chest, and the mismatch makes me uneasy.

The mayor seems to hear it as well, but she doesn't react to it. "Three," she confirms, her voice full of confidence. She turns a scornful eye down to the prisoners. "And if we find more, Premier, I will bring them before you."

He smiles thinly at her. "You do me a great favor, Mayor Elland."

She gives him that wink of hers. "I've known you since you were a boy, Premier. It's the least I can do."

Constantine's gaze slides to the workers kneeling on the floor. "It looks like we've found a few rats in our midst."

My heart tightens. It's a direct call to me. I've been called a Basean rat too many times to miss the pointedness of this particular insult.

But I force myself to keep calm. He doesn't know anything yet, or else he would have mentioned it already. And Mayor Elland is putting up a good front. So I stare at the prisoners too, saying nothing through our bond.

Mayor Elland nods at Constantine. "How should we deal with them, Premier?" she asks in a low voice. "I have my executioners ready. The Chief Architect also says they had to put down two of their Ghosts whose bones weren't setting properly. Shall I simply deliver them to her? She certainly has space for them."

She's trying to save them.

Constantine looks up to meet the mayor's eyes. Some unspoken understanding passes between them, and I feel the Premier's emotions twist slightly between us, there and then gone.

"No," Constantine says. His voice is harsh this morning, rock grating against rock. "My Skyhunter will take care of them here." He shifts his eyes to me. "Now," he addresses me aloud.

I look quickly up at him.

"I have no patience for anything else this morning," he says. The language he uses now is Basean. "Let's make quick order of this, Talin."

He is testing me. No, punishing me. I search his eyes, wondering what he knows. I keep expecting him to say something more to me through our bond, but he doesn't. I turn my gaze to the mayor now. If I'm not mistaken, there's a flicker of what looks like grief in her eyes.

But she makes no movement to intervene.

The boy is so young, but he looks at me without any fear. The older woman is already listless, the spark of hope gone from her eyes, and the third is a man who won't look up from the floor.

I have walked the line enough; I can't afford to disobey Constantine again. There is no way out of this, no chance to seek mercy. So I walk forward without giving myself a chance to hesitate. As I go, I recite a bit of Basean poetry that my mother had once read to me as a child.

The bird wakes early for the morning sun. It waits even on days of rain, knowing just because the sun cannot be seen, that does not mean it isn't there.

I make it quick. It's all the kindness I can offer. My wings flash silver through the air. The soldiers nearby flinch at the speed of my movement. Most people have never seen me execute someone, or the damage I can do when put to use. The prisoners each stiffen, shudder. There is blood.

They slump to the floor. Then, silence.

I look at the bodies, wondering why I can no longer feel the tips of my fingers. Why my exhaustion dulls the pain of executing them. Why I don't pay attention to the blood dripping from my steel wings.

When I look back up, I see that the mayor's eyes are slightly averted, as if she can't bear to watch.

But the Premier, he is staring directly at me.

What rats deserve, he says through our bond, his voice echoing in my mind.

The unsaid part of his words crawls through my body and fills me with dread. What if he knows everything? The Chief Architect, my meeting with Red, the escape of Aramin and Adena? What if he knows what the mayor is up to, and just playing his games with these executions? What if these words are a threat? What will he do to punish me? My mother?

Still, I keep my chin high and match his stare. I've spent six months in Cardinia worrying about how he feels and what he's capable of doing. I know how to handle it.

As guards remove the bodies, I return to my place beside Constantine. The bond between us settles into its usual state, tense and uneasy. I stay calm. He's going to send me out into the city, most likely, to comb every inch of the streets, supervised by teams of soldiers. He's going to want me to be the one who finds Adena and Aramin and ends their lives.

But when he speaks again, that's not what he says. Instead, he turns to me and gives me a bitter smile. "I have another surprise for you this morning, Talin. I think you know why. After all, given what's been happening, I think it's wise to move your mother a bit early. Don't you agree?"

The mayor's gaze flickers to me, and there, I see a hint of fear. She hadn't expected this from him.

I meet Constantine's look without blinking, determined to hold my own. But his words cut straight through my defenses, the claw of it clenching around my heart. He knows.

I didn't free them, I say through our bond.

Of course you didn't, Constantine replies, his voice smooth and sincere.

But when I look at him, all I see are his eyes, dark and impenetrable, searing into me. Searching for secrets.

"Come with me, Talin," he says, gesturing for me to follow him. The other guards fall into step around me. "There's someone I want you to see."

29

TALIN

THE PLACE WHERE CONSTANTINE LEADS US isn't anywhere near the solstice festivities. As the rest of the city remains festooned with banners and people continue to celebrate in the streets, we head to the walls of Cardinia, toward the various rail bridges that arc over the river surrounding the exterior of the city.

Here, along one of the bridges running through the back of the city, there are no banners. No people wander along the outer wall to admire the river. This is an overgrown section of the river, weedy and thick with mud, the bridge crumbling slightly. And when we arrive, there are only a few soldiers standing at the ready, waiting for us.

They have a prisoner with them. It's an older woman, hair gone white as my mother's, with her hands bound firmly in front of her. Basean, judging from the tatters of her clothing. She's on her knees in the middle of the bridge as we approach her, and when she looks up to see the Premier, she starts trembling uncontrollably.

On Constantine's other side, the mayor doesn't miss a step. But as we stop and she shifts to stand next to us, she catches my gaze for a second. She looks helpless. Like she knows something terrible is about to happen.

I don't recognize the prisoner. She's not my mother. But she resembles her so much that I freeze in my tracks behind the Premier, my eyes locked on the bound woman.

What is this? I say through my bond with Constantine.

Beside me, the Premier folds his hands behind his back and glances at one of his soldiers. The man moves toward the prisoner. When Constantine speaks again, it's aloud. "You know your mother benefits or suffers directly from what you choose to do," he says. "And after the events of the past few days, I'm sure this will come as no surprise to you." He shrugs. "At first, I wanted to bring her here so you could see it with your own eyes. After all, that's the only way I can convince you I'm keeping true to my word. But for this punishment, I thought some distance might be instrumental. After all, you might snap, attempting to rescue her once you see what's happening to her." He looks at me. "And I can't have that. So this is my solution."

He nods at the woman, and the soldier strikes her viciously across the face, so hard that she collapses onto the bridge.

The careful walls around my heart crumble. Everything in me twists in agony at the sight.

The mayor stands with her hands folded calmly before her. But in her eyes, I can see an ocean of pain.

"Everything that happens to this woman," Constantine explains, nodding at me, "is also happening to your mother. She is her."

The soldier walks over to the woman as she struggles back up to a sitting position, then kicks her before she can steady herself. She lets out a hoarse wheeze of pain and falls again.

My hands clench so hard that I think I've cut into my palms. *Is this about the arena?* I respond. My rage and terror spark like light in my head, blinding me. *My refusing to execute a Striker?*

Oh, Constantine replies, this time through the link. *I think you know it's about more than that. Your Striker friends are, somehow, loose.*

I told you. I didn't free them.

I don't think you did. Constantine's stare sears into me. *But I think you know who did.*

This isn't about Raina or Mayor Elland; if he suspects that, he hasn't shown any sign of it. But it doesn't matter. He knows something is brewing behind his back.

Beside us, the mayor's hands have tensed in front of her.

I stare at the prisoner as she struggles against the stone ground. Somewhere out there, my mother is experiencing the same thing. It is *my mother* they are kicking to the ground and striking across the face. *My mother* who is bleeding on the ground.

"I want you to think carefully, Skyhunter," Constantine says aloud to me as the soldiers drag the woman back to her feet. One of them twists her arm behind her back. "About what you know and who set the Strikers free."

I don't know. I tremble with the force of my words as I say them through our link. *I only know it wasn't me.*

"Very well." He glances sidelong at me. "Do you know where my brother is right now?"

Is that where Caitoman is? Is that why he's not here with us? That's all it takes for me to conjure a mental image of the General standing beside my mother, the way these soldiers are now with this prisoner. Everything in me trembles.

No, Premier. I look at him, letting him see the rare sight of begging on my face. *Please.*

Constantine looks at his soldiers and nods again. "I asked my brother to give this soldier one of his rings." Sure enough, a gold band gleams on the soldier's hand. "To remind you that when he puts his hands on this woman, my brother is doing the same with your mother."

My eyes widen slightly. *Caitoman* is doing this.

Next to Constantine, the mayor meets my gaze briefly. In that second, I see a dawning realization on her face. She knows where Caitoman went. That means that she knows where my mother is being kept.

But I have no time to dwell on this.

The soldier twists the woman's elbow firmly behind her back.

Then he shoves it up hard. I hear bone snap. The woman screams. The ring flashes.

Somewhere, General Caitoman just shattered my mother's arm.

I fall to my knees at the blow, as if it had struck me instead. The pain roaring through me might as well be my own.

Stop, I tell Constantine. My eyes glow, the blue reflected against the ground. *I'm begging you.*

"Then tell me who did it, Talin."

I don't know!

The soldier goes up to the sobbing woman and kicks her again. My head swims at the sight.

"Tell me who did it, Talin," Constantine says again.

I press my palms against the ground. I can feel the Premier's determination through our bond, his will pressing against the secrets I keep guarded close to my chest. My anger fills every crevice in me, burning through my muscle and steel and skin until I think I'm going to turn into flames. *Could it be*, I hiss through our link, my jaw clenched tight as I glare up at the Premier, *that the Strikers simply freed themselves? That you underestimated their abilities, as you do us, as you do to anyone you think you've conquered? Could it be that they are simply better than what you can throw at them?*

Constantine's his eyes are hard as stone. "I think you need a reminder of why you are my Skyhunter," he replies. "I think you've gotten too bold, your answers those of someone who isn't under my control. I think I've been too lenient with you, Talin. So let this be that reminder."

He looks at his prisoner. One soldiers takes out a knife.

No. I suddenly startle up from the ground as the soldier grabs one of the woman's hands. General Caitoman is grabbing my mother's hand. *Stop. Please, don't.*

But Constantine doesn't issue an order to stop.

Beside him, the mayor suddenly takes a breath and fixes a stern look on the Premier. "Constantine," she says in a calm voice.

I've never heard anyone call him his name to his face. But somehow, Constantine pauses for a moment, his eyes swiveling to the mayor as if he'd once listened to her before.

The woman glares at him. "Remember your own mother, Constantine," she says softly. "And what she would say, were she here."

The words are like an arrow to his chest. I feel his sharp recoil through our link, can see the paling on his gaunt face. For a brief moment, Constantine looks at Mayor Elland not like she's the mayor of his capital, but as if she's his elder, a woman he must once have listened to in the same way he'd listened to his own mother. I look back and forth between them, the world blurred through my tears, hoping desperately that her words were enough.

And for an instant, they seem like they might be. Constantine seems to waver, a rare hesitation on his face. I wonder if he's imagining his mother here. I wonder if he knows that Mayor Elland had loved her.

But then the darkness in his heart clouds his face again, and any softness that might have been there disappears. He looks away from her in disgust.

"But she isn't, is she?" he says. "She's dead. And the dead are useless."

He gives the soldier a nod. The soldier lifts the prisoner's hand right as I take a step forward. For a moment, the woman meets my gaze. She is silently begging me for help, and even as I see nothing but my mother in her, I remember that this prisoner is also her own person, being tortured for no reason other than her mild resemblance to my mother.

The soldier tightens his grip on the knife. Then he brings it to the woman's longest finger and cuts it off.

The woman lets out a piercing wail. Blood runs down her hand.

I turn my face to the ground, unable to bear the sight. I'm trembling violently now.

Constantine's soldiers have observed me every time I've visited my mother. He knows how important it is for us to communicate with our hands. He knows what this cruelty means for us.

Tears are streaming down my face now. My hands have been clawing so hard against the bridge that my fingers are bloody, streaking scarlet against the ground.

Please stop, I beg Constantine. I press my face closer to the ground before him, not caring that all his soldiers see me prostrating like this. It's what he wanted, after all. *Please stop. I'm begging you.*

I hear the sound of Constantine bending down to me, the hush of his robes against the ground. A cool hand touches my chin and brings my face up. I find myself looking straight into his eyes. In them, and through the emotions in our link, I see the truth of my punishment.

It isn't my defiance of him at the arena. It isn't even the escape of the Strikers, although that may have been the catalyst.

It is simply what I said to him in the privacy of that small room in the middle of the night. Because the expression in his eyes right now is the same expression I'd seen on him that night—a wild, nearly terrified rage.

Maybe you're just scared to die.

I look back at him and let all my pain and rage flow. *How can you do this*, I say to him, *and still say you loved your own mother?*

He looks at me. This is his father in him. *Because I know what it feels like to lose her*, he replies. *And I know what that does to you.*

Then he releases me and waves at his soldier to help the prisoner to her feet.

In a daze, I look on as the soldier offers a hand to the prisoner, and when she flinches away from him as she cradles her damaged arm and hand, he grabs her good elbow and forces her back to her feet. Is Caitoman dragging my mother to her feet right now? Or is he continuing with his torture of her, doing more than what he promised his brother he would do? He is capable of anything.

The woman remains hunched, swaying from pain, as the soldiers begin to usher her away, back to whatever wretched prison they've taken her from. And all I can imagine is my own mother doing the same, bent with agony and blood, being led back to wherever they are keeping her.

Mayor Elland watches them go, her own face bleak, whatever thoughts churning through her mind held tightly back as she forces herself to stay calm. All she can do is cast a disappointed look toward Constantine. He makes a point to ignore her gaze, but I can see that it bothers him. The words about his mother have stayed with him.

And as I crouch there, consumed with my own fear and fury, I notice something about the soldier that Constantine had brought here. The one wearing Caitoman's ring.

The ring features the sun and its flares carved in gold around a band. It flashes once in the light and my eyes go to it. In that moment, I remember Raina's ring, a similar sun ring that she'd worn when we first arrived back in the capital.

No, it wasn't a similar ring. It was the *same ring*.

The exact same ring that Caitoman had now given this soldier.

We are guided by light and fated by the sun.

It suddenly occurs to me that General Caitoman was the one who had ordered the switching of Constantine's guards after the assassination attempt.

That he had publicly called out Constantine's weakened state during the banquet on the Sun Dial, so all would see the Premier fallen on the steps. I'd thought it real concern at the time, brother for brother.

Allies in powerful places.

My stomach turns with a sickening lurch. No, it couldn't be. Caitoman and Constantine have an unspoken language between them. They care about each other. Constantine had allowed Red to escape in order to save his brother. And Caitoman . . .

But Caitoman doesn't care about others. Even Constantine had confirmed that. And that means Caitoman doesn't care for Constantine, either, even if his brother might pity him to some extent. Caitoman is a monster. I have seen it enough with my own eyes.

That means Caitoman is part of the rebellion.

I am working on the same side as him.

The Chief Architect and Mayor Elland are planning to dethrone Constantine. But they're not going to overthrow the Federation.

Instead, they're going to help Caitoman take the throne.

30

RED

WHEN THE FEDERATION FIRST ARRESTED ME, they took my father and sister. I still remember seeing the carriage pull up in front of our home, and my father stepping before me to greet the guard dressed in white. My father had walked around me so smoothly. He'd bent down to my ear as he passed and said to me the last words I ever heard from him.

"If you fight them," he'd whispered, "make sure they don't see it coming."

Even now, I think back and marvel at the straightness of his shoulders and the lift of his chin. He knew why they were there, and that he had no way of protecting me and my sister. He could only tell me to find a moment—any moment—to escape.

His final words echo in my thoughts as we hide in the outer limits of Cardinia at dusk. Here, the city dwindles, the storefronts and apartments and parks making way for large factories and turbines. Massive waterwheels churn against the side of the inner walls, powered by a series of irrigation canals running over the top of the walls that pour water endlessly over the wheels. Billows of steam and smoke rise from the factories.

Here, there are no spectators, no crowds on the streets. Instead, I see workers dressed in gray and black, faces smeared with sweat and dirt as they walk in steady lines between buildings inside the factory grounds.

My father had always told me and Laeni to stay away from the edges of Cardinia. This is the prison district, and it runs in a large ring around the city. Criminals deemed unworthy of use in the lab complex come here instead. They are charged rent for their prison cells and must work to pay it off. The numbers never quite add up, though, so you always end up earning less than the rent of your cell costs. Some families manage to scrounge up enough money to pay the debt and help a prisoner finish their sentence. Most never do.

Even without the lengthening evening, we are swathed in shadows from the moment we draw close to the prison district. Towers loom high over us, spewing their steam, and enormous gears churn, generating the electricity that keeps the light bulbs burning bright throughout the city. Most of the workers have cloth draped across their heads to protect themselves from the constant rain of soot that stains the streets.

I guess it's a good thing. At least I have an excuse to hide my face.

A short wall runs around the edge of the prison complex, and as we draw near to it, I see more soldiers there than I've ever seen outside of a warfront. They stand nearly shoulder to shoulder along the wall, their eyes turned out to the city streets. The only breaks come in the shape of a dozen open gates spaced out in regular intervals along the wall, through which lines of prisoners now shuffle back into the complex under heavy guard. They must be returning from work shifts outside the city, cleaning the streets or working in greenhouses outside the prison complex.

Jeran keeps a dark gray cloth looped around his own head, the fabric hiding his face from view, while I do the same. In this evening light, we blend into the shadows at the corner of a street as we watch the lines of prisoners move.

Above us, moving along the balcony ledges of the surrounding buildings, are Aramin and Adena.

I can't help shaking my head in admiration. Even after being captured and subjected to the terror of the arena, they can still glide silently through the shadows of the city, their movements so subtle that sometimes even we lose track of where they are above us. Only now and then do I see a faint glint of light flash at us from the ledges. Adena, already back to crafting her makeshift gadgets, has polished Aramin's newly acquired dagger enough to make it shine like a mirror. She uses it to communicate with us in the darkness, alerting us to where they are without giving away their position to anyone else.

Jeran tilts his face in their direction at Adena's latest signal, then signs to them briefly. He glances at me. "They can see the top of the prison wall from where they are," he whispers to me. "Adena says there are too many guards stationed at too regular of intervals."

As we draw near, I catch myself unconsciously touching the collar of my shirt, underneath which my chest brand lies. Every prisoner has a brand. It tells the guards where they belong inside the complex, and it gains entrance into the complex. From there, they match the prisoner with a complex's manager, who keeps track of who belongs in which prison block. My brand had assigned me to the turbine factories, where I worked ten-hour shifts pushing the pedals that powered the electric generators.

"Not if we find a way to bring those guards over to us," I whisper back. "Give them some room to get in."

Jeran thinks about this for a moment. "Do they keep a written tally of who works inside and outside the complex?" he asks.

I nod. "The workers allowed outside of the complex are tracked in great detail."

He shakes his head, studying the sheer size of this district. It loops all the way around the city. "Even if some of us make it inside, how would we find Talin's mother? That is, if she's here at all? What if they moved her tonight to some other place?"

"They tend to divide the workers by their specialties," I reply. "Talin's mother is skilled in medicine. They might use her for the turbines or they might have her as a nurse to treat injuries the other prisoners sustain from the factories. We should head first for the prison infirmaries."

"And what if they're just holding her in there without assigning her to anything? What if they're just punishing her?"

I shake my head. "Then they wouldn't have taken her here. Constantine would have sent her to the labs. Torture is inefficient for the Federation in this district. They want to get something out of you here."

Jeran nods, his eyes turning to the lines. His focus pauses on one some distance from us. Then he looks back up in Adena's direction and signs again. "I'm telling them your idea of distracting the guards," he whispers to me as he goes.

I wait in silence as Jeran watches for Adena's signals. After a pause, he turns back to me, blushing, and wraps his head scarf tighter around himself.

"What?" I whisper.

Jeran just shakes his head, as if embarrassed. "Nothing," he mutters. "That was Aramin responding this time, not Adena."

"What did he say?"

"Nothing." Jeran shrugs, his blush deepening. "He said he can tell it's me from a mile away, and to readjust my disguise."

Even through Jeran's mumble, I can clearly hear Aramin's gruff affection for him. I smile a little, my eyes darting up to the others. How closely Aramin must watch Jeran to be able to still decipher his little movements and graceful figure.

As I observe them, my mind returns to Talin. Hours earlier, I'd felt a tug of agony through our bond, sharp and bracing despite the distance between us and the fraying of our link. I'd stopped in my tracks, my face turning so pale that Jeran had asked me if I was okay.

The feeling dissipated the instant I'd tried to reach out to her, as if she had closed off her emotions to me. Since then, all I've gotten from her is a thin trickle of her pulse. Even that is laced with tension, everything about her coiled tight like a spring.

Something happened to her, and I don't know what it is.

For once, my other voice attempts to soothe me.

Swallow the fear. Talin is alive, that heartbeat still steady. There is nothing you can do about it except to keep going. You hope for the best, even as you brace for the worst.

I look toward one of the towers looming against the night, a structure built with a narrow slit of a window overhead. "They flash a light through that slit every night," I answer. "It tells the guards to shut the gates."

The night turns darker, until the full moon rises and casts the entire district in its silver glow. We stay where we are, watching the lines outside the prison complex grow and ebb. Every prisoner looks the same—tired, dirty, cheeks sunken. Some of them dare to hum under their breaths. For the most part, the guards don't seem to care.

There are a regular smattering of children among them. Twelve-, thirteen-year-olds, not far in age from when I'd first visited this place. They are the ones with the widest eyes, new to the prisoner life, still looking around and trying to figure out a way to escape. But then they step forward toward the guards at the gate, and their moment of panic subsides. Their faces lower to the ground. And I find myself wondering if I had looked like that. I must have. I remember the way I'd dread seeing the land beyond the gate, a maze of darkness, of churning steel and roaring furnaces. I remember feeling so grateful the day they took me out of the district and to the lab complex.

Wasn't I a fool? How little I knew back then of what would happen to me.

The hours drag on. As the time draws near for the gates to close for the night, I nudge Jeran gently and nod toward the guards. Right before the gates shut, the soldiers are always the least patient. They bounce on their legs, tired from standing guard all night, eager to head back to their quarters for a hot meal and a bed. We watch them snap at the prisoners who aren't moving fast enough, yanking some of them forward, shoving others with the hilts of their blades.

"They are always the most careless around this time," I murmur to Jeran.

He nods in agreement, studying their actions. "They want to go home."

As the lines begin to dwindle, we creep from one shadow to another and edge closer toward the gate. I lower my head and drape the cloth more tightly around me. Jeran does the same. The prison wall draws near before us.

By the time we approach the gate, they are closing it. The four guards managing it are arguing with one another. Sure enough, I immediately spot the insignias around their sleeves. East and southeast city patrols. The ones that had been conspicuously missing from the solstice festivities.

"I've done double shifts this entire week," one snaps.

"You think I haven't done double shifts?"

"Who covered for you last week?" The soldier rolls his eyes as he tucks his gun back at his belt. "All of us here, doing extra hours because of the Premier, and there you were, skipping gate duty to woo your girl."

"She's not even going to marry you, you know," one of the other guards pipes up.

Jeran glances at me. Patrols stationed here at the Premier's personal request. At least poor Danna had been telling the truth.

The offended soldier throws an obscene hand at both of them. "Wait until I do marry her and transfer out of this position," he says. "You'll all be here, sorting prisoners. I'll be having proper meals and sleep up in the thoroughfare district."

Jeran signs up toward Adena and Aramin, then looks at me. "They're heading to that tower," he says, nodding at an apartment complex across from the wall.

Now I see why they're going there. A footbridge runs between several of the nearby buildings. It shouldn't be a way to get across behind the prison's walls, except there is a dead tree, gnarled and twisted, a dozen feet away. It's not an easy jump for anyone to make, especially quietly, but for Strikers? Doable. If they time it just right, they could make it onto the wall's ramparts.

"We'll need to bring the guards on the wall to us and away from those footbridges," I add.

Jeran nods. "They'll wait for us to make our move."

We wait a few more minutes, then step out from the shadows of the buildings to head over to where the soldiers are standing.

One of them immediately narrows his eyes at us, his hands moving to the weapons at his belt. His gaze roams over me. "Lost?" he snaps.

I have a sudden urge to scare him, to spread my steel wings and see their faces change from hostile to terrified. But instead, I swallow and wring my hands.

Another guard shoves me with her baton. "What's this? Speak when you're spoken to. No loitering around the prison district. Everyone knows that."

"I'm sorry," I say, pretending shyness. At least I have a native Karenese accent, something which seems to make them look at us with disinterest. I put a hand on Jeran's shoulder beside me. "My cousin and I, we're looking for an aunt who we think was brought here."

It's a pretty typical scenario, what we've set up. I've seen plenty of people try their luck at the prison district's gates, pleading the cases for their family members to the guards standing by.

The first soldier snorts. "You have questions about specific prisoners, take it up with your local captain."

I take a deep breath, drawing on my own memories of living in Cardinia and the various tours of duty I had in the city. "I would," I say, "except my local captain has been heading up the solstice festivities all week and hasn't been in her complex."

"Who's your local captain?" the soldier asks.

I name someone I remember. "Captain Solamen," I reply.

"Ah." A third guard nods, confirming that I must be a native citizen here. "Solamen hasn't been talking to her blocks in weeks. Too busy with the solstice."

The other two guards seem to lower their stances a bit at that. The first one shrugs at me. "Your unlucky week," he tells us. "Wait until after solstice. You can ask about your aunt to her then."

Jeran pretends to start crying. I shake my head, my voice turning urgent. "No, you don't understand," I tell them. "We can't wait that long. Our aunt suffers from a lung disease. She won't last a few days in this district, and we need to petition for her to be moved. Please. Isn't there anyone I can talk to here? Can you pass along my message?"

The soldier sighs. "No exceptions and no moves. We're all stretched thin these days." He waves his gun at me. "Move along with your cousin. Go back and talk to your local captain."

"I can't!" My voice gets more frustrated, and the other guards tense a little, their hands going back to their weapons. "Please. She'll die here." Up on the wall, two of the nearby sentries turn in our direction too, grateful for a little bit of drama to liven up their moods. Good.

"It's the prison district," the second guard snaps, growing impatient with me. "If she couldn't handle being here, she shouldn't have broken the law."

The third soldier looks at the others, uncertain. "Come on," she says, glancing at Jeran, whose beautiful face looks convincingly piteous. "Isn't there anyone we can direct them to? Captain Mendal is still here for the night. They could talk to him."

The first guard rolls his eyes and pushes us back again. "Get out of here," he snaps. "If we stopped to indulge every desperate family member waiting around here at these gates, we'd never have time to piss in our pots."

I repeat myself again, even more urgently this time, while beside me, Jeran stumbles. He grows weak against my shoulder, and I catch him as he slides faintly against me. I almost want to roll my own eyes at his performance.

The guards blink at him. "What the hell's the matter with your cousin?" the first guard mutters.

"I'm sorry," I say, helping Jeran stand. "He's quite frail from a bad winter last year."

The sympathetic guard starts up again. "I'll go get Mendal."

"Don't you dare," the second guard snaps, shooting her an annoyed glare.

Up on the wall, near the footbridge, I see a slight ripple of motion against the lengthening night. Adena and Aramin are on the move.

The guards along the wall have all shifted in our direction now, intrigued by the spectacle of our inquiry.

"Get out of here, or I'll make sure you both end up in prison with your aunt," the first guard says, now drawing his gun and pointing it directly at us. "You can find out about her condition that way."

The nice guard shoots him an annoyed glance before heading toward us. "Don't mind Erik," she tells me as she escorts us away from the gate. "He's going to have a failed proposal on his hands soon. But you and your cousin need to leave. You can't do anything for your aunt here."

A part of me wants to talk to her some more. She reminds me of who I once was—stuck in this job, trapped in a world that wants me to tag along with its evil. I wonder if she knew Danna, if she would have been someone who'd speak up for me when I was first arrested or someone who would have stood quietly by.

But instead, I resist for a second longer as I pretend to struggle with Jeran's unconscious weight.

When my eyes dart back up to the area near the footbridge, though, I notice that Adena's and Aramin's shadows are no longer anywhere to be seen. They've made their way into the prison, past the walls.

Time for us to go too. I pinch Jeran slightly, forcing him to yelp and stand up again. He blinks, feigning disorientation, as I guide him away from the gate.

"I—I'm sorry," I keep stammering over my shoulder at the guard as she guides us to the other side of the street from the wall. "Thank you. I'm sorry."

Then we turn and walk back into the shadows. As the guard returns to her post behind us and the others settle back into the boredom of their routines, Jeran and I cut down an intersection and make our way toward the footbridge area. We emerge onto the quiet street across from the wall there, near where Adena and Aramin had gone in.

I glare accusingly at Jeran. "You can make yourself surprisingly heavy, you know," I tell him.

He gives me an innocent look. "I wanted to make sure you seemed like you were really struggling."

I roll my eyes at him, then turn to look toward the wall. "Now we wait?" I whisper.

"Now we wait," Jeran confirms.

The night air cuts through my clothes, and I shiver. If they find her, they will find a way to sign to us. And then what? Even if we find her, how do we get her safely out?

Either way, the answer changes nothing for us.

I'll find a way to rescue Talin's mother, or die trying.

31

RED

IT'S CLOSE TO MIDNIGHT WHEN WE FINALLY GET a message from Adena and Aramin.

Jeran sees them first. He rises slightly from our cramped crouch under the deep shadows cast by the footbridge against the adjacent buildings. Then he nudges me and gestures toward the trees nearest the prison wall that are swaying in the night breeze. The silhouette of their branches slices the sky behind them into slivers.

At first, I have no idea what I'm looking at. My vision is keener than Jeran's, sure, but I don't know the many subtle signs he and his Shield have developed over their years together on the warfront. But when Jeran circles a small space before us, I finally see what he does.

One of the branches of the tree isn't moving in the breeze like the rest. It's still, as if being held back by hands, lit from behind by the moon.

"They're here," Jeran whispers. He looks on as the moonlight glitters between the branches.

Now I start to see more too. Against the bright moon is a second, flickering light between the trees, so faint it's nearly overwhelmed by moonlight. It's Adena, flashing Danna's dagger in a distinct pattern.

I tap my fingers against my leg restlessly as Jeran waits for her entire message. In the glow of the night, everything about his expression looks wound tight, and for an instant, I think we've failed. We've followed the wrong clues and ended up at the wrong place.

Then Jeran lets out a slow breath and looks at me. He nods once. "They've found her," he whispers.

Talin's mother. She's here.

Everything in me swells in a tide, and my hands start trembling. I want to shout it through my bond with Talin, tell her exactly where her mother is being held, let her know we've tracked her down against the Premier's every attempt to keep her a secret.

But telling Talin will do none of us any good. It could overwhelm her emotions so drastically that the Premier will suspect her of knowing. And if that happens, he'll have guards on the alert instantly. He'll move her mother again.

I think once more about the sharp pain I'd felt from Talin hours earlier, and dread prickles my skin.

So, with all my strength, I push back my desire to tell her. Instead, I return Jeran's look.

"Is she well?" I ask him.

Jeran looks gravely at me. "She's in bad shape," he tells me. "They've beaten her. One of her hands is heavily bandaged."

I think of the white-haired woman who had once fed us around her humble table in the shanties around Newage, of the way she had smiled at Talin. I think of the young mother who had fought against the Federation when they came storming into Mara's capital, who had faced their onslaught without flinching once.

Was this what triggered Talin's anguish?

I swallow hard and look back at Jeran. "Can they get her out?"

Jeran shakes his head, still deciphering the faint flickers of light against the silhouette. "Not alone," he whispers. He seems to count something silently on his lips. "They say she is under heavy guard, and that they don't think she can walk on her own."

I nod. Then I turn my attention up to the footbridge.

If I take the same path the others did in getting into the prison, I won't be able to get out the same way. Not with Talin's mother injured the way they describe her. Now, I could try to fly her up, but judging from the way my wings have been damaged since Newage, I won't be able to get the lift I need while also carrying her weight.

The other voice in my head rumbles its agreement.

You have to find some other way out.

Jeran takes the lead. As the night shifts and the guards rotate on the wall, we steal through the shadows and up into the trees near the footbridge. Jeran moves like the Deathdancer he is, each step nimble and soundless, crouching in the thickest part of the trees while he watches for a gap between the guards. As one of the guards turns away to talk to another, he leaps from the tree branches onto the wall and rolls immediately off the side, sliding out of view into the prison beyond the wall.

I watch him go, then study the guards on the wall for my own break. Minutes later, I do the same leap. I'm less graceful than Jeran, and my landing against the wall knocks my shoulder painfully against the rock, but I grit my teeth and slide over the side. There, I crouch along the ground before hurrying into the shadows of the prison buildings.

After all, getting into a prison is never the hard part.

I've never been to this area of the prison district before; I've never had a reason to. The enormous turbines that define this region are against the outer wall in the distance, still churning, and the sound of their groaning gears mixes with the slosh of water as they turn. My eyes scan the rest of the space.

Identical, dilapidated stone complexes line the interior of the prison in gray blocks, housing quarters for most of the workers here. There are turbine factories, and from where I stoop, I can catch a glimpse through the windows of workers sweating as they churn the pedals by foot, making the turbines turn. Other buildings are giant storage sheds, their doors swung open. One contains a large water turbine that is being fixed by what looks like teams of prison workers. I can't see what's inside the second one from where I stand.

Then, farther down the road, I see a narrower building looming. It's of the same gray stone, except with a small sign hanging outside over its entrance. The hospital, where they take injured workers to fix them enough so they can continue their labor.

A sick feeling settles in my stomach. I'd thought that perhaps they might have kept Talin's mother in a prison hospital because of her skill set. But she's probably there because she's the patient, healing from her injuries.

A moment later, I see Jeran signing to me from the roof of one of the living complexes. He's warning me to take better cover.

I dart away from the wall and into the shadowed alley between complexes right as two guards walk by from the area of the hospital. As they go, I glance up to see Jeran turning his head pointedly toward the hospital complex. Right as he does, I feel a hand tap me on my shoulder.

I whirl around, ready to strike, but a hand clamps down hard on my wrist before I do. I find myself staring into Adena's dark eyes. She gives me a quick grin.

She is dressed like a Karensan soldier. Moments later, Aramin appears beside her, dressed the same way.

"Guess who stitches these uniforms," she whispers, glancing around at the complexes.

"There are Ghosts everywhere in here," Aramin adds as he nods down the path. "Especially around the hospital. Talin's mother is being held in there."

"You saw her?" I whisper.

Aramin nods. "Through a window. She's being kept on the second floor of it, in her own cell."

Cell. The hospitals in the prison district aren't equipped with typical rooms. They are full of jail cells, the patients behind bars. And Talin's mother must be kept in one crawling with guards.

Up above, Jeran signs down to us.

When he finishes, Adena looks at me. "Can you scale the side of the hospital?"

I nod. If there's anything my strength is still good for, it is for doing something like that tirelessly.

Adena glances up at Jeran. "Then we will take care of the front of the hospital. When we draw the attention, Red, you'll need to get Talin's mother out." She narrows her eyes. "Whatever the cost. Do not look back for us. Do not stop. Get her out of there, so that Talin can be free."

Something in me lurches at her voice. She's telling me to leave them behind.

"I didn't go through all of this just to see you all die," I snap at her.

Aramin tightens his lips. "It was never about us," he replies. "Get her free. Talin is the only one who has a chance to end the Premier's life. We're only here to help."

I stare back at them. They have survived countless rotations at the warfront, capture in Newage during Mara's fall, near death in the arena. And yet this is where they might make their final stand, giving their lives to save the mother of their friend.

And I understand it all. Because that's why I'm here. Because Talin is the one who has gotten me as far as I am. I'm alive because of her. The others followed her in and out of Cardinia. And in the end, she could be the key to changing everything for us.

I nod. Then I place my fist against my chest in the Striker salute. After all, I had taken this oath with Talin. I am her Shield, now and forever, my life intertwined with hers.

"May there be future dawns," Adena says softly.

We whisper it in unison.

The others scatter into the darkness. As they go, I turn my attention up to the second floor of the hospital. I will get to Talin's mother, so help me, or I will die killing everyone standing in my way.

As I steal through the alleys between the prison complexes, I see workers stream in and out of one of the giant storage sheds, working through the night to repair a wheel, while more come out of the second one. My curiosity piques, but I don't stop to watch them closer as I head for the hospital. No time.

Jeran approaches the guards at the front of the hospital, dressed in soldier garb. He speaks to them, bits of his voice coming to me where I am. Flawless Karenese. The guards frown at his words. For a moment, they seem to buy whatever it is that he's telling them, but then one of them shoves him roughly back. Behind him comes Adena. For a moment, they seem taken aback by her uniform. Their voices echo to where I am as she argues with the guards.

I turn my attention back to the building before me. Then I unfurl my wings as far as I can make them go, wincing at the pain of the movement. With a single, broken push, I launch myself up at the wall and begin to climb.

The agony lancing through my back sends shivers of sweat down my limbs, turning me hot and cold. I continue moving, even as a memory shoots through me and my other voice sparks to life.

The day after you invaded Basea, after you failed to shoot Talin and instead allowed your superior to get killed, you'd gone climbing in the woods outside Talin's village to clear your head. You climbed and climbed, your limbs young and strong, pulling yourself up past broad leaves and thick branches until you'd reached the top. You looked down at the village to see Danna and Lei, taking bets on whether a villager would be taken back to Cardinia or shot dead right there. You saw stretchers carrying bodies away and laying them out in neat rows in the streets. Small children ran past lines of soldiers like you and wandered aimlessly in the streets' bloody dirt. You stayed up in the tree for as long as you could, until you finally climbed back down and threw up everything in you behind the tree's roots.

I shake my head, pushing the voice and memories aside, and make it onto the second ledge. It's easier to see things for what they are from a higher vantage point. I look out toward the front of the hospital grounds, where the commotion Jeran started has escalated. Shouts come from below. More guards stream toward where Jeran and Adena stand, arguing with the soldiers.

I keep going. I pull myself higher until I finally reach the window leading into the corridor of the second floor.

Down below, I hear a shot fired.

I ignore it. Then I force one of my steel wings around, slicing through one of the bars of the window. I pull myself through, rolling as I hit the ground.

Inside, the hall is curiously lit with bright, artificial sconces against the walls that cast strange stripes of shadows across the corridor. It looks like a prison, except there are signs of a hospital here and there—the smell of poultices and herbs and medications in the air, the stench of steam burns, of blood and crushed limbs. It mixes with the smell of mint and sugar, creating something sickening.

I find myself instantly reminded of the two victims I'd seen rushed into the lab complex, burned almost beyond recognition.

I can hear the sounds of dozens of guards down this corridor. And at both ends, jaws clicking, claws scraping the floor, are Ghosts.

They sense me before anyone else does. Their eyes dart blindly down the corridor, searching, and their jaws grind, their long ears twitching as they sense the presence of someone who shouldn't be here.

I narrow my eyes, and a smile creeps onto my lips. They had prepared them for someone to come for their valuable prisoner. But I am a Skyhunter. And in my chest, I feel the buildup of my rage, the way it courses into every limb of my body, sets my eyes alight. The way it feeds and fuels me.

This is what Constantine designed me to do, to be an unstoppable war machine.

But he had never intended for me to turn against him. That's the thing about inventing new things. You can only control the genesis of it, not the evolution. And I have evolved.

The instant one of the Ghosts locks eyes on me, I lunge for it. My good wing spreads out, fanning into dozens of steel blades. In a single twist, I slice through the Ghost's arm and turn back around to stab it through its chest. It screams, crumpling against itself, before I finally cut its throat and move on. Another Ghost. I move like a creature of death, cutting through it before it can touch me.

Farther down the hall, in front of the cell where Talin's mother must be kept, the guards are already on the move. They've been preparing for this ever since the Premier captured the woman—knowing that someday there might be a fight for her life. I clench my teeth and hurl myself into the third Ghost.

It doesn't matter how quickly I can move to kill the monsters standing in my way. Talin said they'd been trained to kill her mother if there is any sign of a threat. And now they are unlocking her door, ready to point a gun at her face. I surge forward.

Through my bond, I call out to Talin, hoping she can hear me.

I love you. We are going to get your mother out. I promise.

I think of the moment I'd kissed her in the shadows of the sculptures on the thoroughfare, the moonlight in her eyes. I think of her tears through our link the night after the arena.

Soldiers rush toward me, blades lifted, but I cut through them. One of them manages to slice me deep in the arm. I wince, but the steel that strengthens my body holds up, and the cut that would've gone all the way to the bone instead bites into my muscle. I slash out with my wings—the soldier collapses. My eyes turn back to the cell at the end of the hall.

I hurtle through the corridor.

The soldiers unlock the cell door, shouting at one another to hurry up. One of them lifts a gun and points it straight inside.

"No!" The shout bursts from me, and I realize that it's a shout of desperation for my sister, my father. For the family that I had lost. I surge forward. A shot is fired at me—it hits me in the shoulder. I twist to one side, dodging a second shot, then hurtle into the soldier who had fired at me. The cell door draws near.

The soldier's finger tightens against the gun's trigger.

I hurtle into the guard right as he fires the gun into the cell. My wings slash out, catching anyone in their path. I'm too late, too late—the refrain runs frantically in my head. I've failed to get to Talin's mother. They've shot her.

They've killed her.

We've failed, and Talin's mother has paid the price.

And just as I think this, just as I stagger to the cell door, just as I look in, fearing what I'll see, that I'll witness a familiar woman lying dead on the floor, gunshot wound to her heart—

I look in and see a woman still breathing, lying exhausted with her head against the wall.

I'd hit the soldier right as he fired. He hadn't managed a good shot. Talin's mother is alive. I find myself staring into a face that Talin inherited—that fierce gaze, the proud tilt of her chin, a mixture of both fearlessness and vulnerability. It is the face that birthed the one I love.

What have they done to her? Her face is black and blue, and her left eye is swollen shut. One of her hands is bandaged, the cloth bloody, and her arm is slung in a cast as if it had been badly broken.

In an instant, I know this is what had caused Talin so much agony hours earlier. She had known what they'd done to her mother. I'm glad that Talin isn't here to see her like this. My breath escapes in a rush as I hurry to her side.

Even though she is injured, that fire hasn't died. At the sight of me, her mouth crooks up in a slight smile. The light of recognition flickers in her eyes.

"You," she croaks out in Maran, then frowns. "You haven't been eating well."

She'd just gone through torture, but the first thing out of her is concern that I'm not eating enough.

I can't help smiling at her, in spite of everything. "I hope I get another of your meals, ma'am," I tell her. "Let's go."

"Your language has improved a little," she manages to say as I fold my wings away and hoist her onto my back. She lets out a groan of pain as she gingerly adjusts her cast against me.

As I head out, other guards catch up to us. I grit my teeth and lunge at the first one, knocking him in the head with my own. He stumbles back, losing his grip on his gun. I seize it from him and fire a shot back. It hits him hard in the shoulder, a huge, heavy bullet that does enough damage to leave him collapsed and screaming. This is the kind of weapon they were going to use on Talin's mother?

Another swings a blade at us—I duck low, then encircle Talin's mother with my arms and shield her with my body. We run down the steps.

An alarm is blaring somewhere, a horn that makes my head ring. I recognize the sound—I'd participated in drills for this when I was still a young soldier. It means all hands on deck. It means we are about to be surrounded by soldiers. Surely the word is being passed down in some urgent line somewhere—before long, Constantine will know that we struck the prison district. This will no longer be a secret. But if we can make it out, it won't matter. Because we'll have Talin's mother, and Talin will be freed.

As I bolt down the stairs, voices echo from above the stairwell and below.

More and more soldiers are appearing. I hurtle into them at the bottom of the staircase, my body curling protectively around the woman in my arms as I extend my wings as far as they can go, striking out, slashing anyone in my way. The anger in me courses through my veins like fire.

Constantine will tear through families, over and over and over again, destroy our lives and loved ones all as part of his strategy to win. He will do it until the day he dies, unless we can stop him.

I turn my glowing eyes on a terrified soldier. So help me, I will get Talin's mother out of here alive. Let this be the last time Constantine triumphs over our lives.

Another soldier manages to get close, his eyes focused on the precious prisoner in my arms, and stabs out with a dagger. I duck into a ball. The dagger slashes open the top of my shoulder near my neck. I growl at the sting of it before lashing out with my wing at him. A scream. Blood.

I hurtle through the bottom floor of the prison. The commotion has stirred up the other prisoners held here, and I hear their desperate pleas as I rush through the guards. Their hands reach out toward me, begging for someone to hear them. I catch glimpses of those injured, with their bandaged arms and faces, some scalded from working in the prison factories, others scarred or missing limbs from the dangerous work in the turbines. I force myself to look away, trying to stay out of reach from their outstretched arms as I cut and slash.

Then there is a whirl of a uniform, followed by a blurred figure charging into the fray. I pause in my assault long enough to catch a glimpse of Aramin's vicious face, his expression wild and alight with battle fury. He seizes a blade from one soldier and hurls it straight into another. His lips are twisted into a warlike smile.

Ahead, I glimpse the front courtyard of the hospital. One look is all it takes for me to know that we can't possibly make it out of the prison district with just the four of us fighting. Even with my help, I am still a broken Skyhunter, and there are too many soldiers crowding the front of the building. And soon, Constantine will get word of what's happening here. Maybe he's already sent more patrols our way.

My gaze darts wildly around at the space, searching for a way we can still escape. In my arms, Talin's mother gives me a sad smile.

"I'm sorry, Redlen," she says. "I've been the cause of so much pain."

I glare at her. "Don't say it," I snap. "We're going to get you back to your daughter."

But even as I say it, I see Jeran standing against the wall on the other side of the hospital, facing a tight circle of soldiers all pointing their guns at him. Adena struggles toward me through the fray, cutting wildly at anyone who dares to come close until she stands in front of me, her back to me and Talin's mother as we huddle against the wall of the hospital. She has her teeth bared, and her eyes are slits. She holds two guns out in front of her. Nearby, Aramin spots Jeran and shouts something desperate at him. The Firstblade then hurls himself at the closest soldiers as one of them fires a bullet that catches him in his forearm.

I'm not going to make it.

That's when I see the giant storage shed ahead, one of the ones that we'd passed. The door to it is still ajar, but this time, I'm at an angle where I can see what's inside.

This one doesn't contain the giant turbine gears that the others did.

Instead, it contains the artifact that I'd seen loaded onto the train near Newage.

Hadn't those guards said they needed to move it somewhere where it couldn't cause significant harm? Of course they would store it here, in the prison district. Of course they would allow prisoners to work on dismantling the object, let them absorb the dangers of working near that thing. No significant harm if it's happening to these people.

My gaze hitches on the exposed belly of the artifact.

I make the decision in a split second.

Everything seems to happen in slow motion. I put Talin's mother down behind Adena. "Get down, as low as you can!" I shout to Adena. "And protect her at all costs!" Toward Aramin, I wave a hand at him, telling him to do the same. Jeran glances at me, meeting my eyes once.

Then, without looking back, I take off at a run toward the storage shed.

I feel the slash of blades against me as I go. I strike out with my wings. I don't stop to think. I just shut my eyes and charge straight through the lines of soldiers until I near the shed. They've been dismantling the interior of the object, which is composed of hundreds of smaller cylinders. In its core, it emits a faint blue glow.

If you are going to die in a final stance, take this out with you.

So I skid to a halt and lift the gun I'd taken from a soldier. I aim it straight at the core of the object.

As I approach, I see the remaining soldiers standing near it scatter in all directions.

I fire, then turn and hurtle back to the others. My wings stretch out, ready to shield Adena and Talin's mother where they stand. Nearby, Jeran sees my move and throws himself flat to the ground. "Aramin!" he screams out.

The word is cut off by the blast that follows.

The explosion rocks the ground.

The heat of the flame is so hot that it looks white.

I feel it scorch my back and throw me forward. My wings bend from the force of it, and I shriek in agony as the pain lances through my entire body. I hit the ground and tumble over and over again. The world spins all around me, a blur of orange and white and blue fire. I force myself back onto my feet, then throw my wings open as far as I can and shield the crouched figures of Adena and Talin's mother.

Rubble hits my back, tearing against my body. Everything blurs around me. The pain sears me, white-hot, and I think for sure that my back must be on fire. I squeeze my eyes shut and scream. I'm going to die.

My ears ring. Sounds muffle.

I don't know how long it's been. Time seems to stand still.

I open my eyes a little. When I glimpse my wings, arched protectively over Adena and Talin's mother, I see that the edges of my steel feathers have melted from the heat.

It's supposed to be impossible to melt this steel.

For a horrifying moment, I think they've died.

Then I see Talin's mother stir, her eyes blinking up at me. Adena shifts against her, her arms still thrown protectively around the woman.

We stare at one another, breathing heavily.

"Are you all right?" I murmur to them both.

Adena nods tentatively, then glances between my ruined feathers at the carnage behind me. I glance over my shoulder to see the shed completely destroyed, the artifact lying in fragments all around the district. The scattered, ruined little cylinders bring to mind the wood engraving I'd seen at the museum. The sides of the buildings nearest it are scorched. And as for the soldiers caught in the heat of that blast—

—they aren't just dead. They are charred to ash.

The destruction stretches across the prison district and into the buildings and streets beyond, in a massive radius.

Never, among all the weapons I've ever witnessed the Federation use, have I seen one that can cause this level of destruction with a single blow.

Fire, as if sent from the sun.

I search frantically for Aramin and Jeran. At first I can't find them—but then I see Aramin stumble out from a crumbled pile of bricks near the side of the hospital, where one wall has partially collapsed. He is bloody, injured in a dozen places, but alive. At his side, wounded but still breathing, is Jeran. We are all burned, scalded by the explosion of this strange object. Maybe we are all injured even more than we know.

I should be relieved, but all I feel is numb. All I see in my mind is the image of those bleeding workers. This is your fate, a creature of destruction. You will always find a way.

But for now, I hurl myself forward. We are alive. We will live to fight another day. And we have Talin's mother with us.

I go to Adena and lift Talin's mother into my arms, ignoring the agony of my own injuries. The others hurry beside me. No one says a word. We only know we have to get out of here before reinforcements arrive. Along with that is a singular, searing goal.

Tell Talin about her mother. And see Talin burst free of her chains.

As I think this, a few soldiers appear at the destroyed entrance to the prison gate.

I feel exhaustion course through me at the sight of them. Constantine's soldiers have arrived at the scene already. But even as I think it, one of the soldiers comes up to us holding his arms out, no weapon in sight. Another does the same.

As they do, a woman with silver-gray hair hurries between them toward us. She nods at me as she reaches us. Her silks are fine, her stance regal. A Karensan noble. And her eyes are fixed on me with an intense urgency.

"Hurry now," she says to us. "Come with me. We don't have much time."

32

TALIN

AFTER THE TRAUMATIC SCENE ON THE BRIDGE, I retreat to my bedchamber. Everything in me is shaking. I don't even bother to hide my emotions anymore. The walls around my heart are gone, and in their place is my bare grief and pain and fury. They roil through me for hours as I pace restlessly in my room.

Let Constantine feel it. That's what he wants anyway, isn't it? To know that he's broken me down?

Let him. I don't care.

Somewhere in the city, General Caitoman has tortured my mother. And the rebellion that I'd thought was worth helping has instead been supporting that same man, aiming to make him the next Premier.

Constantine is a monstrous leader. But Caitoman will be worse.

How could I have aided him? How could I not know?

General Caitoman, the same man who terrorized victims in Mara. Who tortures prisoners. Who smiled when he ordered me to do atrocious things for the Premier.

The thought festers within me.

Have I been working with someone who has no intention of ending Karensa's regime, after all? Replacing one Tyrus with another, one who is even crueler. If they succeed, then what? Caitoman is left to be the ruler of the Federation? Will I just serve him as his Skyhunter? What would my freedom even mean? Where would we go? Will our countries still all be under the Federation's rule?

All my rage rises. I want to destroy everything. I want to tear everything apart with my bare hands. My wings unfurl, extend. The light from my furious eyes reflects off the walls.

It is in this state that I hear my door open and shut.

I whirl to see Mayor Elland standing there.

Her eyes turn wary as she takes me in. Seeing her now makes me even angrier. I bare my teeth and stalk toward her. I could kill her right now. Kill them all, for betraying me.

The mayor sees me coming and holds a hand out to stop me. I snarl, ready to shove her arm aside and push her against the wall.

"I have your mother," she says to me.

I stop in mid-motion, confused. What did she say?

When I stay frozen, my hand still held aloft, the mayor tightens her lips and nods at me, her hand still up. "I have your mother," she repeats, emphasizing each word meaningfully as if she's afraid I might not understand. "Some of my spies were in the General's patrol today, after the guard rotation. Constantine gave her location away to me when he said that his brother was with her. She is now at my estate."

All my breath escapes me now. My mother? My *mother*. All the strength I'd felt moments earlier, that I'd been so ready to direct at the mayor, now crumbles in on itself, and my knees go weak. My limbs suddenly feel numb, and for a moment, I wonder if I'm going to collapse. My gaze returns to the mayor, all my fury sucked out and replaced with bewilderment.

She gives me a tragic smile. "She's resting from her injuries." At that, she winces. The memories of what happened earlier today flood through me in a fresh wave of pain.

So it did happen, then. Constantine had made good on his word—Caitoman made sure of it. A whisper of a sob escapes me, and my knees really do give way. I sink to the floor.

"I'm sorry, Talin," the mayor murmurs to me as she kneels before me.

"When can I see her?" I sign, not knowing how else to communicate with her.

The mayor shakes her head at me, indicating she doesn't understand, before reaching into her robe and pulling out a small booklet of paper and an ink pen. "Write the best you can," she whispers.

I stare at her, suspicious, before taking the paper and pen and gathering my limited knowledge of written Karenese.

When? See mother? I write.

"After the arena," she replies.

The spark of anger in me rises again, and I clench my jaw. I don't even bother writing anything down for her this time—instead, I shove a finger at her chest and then gesture to myself, putting my hands up in impatience.

"No, you're going to wait," the mayor snaps. "It's too dangerous. You think it was easy for me to make my way to you here, to give you this news? The Premier can feel his power being squeezed all around him, can sense an imminent collapse. He's never more dangerous than he is now. He's—"

The mayor bows her head. "I'm sorry, Talin. Constantine . . . he's . . ." She pauses in her words and shakes her head. In that gesture, I see an ocean of regret, a heartbreak that's lasted decades, born from her watching a little boy grow up into the cruel image of his own father.

"Raina de Balman is missing," she finally says in a low voice.

An icy chill runs down my spine. This is the real reason why she's here, and why it's too dangerous for me to see my mother right now.

When? I write.

"Since last night. She has not responded to my letters nor opened the lab institute's gates to see me. I'm greeted only by a lab worker when I go there."

I think of the ring, of Caitoman's ties with Raina, and my eyes darken at the mayor. *General Caitoman?* I write.

The mayor frowns at me. "What do you mean?"

The anger comes out in my harsh writing. *You work with General Caitoman. You all work for him.*

She stares at me, as if not quite believing that she understands what I'm writing. "Why do you think Caitoman has anything to do with our plans?" she whispers.

I stare coldly at her. Then I sketch a quick, rough image of the ring, with sunrays on it. Above it, I write, *Raina's ring. Caitoman's ring. Raina's ring is the same ring that Caitoman gave to the soldier that tortured my mother.*

I don't know what I expect to see on the mayor's face. Realization, perhaps, that I've uncovered their ruse. Fear of me.

But all I see is confusion. She shakes her head. "You're mistaken," she says. "Caitoman is one of our targets."

I take a step closer to her. Then I write another phrase on the paper. *You and Raina have different plans.*

The truth seems to hit her then, at the same time it hits me.

The two women had always been at odds.

"Tell me when you saw the sun ring on the Chief Architect," the mayor says slowly.

I struggle for the right Karenese words before I write a date down. The date I'd returned to the capital with Constantine.

Mayor Elland searches my gaze, as if questioning for a moment whether I'm the one who shouldn't be trusted.

I do the same, but what I find is genuine surprise. Then I write, *You never knew.*

Her expression gives me all the answers I need. The mayor didn't know that Raina was working with General Caitoman. Raina had been planning behind all our backs this entire time, had told us she was working as part of the rebellion while helping to install Caitoman as the new ruler. And it makes sense. Why wouldn't he try it? General Caitoman has control over significant parts of the Federation's military. He's the son rejected for being a bastard. And he must have promised Raina the safety of her own family.

Raina had always worked for herself instead of a greater cause. The mayor should've known. I should've known.

Raina had been the one to inflict pain on us in order to protect her family. So had I, of course—I am willing, after all, to be Constantine's Skyhunter in order to save my mother. But Raina had purposely withheld Caitoman's name. She had told me it was to protect each of us from the other, that if one of us were discovered, it would not mean the end for the others.

Maybe she had withheld his name all along because she knows what I would think.

What do we do? I want to say to Mayor Elland. Instead, I hold my hands up at her and shake my head.

She's silent for a moment, thinking rapidly. Then she looks at me. "Stay the course," she says. "Constantine insists that the arena's game will go on. You will attend and wait for my signal to act against the Premier."

I start to sign before I remember that she can't understand. What's the point of continuing with our plans if they were compromised from the start?

But Mayor Elland looks like she knows what I'm thinking. She puts a firm hand on my shoulder. "Listen to me, Talin," she says firmly. "Stay the course. Do you understand?"

I scowl at her and start shaking my head again. But she squeezes my shoulder tightly. "There are too many pieces in place. I have a plan." Her eyes are dark and resolute now, filled with some grim sense of justice. "You *will* see your mother again. You just have to trust me."

• • •

I don't see Constantine at any point during these early morning hours. He doesn't speak to me through our bond. Instead, I'm escorted out of the palace and ride to the arena. As we go, I see patrols hurrying through the city's thoroughfares toward the edges of the city. Off in the distance, the sky takes on an eerie green glow, as if the day will bring with it a terrible new era. Something has happened out there—I can feel a tremor in the ground, like the earthquakes that occasionally rumbled in Mara.

I fixate on the sky's strange color through the window of our carriage, my heart in my throat. A terrible tension comes through my link with Red. Has Constantine found out about him? About the mayor? Has General Caitoman planned something else with Raina?

Worst of all—has anyone discovered my mother at the mayor's estate?

I want desperately to reach out to Red, but I don't dare to. Not with everything up in the air, not with even Mayor Elland tense with the danger hanging over us. Over this whole city. What if Raina had never weakened my bond to Constantine? What if she'd been working this entire time to hand me over to Caitoman as his Skyhunter?

The memory of the Sun Dial banquet comes roaring back to me, and I see the moment when Caitoman had seized my arm and looked at me with those soulless eyes of his. Constantine forced him to back away, telling him that I was not his Skyhunter.

But that may soon change.

Are you okay? I want to ask Red. *Are you hurt? Have you been captured? What about the others?*

My guards are stoic, their faces turned away from me. I even find myself calling desperately to Constantine through our bond, my inner voice pleading.

I'm begging you, I say to him. *Please, Premier. Please. What have you done to my mother?*

Let him believe that I don't know my mother has been taken somewhere else. But he doesn't answer me right away.

Finally, when he does, his voice comes through our bond like an icy wind.

Soon it will all be over, Talin.

I don't know what he means by that. But before I can ask, I can feel his emotions curling back in against him, hidden behind steel. He will say nothing more to me.

I don't know how to feel. I don't know what to do. I've been left adrift, and the feeling of being alone and unmoored makes my head spin.

As we pull to a stop under the arena's looming arches, the soldiers open the carriage door for me and I step out, forcing myself to put one foot in front of the other.

What could Mayor Elland possibly do? What are her plans that I must trust?

I'm so tired of trusting. So tired of relying on others. Maybe it was a mistake all along, putting my faith in those who don't put their faith in me.

The morning light sifting into my holding room tilts against the floor. I pace like a caged animal, trying to keep the panic inside me from pouring out. As the time ticks on, the weight on my heart grows heavier, and my fear stirs like a living thing.

I count out each minute to keep track of the time. I pace some more, trying to keep my emotions from spilling over. I reach out to Red, with no luck. I reach out to Constantine.

No one answers me.

Another hour.

I pause over and over again to look out through my holding room's bars, certain I will see some familiar figure striding down the hallway—Raina, perhaps, or the mayor, or Constantine. Even Red and Jeran. Are they well?

I imagine Caitoman approaching and tighten my hands against the bars. But instead, all I see are guards.

Another hour. I bite back tears and wait. The light outside my holding room brightens as the morning drags on, streaming through the arches of the arena. The color against my floor turns from dark to pale gray. The sounds of the city stirring to life for the final solstice day reach my ears.

I wait for Mayor Elland to appear, to give me any final words or warnings. She doesn't.

The crowds have gathered outside the arena by now, and I hear the stir of them echo throughout the entire structure. Within it are waves of unrest—a palpable sense of tension rising from the audience in a way that feels more tangible to me than before. There have been uneasy stirrings in Cardinia since I first arrived, but today . . . today feels different. There is a charge in the air, like the humidity before a storm.

The lightning is there, just waiting to strike. And when it does, it will illuminate the city like a match.

Then one of the guards is before me, nodding at me. "It's time, Skyhunter," she tells me, then gives me a bow of her head.

As she says the words, I hear the gate on the other side of my holding room start to slide open. I turn back and squint as bright morning light filters in from the other side. With it comes a blast of fresh air, and the roars from the arena suddenly turn deafening.

My heart feels like it might break. I am alone. I am going to look up into the stands and see Constantine standing there with the Chief Architect at his side, his brother on the other. Maybe I will see the other Skyhunters standing at the ready.

What will happen next, I can only guess.

Then the gate opens completely, the light engulfs me, the sounds of the arena suddenly amplify into chaos . . .

. . . and I find myself walking out into an empty arena floor.

No mazes. No Ghosts. Nothing else is here . . . except two prisoners with their faces covered by cloth. Behind them stand two soldiers, each dressed as executioners. The arena itself is a cacophony of shouts, angry and bewildered and excited. No one knows exactly what is about to happen.

My heart starts to hammer. *Red and Jeran*, I think immediately. They've been captured, and I will be forced to watch them executed in this arena.

Or it will be Adena and Aramin. It will be someone I love.

Or it will be my mother.

That's my next thought, and the idea makes my stomach clench. No, let me not be forced to execute my own mother.

But then I notice the prisoners' clothes. They are Karensan, and not rags, but fine silks that have been shredded and dirtied. One is a woman with white skin, her hands bound firmly behind her back. The other is a man with brown hair, well-built like a soldier.

Like a general.

I frown, and for a moment I'm confused. My eyes finally go up to the balcony where Constantine always is, seated with his brother and his Chief Architect, and—lately—with me.

But the balcony is completely empty.

Constantine knows about our plans. He isn't here.

It doesn't mean he isn't witnessing this scene from somewhere, though, because an instant after my realization, I hear his voice in my head. He is ice cold, his anger a blade he slides against my mind, anguish bleeding in its wake.

You thought I didn't know, he says.

The executioners reach up and pull the cloths off the prisoners' faces.

I don't see Aramin or Adena or Red standing before me. I see Caitoman Tyrus and Raina de Balman.

They are bound and gagged, their faces bruised from what must have been a night in the prison. Raina is trembling all over, but the deep emptiness in her eyes tells me exactly what has happened to her family. Her son, her husband. They have already been killed by the Premier for her scheming.

Her plot to replace Constantine with Caitoman. None of that matters now.

And in this moment, I know that Mayor Elland must have tipped Constantine off about their plot.

The din in the arena quiets abruptly as the audience realizes who they are looking at. The General of the Karensa Federation. The Chief Architect. Two people that the city has seen standing beside the Premier all their lives. What are they doing here, bound and gagged?

Raina stares at me with tears in her eyes. Strangely, there is no sense of pleading in her gaze. Instead, I see something that resembles a farewell, as if she has always known she would end this way. She has spent her entire life creating monsters for the Federation. But in the end, they have still destroyed all that she holds dear.

I could risk everything right now. Lunge forward, protect them, and serve this rebellion. I could do it. I'm close enough. In this moment, I can choose between the Premier and a different future.

But I don't move. I can't. I'm tired of being everyone's pawn, moved from place to place, goal to goal, kept in the dark. I'm tired of having so much power and no way to wield it. I'm tired of false promises, of my mother used against me.

So I only look at the face of the woman who had helped the Federation destroy so much. I only stare at the face of the man who must have smiled as he tormented my mother.

Everything happens in the span of a second.

The executioners shoot each of them from behind.

Their heads rock forward. They pitch to the ground.

Dead.

And it is all over.

A collective gasp ripples through the audience. Followed by startled screams. An undulation of indignant shouts from those who had expected more of a spectacle.

But most of all, there is the roar that comes with unrest.

With rebellion.

All around me, the arena explodes in chaos. People are on their feet, shouting their disbelief and anger, throwing things down at the center of the stage. They are the other rebels that must have worked with Mayor Elland and the rest of the rebellion, other teams unknown to me, those simmering in unrest throughout the city, waiting for a signal, hoping for a chance to take down the Premier. They are the reason why I'd felt the crowds were uneasy today. They've all gathered here, hoping initially to explode in a rebellion against the Premier. But instead, they have witnessed the deaths of two of their leaders.

This is a part of Mayor Elland's plans.

I stare, numbed, around the arena at the unrest stirring to life before me. I remember that the rebellion is larger than I think. The edges of the Karensa Federation are beginning to fray, and for the first time, I see it for myself here, in the agitated crowds.

Mayor Elland was right. The rebellion hadn't failed after all. She has simply built up the silo of gunpowder and then dropped a match in it.

Constantine's voice reappears in my mind. In it, I hear something raw and cold and vicious. It is the sound of a man who has just killed the engineer of his entire empire. It is the sound of someone who has just ordered the execution of a brother he had loved. Who is now truly alone.

I do what I want, Constantine tells me. His voice seems to bleed.

The people will rip your city apart for this, I tell him.

I can almost see the tight, bitter smile on his face as he answers: *Let them.*

This is why he isn't here today—he knew the rebellion was set up for this, that I would be a part of it. He wanted me to see it happen before my own eyes. He wants me to know how stupid it was for anyone to challenge his regime. That even his Chief Architect—even his own brother—won't be spared.

And only then do I see the soldiers swarming the bottom gates around the arena. They are sealing them off. The gates are sliding closed, even as more and more scarlet-clad troops pour into the arena. Hundreds. No, thousands of them. With them come Ghosts, gnashing their overextended teeth in fury. At the sight of them, the stands still, then turn louder. I see some people starting to climb over others as they realize what is about to happen.

I'm sorry we have to end like this, Talin, Constantine says to me. *But it is what it is.*

Too late, I sense a person at my back. I whirl on the figure, but already I feel the stab of something sharp and strong in my neck. A pain hits my veins like nothing else I've ever felt before. Not even during my transformation. Not even when I saw the prisoner meant to be my mother tortured before me. It burns through my body like liquid fire.

I collapse to my hands and knees. It's poison. I know it. It surges through me. My vision blurs. I look around at the chaotic arena and sense my bond with Constantine shudder.

Memories flash before my eyes. I think of my mother, my father, Basea. Corian. The Strikers. Red. The panic in me rises to a fever pitch, and I try in vain to command my poisoned limbs to react, but I can't.

Maybe my mother is already dead too. Maybe Mayor Elland had been lying, after all. Maybe Constantine has ordered her killed, just like Raina's family.

Around the arena, the soldiers take their positions. They open fire.

Through my hazy vision, I see someone else suddenly barrel into the person standing over me. Someone with metallic-silver hair, eyes so dark blue they look black.

Red?

I think I am dreaming, but I hold up my hand to his face anyway. He's saying something to me. It takes me another second to understand his accented Maran.

"Your mother's with us, Talin," he's saying. "She's safe."

My mother? It can't be true. I try to focus on his face, but there's too much happening around me. Then the world is fading away, and I drop into a maw of darkness, the screams around the arena still echoing in my mind.

33

RED

EVERYTHING AROUND US SEEMS TO BE A BLUR— fires in the streets where only a day earlier there had been celebrations, flags and banners burning where before red paper had rained down in festive strings. All of Cardinia has descended into chaos. The rebels that Talin had promised may have lost their leaders, but that has not kept them from bursting out into the city. The unrest that we had sensed when we first arrived in the capital has exploded into a full-blown revolution. There are soldiers on every corner, and what seems like every Ghost in the entire Federation has been released into the city, jaws open and milky eyes searching, ears tuned toward any human nearby.

Talin does not move. She does not speak through our bond. She lies limply in my arms as our carriage rushes us back to the estate of Mayor Elland, the woman who found us and fetched us from the damaged prison.

I shake her, shouting at her, trying to get her to stay awake, but her head only lolls to one side, her eyes unfocused as we jostle up the path to the mayor's gate.

She's going to die. What did Constantine's soldier inject her with? I stare in horror at Talin's face, the bluish hue of her lips and the tips of her ears, utterly helpless.

The gate opens for us, then quickly closes. Guards swarm the path protectively behind us. Several servants rush immediately toward the carriage as it comes to a halt in front of the estate. But even though Talin is the one barely conscious, no one dares to approach her.

At last, I see Mayor Elland rushing down the steps and hurrying toward us. "Aside, aside!" she says impatiently as I step out of the carriage with Talin in my arms. Beside the mayor runs a young woman in a lab coat, one of the Chief Architect's former assistants.

And with them, her white hair pulled tightly back, her broken arm still in a sling, is Talin's mother, rushing to be with her daughter.

"The soldiers injected her with a poison," I say in a rush as her mother reaches us.

Talin's mother chokes out a sob at the sight of her, then starts ushering us inside. "She's still breathing," she says in a rush.

"She's ice cold," I add.

"It's a calming serum," the lab worker tells us as we burst into the estate's main hall and into a dining room. A table has already been cleared for us.

"What for?" the mayor asks.

"The Chief Architect used to keep it on hand in case any of our Skyhunter candidates became overwhelmed and aggressive," the worker answers. "It's designed to put them into an unconscious state. Not to kill." She tightens her lips as I gingerly lay Talin down. "But it will if she doesn't receive a tonic soon to counter it. It's not a formula meant to stay in her bloodstream for long."

Talin's mother looks sharply at her. "Do you have some of it?"

"We have some supplies from the lab complex," she says hurriedly, waving at another worker in a white coat to run. "We couldn't grab everything before the city went to pieces. Go. *Go!*" she snaps at the other assistant.

Beside the table, Talin's mother grabs her limp hand and leans down to whisper continuously in her ear. On her other side, Adena stands helplessly, looking on while Aramin keeps a hand on Jeran's shoulder and watches, the two of them pressed gently to each other side by side. I can only watch.

After a while, I step out. It's too much to see Talin like this. She had seemed unstoppable, had saved me so many times that, even after all she's suffered, I've come to see her as invincible. And yet, here she is, pale and blue, her skin as cold as the ground.

"She'll make it," the mayor says as she approaches my side.

"I know," I answer, my voice a growl. I still don't dare look back.

"Raina told me how few of you make it into the Skyhunter program," she goes on, folding her arms in front of her and giving me a stern look. "None of you go easily. It's your defining trait. She'll pull through, if only by sheer force of will. And if she's anything like that mother of hers, she'll be up and ravenous by dinnertime."

"And then what?"

The weight of the loss of her allies seems to pull her shoulders down, and for a moment, the mayor looks lost.

But the hesitation lasts only for the blink of an eye. Then she turns her attention back to me and sniffs. "And then we do something about the mess that you are," she retorts, glancing at what must be a mass of burns and dried blood on my back.

The mention of my injuries seems to suddenly remind me, and I wince as if on cue as the pain of it finally hits me. My back feels like it's been set on fire.

"I've got a makeshift infirmary set up in the back courtyard," she goes on. "Tend to yourself as needed. We'll gather this evening to discuss our next steps." She reaches up to touch my chin, and the motherly confidence of her gesture sends a pang through me for all the missing pieces of my family. "You may be a Skyhunter, if a broken one. But you still need to rest up and eat. Understand?"

"Understood, ma'am," I respond.

"Ma'am," she scoffs, releasing me. "I haven't been called ma'am in a decade." She nods toward the dining room, where the workers administer to Talin. "Go on. I know where you want to be."

I head back into the room and hurry to the side of the table, where Talin still lies unconscious, breathing slowly. The lab worker who had first seen her is now injecting a white tonic into Talin's arm. Talin's mother calls for a basin of hot water, then presses a wet cloth to her daughter's forehead and chest to warm her.

I take Talin's hand and squeeze it. Through our bond, there's still only silence—but the beat of her heart comes through. At least that sounds strong.

Talin, I say to her, even though I'm not sure how much she can hear. *We're all here. All of us.*

I hesitate, pushing down the lump that rises in my throat.

And I love you, I add to her. She doesn't stir. *I love you.*

34

TALIN

I LOVE YOU. I LOVE YOU.

I hear Red as if from a vast distance. I try to turn toward him, but everything in me feels made of steel.

Other voices are familiar too. Jeran. Aramin. And Adena—her rapid talk, her falling into her meticulous habits in times of stress. Everything in me yearns to wake up to see them. What is she so scared of right now? They are talking about me. I can hear my name on their tongues.

And suddenly I am on the warfront again, the memories hazy around me. I am a young Striker, newly anointed, and Corian and I are returning from an exhausting day patrolling the border. I am sitting around a fire, laughing with Adena and Jeran until tears stream down my cheeks. I am practicing with Aramin, who is showing me a complicated maneuver with my daggers. I am pointing at the stars with the others, all of us lying in a row, picking out constellations and wondering if the Early Ones had left to live there.

I am younger, full of anger and hope, and surrounded by friends. I am with the first true friends of my life. I am home.

I yearn now toward their voices hovering above me. It doesn't matter where I am. They are all here. We are all together. This is home.

"Talin? Talin!"

And now I can see Adena's worried face, the way her eyes light up at the sight of me. The world blurs, sharpens. Jeran has the biggest smile I've ever seen, one that highlights every last bit of his beauty, and nearby, Aramin lets out a long breath of relief.

They are here.

I look at Adena and want to move my fingers, tell her how sorry I am for being unable to save them from the train and the arena. My limbs feel like they're dragging through mud. But it doesn't matter, because Adena throws her arms around me in an embrace. All her warmth hits me at once, and I'm fully awake, I'm laughing through my tears, I'm pulling my groggy arms around her in a hug.

"Damn it all to hell, Talin," she exclaims, "but you sure like to take your time."

"Leave her alone," Jeran says. He's holding one of my hands. "She's just coming to."

There's a scuffle and more squabbling, and I want to laugh at the music of it.

"All of you, give her some space," Aramin says in his gruff voice, even though I can see his smile too.

And Red. Red is here, his smile shyer, his eyes locked on mine. He is holding my other hand, I realize, and I squeeze my fingers tight around his.

Hey, he says through our bond.

Hey, I answer, relishing this bridge of ours.

"Oh!" Jeran suddenly straightens and steps back. "Step back. Let her in."

It is the last voice that I hear the clearest, that pulls me completely out of this strange fog of my mind. It is a voice that I've talked to over many a simple meal of fragrant rice and chicken, of steaming buns and hot tea. It is a voice that has come home humming, a deer slung over her back. It is a voice that I followed out of a burning homeland and across a dark plain, over a bridge that led us to safety. It's a voice that once told me, *It's okay, baby. It's okay.*

It is my mother, and she is right here, hovering somewhere over me, her warm, familiar hand encasing mine.

I turn my head and find myself looking up into her eyes. Her white hair. The smile that breaks across her face at the sight of me.

The mayor had told the truth. My mother is here. Alive and well.

The tide in my chest crests and everything in my heart breaks wide open. The anguish that has held me tight since we were first captured loosens in a single go. I am a little girl again. I manage to lift my arms to her as she bends down to embrace me with her good arm. My tears come in a rush.

Mama. My lips form the word silently, and a hoarse whisper of a sob emerges from my throat. *Mama, mama.*

And she wraps me in her warm embrace.

"It's okay, baby," she whispers in my ear as I weep. "It's okay. I'm here."

35

RED

I DON'T EVEN REALIZE HOW MANY INJURIES I have until I start getting them treated in the mayor's courtyard. They pour stinging liquid down my back and somehow I stay stoic through it all, my fingers clawing against the ground in agony. They wrap me in tight bandages.

I don't care. It doesn't matter, because Talin has woken up. She's survived.

Hours later, I see her picking through the people scattered across the steps leading out from the estate's back door, her arm still looped through her mother's, the two of them inseparable. Beside them, the mayor speaks to her in low voices. Some color has returned to Talin's cheeks, although she looks paler than she should.

For a while, I say nothing. I just admire her as she goes. Even after everything, she moves with that grace trained into her by the Striker forces, as if she is gliding through a forest floor without a sound. Her dark hair is pulled back up into a messy version of her warrior knot. A few strands fall around her face, framing it.

I can't look away from her. I never want to look away again.

Jeran grins from beside me. "This is the happiest you've been since we left for Cardinia," he says. "And we're all gravely injured and losing a war."

I give him a bemused look. "I'll take what I can get," I say, nodding slightly at Aramin sitting beside him, sipping gingerly at a cup of hot tea. "Eh, Jeran?"

Jeran blushes, but he doesn't look away. Instead, he seems to shift unconsciously in the Firstblade's direction.

Nearby, Adena straightens from sharpening a dagger incessantly. "Save up your strength, boys," she tells us, her eyes roaming over the white bandages looping around my torso. "We won't get to stay up here for long. The mayor won't be able to hide her involvement with these rebels forever, and soon Constantine will be on us. We don't have infinite rebel guards at the gates, you know."

As she speaks, Talin catches sight of us. Her eyes go straight to me, and the link between us pulls tight. She smiles faintly. My heart leaps.

She and her mother come to a stop near us.

I haven't even finished nodding to them both in greeting before her mother unloops her arm from her daughter long enough to tilt my chin up with her good hand. She turns my face slightly, frowning.

"So many cuts," she mutters to me in Maran.

"I'll be okay, ma'am," I reply, shrugging off my healing scrapes from the prison district battle.

She just studies me some more before shaking her head. "You need some poultices. Young soldiers like you never seek out enough help. I'll ask the mayor if she grows any yarrow."

Talin looks on, seemingly amused, as her mother then turns away from us to check on Adena's bruises. Then she sits down on the step beside me and gives me a smile.

Hello, she says to me.

To be close enough to her again that I can communicate, to once more hear her voice through my bond, strong and steady.

It brings tears to my eyes. I laugh a little and look down, embarrassed, and blink rapidly as if to get rid of them.

Hello, I answer back through our link.

The sound of my voice in her mind must startle her too, because her smile widens and her eyes gleam in the fading light. She looks like she wants to tell me something more, hesitates, then smiles again, shyer this time.

Your mother's doing well? I ask her. *Her hand . . . ?*

Talin glances over her shoulder to where Adena is now complaining gently about her mother's concern. *She will be*, she answers. *She never tells me about her pains. But she's happy to see us all here.*

My lips twitch in a small smile. *If the Federation let her, she could have this entire nation sorted out before sunset.*

I believe it, Talin replies with a whisper of a laugh. Then she glances with concern at my bandages. *Your back*, she says.

I just turn so that my bandaged back is facing her. *Why?* I ask, glancing over my shoulder at her. *Does it look bad?*

She tilts her head playfully at me. *Not your best look.*

I'll grow out of it.

She smiles, then looks over to where Adena moans halfheartedly as Talin's mother rewraps a bandage around a cut on the Striker's arm. On impulse, I reach out to take Talin's hand gently in mine.

Touching her. The real her, here, in the flesh. It feels so good. My hand tightens around her fingers, and she squeezes back.

Thank you, Talin says after a pause. Her smile is gone now, replaced by a grave expression. *I never thought I'd see her again. And then you got her out of there.*

I hesitate, bashful now myself, unsure what to say. *We needed you here,* I say. *With the rebellion, not at Constantine's side.*

Talin's emotions waver through our bond, and I suddenly curse myself. Nicely done, Red. Tell her more about how the only reason you saved her mother was because you needed her to fight for the rebellion.

I clear my throat and prepare to tell her the real reason—but the mayor is taking a seat near us in the courtyard, and everyone around her hushes, turning in her direction to hear what she has to say. My moment passes. I force my answer down as Talin turns toward the mayor too. Our hands slide free.

Mayor Elland looks weary, tired in a way that seems unlike her. Still, when she speaks, her voice is strong and steady. "The Premier knows the edges of his Federation are crumbling," she tells us. Beside me, Jeran translates in a soft voice to Aramin and Adena. "He knew the rebellion was stirring here in the capital, poisoning his authority. That's what he meant the slaughter in the arena to be—a warning."

A slaughter, Talin's voice comes through our bond, alarmed. And I remember that she wasn't awake during the killing.

I give her a grave nod. *A slaughter*, I answer. I decide not to recount the way Constantine blocked the entrances and exits of the arena, then sent his soldiers in to do his bidding. How many dead there were.

Talin's heart twists, and I feel the twinge of agony from her.

"How did Constantine know we planned to make a move today?" someone asks.

"Because I told him," the mayor replies.

There's silence. Some in the crowd know; I can tell because they don't react. Others suck in their breath sharply.

"I told him about the betrayal of his Chief Architect and his brother," the mayor goes on, her eyes narrowing. "Raina's mistake was in keeping her alliance with General Caitoman a secret. We are not here to hand power over to another Tyrus."

There is a murmur of agreement.

"His mistake," Jeran chimes in at the mayor's words. "Without killing every rebel, he has simply made them martyrs."

"But where do we go from here?" Adena asks as Jeran translates. "We've lost the element of surprise, now your original plans have been scrapped."

Another rebel nods and speaks up. "She's right. Constantine has retreated to hell knows where. We'll have to find a way to root him out."

"I know where he is."

Talin signs her words in Maran, and Jeran speaks up for her, interpreting for everyone to hear. At that, every eye turns to her.

The mayor watches her. "You feel him right now through your bond with him?" she asks.

Talin's signs are cutting and angry now, and within them, I see hints of all she has suffered under the Premier's control. "When he wants to be alone, he retreats to his greenhouse across from the palace grounds."

The mayor nods in understanding. "Of course he would," she says.

"Why do you say that?" I ask.

The mayor is quiet for a moment, as if remembering something from long ago. Finally, she says, "The Premier's mother ordered the building of that greenhouse. It was her sanctuary. I remember Constantine playing along the paths inside."

The Premier's mother. I hadn't thought much of who she must have been. A silence follows her words, and in that silence, I hear the truth of how the mayor might have hated Constantine's father, and why she has come to support the rebels' cause.

There's an unspoken understanding that passes between Talin and the mayor, although I don't know what it is. Then Talin signs, "Constantine has a private chamber in that greenhouse."

"A private chamber?" the mayor asks as Jeran translates.

"I wouldn't have known if I didn't stumble upon him there myself," she answers.

"Are you sure he would be there now?"

Talin's eyes flutter closed for a second, then open again. "I can feel his heartbeat," she replies. "I'm willing to bet on it. It's too close for him to have left the capital."

Aramin nods at that. "We saw the number of patrols still stationed around the palace. Too many for there to be no one to protect."

"We still have many supporters in the city," a rebel tells us in a low voice. "Many who are alive and strong enough to fight. They're all out there in the streets. What can we do to help them?"

"Arm them," the mayor replies. "Send out equipment, weapons and food, medicine and bandages."

"There are too many of Constantine's loyalists still in the city," another rebel says. "What happens if they come targeting these gates? They'll find out soon that you're harboring us all here."

In the momentary silence after, Talin's mother speaks up in Maran. "Well then. It means we have to root the Premier out before he can do the same to us. Isn't that right?"

Jeran interprets her words to the rest of us, his voice ringing out clear in the air.

The mayor nods, smiling at the woman's words before addressing the rest of us. "You heard her. We do what we can control. We will get to Constantine. There is no alternative."

"You once said you pitied the Premier," Talin suddenly signs. "Do you still feel that?"

As the mayor listens to Jeran repeat the question in Karenese, everyone quiets. The mayor stares listlessly into space, thinking her answer carefully through. Then she looks back at Talin. "The boy I once pitied is no more," she says. "We are going to end his regime." Her lips tighten. "And end him."

If Constantine dies, the Federation goes with him. There is no one else now. No Caitoman, no heir. Without Constantine, the Federation's standing on the Tyrus name will end.

"I will get to him," Talin signs.

Jeran looks sharply at her, then translates her words for all to hear. Talin doesn't flinch from the attention around her.

"It has always been my fate to face him in the end," she adds.

"I will go with you," I say aloud. Talin stares at me, searching my gaze, but I just nod and repeat it. "I will go with you, and we'll make sure to end this once and for all."

"Rest first," Mayor Elland says, and we all quiet, as if she has just reminded us how tired we all are. "The palace is too thick with soldiers right now, and you'll do no one any good if you're exhausted. We'll make our decisions later."

36

TALIN

WE GRADUALLY DISPERSE AFTER THE MAYOR'S servants bring us dinner on the courtyard terrace. As evening falls, I rise and pick my way back through the clusters of rebels. The mayor is speaking quietly with several of those leading the other rebels. Her voice remains steady, but I can see how this has all taken a toll on her. She had been the one who'd grieved her servants in the palace atrium, the three lives I'd taken in order to satisfy Constantine. At the memory, I feel the shame and trauma heavy in my own heart. My hands still feel stained with blood. How must *she* feel? How many friends had she lost in the arena's massacre? All those lives, sacrificed likely because of Raina and Caitoman's betrayal.

Maybe she grieves for Raina too, will feel a lifetime of guilt for telling Constantine to arrest them. Maybe she and the Chief Architect had been true friends, if opposed in their beliefs.

Nearby, Adena argues with a soldier about what tools she needs by morning in order to make a series of distractions that can help us break into the palace tomorrow. Somehow, even after everything that has happened, she finds a way to dive into productivity. Even though her shoulders are slumped in exhaustion as she reaches her room, she still pulls two blades from her belt and sets into polishing them in preparation for tomorrow.

"What?" she mumbles when she sees me looking.

I just smile and shake my head. She rolls her eyes, but I can see the hint of a grin at the edges of her lips. It's the return of our old rhythm, and I find myself leaning into her warmth. I watch her a moment longer, admiring the grace of her hands, before moving on.

Jeran talks in soft voices with Aramin. I notice them sitting across from each other in one of their chambers, their hands close enough to touch, and pause, lingering for a moment to see the look that passes between them. Jeran says something to Aramin, a question. Aramin's brows lift in surprise, and then he laughs. I do not think I ever remember him laughing. Jeran seems surprised by the sound too, but then he smiles, leaning unconsciously into the figure of his former Firstblade.

I turn away from them and continue down the hall. It takes me a moment to realize that I'm looking for Red. He had left for the inner rooms of the estate earlier, to get his bandages changed, and I hadn't seen him since.

As I head inside, my mother looks up from where she's helping another rebel with an injured hand. She shoots me a brief smile, signing to me with her good hand that she's fine, that I should go look for Red.

A fresh surge of anger comes through me as I glance again at her bandaged hand. Constantine's cruelty is always intentional and targeted. He knew what damaging my mother's hands could do to the way we communicated, that it would forever remind me of what had happened to her. I chew my inner cheek as I head inside, trying to ignore the tug of Constantine's mind forever at the other end of our bond.

Through our link, I sense Red's heartbeat, steady and reliable as ever. I quiet, listening for it, wondering if he wants to be alone, before I finally notice it becoming more prominent the closer I edge to the window overlooking the estate's back courtyard. Outside, the tumultuous evening has settled into night, and against the sky, I can still see the faint glow of fires coming from the inner city. In a couple of hours, we will head back out there, ready to commit ourselves to ending the Premier once and for all. But right now, we are here in this strange suspension of time, an odd peace against the chaos beyond.

By the time I make my way out of the house and into the courtyard, a few stars have begun winking into existence. A cool breeze combs through my hair. I close my eyes, letting myself take a long, slow breath for the first time in a long time, and for a moment, I can pretend that I'm back in Mara, crouched outside my mother's old home in the shanties around Newage, listening for the croaking of frogs and trying to bring one home in a jar.

If I look to the horizon right now, would I see that house silhouetted against the night? Would I see the glow of warm light spilling out onto a dirt path?

I open my eyes. The home behind me is not my home; the steps leading up to the back entrance are unfamiliar, and the flowers in the garden are not the ones that my mother would have spent lazy summer days gathering in a basket.

I stand there for a moment, letting myself feel the loss. Only after a while do I realize that I had closed my eyes and dreamed not of Basea, but of Mara. That somehow, the country of my childhood was not what appeared first in my mind, but the place that I'd defended with my blood and sweat.

There had been a time when I would fall so deeply into the pit of my memories that I never wanted to climb out again. But now I turn away from the house and back toward the rest of the sprawling garden, searching idly for Red. Maybe he doesn't want to be bothered, and the realization makes me hesitate. I don't know why I'm out here looking for him. I should be getting a couple hours rest too, before we have to head out into the flames again.

As if he sensed the uncertainty trickling through me, Red's voice appears in my thoughts.

There's a hidden grove in the back of the garden, he says.

His voice warms me, and I find it easier to push away the pain of old memories by following him instead. In the darkening night, I head through the winding path carved through the grass until I reach a thicket of trees lining the end of the mayor's property. The breeze is cooler here, funneled through the tree trunks, and I follow the current of it instinctively until I find myself staring at a pomegranate grove at the end of the thicket. Their bushy branches grow so close and thickly together that they seem to form a wall. Fruit hangs fat and red on their limbs.

Here, Red's pulse becomes a more pronounced drumbeat in my chest. I crouch, finding a small opening in the grove, and step inside.

It's darker in here, the branches crowding out what light might be filtering over from the house, but I have no trouble seeing the small clearing of thick grass in the center of this grove, then the figure curled tightly within it. Red is sitting with his legs crossed, his torso freshly wrapped with bandages underneath a coat, and his face is tilted up at the sky.

When I look up, I understand what he's looking at. The branches have blocked out enough light so that the stars in here are more visible, and from this vantage point, it looks like the rest of the world has faded away to leave only this circle of leaves overhead, enveloping for us this piece of pristine sky.

Red doesn't turn at my entrance, but in the dimness, I see him shift slightly so that I can come to sit beside him.

I needed to go somewhere to clear my head, he tells me, his face still pointed upward. I can see a hint of his lashes framed against the night. *Found this place. Have you ever eaten pomegranates?*

I shake my head. *Once.*

I heard the Early Ones have a story about them, you know. Pomegranates.

That they do not, in fact, lodge in your teeth?

He smiles slightly at me. *That they were once used to tempt a girl trapped in a place called the Underworld, where the dead are.*

I make a face and wonder if he can sense it through our link. *What a thing to tempt someone with.*

At that, Red glances away from the sky to meet my eyes for a moment. His lips curve into a smile. *I'll take them if you don't want them*, he answers.

I join his side. We stay very still, and I let myself think about the nearness of him, the warmth emanating from his body, the brush of his arm against mine. He has been broken down and rebuilt, just as I had, had survived indescribable trauma, but it has not destroyed who he is. He is still the boy I've come to know, at once brave and mischievous and naïve, taking the world in.

I wonder if sitting in a grove of them connects us a bit to that Underworld, he finally says.

To the dead?

He nods slightly. I feel, rather than see, his movement in the shift of his body. *We might not succeed in getting to Constantine*, he says. *Maybe we will fail, and Constantine's armies will rally around us, slaughter us all before we can take him down.*

I hear the question in his voice, and answer, *But?*

But what if we win? He turns to look at me now. *What if we do reach the Premier and end his life? What will happen to the Federation then? What will happen to the rest of the lands—Mara, Basea, every territory conquered and brutalized?*

I know what he's afraid to say. If we do succeed in killing the Premier, if we end his regime, how will this world splinter? Will we really be able to return to where we once lived and see it rebuilt for us? What are we returning to, exactly?

I don't know, I admit. *Maybe nothing. Maybe something else will replace the Premier and everything will keep on going as it has.*

Red nods slightly. Then he wipes a hand subtly across his cheek. When I look closer, I realize that he's wiping tears away.

Maybe he is dwelling on the pain of his own past, just as I had.

I wait as he releases his sorrow. The currents of his grief wash against my heart, again and again, and I have no way of reaching out and stopping it. I don't have a right to. Instead, I listen and feel his pain mix with mine.

After a while, Red leans closer to me. *He's afraid of you*, he tells me. *He's afraid of us both. He's afraid of everything he has ever destroyed, of all the harm in the world coming back onto him. His time is ending, Talin. I promise.*

I nod, and within the grief hollowing my heart, I can feel the burning of a flame. To my surprise, something about that flame brings a lump to my throat.

Red, I say to him now. *I'm sorry.*

He blinks at me. *Sorry for what?*

I thought I understood everything you went through as a Skyhunter. I didn't.

He quiets for a moment, and then takes my hand. *You are the reason I live*, he tells me. *And as long as I have this life, I will dedicate it to you. I will be at your side in any battle, whether out there at the palace gates or here, in this grove, in your heart. You saved me. I owe everything to you, Talin. Remember that.*

His words flood me with warmth. Without him and the others, my mother might never have made it out of the prison district. Never survived the horrors Constantine inflicted on her. But here she is, after all she has suffered, still able to feed that flame. Still ready to head out and fight.

None of us could have made it this far without each other. And yet, here we are.

In the darkness, my gaze finds his. *Maybe*, I say, haltingly, *maybe someday, after we get out of here, that is, if we survive . . .*

We will survive, he tells me firmly. Then he pulls me to him and kisses me.

We had sat at opposite ends of a bathhouse before, each dwelling on thoughts of the other. We had kissed once in a dream state, something that felt so tangible that I thought it was real. We had shared a stolen kiss in the shadows of a thoroughfare street, afraid for more. But this moment is different. Not stolen. Not in fear. Just . . . us.

Red's lips on mine, our bodies close together, here in a real grove under a real night sky. He leans into my touch, then wraps his arms around my waist. I kiss him harder in return, my breaths shallow. In spite of his grief, I feel safe in his arms, unbreakable. He shifts to kiss my cheeks, then the line of my jaw, then my neck.

I run my hands down his arms, then gently against the bandages wrapping his sides. His movements turn faltering now, his gaze shy. He is new to all this, I realize, having spent most of his youth trapped in the lab institute. So I stop and take his hands in mine, then guide him. We say nothing to each other. There is no need to.

The Federation can do everything in its power to destroy the bonds that tie family together, human decency, love. But it cannot break it. There is a level of power in this small, intimate moment that Constantine, with all his armies and his experiments, can never touch. Here, we are invincible.

Red kisses me again. I can feel the edge of my shirt sliding up. My hands run along his skin, feeling his scars from the traumas inflicted on him, sensing the human beyond that that the trauma couldn't touch. He lets me slide his coat off before he tugs my own shirt up over my head.

He is so warm. I feel myself falling into his embrace, and then I realize that I am lying in the grass, and he is hovering above me, his face perfect and framed by stars, his hair brushing the side of my face.

I don't know, really, if this is love. It is a feeling they have tried to rob me of for so long. But if this isn't love, I don't want it. Red here in my arms, the quiet of the world around us, the secrecy of this moment.

This is what I want.

Afterward, we are quiet. His fingers comb through my hair. His breath is warm against my cheeks. We stare up at the stars together, neither of us willing to speak, each afraid to break the spell. Soon we will have to leave this magical place, but for now, we stay enveloped in our private cocoon and try to imagine that this is the world we live in. I look from the stars to him. Red's eyes are distant. Despite our link, I can't guess at what he's thinking. I wonder if he is imagining some future that has us in it. I'm afraid to think it, but I still dare myself to.

The Premier can conquer every nation in the world in his desire for power. He can try to erase who we are, our love for our families, our devotion to each other, everything that matters. After all, the Karensans care only about Infinite Destiny, their desperate quest to touch every inch of the land.

But there are some powers you can't have.

37

TALIN

I DON'T WANT TO LEAVE THE THICKET. I CAN'T even remember the last time I felt this close to someone else or savored the sense of security it could bring. Red's breathing is even and light. I lie against his arm and stare up at the night sky, trying to memorize the constellations. Our limbs are still tangled together, the heat of him still rippling through me. He brushes an idle hand along my arm. I run strands of his hair through my fingers, wondering what it must have felt like before his Skyhunter transformation turned the hair metallic and brittle.

It used to be light brown, he tells me through our link.

It's the first thing he's said to me in a while, and I turn my head so I can see his face. *And soft as feathers, I'm sure*, I tease.

Oh, it's a tragedy you'll never know. He glances sidelong at me.

I murmur a laugh, and it feels so good that I tell myself to remember it forever. When I look at him again, he's smiling serenely. I can feel the ebb and flow of his emotions against my thoughts. Some of them make me blush. Under it, though, he's tense, and I know the feeling because it bubbles within me too.

The instant we step out of this space, the rest of the world returns.

Finally, Red lets out an uncomfortable cough and stirs so that he can look at me. *Can you . . .* , he begins, then stops, as if he doesn't know how to continue. I can feel where he's going, though. *Can you sense Constantine right now?*

I reluctantly let my thoughts loose and force myself to concentrate on the ever-present beating of the Premier's heart in my mind. *Always*, I tell Red after a pause.

Can you sense his emotions?

He is being careful with them, I answer, *just as I am. But I think he's afraid.*

At that, Red snorts in disbelief. *I hope he's cowering in some corner.*

I'm quiet. I think about the night I'd found him in that secret chamber in his greenhouse, his hunched figure over his desk, all those frantic maps and drawings pinned above him. I think of the dark circles under his eyes, the constant undercurrent of his fear that his time is coming to an end.

He's still just a man, I finally reply. *And he comes with all its insecurities.*

Red senses the sober emotion in me and turns to look at me. *What do you think his next move will be?*

He knows Cardinia will fall, I answer. *And survival has always been his goal. We just have to get to him before he finds a way to escape.*

Red narrows his eyes. *He won't escape. We'll trail him until he's cornered.*

He's always been good at blocking his feelings from me. I give him a grim smile. *But I've sensed something new from him lately.*

What is it?

Uncertainty.

It's enough to make Red tighten his grip against my arm. A trickle of hope, wary and strained, comes from him.

Well, he answers. *It's something.*

Adena's voice rings out from somewhere across the garden. It's the sound of her that finally stirs us out of each other's arms, suddenly feeling light and awkward. I look in the direction of her calls, pinpointing where she's coming from, then begin to pull my clothes back on. Red moves quickly and quietly beside me. Our moment is over, but I still feel the warmth lingering between us like a rope, tugging tight.

By the time we hurry out of the thicket, Adena has already made her way to the beginning of the grove of trees. She lets out a relieved sigh at the sight of us, then points back toward the estate.

"Jeran's already out there," she says breathlessly. "We could use your help." She pauses to squint at us. "You two were gone for a while."

I concentrate on tying my hair back up while Red coughs. "Talin was telling me about the palace's layout," Red says. "I know the palace's layout a little, of course, ah, but she—"

Adena sighs. "I'm just kidding. I know what you were both doing out here."

I glare at her, while Red turns scarlet. But Adena's already moved on, her cheeky grin dropping to make way for the serious version of herself. "We have to hurry."

A sickening feeling shoots through me. "Why? What for?"

But when Adena glances back at me, her eyes are alight with possibility. I can see the gears turning in her. "The other artifact," she replies. "Remember? A rebel has located it."

At that, Red straightens. "Where?" he asks.

"At the other end of the city's prisons." Adena hesitates as she recalls what she was told. "Among their textile factories."

The diversion we need to block Constantine's main escape route. This could be it.

"You want to use it for the palace?" Red says.

"Exactly," Adena replies

He shakes his head at her. "It's far too heavy to move in time. We'd need more of our people than we can spare. Besides, it's too hard to control. You remember the first blast. That thing could take out the entire palace if it's put close enough—along with everything in its radius."

"I don't need all of it." Adena pulls out a few of the small cylinders from her pocket that she had carefully wrapped in bits of rubber and lead shielding. "Get me there, and I can disassemble it into smaller pieces without setting it off."

"How can you be sure?"

She holds up one of the small cylinders. "That first one? I saw how their workers were unloading pieces of it before you detonated it. If we can grab enough fragments, we can lay out a strategic set of smaller, controlled explosions. Set them off as we need to."

"Can you do it quickly?" I sign to her.

"If I have help," she replies. "Could use your strength. But we have to go now. There are already signs at the palace of Constantine on the move. Rotations of soldiers."

Fear shoots through my chest, and as if on cue, I feel Constantine's moods stir within me. A darkness fills the space between my ribs. He is making plans.

• • •

There's already a carriage waiting for us at the front entrance to the estate. Adena hops in, scooting over to make room for us. Jeran is already inside, along with Aramin. Scarcely have we all settled in when the carriage jerks forward, taking off toward the other end of the city.

I can see the scattered fires stark against the sky, haloing the horizon with red and gold. As we draw closer to the city center, the crowds grow thicker, until it becomes impossible for us to go any farther. Most of the people in the city are not soldiers, who have retreated to the palace. Still, I stare out at the scene of rebels with rising fear.

"Detour," Red calls out as our carriage screeches to a stop at a blockade. Already, the exchange of gunfire and the clang of metal on metal ring out as rebels on one side of the blockade clash with Constantine's troops. "We have to take the west thoroughfare road."

"Do we know if that's blocked too?" Aramin says.

I suddenly leap out of the carriage. "We need a view from the skies," I sign hurriedly at them before shutting the carriage door. There in the street, I crouch and unfurl my wings.

Some startled shouts ring out as a few witness me. I feel a bullet ping off my steel blades. Inside the carriage, Jeran already urges our driver in Karenese to turn around. As they do, I gather my strength and burst into the air. The world diminishes below me.

The entire city is in flames. The fires dot the landscape in orange and gold, and from up here, the sight takes my breath away. Just days earlier, Cardinia had seemed like an impenetrable stronghold. Now, it looks like a sea of chaos.

I soar through the night sky, stay just above their carriage.

Turn west here, Red instructs me through our bond, and I swerve.

Down below, I spot a cluster of Constantine's soldiers, their scarlet uniforms gathered along a street. Ghosts snap their jaws among them, lunging forward to attack some rebels who have turned and fled down the opposite end of the street.

I turn sharply. *Not here*, I call to Red through our bond. *Stop. Go several more blocks.*

He hears me, and a vein of trust shoots through our link. Down below, the carriage comes to an abrupt halt before it turns back and continues going. Some of the troops spot the carriage. A contingent of them breaks formation to pursue them and the hulking shapes of Ghosts follow.

My eyes search for the next possible path until I finally find it. I tell Red to turn the carriage in its direction.

As they turn, the soldiers catch up to them from behind.

All the anger in me wells up, and suddenly I dive, narrowing my steel wings and pointing myself toward them. This time, no one is commanding me. No Premier is ordering me to strike down prisoners. *I* am my own Skyhunter.

The soldiers look up and see me coming too late. I barrel into them, cutting through guard and Ghost alike. One of the Ghosts twists, its teeth closing on my wing, but I turn in a tight formation. My blades slice through it, and I hear it shriek in response. I land, skidding across the ground to a stop, my eyes glowing.

The carriage hurtles onward. As they turn the corner behind me, I arc my wings protectively around myself—then shoot back up into the sky.

I feel invincible here. The joy of it surges through me until I am drunk from the rush of it all. This is the danger that Raina had warned me of—that once I got this taste of being a Skyhunter, I will only want more of it.

It is this thought that pulls back my emotions. I feel sick suddenly, and angle my flight in the sky back toward the carriage. My head swims. I can smell the tang of blood on my wings.

Do not let yourself get used to this smell, I tell myself.

And, without warning, I hear Constantine in my head.

You will, he says to me. *In time, you will love it.*

There is something wild and vicious about his voice this time, like he is delighted to feel the fear that has just hummed through me, knows that the spike of joy I'd felt aligned with the killing of others.

My hands clench beside me. *I will end you first*, I tell him.

But all I feel from him in response is a trickle of dark amusement.

At last, the carriage passes through the city center. The farther we go, the more scattered the fires. We veer down one path after another, avoiding other blockades. Finally, the dark ring of the prison district looms along Cardinia's wall.

The carriage comes to a halt nearby. I land beside it as everyone jumps out. Already, there is a crowd outside one of the prison's gates, which has been thrown wide open. Rebels are here, flooding in and out.

Adena darts through the crowd, pushing them back whenever she can. "Get back, get back!" she shouts. "None of you have the right gear! Get *back*!"

We manage to carve a swath through the masses until we break past the gate and into the prison district.

Textile mills loom all around us. In the center of them all, left in the middle of the path, is the cylinder taken from Mara, lying on its side.

The rebels have erected a makeshift pulley system to drag the cylinder out, but there are far too few of them to get the object onto a platform they've brought.

Jeran rushes ahead of us, seemingly unhindered by the weight of the vest strapped around his chest. Adena hurries beside him. Together, they reach the base of the cylinder and slide into a Striker formation almost without thinking. Jeran kneels, puts his hands together, and Adena steps onto it, kicking off with his assistance. She lands nimbly on top of the cylinder, then whips out a tool and starts immediately prying loose its circular cover.

Aramin rushes forward with a long rope to secure around the structure. He tosses it up to Adena, who wraps it around the top of the cover and throws the end down to where Jeran and Aramin pull it tight. As they work, Jeran calls out instructions in Karenese to the rebels around us, telling them to get into position to pull.

Red and I step forward. I feel my Skyhunter power coursing through me, and through our bond, I know Red is gathering his strength too. Our eyes glow a faint blue as we reach the end of the rope.

Suddenly I'm reminded of my days spent out in the scrapyards of Newage, balancing from one stack of metal to another, memorizing the feeling of that shifting landscape as it groaned and yawned beneath my feet. Getting a handle for the weights and objects around me. Now I grab the end of the rope with Red positioned in front of me, then look up at Adena for her signal.

She signs to us to move, then scrambles backward on the cylinder.

Pull, I call to Red through our link, and he raises the shout to the others.

"Pull!" he says.

We all throw our weight back.

Even with two Skyhunters, even with a dozen others helping us, the cover barely budges. I shut my eyes and throw my strength against the rope. My wings expand behind me. All around us, people jump out of the way.

We throw our weight against the cover again and again. On the fourth pull, it finally slides off, falling to the ground in a shuddering groan of metal. Everyone scatters as the object hits and sends up a shower of dust. Revealing its interior, full of the smaller cylinders that Adena had collected.

All around it, the rebels swarm, gathering curiously to see this mysterious object that their Premier seemed interested in enough to haul all the way back from Mara.

Adena slides off the side of the cylinder with a grin. She runs up to us. "The Early Ones were out of their ancient minds," she mutters, looking back in fascination at the object. "But they might just save us all in the end."

My gaze turns briefly to the silhouette of the palace off in the distance, through the open prison gate. What would the Early Ones think of everything we have taken from their creations, everything that has been mutilated from their original intent?

Or maybe their own intents were never pure either. Maybe we are exactly like them, and they were exactly like us.

"Trust me, Talin," Adena says as she notices my stare. For a moment, we all look back. Her eyes glint with the need for revenge. "We are going to turn it to ash."

Raina had told me this could be the real ending of the war. And even though I never agreed with how she wanted to do it, even though she was the one who inflicted all of my pain on me, I can still feel those words echo in my mind. This is the ending we were meant to have.

I turn back to Adena with a grim nod. "Tell us how we should set up the palace."

38

RED

DAWN BREAKS ON A CITY AT THE BRINK.

The streets, once crowded with festivities and noise, are now littered with ash and blood. There aren't enough medics in all Cardinia to wrestle with the bodies of both Federation soldiers and those they've killed. Fires still burn in dozens of structures, one factory so ablaze its collapse sends a shudder through the entire city.

I wait stiffly at the east gate of the palace. Around me must be a crowd of thousands of rebels, armed with anything and everything they've been able to get their hands on, stationed a good hundred feet from where flanks of Federation soldiers stand thick in preparation to defend the Premier. When I look at the top of the palace, it is lined so heavily with soldiers—all of them with their guns and arrows trained down on us—I can't tell where one soldier ends and the next begins.

Adena has gone to organize where to set and detonate the explosives around the palace. Our signal to act. Somewhere among the rooftops near the palace, Aramin and Jeran are crouched and waiting for my signal. Talin is among the rebels, invisible among their crush of bodies, watching for the right time to move.

The sheer number of rebels gathering here is what we're relying on, but still, I look at their numbers and feel something sinking in me. Mayor Elland had sent word out among them to surround the palace and send up an alert if there's any sign of the Premier attempting to leave its perimeters. When ready and directed, they should flood the east gate.

I look at those around me. In a mass, they may seem a faceless sea of people, but I take in those around me and wonder what they've seen, who they might have lost. We are going to use the sheer number of their bodies to try to break through the line of soldiers. Once inside the palace, Talin will have a chance at hunting down the Premier—but alone? In order to give her a chance to get in, we need to stage a large-enough distraction.

The light begins to brighten the city, casting the palace's domes in hues of pink and gold. In the street, the rebels' chants grow louder. Is this what overthrowing a ruler looks like? Was this what had brought the Early Ones down?

Behind me, I sense a ripple of Talin's emotions.

Almost time, she says to me.

I'm quiet, taking in her words. The memory of her lying next to me is still imprinted sharply in my mind, and I close my eyes for a moment, wishing I could return to the comfort of her embrace.

Don't look back, I tell her after a moment. *Just keep moving. I'll be right here.*

Talin doesn't answer right away, but when she does, her voice is calm and warm. *I know.*

Through our link, I can tell that she is calculating her fears, her emotions cycling in the same way they do right before a Ghost attack. She had once told me about the way Strikers train—once you make the first move, you must keep going.

Once we begin, we will have to finish what we started here. There is no going back, no returning to the thicket in the trees.

Suddenly, I feel a slight rumble in the earth beneath my feet.

I still, listening, and then turn my head slightly toward the palace. Nothing happens for a while. The rebels stop too, and with them, the Federation soldiers shuffle. I can see them looking at one another, their frozen faces twitching in sudden uncertainty.

For a while, I think that I've mistaken what I felt.

Then the loudest boom I've ever heard in my life reverberates across the city, followed by a rush of hot wind so powerful I'm nearly knocked to my feet. Everyone around us—rebel, soldier—falls to their knees. And there, on the other side of the palace, I see a ball of orange and red rise blinding into the lightening sky, the clouds of the explosion swallowing itself over and over as it grows. The earth rumbles and shakes and sighs, as if the plates of the land itself are shifting.

And, to my horrified awe, I see a shaft of faint blue light shoot up into the horizon from the source of the explosion. It glows brightly, illuminating the clouds, before it fades away as quickly as it came.

Whatever was inside that cylinder, it is powerful enough to have its heat felt from here.

Adena. Was she far from the explosion? What if she'd miscalculated?

All around us, the rebels move. They flood toward me from the north and west and south gates, masses and masses of them, a sudden crowding that swells our ranks. I feel everyone jostling in, brandishing their weapons against the soldiers before them, who suddenly have gone pale. They hoist their guns higher at us, trying to figure out where best to aim, but there are so many of us that I can smell their sudden fear. My own heart leaps.

The first move has been made. There is no turning back now.

I love you, I tell Talin through our link.

I love you, Talin answers back, and her words fill every inch of me with light.

I focus my attention on the soldiers before us, and tense. The rebels gather behind and alongside me. Then I lunge forward at the soldiers and their screaming Ghosts as everyone around me surges forward at the same time.

Soldiers shoot the first row of us almost immediately. I see them fall before the gunfire. But the next wave—we—run forward relentlessly, outpacing the fallen and charging forward into the mix. The soldiers fire again, and more collapse at our feet—but we are closer now. I put all my strength into the attack. Then I'm out in front, and the first soldier widens his eyes at the sight of me before throwing his hands up in panic.

I barrel into him, flinging him across the courtyard, and throw all my weight into attacking the Ghost behind him. The creature shrieks, clawing for me, but I twist, my broken wings still shearing right through its body. A cold sweat breaks out all over my body at the pain of the strike, but I blink away the tears and lunge out again. Soldiers fall around me like wheat in a field. Ghosts rush toward me. In a blur, the east and west flanks of soldiers try to close in around me, separating me from the others. But in the next instant, rebels clash into both sides, weapons swinging—axes, kitchen knives, canes and door bolts, guns, planks of wood, homemade arrows. They use anything they can get. The soldiers fight back, cutting them down—but there are too many of us here in this moment.

A Ghost bites down hard on one of my wings. The pain lances through me like a spear through my back. I twist in time to see the same Ghost's claws swipe down at me. Every one of my limbs tingles. I rush forward at it again, wielding my damaged wings, and cut into its leg. It loses its balance and lurches to one side.

We push and push against the flanks of soldiers. I rush forward again. Their ranks thin slightly before us. They seem to understand what we're doing, and I can hear them shouting desperately at one another, calling for the rest of the guards around the palace to abandon their posts and help them here. But it's too little, too late. I can see the courtyard beyond the masses of soldiers. I strike out with the metal blades of my wings. Soldiers go down before them in a wave.

The rebels push again. The soldiers try to close the widening gap. But we keep going until—finally—I see a glimpse of a clear path between the soldiers.

Talin! I realize I'm calling for her in our link. *Talin!*

She doesn't answer—but she doesn't have to. Because one second she's somewhere invisible behind me, and the next she's surging past me. The soldiers have no way to stop her. She cuts right past them and slaughters the first Ghost that dares to cross her path.

Up on the roof, the soldiers open fire. Their aim is uncertain when Talin moves so quickly, but one of the bullets catches her on the shoulder. The sting trickles through her right to me, and I find myself twisting as if the injury were mine. My heart leaps in fear for her. But she ignores it—doesn't even look at it—and hurtles toward the side entrance to the palace.

Behind us, the ranks of soldiers begin to close again. The rebels are being pushed back as the swell of soldiers strengthens. Off in the distance, I can still hear the roar from the fires set by the explosion. A faint tide of hope fills me. We are going to do it. We are going to get into the palace. Talin is going to hunt down the Premier, and there's nothing he can do to stop us.

And just then—

—right as I feel the first tenuous hint of victory—

—a silhouette on the rooftop catches my eye.

I halt, my gaze darting up. No. I couldn't have seen it. Could I?

But it's unmistakable. Outlined against the red dawn, with wings outstretched, are two other Skyhunters. Their eyes glow blue in the dim light.

Everything in me turns to ice.

Constantine had these weapons lying in wait. Of *course* he had.

I look at Talin in a panic and start shouting for her. "Talin!" I scream. I do the same through our link.

Talin! Talin! Look out!

She glances at me over her shoulder, her run faltering for just a second. Then she looks up to where my eyes are focused. She sees the other Skyhunters.

Her face drains of color.

I don't think. I bolt forward. I break rank and surge ahead just as the first of the Skyhunters hurtles into the air. The other voice in me rises now.

Your only purpose is to give Talin time. And that, you are going to do to the very end.

You grit your teeth and whisper a verse of forgiveness for everything wrong you've ever done. Every innocent life you've ever taken. It is not unlike what your father said when the guards came for you. It is the same phrase you've used under your breath many times in battle, whenever you were forced to lift your gun or blade or arrows to cut down a civilian. Their eyes haunt you now.

The first Skyhunter comes soaring down at me, wings spread, his eyes ready to murder.

My wings are broken. My back is a mass of wounds. But I feel no fear. Right now, there is only one person who needs every bit of protection I can offer her. Talin.

This is your redemption.

39

TALIN

THE TWO SKYHUNTERS FROM BACK AT THE LAB complex, when Raina showed me around. How could I have forgotten about them?

I look back and, in horror, see Red barrel forward to face the first of them. He's buying me time.

Red! I scream through our link, but I know it's no use. No time to waste now—and certainly not when Red is risking his life to give me that time.

I tear my eyes away as Red clashes with the first Skyhunter. I rush into the door. A gush of cool air greets me as I hurtle into the palace.

The instant I set foot in here, I feel the weight of Constantine's presence. It's so strong I'm not even sure if it's just through our bond. Perhaps it has always haunted every hall of this palace, the whisper of his legacy in every tile and stone and wall of this forsaken place. But the beat of his heart turns into a drum in my chest as I hurry down the corridor that widens into the main atrium of the palace, until I almost mistake it as my own.

Come out, Constantine, I tell him through our link as I head down the path. My anger is a fire in my mind now. *You've lost.*

He doesn't answer, but I can feel the shift of his emotions, the hate in his heart. It is strong here, echoing off the walls. At least he's still trapped.

Somewhere behind me comes Red—but almost as soon as I feel his energy follow me in, something attacks him, sending him crashing against a wall. I wince as I feel agony lance through his body and tremble through our link, and turn around long enough to see him struggle with a Skyhunter.

He shoots me a grim look before he bares his teeth at the Skyhunter and attacks him.

Go, he tells me, his voice a hammer through our link. *Go!*

Constantine. I have to find him. I tear my eyes away from Red and force myself to continue down the hall. The space opens into the soaring ceiling of the atrium. I'm so used to seeing this space speckled with sunlight that at first it looks completely unfamiliar—the sky through the glass ceiling is dark and churning, fires burning around the city casting the sky in shades of crimson. It gives the entire space a scarlet glow.

Bullets fire at me from somewhere high on the balcony. I glance up, my eyes narrowing, to see snipers positioned between the banisters, their weapons aimed down at me. They cringe at my stare, then back away from the edge. At the same time, I hear the unmistakable growls of Ghosts emerging from the shadows of columns around me. Their milky eyes roll at me, and blood drips down their chins.

Everything around me moves like I'm in a dream. The Ghosts seem to float, dragging through the air, as they move. Their muscles crack, bleeding and raw. I am on the warfront again, Corian at my side, fighting for survival. Through my link with Red, I feel currents of his own fury as he fights farther down the hall, pain rippling through him with each strike from the enemy Skyhunter.

One of the Ghosts near me lunges, its fangs seeking out my arm. I dart to one side, then launch into the air and fatally cut its neck with my wings. If it bit my flesh, would I transform eventually? Can a Skyhunter like me turn into a Ghost? Then its blood spills on the floor around me, and I turn my concentration toward the others. Their screams echo through the room. Another bullet flies from somewhere above and hits me in the upper back. I flinch at the strike—even though it doesn't penetrate my body in the same way as it does a normal human—I still feel the pain, followed by the sharp smell of my own blood. I cut through another Ghost, then launch into the air and hurl myself at the banisters. As I reach the balcony, I arc my wings protectively around myself.

I smash through the banisters. The guards lose all their nerve at the sight of me, and flee. As I stare at them racing down the hall, Constantine's voice comes to me through our bond, haunting and cold.

It's such a shame, Talin.

His words send a chill down my spine. I look around me, as if I can see him.

You were my strongest Skyhunter.

The halls are bathed in that ominous red from the sky through the glass ceiling. I start running again, trying to pinpoint Constantine's location through our link as I hang on to his words.

What will you do when my new Skyhunters tear you apart? he asks me.

They won't, I answer. *Because by the time they arrive, you'll be dead. They'll have no one to fight for.*

You won't bring down this Federation alone, Talin.

I am not alone. My teeth clench into a grim smile. *But you are.*

Constantine doesn't answer that. But as I reach the end of the hall and draw near the stairs, his voice comes back to me. Suddenly, I feel like I can sense his heartbeat strong and unrelenting here.

I turn my eyes up to the glass ceiling, then to the staircase that winds high, ending through a door that leads out onto the roof.

It's a trap. I can feel it in my bones, the tingle of something sinister and knowing from him. He doesn't try to hide it either. He knows this is the only reason I've come inside, that everything about our plan centers around me getting close enough to kill him. Down below, the atrium floods with soldiers. Their boots echo down every path, and I hear them coming up every stairway. Ghosts scream alongside them.

From somewhere below, Red calls out to me in desperation. *Don't go!* he shouts through our link. *They'll trap you up there!*

But we don't have the time to wait any longer. I clench my hands into fists and think about my mother outside with the other rebels, launching arrows into the melee. None of us should be here. It is all one big trap.

But I'm done being afraid.

I push away the feeling of Red's terror and launch up at the stairway.

I burst through the door and onto the roof. It's one vast expanse of flat stone broken by the glass ceiling in its center. No sooner than I emerge, another bullet hits my arm and sends me careening backward. My wings arc instinctively—I feel and hear the pings of more bullets against the metal. I close my eyes and let my Striker training take over. It is a midnight forest; I am hunting Ghosts by sound alone. I concentrate on the direction of the bullets, then paint in my mind a picture of where they're coming from. I remind myself that his guards fear me more than I fear them. And I launch through the air at them.

I cut down soldier after soldier. Others run from me, dropping their weapons as they go. Even they must know that this battle can only end with me facing their Premier. My eyes glow as the fury within me rises.

And then I see him. He's standing in the middle of the roof, from a spot where he can still see beyond the edge of the palace to the masses of rebels pushing back against his soldiers below. At first glance, Constantine looks alone. He stands straight, his hands folded behind his back, the black and scarlet of his uniform reminding me of the first time I'd ever seen him silhouetted against a burning sky.

His eyes, as piercing and fierce as ever, are focused directly on me.

He gives me a smile. *Hello, Talin.*

Something barrels into me from behind. It hits me so hard that my vision turns black for an instant before I shake myself awake and find myself hurtling through the air. I twist, landing on my feet, then crouch low.

To see two Skyhunters rushing at me.

40

RED

I FEEL THE PRESENCE OF THE OTHER SKYHUNTERS confronting Talin without even seeing a vision through her eyes. The spike of her emotions tells me everything I need to know.

She's going to face them alone up there.

They're going to kill her.

How many Skyhunters has Constantine been working on? Was he in the process of building an entire army?

The thought sends a ripple of animal strength through me. I duck as the Skyhunter attacking me sheers his wings at me, seeking my throat. Then I run. As the other Skyhunter gives chase, I speed up, pointing my boots in the direction of the atrium. Everything is cast in a shade of crimson. There are soldiers everywhere, all bathed in the bloody light. They hesitate at the sight of me—and I realize that, for a split second, they can't tell the difference between me and the other Skyhunters, thinking that both of us are war machines loyal to the Premier. I take advantage of their confusion to barrel past them. Behind me, the Skyhunter draws near.

As he reaches me, I suddenly halt and twist around, grabbing for one of his wings. He shoots me a furious look of surprise—my hand closes around one of his bladed feathers. It cuts deep into my palm. I ignore the sharp pain, then use the momentum of his movement to swing around until I've leaped onto his back, then grab the edge of his wing with my other hand too.

He twists, frustrated, trying to reach me. We spin in a mad, chaotic circle in midair. Then he does what I want him to do—he launches upward, right at the glass ceiling. His wings curl forward to protect himself.

I shut my eyes and brace myself.

He hits the ceiling with all the force of an explosion. Glass shatters in every direction—shards rain down to the atrium below us as we burst onto the roof. The impact nearly knocks me off his back, but somehow I manage to hang on as he twists again and again to reach me. Finally, he hurtles to the roof, turning so that his back will take the impact.

I let go the instant we hit. The force knocks the breath from me. My body rolls—the world spins furiously around me. I shake my head, then glance up for an instant to see Constantine's lone figure standing at the other end of the roof from us.

But it's not him that my eyes jump to. It's Talin. She's in midair, struggling to fight two Skyhunters at once.

I can't get to her fast enough to protect her. All I have time to do is leap to my feet, still gasping, and send a searing message through our link. *Talin.* All I can say is her name. For an instant, I feel her response come through the bond—a trembling, angry, terrified tremor.

At least she knows I'm here.

But it's all she can do. Because in the next moment, she arcs back in agony as one of the Skyhunters grabs her by the throat.

And as I look on in horror, the second Skyhunter grabs one of her wings and—in a single, violent gesture—rips it completely from her back.

41

TALIN

THE PAIN IS WORSE THAN ANY EXPERIMENT Raina put me through during my transformation. Worse than the nights I spent trembling and sweating. It feels like my body has split into two, like someone has taken a sword and jammed it into my back, then ripped out my bones.

My mind goes blank from the trauma. My eyes widen and my mouth opens in a silent scream. I arc backward as the pain rips through me in a violent wave. My balance suddenly feels off—part of me feels too light, lighter than the rest. The girl releases me, and I feel myself falling. From somewhere, I hear an anguished cry.

Red? Is he here?

As I hit the surface of the roof, I glimpse the two other Skyhunters. Vaguely, I realize what must have happened to me. They have torn off one of my wings.

The forceful hand seizes my back again. I have no strength in this moment to defend myself. My body is swimming in too much pain. All I manage to do is look out across the roof to see Red racing toward me, shouting my name, before the Skyhunter grabs my remaining wing and tears the metal from my back.

Stars explode in my vision. I crumple to the ground, tasting blood in my mouth as my lip scrapes hard against the stone. Constantine's voice comes to me from somewhere.

It's the end, Talin.

There is real grief in his voice, as if he regrets losing something he had worked so hard on. I clench my teeth and, through my swimming vision, look to my side to see the second Skyhunter rush to crouch beside me. She arcs her wings and reaches out to seize me, as if to pull me forward and impale me on her bladed feathers.

I don't know what I do. Sometimes the mind is a curious thing when it tries to protect itself. But as she pulls me toward her, I manage to twist around so that the Skyhunter at my back is forced to move with me. My body is slick with my own blood, turning me slippery. As I go, I slide out of her grasp and throw myself flat on the roof.

Her wing, instead of impaling me, stabs straight into the chest of the second Skyhunter.

A shudder wracks him. He drops the bloody wing he had ripped from my back, then stares down in dumb shock at the steel feathers of his Skyhunter partner that have entered his chest and exited through his back.

For the first time since I came up here, I feel a tremor of surprise and anger come from Constantine. It's all I manage to grasp. Over me, the impaled Skyhunter drops to his knees as his partner pulls out her wing in stunned surprise. Then the hurt Skyhunter falls heavily. He stills. Blood pools underneath him.

Who was he? Who are his loved ones that he'd been forced to fight for?

My head swims. I feel my limbs grow weak, as if they're moving through water. I don't know how much blood I've lost. I don't even know to feel relief or joy at the death of the other Skyhunter. Somehow, in the midst of all my feelings, I find myself grieving for him.

The female Skyhunter turns her rage on me. Before she can reach me, though, I feel Red's presence near. Then he's here, really here, all his strength and fury barreling into the Skyhunter. The two of them tumble into a rolling heap.

I am so tired. I could lie down right here and sleep. My blurring vision sweeps the roof, searching for Constantine before I finally see him standing some distance away. No, he is already moving. He's running away from me. I blink, trying to comprehend what I'm seeing. Everything in my mind feels so slow.

Constantine is running away because, for the first time in his life, he knows he's lost.

I find my last vestiges of strength within. They have been buried deep in my chest, locked tightly away since childhood, since the night that Karensan troops burst into my family's home and killed my father. They remained buried as I ran across the grassland at midnight with my mother, for nights and nights on end. That strength has been stored away since I fled across Mara's bridges with my mother and crouched on the other end to watch the Marans cut their bridges down. The strength has been untouched, idle during all the years I've fought at the warfront, defending Mara even as she didn't defend me. That strength is still inside me, shielded behind walls. Waiting for the moment when I would need every last bit of it.

This is that time.

As Red struggles with the Skyhunter behind me, I push myself onto my feet. Blood stains my hands and arms, stains everything. I trip over scarlet rivers as I go. Somehow, I break into a run. One of my daggers is clutched in my hand. I hold it tightly, afraid the blood will make it slip from my grasp, and I run toward Constantine.

Without his war machines at his side, he is weak. I'm reminded of all the times I had to steady him against my arm as he walked, the frail, human set of his body, his vulnerable nights when he couldn't sleep. Now he runs, and as he does, I see him for what he really is: a dying young man, hanging desperately on to the shreds of a Federation he cannot hold together, the end of his father's legacy—and his own. I realize this is what I feel through our bond now. His true, grieving realization that this is the end. That he is about to meet his greatest fear.

He is too weak to run fast. Even in my injured state, I catch up to him. He turns around, teeth bared, slashing out at me with his own knife—but I don't care. One of my hands comes up and I pull him toward me.

I meet his eyes. He stares back at me with a wide expression, and I find myself wondering if this is what he looked like as a child.

Then I take my dagger and stab him in the heart.

His body goes stiff. I hear him take a rasping breath, as if he's still—even now, at the end—shocked that I did it. He leans heavily against me, the blade digging deeper as he does. The pain that trembles through him hits me in a wave, and I feel my own legs in danger of buckling. It occurs to me he must have felt a hint of my agony, too, when the Skyhunters ripped my wings from my back. That was the grief he felt. As if a part of himself had died.

I feel that same grief now. I feel that steady heartbeat of his—an ever-present part of me for so long—shudder and turn erratic, beating frantically as if speeding up might keep it from bleeding out.

Then Constantine's legs finally give way, and he falls. I collapse at the same time. As I fight to hold myself up on hands and knees, I meet his gaze for the last time.

He stares at me like a frightened child. Death, the thing he feared the most, has finally come to claim him. A thin trickle of blood runs down the side of his mouth, even as his lips still murmur something. I can't hear what he's trying to say, but through our link, I know.

My Infinite Destiny. Even in his dying state, his voice echoes through my mind.

Then the voice in my head fades. The beat of his heart fades. The link binding us snaps, and I find myself suddenly without his presence in me as his body goes limp. His eyes turn vacant.

Then Constantine, the young Premier of the Karensa Federation, is staring at nothing at all.

The strength that had magically held me up now ebbs to nothing. I'm aware of the agony coursing through me, the blood that's still gushing from my back and staining everything red. I give in to it and fall to my side. The stone roof is cold and hard beneath my cheek. The world grays, turns muffled and tilted.

Somewhere in it, Red emerges. Had he won his own battle? He is bloody and wounded, he is limping, but he is moving toward me. I smile at his approach, every part of me yearning for him. He kneels down beside me, his hands running gingerly down my arms, but he's too afraid to lift me. He knows the damage that has ravaged my back. Off in the distance, I can hear the chants of the people.

Red's hands touch the sides of my face. I close my eyes for a moment, sighing, savoring the feel of those rough palms gentle against me. Maybe things will be all right now. I feel so tired.

Talin. Talin. He is speaking through our bond to me, maybe because it is all I can hear right now. When I look up at him, there are tears in his eyes, running down his face, dripping from his chin. He bows his head before me and I feel his breath warm and shaking against my face.

You did it. He says it over and over so that I finally understand him. *He's gone. You did it.*

I don't know what I did. I don't know what will happen after this.

And everything in me grieves at the thought that I might never find out, that in spite of everything, I will not be able to leave this place and see my mother again.

I manage to reach up and touch Red's face with my hands. They are shaking so hard. He presses his own hands firmly against mine, and I'm grateful I can still feel their warmth.

Stay awake, Talin.

I'm trying, I tell him. *I'm trying.*

There is so much ahead for you.

I try to hold on to his words. There is so much that could be ahead for me, for us, for this world. Even when it is burning down, even when we are lying in blood, dying, too weak to do anything more than concentrate on taking one breath at a time. I blink, blink again. Red is still here. I pull him to me, think that I feel his lips touch mine.

I love you.

Save it, so you can tell me again later.

I love you.

I love you.

Through our link, I can feel the strength and light of his life coursing into mine, his heart beating for mine, keeping me afloat. I hang on to him with everything left in me, even as the corners of the world finally fade. There is the scarlet sky, the sound of shouts from below. There is Red.

Maybe there is nothing else ahead for us. Maybe there is only this.

42

RED

ONCE, I'D THOUGHT THIS CITY WAS BEAUTIFUL. Now it looks like the end. The sky is bleeding, fires rage against the horizon, and the streets are smeared with blood from rebels and soldiers and Ghosts alike.

I can still feel Talin's heartbeat through our link, and I take comfort in the fact that we are bonded. Down below, I think I catch a glimpse of Aramin and Jeran fighting side by side—and then of Talin's mother cutting a line through the pandemonium.

The people need to see—I remember thinking as I come back into my body—they need to know that Constantine is dead.

I leave Talin's side for an instant and drag Constantine's lifeless form up, then carry him to the edge of the roof. There, I hold him up.

No one sees me at first. Then, someone shouts and points up at me. Her cry alerts another, who does the same. Another person joins in, and then another, and then the soldiers see. The clashes around the palace turn stilted, halt, restart in fits of chaos. But more and more people see who I am holding.

"Constantine is dead!" I call out, my voice harsh with tears. "The Premier is dead!"

As the chant rises over the din of fighting and flames, I lay Constantine's body down at the edge of the roof and return to Talin's side. I hoist her up over my shoulder, trying not to further injure her back.

Only then do I see someone familiar appear on the roof. It's Talin's mother, followed closely by Adena, the two of them bursting out from the stairway and rushing toward me. Behind them come a disorganized line of rebels. All I can think is that it must mean they have overtaken the palace.

The thought sends me to my knees. I crumple slowly and wait as Talin's mother and Adena reach us. I must have tried to say something to them—explaining what happened to Talin—because Adena immediately pulls off her own jacket and starts to wrap Talin's back tightly. Talin's mother leans over to me, shouting.

"She needs blood," the woman says. She and Adena help me steady Talin's body as I gingerly lift her in my arms. "We need to get her downstairs!"

We leave the roof. As I start to descend the stairs, I cast a final glance over my shoulder. Constantine's body stays there on the edge of the roof, alone and undefended, just an object to be gawked at and pointed to by the crowds below. All the destruction he has caused, all the lives he has destroyed—but in the end, he is just a lone, frail figure, another body. And in time, like all bodies, he too will vanish into dust.

Think of all that a single person can do. All the indescribable good. All the unspeakable evil.

• • •

There is a moment in the hospital of the inner city when I think Talin has died. Her heartbeat grows so faint that I can barely detect it. Outside, the city is flooded with the chaos that comes from the end of an era. When I look out the window, I see people tearing down a statue of Constantine's father that has been in the center of the Solstice Circle for as long as I can remember. People from every conquered nation have dared to appear in the streets today, many of them crouched, weeping, before the monuments stolen from their countries and now adorning the main thoroughfare.

As the chaos sweeps through the streets, I stay by Talin's side. A nurse from the former lab institute has already come by to set up an infusion of liquids into her body. Sometimes her heart quiets so much that I have to lean my head against her chest to hear her pulse for myself. Her mother stands beside her, her steady hands carefully sewing the horrendous wounds that Talin has sustained on her back. Beside her, Adena assists, occasionally looking at Talin's face in the hopes that she might wake up.

I don't know what time it is when Jeran and Aramin walk through the hospital door to see us. The day has come and gone, and night has fallen over the city again. Outside, Cardinia still sounds like a roar, but I see fewer soldiers clashing in the streets. Instead, there are arrests, and rebels waving the flags from a dozen fallen nations. The flag of the Karensa Federation burns everywhere.

"I heard about what happened," Jeran says as a greeting as they stop at Talin's side. He is drenched in sweat and blood, but otherwise, he looks well, his face smeared with ash.

Adena shakes her head. "She's lost a lot of blood. I don't know when she might wake up."

Aramin doesn't say anything at first. Instead, he just watches her chest rise and fall, as if silently counting her breaths. I observe his face quietly before I nod at them both. "What's happening out there?" I ask.

Jeran looks at me. "Those still loyal to Constantine stood down almost the instant you brought his body to the edge of the palace roof. Everyone knows the Premier is dead."

"Now what?" Adena asks quietly, her eyes going from me to Jeran to Aramin.

We are silent. None of us know. It doesn't feel real that the capital of the Federation has fallen to rebels, the victims of all of those it had conquered and ruled. What happens after this? The Premier is dead; his brother is dead; there is no heir. Where do they go from here?

Aramin is the first one to speak. His voice is hoarse, as if he has been crying. "We may not know for a long time," he says. "Maybe that's a good thing. Let the people *feel.* Only then can we stop to think about what comes next."

We sit, indulging in another round of silence. I find myself feeling grateful that there is no discomfort in this silence. It is the sound of friends who have been through everything together. And in this moment, we are all waiting for the same thing. Our eyes linger on Talin, watching her every breath, watching her eyes, watching for the slightest hint.

Her hand is tucked in mine. But she does not squeeze back.

• • •

Talin's mother stays the entire time. So do I. We never leave her side—even though her mother tries frequently to make me go.

"Look at you," she scolds, waving her hands impatiently at me one morning. "Get out of here, get some air, get some food."

"I could say the same for you, ma'am," I answer, refusing to budge.

She sighs and shakes her head at me. "Stubborn young things," she mutters as she turns back to stare at her daughter's face.

"Weren't you too?" I ask her after a while.

She doesn't answer right away, but I catch a faint smile on her lips. "Ah," she says sorrowfully. "There is nothing in the world I can say to send you away, is there?"

"I'm afraid not."

She touches her daughter's face gently, and I find myself imagining a small Talin and her younger mother.

"I suppose love is a stubborn thing," she finally says.

Adena disappears for a stretch, off to survey the remains near the lab complex. She is still unsure what exactly happened when they detonated the cylinder, or what the blue shaft of light that shot into the air when it went off means. Already, several rebels have died, burning to death over the span of a day in the same way that I'd seen before with those poor workers. The land around the lab complex, she tells us, is charred so badly that everything—stone and steel and earth—has melted together into a single mass. Whatever the energy source was meant to do for the Early Ones, they had buried it deep in the earth, as if they'd never wanted it to be found again. Now I know why.

Sometimes I see Aramin and Jeran outside the window, wandering the courtyard outside the hospital restlessly, their heads together as they talk. At one point, late in the evening, I see Aramin take Jeran's hands in his and bring him close for a kiss. My hand tightens around Talin's.

At some point, I fall asleep beside her. In my dream, I am again walking down the bright, narrow tunnel toward the end, where I see Talin waiting for me. But I walk and walk and walk, and the tunnel goes on and on and on, and I never reach her. Somewhere down there, I can hear the faint steadiness of her breathing. She's still there. But she doesn't answer.

I wonder if I will continue to walk in this dream forever. As I go, I remember the way she extended her hand to me in the Striker arena, then the way she reached for me on the battlefield. She had come to my rescue the first time we'd failed to escape the lab complex.

Talin, I say, calling her name over and over through our link, listening for her response.

I wait. The day changes again. Night becomes morning becomes night. Our friends rotate in and out of the room. Talin's mother sleeps, exhausted, nearby. Outside the window, the chants continue. I drift in and out of my own dreams, and in every dream, I walk down the tunnel and call Talin's name.

I call and call and call.

Then, finally, on the morning of the fourth day, I call for her. *Talin*, I say through our bond.

And I stir awake to see her eyes open, clear and vibrant, staring directly at me. She smiles faintly.

Hello, Red, she answers.

43

TALIN

STEELSTRIKER.

That's what Red says they've been calling me in the streets. The Striker from Mara, turned into a Skyhunter, reinforced by steel in her bones. A warrior. A savior. A human who is not human.

By now, the news that I was the one who plunged a dagger into Constantine's heart has spread: one of the Premier's own Skyhunters, freed of her bonds, turned on him and ended the Tyrus rule in a single blow. The corners of the Federation—Tanapeg and Carreal and others—have already frayed in response to the Premier's death. I've heard another territory is now claiming itself as independent.

At night, I can hear chants of my name rise and fall in the streets outside. I can't tell if I'm dreaming or awake when I hear them.

Empire breaker. Steelstriker. Skyhunter.

Another name to add to my list.

It's a strange feeling, knowing that Constantine is no longer on the other end of my mind. There is no one to tell me that my mother's life depends on what I do. She is here, beside me. So is Red and Jeran and Adena and Aramin. They rotate in and out of my room at such regular intervals that I quickly begin to anticipate their arrivals, my heart quickening in a different way as each hour brings a different friend to my side.

But even as the days turn into weeks, my mother never moves. Every time I drift off into sleep and wake, she is there, tut-tutting over the color of my cheeks or how much food I've left behind on the tray. A new bowl of porridge will be there, or a pot of simmering meat stew, or a savory bun filled with chicken and vegetables. I don't know how she gets the ingredients or where or when she cooks, but somehow, like she did in Mara, she always finds a way.

"They say you're recovering well," she tells me in Basean this morning, as I wake to the aroma of chicken stew and warm sweet rolls.

The constant, searing pain in my back says otherwise. "They say I may never fight again," I sign.

"I sincerely hope you never do," my mother signs in return, but her eyes are gentle. She knows that the war has left behind wounds in me that will never heal, but that it also brought me some of the greatest joys I've ever known. I've found the people who would stand shoulder to shoulder with me. We've made it, together, to the other side.

My mother sits in silence as I eat. From here, we get a good view of the city center. Karensan troops are still everywhere, but they are busy directing workers to repair the damage from the fights and preventing scuffles from breaking out on the streets. Others are handing out food to lines of people who have seen their markets burn down. Still others stand idle, wandering restlessly from one end of the Circle to the other.

Their expressions look lost. Who are they now, if not servants to the Premier? What do you do after the regime you've served topples to the ground?

"Do you know what else they say?" she tells me after I've finished eating.

I look at her. "What?"

My mother rises, taking the empty food tray. As she does, she glances sidelong at me.

"They say you should fill the Premier's vacancy."

Then, before I can answer, she turns away, leaving me alone to gather my thoughts.

My gaze shifts to the window.

They have been without a dictator for mere weeks, and already they are prepared for someone else to step into their late Premier's shoes. Karensa is a Federation where they have been taught to value the strength of their rulers. Well, they've seen that strength in me. A Skyhunter is a Skyhunter, seemingly invincible. They believe me capable of ruling them the right way, taking over a regime that had been evil and turning it good.

I want to laugh, laugh, and laugh until tears stream down my face, until I cry.

They don't understand what they're looking for.

Goodness can be no single leader. No solitary person.

Goodness is friends who stick by you, even when they fear you're lost. It's mothers who fight for their daughters. It's believing in something better—and taking action to make it reality. It's love, untainted and pure.

Goodness is a garden that provides life to thousands of blooms. It does not rule. It gives.

• • •

Another week blurs by.

One sunny morning, as my mother sits at my bedside and talks to me softly, I feel Red's presence approaching us from down the hall. I turn away from my mother and toward the door, then straighten as Red walks in with several Karensan soldiers. The sight of him is a comfort, as always, but today, seeing the red coats still sends a flutter of fear through me. I tense.

It's okay, Red's voice echoes in my mind. His eyes meet mine, then skip to the woman standing to his right.

Mayor Elland.

My mother narrows her eyes, annoyed with them for disturbing her daughter's rest, and Mayor Elland clears her throat. I almost laugh at the way that my mother can make even the mayor hesitate in her boots.

"Talin Kanami," the woman greets us. "Glad to see you doing well."

I just give her a single nod, then wait for her to continue.

She approaches us, then takes a seat beside my mother before facing me. "How do you feel?"

I tilt my head slightly at her. "Strong enough," I sign, letting Red translate. "I should be back on my feet soon."

"Good."

"Why is that good?" I eye her. "What do you need?"

She glances briefly at my mother, who simply sits back in her chair and regards the woman with an icy stare. Then the mayor lets out her breath and leans forward on her knees. She fixes her eyes on me.

"The Karensa Federation is leaderless," she says. "I currently manage the affairs inside Cardinia, but there is a need to fill the Premier's seat."

"The people are calling you Steelstriker, Talin," Red adds. "They know what you did on the roof of the palace, and your name is on their lips at all hours."

I look back at the mayor, who gives me a nod. "I've heard the same in the streets. Many are calling for us to appoint a new leader soon."

A new leader for the Federation.

I frown at Mayor Elland. "I'm surprised you aren't stepping into the role."

She shrugs. "I have no interest in ruling the entire Federation," she replies. "I'll let that honor fall to someone else. I've done enough."

Red comes over to my bedside. His fingertips brush mine, and through our link, I hear his voice, followed by a rush of warmth.

You don't have to do anything, he insists. *There's simply a lot of support for you.*

I stop myself before I can respond, letting the words sit in my own heart. *If I step forward to lead the Federation, what will happen to us?* He will have no choice but to step up with me. We could control the Federation together, side by side, sitting at the top of a system that had once brought each of us so much suffering.

But to him, all I say through our link is, *I know.*

Mayor Elland leans toward me. I remember the first time I'd ever seen this woman, her warm, lively eyes greeting me, the straight confidence of her shoulders. She gives me a small smile. "You are a force to be reckoned with, Talin, and we could certainly use your strength. I won't be ruling the Federation, but perhaps you would be open to working alongside me and other like-minded nobles, guiding an intimate circle who will help chart this Federation's course."

The potential in her words lingers with me, sparking in my heart. Never in my life have I been invited to create this kind of change.

I could transform every law in this entire Federation. We could punish every war criminal, order the execution of all who fought for Constantine and carried out his orders. I could root out every last person—soldier, civilian, worker—who tormented Karensa's conquered territories, finally unleash all the anguish pent up in me against those who deserve it.

I could become what Constantine had striven for.

I'm quiet for a while. Outside, I can hear the occasional chant breaking out in the streets even as soldiers bustle back and forth.

Finally, I sign, "Then let me speak before your circle."

The mayor smiles a little. She looks uncertain that I've accepted her invitation, but she doesn't question it. She doesn't cower away from me in fear of my Skyhunter strengths. She just bows her head once.

"I'll gather the others," she says.

My mother looks at me without a word. Even though I've given no response, she can already see the answer in my eyes.

• • •

Later that evening, I leave my bed for the first time in weeks. Everything in me aches—my back still feels tender from the damage that Constantine's Skyhunters had inflicted, and my dozens of other, smaller wounds still smart, pulling and stretching me in the wrong ways as I join a small council seated in the atrium of the late Premier's palace.

It's surreal to be back here. I'd seen blood smeared across these marble tiles, had been forced to serve Constantine and kill while the light streamed down through the magnificent glass ceiling above.

Now it is a serene space lit by a spring sun, and I stand in the middle of a half circle of Karensan nobles. Funny, isn't it, how different the same place can look.

I recognize some of them. There's Mayor Elland, of course. Red and my mother have also been given the courtesy of seats in this half circle, along with Adena, Aramin, and Jeran. They are here with several of Constantine's former advisors that the mayor must have deemed worthy of being here. There are a couple of her rebel allies.

What a strange mix we all are.

Now, as the mayor greets me with a formal nod, Red rises from his seat to stand next to me. His hand brushes against mine, and my fingers reach to touch his, searching for his strength.

"Welcome, Steelstriker," Mayor Elland says. "We are ready to listen to what you have to tell us."

I don't need to ask her what she wants to hear from me. They want to know if I will help them lead the Karensa Federation into its new era. What will it become now, without its late Premier? What comes after the Tyrus family?

I look from the mayor to my mother, to my Striker companions, and then to Red. I envision a lifetime living in the palace of Cardinia, walking the same halls that I had once walked when I was trapped under Constantine's rule. I imagine a future undoing the travesties that Constantine and his father before him committed, to spend the rest of my life revisiting grief over and over again. I see a life defined by my past, haunted by dreams of burning homes and boys with guns and bridges collapsing into the night.

I think of how far the Federation still has to go, and what it will take to bring it there.

When I answer, I respond through my link with Red. He voices my words aloud in steady Karenese to the others.

"I happily accept the task of leading the Karensa Federation into its next life," I tell them.

The mayor smiles, and the others nod along, ready to bring their hands together for me, eager to work together.

"And my first command in leading this effort," I continue signing as I meet the mayor's eyes, "is to break the Federation apart."

The few scattered claps that had started now pause, silence. I see a few surprised blinks.

They weren't expecting this.

"This is your world, not mine," I sign to them. Red's voice rings out strong. "I don't want to be a part of this. I never wanted to be a part of this, and neither did any of the nations that Karensa conquered. None of us were asked to join this. We were brought here."

The mayor nods at my words, even as her lips tighten. After a lifetime in her position, it must be surprising to her to see someone refuse power. Beside her comes a faint murmur from the advisory council.

"Then what do you want, Talin?" she asks me.

What do you want, Talin? It is a question I have heard so rarely that for a moment I'm not even sure how to answer.

"What I want," I sign, "is for the Karensa Federation to free every territory that it has ever conquered, restore to each of them their autonomy. I want the people of Basea to be able to return to Basea, if they so choose. I want Mara's borders to be restored. I want Karensa to give back everything it ever took—every statue, every structure, every piece that ever belonged to someone else. I want every former nation to become its own nation again, ruled by its own government, free to do as they will. As they always should have been. Take the power you want to grant me, and give it to those who should have had it all along."

"Then the Federation will disappear," one of the advisors says incredulously.

"So be it," I answer.

Mayor Elland listens carefully to me. I know she thinks some of these wishes are impossible, but even more so, I think she knows that they aren't at all. That these are things they should have done a long time ago. One of the others on the council looks like he's about to stand up and speak, but the mayor holds a hand up. He quiets, then settles back down.

"And what about *you*, Talin?" she asks. "What do you want your role to be in all this?"

I give her a soft, steady smile. "It is not my responsibility to undo the Federation's crimes," I answer. "I just want to go home."

My words must hit something hidden deep in her, because she smiles some secret smile, and I wonder for a moment if it's a smile that she used to share with Constantine's mother, the queen who had once been a girl who lost everything. Whatever it is that goes through the mayor's head, she doesn't share it with me. But she bows her head anyway.

"We will do as you've said," she answers.

And in that gesture, I feel something more genuine than anything a Karensan noble has ever done. There is grief in her movement, an acknowledgment. And a resolve.

A couple of the advisors seem to choke in surprise at the mayor's reply. But others hold steady, as if acknowledging they will go along with her. In the half circle, I see Adena grin at me. Jeran and Aramin exchange a small smile. And my mother looks at me as she always has, with the unwavering assurance that she will always be here.

Red touches my hand beside me, as if it's something he's done all his life. *You said you want to go home*, he tells me through our bond. His eyes, soaked in that beautiful deep blue, turn down to me. *Where's home?*

I think of the night when Red and I met each other in our dreams, when we connected through our unconscious minds. I think of Red telling me to envision a place that brings me peace, that can still the surface of my heart into contentment.

I think of that old avenue from my childhood, shaded by the wide-brimmed leaves of ancient trees, and of us sitting together in one of those branches, our lips sticky with watermelon juice. I picture windows letting in the light and the colors of flowering plants, the breeze dancing through the trees and showering our rooftop with curtains of dew. A butterfly chrysalis hanging on a twig, suspended in a glass jar under the light. My father's deep chuckle. Then I think of the warfront in Mara, of the warmth of the Strikers' mess hall, the arena where we used to train, the memories of sitting in a row on a wall with one another. I think of Red and me, each of us resting in a warm, hazy pool, separated but not separated at all.

It isn't a place, I answer as I squeeze his hand back.

It is a feeling. A people.

It is those I'm brave enough to open my heart to, and those who open their hearts back.

It is us.

44

TALIN

IT IS ANOTHER FEW WEEKS BEFORE I'M ABLE to move around regularly. My muscles are weak from resting for so long, and when I walk, I tremble, but Red is there, holding me steady. My mother continues to stay at my side, gossiping with me late into the night about what she hears is happening outside the city. Gradually, she allows me longer and longer intervals on my own. I can now take comfort in the peace of these moments of solitude. My friends come and go in their regular intervals.

And then, one morning, I find myself waking up before dawn, my room still awash in deep blue light.

I toss and turn for a while before I finally sit up with a sigh. Then I swing my legs over the side of my bed and change out of my loose white shirt and wide dark pants. I switch to a Striker uniform, cleaned and tailored for me and hung neatly in my wardrobe. The familiar weight of the fabrics makes me smile.

The hall is cool and dark. A few nurses bustle here and there, but others are asleep, and most don't bother me. One recognizes me and looks like she wants to say something, then stops. They know what I've been through. The last thing they want to do is tell me where to go and what to do.

I give her a brief smile, hoping she understands it as *I won't be long.* She blinks at me, then responds with a subtle nod. She leaves me alone to continue down the hall.

The dawn is already making way for day by the time I step outside. I close my eyes for a moment, relishing the bite of a cool breeze against my skin, and breathe deeply. The aches in my back, my still-healing wounds, seem to recede for a moment, and for the first time since I left Basea, since my mother and I fled into Mara's borders, I feel light. Soldiers dot the thoroughfare, but otherwise the city seems quieter than I've ever seen it.

From somewhere high above me, I hear the faint, unmistakable sound of Adena's voice. I turn my head up to the roof of the hospital. The stairs against the side of the building lead up there, and as if on instinct, I head toward them, searching as I used to do as a Striker for the highest vantage point.

The stairs tire me faster than they should, but I still make my way to the top. And there, instead of seeing an empty ledge, I come upon Adena sitting beside Jeran, speaking in a low, rapid voice as she demonstrates the clips on a belt she has designed. On Jeran's other side, Aramin crouches against the ledge and stares down at a crew working to disassemble one of the hundreds of structures lining the main thoroughfare. Jeran leans back on his hands, answers Adena now and then as she turns the belt in her hands. As I watch them, I realize that the slowly emerging dawn has outlined their bodies in pale blue, casting them in light so fine that I'm afraid they might disappear before my eyes.

Aramin is the first to look toward me. As if tied to him, Jeran lifts his gaze too. Adena pauses in mid-sentence as I approach them, then breaks into a smile.

"Look at you," she says, leaning back to take me in, then motions me to sit with them. "Should you be walking around this much? Don't pitch over the side of the ledge, now—I don't want to leap after you."

I roll my eyes at her, then settle gingerly at her side and stare out at the warming horizon. It is an unfamiliar one—the curves of distant ruins from the Early Ones are nearly lost amid the towers of Cardinia and the domes of its many exhibition halls. But the sun begins to rise over it, just as it will soon be doing over Basea. Over Mara and Newage, where we once used to sit in a line on top of the Striker complex to greet the morning together.

We all fall silent now. The breeze carries with it something nostalgic. The memory of a different time. I find myself looking from the brightening horizon to my companions, soaking in the comfort of their presence. Adena still has some burn marks on her arms and cheeks from the blast at the lab complex. Jeran's scars are healing, his arm still in a cast. Aramin's face, ravaged with a vicious cut from the final night of battle, looks subdued.

But we are all still here.

The feeling of Red's presence, followed by a slight sound near the steps, makes me turn my attention toward him. I see him emerge on the rooftop too, his eyes softening in relief at the sight of me. He doesn't say a word. Instead, he walks quietly over to me, and we twine our hands together as if we were meant to do it all our lives.

Somehow, broken and unbound and rebound, we have survived. And as the first hint of sun peeks over the edge of the horizon, washing the city in a ray of gold, I lift my hands and sign.

"May there be future dawns."

The others all answer with the same sign. Even Red does. "May there be future dawns."

I turn my eyes up, watching the light overtake the sky.

May there be future dawns forever.

FIVE YEARS LATER

45

TALIN

ONCE, YEARS AGO, THERE WAS A SET OF DOUBLE walls that encircled Newage's Inner City. They were built in a time long before us, by the Early Ones, and they used to protect the city against the war beasts that the Karensa Federation used to defeat us. Those of us, like my mother, who lived on the outer side of the walls, saw them differently.

But they are gone now. Instead, Newage's Inner City and Outer City look more like a gradient, a gradual shift from busy, winding streets adorned with black-and-white architecture to greener expanses of courtyards and land fenced in by rows of houses, space that extends still more into pastures and farms, then finally into open countryside.

The warfront, too, is gone. I'd spent so many years patrolling our border I can hardly believe it's no longer there. Instead, there is nothing but forest. There are no Ghosts roaming through those lands, no grinding of teeth we must listen for. There is nothing but another country on the other side.

I observe this as our train winds its way along the outskirts of Newage until it finally turns south through Mara, leaving it behind and entering the hills of northern Basea. Beside me, Red sits with his shoulder gently touching mine, our hands twined as always. In his arms is a basket bearing all sorts of seeds, buds of flowers carefully wrapped, sacks of crushed eggshells. Gifts from the garden that Jeran and Aramin have been cultivating behind their home in Newage's National Hall, a few miles away from where the Striker arena still stands.

Aramin has been reinstated as the Firstblade of Mara's Striker forces. But there are no groups of Ghosts to fight anymore, no Federation to face. The Strikers pass on the most useful of their knowledge to other soldiers, and sometimes they are called on when a lone, stray Ghost is found wandering somewhere. But there are no new recruits in training. Maybe in a generation, there won't be a need for Strikers at all. So Aramin instead spends half of his time advising Jeran, the newly elected Speaker of Mara, offering him guidance on how to use the Striker forces to help repair parts of the country that have been broken.

The formula of crushed eggshells is from Adena, some new fertilizer she's developed that she wants my mother to try with her plants. Adena has left the Striker forces, concentrating her efforts on innovating new ways of improving the city with her own lab funded by Newage's Senate. She has outfitted the apartment Red and I share as an additional experimental space, installing it with all manner of piping systems and energy bulbs. Some inventions from the Karensa Federation have been worth adopting, at least.

I turn my attention back to the basket of ingredients. Spices difficult to find in Basea, nuts and seeds and dried herbs that grow wild in Mara's cool forests. My gaze drifts to my arm. I idly touch my skin, noting the unnatural hardness beneath it, the result of my Skyhunter transformation from years ago. My back has never healed quite right; the scars crisscross hideously across my skin. My ravaged body means I will never fight again. Sometimes, I find myself jolting awake beside Red in the middle of the night, sweating and shaking, my dreams haunted by memories of glass walls and sharp needles. But every year, the dreams fade a little more. Maybe someday, like the Strikers, they won't exist at all. Other than that, I've healed, come to terms with what I am now. It's something I bear with my chin high.

I had once been a Skyhunter, but I survived it.

Hours pass. I focus on the changing landscape outside. Once, some years ago, this land belonged to the Karensa Federation. I had ridden along this same track and seen towns draped in Karensan flags, scarlet-clad soldiers waiting at every stop. Now, though, those flags are gone, replaced instead with Basea's flag. I have only a vague recollection of them, but now they are everywhere, bold green and yellow, like the ground in summer.

By the time we arrive in Sur Kama, the sun has already begun to set. We get off the train onto a platform shrouded in billowing steam. The town doesn't look like the one from my childhood, the one that was destroyed. The one I remember had streets lined with thick trees, their branches arching so low that you could simply pull yourself up into their crooks and idle away. Those trees are long gone now, burned away when the Federation first conquered it. But now there are new trees, young and willowy and pale green, stretching up to the sky in neat rows along every boulevard. True to our heritage, the streets overflow with thickly flowering plants, bushes thick and lush along every corner.

My heartbeat quickens as we leave behind the main streets and turn into a smaller neighborhood. Now I start to recognize a few sights. There is the street stall I used to visit when I was small, the one selling frozen cubes of sweet strawberry juice and ice-cold watermelon slices. The one I'd envisioned once in a dream with Red. It is there again, and at the sight of it, I feel a rush of those old memories come back to me: my hand tucked neatly inside my mother's and the juice sticky on my lips. The homes are like I remember, albeit newly built; rows of small, neat rectangles surrounded on all sides by flowers and trees. Their doors, as they always were when I was little, are open, the neighbors familiar enough with one another that no one feels a need to lock them.

Red smiles in wonder as he walks alongside me, and for a moment, I feel like he is returning to a childhood too.

And then I see my mother's house.

It is a little different, of course. Its colors are blue and white, the sides not covered yet in thick curtains of green ivy, the stones and roof too new to have that sunbaked quality to them. The trees she has planted around the house are still young, brilliant green and bold and straight. But the flowers are blooming in enormous patterns of yellow and white, and the front door is wide-open.

Standing there in the front entrance is my mother, both how I remember her and how she is now, her hair pulled neatly back and her piercing eyes focused on us, her smile a sight of joy. I find myself breaking into a smile. A laugh bubbles in my chest. She waves. We wave back.

Beside me, Red smiles. *Is this your peace?* he asks me through our link.

I open my heart and let the light in. *It is better*, I answer.

ACKNOWLEDGMENTS

***SKYHUNTER* AND *STEELSTRIKER* ARE DARK** books, written in dark times: during the throes of a horrific American presidency and during a pandemic that devastated the entire world. My stories are always a snapshot of who I was and what was happening around me, so in many ways, this duology are the most difficult books I've ever written and of which I'm proudest. I could not have done it without a crew of wonderful people at my side.

My deepest gratitude to my editors, Jen Besser and Kate Meltzer. Kate, you are such a brilliant, kind, and wise soul, and I'm so lucky to work with you. Jen, I could write a thousand acknowledgments and never thank you enough. You are one of the best people I've ever known. What a gift it is to be your author and your friend. To Luisa Beguiristaín, I am eternally grateful for your sharp eye and kind words. To Anne Heausler, what can I say? All these years together, and every book with you is a delight. Thank you.

To Kristin Nelson, agent extraordinaire and steadfast captain of our ship, I could never do this without you. Thank you and the entire NLA team for keeping me inspired and sticking by me through these difficult years. To the wonderful Jenny Meyer: Thank you so much to you and your team for supporting me internationally.

To the incredible Macmillan Children's team: Allison Verost, Kristin Dulaney, Molly B. Ellis, Kelsey Marrujo, Mariel Dawson, Kathryn Little, Katie Quinn, Teresa Ferraiolo, Melissa Zar, and Cynthia Lliguichuzhca. Thank you all so much for your warmth, support, and guidance—

especially through this time. I can't even imagine the challenges happening behind the scenes, but you all kept the engine running and our books going and our readers prioritized. No small feat in any year—but certainly not in 2020 and 2021! You are warriors.

Aurora Parlagreco and Novans V. Adikresna: *Steelstriker* takes my breath away every time I look at it. I'm so grateful to have your talent grace this cover. Deepest thank-you to Beth Clark and Rodica Prato for the gorgeous map and insert, and for bringing the world to life.

Thank you so much to every single one of my international publishers for having faith in my books and taking a chance on me. I cannot exaggerate what it means to me to work with you all. A special thank-you to Leo Teti and your team: Although I am so sad we didn't get to meet last year, I hope we get to in the future. Wishing you all well.

To my friends—I'm more grateful than ever to have you all in my life. Thank you for existing and for being yourselves. To my husband, Primo, and our little one: If there must be a pandemic, I am thankful to spend it with you both. I love you more than words can say.

To the librarians, booksellers, and teachers around the world: What a couple of years. I'm so sorry for all you've had to weather. Thank you from the bottom of my heart for the important work you do.

And, of course, to my readers. What a burden you all have carried throughout this pandemic. I mourn with you, I am grateful for you, and I hope to see many of your faces in person soon. As goes the poem Talin remembers from her childhood: *Just because the sun cannot be seen, that does not mean it isn't there.* I hope we will reach the times of sun.

May there always be future dawns.